PENGUIN  CLASSICS

THE STORY OF THE STONE
Vol. 5

ADVISORY EDITOR: BETTY RADICE

CAO XUEQIN (?1715–63) was born into a family that for three generations held the office of Commissioner of Imperial Textiles in Nanking,
a family so wealthy that they were able to entertain the Emperor Kangxi
four times. But calamity overtook them and their property was confiscated. Cao Xueqin was living in poverty near Peking when he wrote
his famous novel *The Story of the Stone* (also known as *The Dream of the
Red Chamber*), of which this is the fifth volume. The first four volumes,
The Golden Days, *The Crab-Flower Club*, *The Warning Voice* and *The Debt
of Tears*, are also published in the Penguin Classics.

GAO E (?1740–1815) was a Chinese Bannerman of the Bordered Yellow
Banner, who for the last twenty years of his life worked in the Grand
Secretariat and the Censorate in Peking. In 1792 he and his friend
Cheng Weiyuan published for the first time a complete version of *The
Story of the Stone* in 120 chapters. Previously handwritten copies of the
novel had circulated, which ended with the eightieth chapter. Cheng
and Gao claimed that they edited the last forty chapters of their complete
version from a fragmentary manuscript by the original author.

JOHN MINFORD was born in 1946. He studied Chinese at Oxford and
at the Australian National University, taught in the People's Republic
of China (1980–82), and is at present director of the Research Centre
for Translation in the Chinese University of Hong Kong.

THE STORY OF THE STONE

A CHINESE NOVEL BY

CAO XUEQIN

IN FIVE VOLUMES

*

VOLUME 5

'THE DREAMER WAKES'

EDITED BY

GAO E

*

TRANSLATED BY

JOHN MINFORD

PENGUIN BOOKS

Penguin Books Ltd, Harmondsworth, Middlesex, England
Viking Penguin Inc., 40 West 23rd Street, New York, New York 10010, U.S.A.
Penguin Books Australia Ltd, Ringwood, Victoria, Australia
Penguin Books Canada Limited, 2801 John Street, Markham, Ontario, Canada L3R 1B4
Penguin Books (N.Z.) Ltd, 182–190 Wairau Road, Auckland 10, New Zealand

This translation first published 1986

Copyright © John Minford, 1986
All rights reserved

Made and printed in Great Britain by
Richard Clay (The Chaucer Press) Ltd,
Bungay, Suffolk
Typeset in 10/11½ Monophoto Garamond

FOR EMMA, LUKE, DANIEL AND LAURA

CONTENTS

8   CONTENTS

NOTE ON SPELLING

Chinese proper names in this book are spelled in accordance with a system invented by the Chinese and used internationally, which is known by its Chinese name of *Pinyin*. A full explanation of this system will be found overleaf, but for the benefit of readers who find systems of spelling and pronunciation tedious and hard to follow a short list is given below of those letters whose Pinyin values are quite different from the sounds they normally represent in English, together with their approximate English equivalents. Mastery of this short list should ensure that the names, even if mispronounced, are no longer unpronounceable.

$$c = ts$$
$$q = ch$$
$$x = sh$$
$$z = dz$$
$$zh = j$$

CHINESE SYLLABLES

The syllables of Chinese are made up of one or more of the following elements:

1. an initial consonant (b.c.ch.d.f.g.h.j.k.l.m.n.p.q.r.s.sh.t.w.x.y.z.zh)
2. a semivowel (i or u)
3. an open vowel (a.e.i.o.u.ü), *or*
   a closed vowel (an.ang.en.eng.in.ing.ong.un), *or*
   a diphthong (ai.ao.ei.ou)

The combinations found are:

3 on its own (e.g. *e, an, ai*)
1 + 3 (e.g. *ba, xing, hao*)
1 + 2 + 3 (e.g. *xue, qiang, biao*)

INITIAL CONSONANTS

Apart from c = *ts* and z = *dz* and r, which is the Southern English *r* with a slight buzz added, the only initial consonants likely to give an English speaker much trouble are the two groups

j q x   and   zh ch sh

Both groups sound somewhat like English *j ch sh*; but whereas j q x are articulated much farther *forward* in the mouth than our *j ch sh*, the sounds zh ch sh are made in a 'retroflexed' position much farther *back*. This means that to our ears j sounds halfway between our *j* and *dz*, q halfway between our *ch* and *ts*, and x halfway between our *sh* and *s*; whilst zh ch sh sound somewhat as *jr, chr, shr* would do if all three combinations and not only the last one were found in English.

Needless to say, if difficulty is experienced in making the distinction, it is always possible to pronounce both groups like English *j*, *ch*, *sh*, as has already, by implication, been suggested overleaf.

SEMIVOWELS

The semivowel i 'palatalizes' the preceding consonant: i.e. it makes a *y* sound after it, like the *i* in *onion* (e.g. **Jia Lian**)

The semivowel u 'labializes' the preceding consonant: i.e. it makes a *w* sound after it, like the *u* in *assuages* (e.g. **Ning-gu**o)

VOWELS AND DIPHTHONGS

i, Open Vowels

a   is a long *ah* like *a* in *father* (e.g. Jia)

e   on its own or after any consonant other than y is like the sound in French *oeuf* or the *er*, *ir*, *ur* sound of Southern English
         (e.g. Gao **E**, Jia She)

e   after y or a semivowel is like the *e* of *egg*
         (e.g. Qin Bang-y**e**, Xu**e** Pan)

i   after b.d.j.l.m.n.p.q.t.x.y is the long Italian *i* or English *ee* as in *see*
         (e.g. Nannie L**i**)

i   after zh.ch.sh.z.c.s.r is a strangled sound somewhere between the *u* of *suppose* and vocalized *r* (e.g. Shi-yin)

i   after semivowel u is pronounced like *ay* in *sway* (e.g. Li Gu**i**)

o   is the *au* of *author* (e.g. Duo)

u   after semivowel i and all consonants except j.q.x.y. is pronounced like Italian *u* or English *oo* in *too* (e.g. **Bu** Gu-xi**u**)

u   after j.q.x.y and ü after l or n is the narrow French *u* or German *ü*, for which there is no English equivalent
         (e.g. Bao-y**u**, Nü-wa)

ii. Closed Vowels

an   after semivowel u or any consonant other than y is like *an* in German *Mann* or *un* in Southern English *fun* (e.g. Yu**an**-chun, Sh**an** Ping-ren)

an   after y or semivowel i is like *en* in *hen* (e.g. Zhi-y**an**-zhai, Jia Li**an**)

ang   whatever it follows, invariably has the long *a* of *father* (e.g. Jia Qi**ang**)

en, eng   the e in these combinations is always a short, neutral sound like *a* in *ago* or the first *e* in *believe* (e.g. Cousin Zh**en**, Xi-f**eng**)

in, ing   short *i* as in *sin*, *sing* (e.g. Shi-y**in**, Lady X**ing**)

ong   the o is like the short *oo* of Southern English *book* (e.g. Jia C**ong**)

un   the rule for the closed u is similar to the rule for the open one: after j.q.x.y it is the narrow French *u* of *rue*; after anything else it resembles the short English *oo* of *book* (e.g. Jia Y**un**, Ying-chun)

iii. Diphthongs

ai   like the sound in English *lie*, *high*, *mine* (e.g. **Dai**-yu)

ao   like the sound in *how* or *bough* (e.g. **Bao**-yu)

ei   like the sound in *day* or *mate* (e.g. **Bei**-jing)

ou   like the sound in *old* or *bowl* (e.g. **Gou**-er)

The syllable er, sometimes found as the second element in names, is a peculiarity of the Pekingese dialect which lies outside this system. It sounds somewhat like the word *err* pronounced with a broad West Country accent.

PREFACE

Readers who have come this far, and who have already had to wait so long for this final instalment, will be impatient of further delay. This is therefore not the right moment to hold them back. But I must nevertheless do something to qualify the too sweeping judgement of this ending expressed in my preface to *The Debt of Tears*. While there is undeniably 'something missing', and while I still believe this to be a fragmentary original fleshed out by a later editor (or editors), I am less and less certain *what* exactly that 'missing something' is, and more and more convinced that the text we have succeeds in bringing Cao Xueqin's dream to a fitting conclusion.

'The tears one owed have all been shed'; now in this fifth volume 'the tree falls, and the monkeys scatter'. This is the working of karma:

> Wrongs suffered have the wrongs done expiated;
> The couplings and the sunderings were fated.

One by one events come to pass that were riddlingly foretold in the 'Dream of Golden Days', that haunting song-and-dance suite staged for Jia Bao-yu's benefit by the fairy Disenchantment in the fifth chapter. For scholarly purists the fulfilment of those prophecies is not literal enough, the reversal of fortune not sufficiently extreme. And yet surely it is still a saga filled with human suffering. There is little comfort in these pages. One by one

> The disillusioned to their convents fly,
> The still deluded miserably die.

We witness death (sometimes brief and poignant, more often protracted and harrowing); ruin (nowhere in Chinese literature is there such a well inventoried chronicle of a family's 'confiscation'); disappointment in marriage; the corruption, recorded in documentary detail, of an eighteenth-century provincial tax-collector; the pampered decadence and vicious intriguing of the sons of the rich; the subtly depicted growth of superstition in the crumbling fabric of a noble household.

Against this multifarious backdrop we never lose sight of the protagonist. Jia Bao-yu weaves his way through these events like a sleep-walker, and finally through a dream-vision is awakened to the realization that life itself is but a dream, that

> All is insubstantial, doomed to pass,
> As moonlight mirrored in the water,
> Or flowers reflected in a glass.

The story of his progress to enlightenment, of the return of the Stone to its otherworldly home at the foot of Greensickness Peak, is told with such zaniness and with such an absence of sentimentality that we can easily believe in its truth. It is not a pretext for a plot. It is not a schematic progress, or a series of predictable steps along a stereotyped pilgrim's path, but a hard-won personal discovery proceeding from the inertia of bereavement, through a long convalescence, a dark night of the soul, to a crisis in which that soul is lifted above the seemingly endless wheel of suffering.

At the very last it is as though we, the readers, have also passed through a dream, have shared a vision in scroll form, bright woodblock impressions of everyday life alternating with the inksplash fantasies of a Yangzhou eccentric. The familar faces come on for their final call and then fade into the snow,

> Like birds who, having fed, to the woods repair,
> Leaving the landscape desolate and bare.

*

In translating this last part of the novel, I have again received help from many kind friends over the years. My wife Rachel May read and typed the first part of this volume with her usual fastidious attention to detail, and made many judicious emendations. Mrs Margaret Chung typed the last chapters with great skill and diligence. I must thank once more Dr David Hawkes and Professor Liu Ts'un-yan for listening to my endless queries, and Professor Yang Qinghua of Tientsin for reading through with me an earlier draft in its entirety and making several helpful suggestions for its improvement. Professor Pang Bingjun, also of Tientsin, has shared with me, during many a lively conversation, insights into translation, *The Stone* and Chinese culture in general. Professor P'an Ch'ung-kwei very generously sent me a copy of his new and sumptuously printed edition of the 120-chapter corrected draft (published in Taipeh in

June 1983), while some years earlier Dr Richard Rigby kindly supplied me from Japan with a copy of Itō Sōhei's *Kōrōmu*.

In Hong Kong Mr Stephen Soong has come to my rescue many a time, while Professor Ambrose King provided me, in 1982, with a much-needed month's respite from my teaching duties by having me as a Visiting Scholar at New Asia College.

Finally I would like to thank two Chinese friends, one young, one elderly, who for different reasons must remain anonymous. The first initiated me in 1966 into the deep spell that this novel has cast over generations of Chinese readers, and at the same time warned me to keep well away. I ignored the warning. The second is a direct descendant of one of China's most illustrious families, a family much vilified by the present regime. He is a man of great courage and independence of mind, who suffered imprisonment (and much else) in the fifties. Meeting with him in his tiny backstreet flat and talking animatedly over endless cups of wine about some little heirloom that the government had just seen fit to restore to him, some scrap of painting from what had been a magnificent collection, always made me think of Cao Xueqin in the Western Hills, brooding over his dream of vanished splendour, piecing together *The Stone*. My friend related with great humour the story of how he had been taken by his Overseas Chinese brother to visit the local antique shop – he himself had never been inside it before, as the shop was only open to holders of foreign passports. The two of them had the time of their lives wandering around the shop and identifying their family possessions – all of which had been confiscated during the Cultural Revolution and all of which had officially been restored! In the telling of the story there was no trace of rancour. Only warmth, humour, and wisdom. He is an unforgettable man, a man of character and substance. Once we were walking together past the site of his grandfather's mansion, now mostly demolished and occupied by some dark satanic mill. A momentary shadow crossed his face. Then he laughed. 'Twenty years ago I still used to feel great bitterness whenever I walked along this street. But gradually as the years went by the pain was numbed and everything, past and present, seemed more and more like a dream. Now I just laugh!'

Hong Kong,
1985

CHAPTER 99

*Unscrupulous minions make use of their master's virtue
to conceal a multitude of sins
And Jia Zheng is alarmed to read his nephew's name
in the 'Peking Gazette'*

TO CONTINUE OUR STORY

We told in our previous volume how Xi-feng, finding Grandmother Jia and Aunt Xue somewhat cast down by the mention of Dai-yu's death, had endeavoured to raise their spirits with a humorous anecdote.

'Who else could it be,' she finally managed to say, after much incapacitating mirth, 'but our newly married couple!'

'Well – what about them?' asked Grandmother Jia.

Xi-feng began mimicking again.

'Here sits one, here stands t'other . . . One bends this-a-way, one turns that-a-way . . . One . . .'

Grandmother Jia interrupted her with a loud laugh.

'For heaven's sake get on with the story! If we have to watch *you* any more, it'll be the death of us!'

'Yes, do stop all this monkeying around,' said Aunt Xue, laughing in spite of herself, 'and get on with your story.'

Xi-feng began again:

'Just now, I was passing through Cousin Bao-yu's apartment when I heard the sound of laughter coming from inside; and wondering who it could be, I took a peep through a little hole in the paper casement. There was Cousin Chai sitting on the edge of the kang, with Bao-yu standing in front of her, holding her sleeve and imploring her: "Oh, Coz! Why won't you *speak* to me? A word from you and I know I should be completely cured!" But she turned away and seemed bent on taking no notice of him whatsoever. He bowed to her, and then came still closer and took hold of her dress, which she tugged away from him at once. You know how unsteady on his feet Bao-yu has been since his last illness – well, with this tug he just tumbled right on top of her! She flushed and cried out: "You're worse than ever! You haven't a scrap of *dignity*!" '

At this both Grandmother Jia and Aunt Xue burst out laughing again. Xi-feng went on:

'Then Bao stood up and grinned. "At least I tripped you into *speaking* to me!" he said.'

'My daughter certainly has her foibles,' said Aunt Xue, with a good-humoured smile. 'Now that they're married there's really nothing against a bit of harmless fun. If she could but see her cousin Lian and you, my dear, when the two of you get started . . .'

Xi-feng blushed.

'Honestly!' she protested laughingly. 'I tell a story to raise your spirits and you turn it against me.'

'Chai is quite right to behave as she does,' put in Grandmother Jia with a chuckle. 'I don't deny that marriage should be based on affection; but there should always be a sense of proportion. I'm glad Chai sets such store by dignity, and it saddens me that Bao-yu should still be such a silly boy – though from some of the things you tell me it seems that he may be improving. Well – any more stories?'

'Soon there will be no lack of them,' replied Xi-feng. 'When their marriage is consummated, and Bao-yu presents his mother-in-law with a grandchild . . .'

'You monkey!' exclaimed Grandmother Jia. 'Thinking of your Cousin Lin's death made us both feel sad, and it was thoughtful of you to want to cheer us up. But now you're going too far. Would you have us forget her altogether? You'd better watch your step. She was never very fond of you while she was alive, and you'd be well advised not to go walking in the Garden alone after this, or her ghost may pounce on you and try to take its revenge!'

'But she never bore a grudge against me,' countered Xi-feng with a smile. 'It was Bao-yu she cursed with her dying breath.'

Grandmother Jia and Aunt Xue took this to be another of her witticisms, and ignored it:

'Don't talk such nonsense. Now off you go and find someone to choose a lucky day for your cousin Bao's party.'

'Yes, Grannie.' After a little more chat Xi-feng went on her way. She despatched one of the servants to consult the almanac; and on the chosen day, the family duly celebrated the (formal if not actual) 'consummation' of Bao-yu and Bao-chai's marriage, and entertained their guests with a banquet and plays. But of this our narrative omits further details.

*

It turns instead to the convalescent Bao-yu.

From time to time Bao-chai would pick up one of his books and engage him in conversation about it, and on these occasions Bao-yu was sufficiently *compos mentis* to sustain a desultory dialogue of sorts. But his mind was unquestionably duller than it had been, a deterioration he himself was unable to account for. Bao-chai argued with herself that the cause lay in the loss of his Magic Jade, but Aroma was less philosophical, and frequently took him to task:

'Where have your wits fled to? If only it was that old weakness of yours that had left you! But you seem to have kept *that* and lost your wits instead!'

Bao-yu did not let remarks such as this rile him, and responded with an inane grin. If he ever showed signs of letting his wild streak get the better of him, he allowed himself to be restrained by Bao-chai's good sense, while as time went by Aroma rebuked him less and less, and confined herself instead to ministering to his practical needs. His other maids had always respected Bao-chai's quiet, demure manner, and now that she was their mistress her gentle and friendly nature won their willing obedience.

Beneath this apparent calm, Bao-yu continued to feel a deep sense of restlessness, and in particular a recurring desire to visit the Garden. Grandmother Jia and the other ladies were afraid that such an expedition might expose him to a chill or fever of some kind, and that the Garden's surroundings would have too gloomy and depressing an effect on his spirits. Dai-yu's coffin was already lodged in a temple outside the city walls, but the Naiad's House and the memories associated with it would be sure to cause him renewed distress and bring on a relapse. So they forbade him to go. Most of the Garden was now deserted. Of Bao-yu's cousins, Bao-qin had already moved out to live with Aunt Xue, while Shi Xiang-yun had gone home on her uncle's return to the capital, and seldom visited the Jias now that the date of her own wedding had been settled. She had been present on Bao-yu's wedding-day and more recently on the day of the party, but on both occasions she had stayed with Grandmother Jia; and her awareness that Bao-yu was now a married man, and she herself betrothed, had inhibited her from indulging in any of her old high-spirited banter. When she saw the newly wed couple, she talked to Bao-chai but scarcely said more than a polite 'hello' to Bao-yu. Xing Xiu-yan had moved in with her aunt Lady Xing after Ying-chun's marriage, while the two Li sisters only ever visited the Garden with their mother, and then would stay for a couple of days with Li Wan before returning home. The only Garden residents proper were now Li Wan, Tan-chun and Xi-chun. Grandmother Jia had wanted the three of them to move in with her, but with Yuan-chun's death and all the subsequent family excitements of one kind or another, she had not been able to find time to make the necessary arrangements; and now the weather was growing warmer daily and the Garden was beginning to seem less dreary, so she decided to leave things as they were until the autumn. But we anticipate.

*

Jia Zheng had set off for his new provincial posting, travelling by day and resting by night, accompanied by the various aides and secretaries he had engaged before his departure. On his arrival at the provincial capital, he reported to his superiors and immediately proceeded to his new yamen to take ceremonial possession of the official seal and to assume office. His first administrative action was to take stock of the grain lying in all the granaries of the sub-prefectures and shires under his jurisdiction.

Jia Zheng's previous experience as an official had been mainly in the capital, and had been restricted moreover to the theoretical aspects of the metropolitan bureaucracy. His one provincial appointment had been as an Examiner, and his responsibilities then were of a purely academic nature. He therefore had no first-hand knowledge of the practicalities of provincial administration, let alone of the forms of corruption widely tolerated – the cuts taken by middlemen, or the extortion practised on the ignorant peasantry, to mention but two. He knew of such things in theory only, as evils to be avoided, and was adamant that his would be an incorruptible administration. On arrival he consulted with his private secretaries and issued a public notice strictly forbidding malpractice of any kind, and announcing that any instance of it would be investigated and reported to the authorities.

At first the locally employed clerks were overawed and tried their utmost to ingratiate themselves with the new incumbent, only to discover that the man they were dealing with was totally inflexible. As for Jia Zheng's family servants, they, after years of unprofitable service in the capital, had rubbed their hands with glee at the news of their master's provincial posting and, on the strength of their anticipated profits, had borrowed money to buy clothes and equip themselves in a manner befitting their new station. Money would fall into the laps of a Grain Intendant's staff. Or so they had assumed. But now all their plans were being foiled by their master's blind insistence on enforcing the regulations to the last letter and by his obstinate refusal to accept a single one of the bribes offered by the sub-prefects and magistrates.

The porter, head clerk and other local staff in the yamen made a few mental calculations:

'If this lasts another fortnight, we'll have pawned all our clothes, and our creditors will start to press for payment; what will we do then? There's good money staring us in the face out there, if we could only lay our hands on it!'

When these locals voiced their concern to the newly arrived staff whom Jia Zheng had personally recruited in the capital, they met with an indignant response:

'*You* haven't staked your last penny on this venture – *we*'re the ones that should be complaining, not you! We paid money to get our jobs, and here we are after more than a month with nothing to show for it. At this rate we won't break even. We might as well hand in our notices tomorrow.'

Which is exactly what they did. The following day they went in a body and tendered their resignations to a bewildered Jia Zheng, who commented somewhat naïvely:

'Very well. You were free to come. You are free to return. If you find it uncongenial here, please feel under no obligation to stay.'

This group went grumbling on their way. The family servants next held a council of war among themselves:

'It's all very well for *them*. *They*'re free to go. But what about *us*? We can't leave even if we want to.'

Among these servants was a porter by the name of Li Shi (Ten), who soon took a prominent part in the debate.

'You chickens!' he scoffed. 'Don't be so helpless! While that "contract" mob was here I wasn't going to say anything; but now that they've pushed off, I don't mind showing you a trick or two! I'll soon have that Master of ours eating out of the palm of my hand! But you've got to back me up. Stick together, and we can all go home with our pockets full. Of course, if you'd rather keep out of this, that's all right by me. I can manage. I can get the better of you lot any day!'

'Come on, Ten old mate! We're depending on you!' groaned the others. 'You know you're the one the Master trusts. If you won't help us, we're done for!'

'All right. But *you*'ve got to trust me too. Don't leave me to do all the dirty work and bring in the money, and then turn on me and say I've taken more than my fair share.'

'No chance of *that*. You know we're broke. Anything's better than nothing.'

As they were speaking, the granary clerk came in, and asked for Mr Zhou. Ten, who was lounging complacently in a chair with one foot propped on his other knee and his chest puffed out, asked him what his business was with Mr Zhou. The clerk stood to attention with his hands at his sides and smiled uneasily.

'The new Intendant has been in office more than a month now,' he replied, 'but not a single granary's been opened to take in the tax-grain. The local magistrates have been made to feel uncomfortable by all his stern pronouncements. They've been quite put off from entering into the usual – how shall I put it? – negotiations. Now, if the grain is not going to be taken in and delivered on time, what's the point of *your* being here at all?'

'What a ridiculous question!' said Ten. 'Our Master the Intendant is a man of his word. Of course he'll meet his commitments. As a matter of fact he was about to issue the Reminders a couple of days ago, but on my advice they were postponed. Now, tell me what you *really* wanted to see Zhou about?'

Clerk: 'Oh, that was it . . . the Reminders. Nothing else . . .'

Ten: 'Nonsense! Don't try to fool me with that, my lad! And don't come sneaking in here with any nifty little plans, or I'll tell the Intendant to beat you and take your job away.'

Clerk: 'My family has served in this yamen for three generations; I've got a decent position here, I manage to make an honest living. I don't mind going by the book until this Intendant gets promoted and moved somewhere else. I'm not like that beggarly lot who've just left.'

He took formal leave of Li Ten:

'I'd best be going now, sir.'

Ten stood up, all smiles:

'Come on now, can't you take a joke? No need to get rattled by a few words . . .'

'I'm not rattled. I just don't want to say anything that might compromise you, sir.'

Ten walked over to the clerk and took him confidentially by the hand:

'Tell me, what's your name?'

'Zhan Hui,* sir,' replied the clerk nervously. 'I spent quite a few years up in the capital myself when I was a boy.'

'Mr Zhan! Why, of course! I've heard of you. Come now, we're all in this together. If there's something you want to talk to me about, why not drop by this evening and we can have a nice little chat.'

'We all know how capable you are, Mr Li,' replied the clerk aloud, with a sigh of relief. 'Why, you really had me worried there for a minute!'

He left amidst general laughter.

That evening Zhan returned and he and Li were closeted together deep into the night. The next day, when Li found some pretext to call on Jia Zheng, and hinted at some of the 'measures' he had in mind, predictably he received a stern reprimand.

The following day, Jia Zheng was due to pay a formal visit in the town, and he issued orders for his retinue to make themselves ready. A considerable interval of time elapsed, and the gong in the inner yamen was struck three times, but still there was no sign of anyone to beat the drum in the main hall. Someone was finally found to perform this duty, and Jia Zheng came walking out of his private chambers with measured stride, to find that there was only one attendant waiting for him, instead of the usual team of runners and criers. Resolving not to pursue this dereliction for the time being, Jia Zheng stepped into the sedan at the foot of the terrace and waited for his chair-bearers. Another long interval elapsed before these had all assembled and were ready to carry him out of the yamen, and the Intendant's solemn departure was then announced by a single feeble report from the cannon, while a grand total of two members of the ceremonial band, a drummer and a bugler, put in a forlorn appearance on the bandstand. Jia Zheng was now extremely annoyed.

* Homophone for 'bribery'.

'Things have been in perfect order until today. What's the meaning of this shambles?'

His insignia-bearers, such as they were, straggled across the road in an unseemly fashion. Jia Zheng concluded his visit as best he could, and immediately upon his return summoned the defaulters and threatened them with a flogging. Some pleaded that they had been unable to attend because they lacked the requisite headgear, others that they had been forced to pawn their uniforms, while some claimed that they had not eaten for three days and were therefore too weak for heavy carrying duties. Jia Zheng vented his anger on them verbally, ordered a couple of them to be flogged and left it at that.

The next day the chief cook came asking for more money, and Jia Zheng had to provide him with some of the personal reserve he had brought with him from home. From then on, one such incident followed another and it soon became apparent that most departments of his provincial yamen were in total disarray. In the end he was driven to send for Porter Li, and asked him outright:

'What's come over my staff? You must try to instil some sense of discipline in them. And another thing: my reserve of cash has run out, and it will be some time before my salary arrives from the Provincial Treasurer's office, so we shall have to send home for extra funds.'

'I've had words with the staff almost every day, sir,' replied Li. 'But I can't do a thing with them. They seem to have lost all interest in their work. Gone to pieces, sir. As for the money, may I ask how much you will be requiring? I understand the Viceroy has a birthday coming up in a few days' time, and the Prefects and Circuit Intendants are mostly giving four-figure donations. How much will you be sending, sir?'

Jia Zheng: 'You should have told me of this earlier.'

Li: 'With respect, sir, it's the fault of the local mandarins. They've not kept you informed. It's because we're new here and haven't made any effort to get to know them. It wouldn't surprise me if they had an eye on your job and were even hoping you would fail to attend the Viceroy's birthday altogether, sir . . .'

Jia Zheng: 'That's preposterous! I was appointed by His Majesty. I am hardly to be relieved of my post for not attending the Viceroy's birthday!'

Li (with a smile): 'That's all very well, sir. The trouble is that with the capital such a long way off, His Majesty relies on the Viceroy for all his information. If the Viceroy speaks ill of a person, there's not much hope of that person being able to defend himself, whatever the truth might be. Now I'm sure Her Old Ladyship and Their Ladyships want to see you do well for yourself here . . .'

Jia Zheng began to see what he was driving at:

'Why couldn't you have said all this before?'

Li: 'At first I didn't dare, sir. Seeing that you asked me, it would have been wrong of me not to speak up. But I'm sure what I've got to say is only going to make you angry.'

Jia Zheng: 'Not if it is reasonable. Go on.'

Li: 'Well, sir: the truth of the matter is that the staff in a Grain Intendant's yamen expect to make a bit on the side. Your clerks and runners have all paid money for their jobs. They've got families to look after and livings to earn. And so far as they're concerned, sir, since you've been here, all you've done is set the local people grumbling.'

Jia Zheng: 'What do you mean? Grumbling about what?'

Li: 'The way the locals see it is quite simple. Officials all behave like that when they first arrive. The stricter they sound, the more certain it is that they're on the squeeze, trying to browbeat the mandarins working in the district. When the time comes for the tax-grain to be collected, the yamen staff will repeat your instructions, they'll swear that they're not allowed to take a penny; and it will only mean a lot of unnecessary trouble and delay for the country people, who'd much rather have things the old way – pay up a bit and get the whole thing over and done with as quickly as possible. So, in short, instead of speaking well of you, they just complain that you haven't understood their situation.

'Look at that smart relation of yours, sir – that Mr Jia Yu-cun you've always been so friendly with. In a few years he's done very well for himself, and all because he's shrewd. He's got a good sense of what's what in the world, he knows how to handle his superiors and staff and how to keep everything running smoothly . . .'

Jia Zheng: 'This is ridiculous! Are you suggesting that I possess no such sense? Harmony is one thing: but I draw the line at collusion!'

Li: 'It's only my concern for you that causes me to speak my mind, sir. If I stand by and let you carry on like this, if I don't even warn you and if your career is ruined as a result, you'll think very poorly of me.'

Jia Zheng: 'Well: what precisely are you suggesting?'

Li: 'My advice is to take immediate action; do the sensible thing, secure your own interests *now*, while you're in your prime and still in favour at court, and while Her Old Ladyship still enjoys good health. Otherwise, before the year's out, you may find you've used all your own funds to cover official expenses. No one in the government service will have the slightest sympathy for you then. No one will believe that you're poor. They'll all think that you're sitting on a secret pile of money; and if anything goes wrong, none of them will come forward to help you. You'll find it impossible to clear yourself, and by then it'll be too late to wish you'd followed my advice.'

Jia Zheng: 'In short, what you are saying is that I must allow myself to be corrupted! The consequences for myself of such a de-reliction of duty, even death itself, I consider as nothing compared with the disgrace that would tarnish my family's honour.'

Li: 'You're a wise man, sir. If it's family honour you're bothered about, then think back for a moment to that group of officials who got themselves into such disgrace a few years ago; good friends of yours they were, good men, men you used to call "above corruption". Where's *their* family honour now? But certain other relatives of yours, men you used to call "downright rogues", have done very well for themselves, gone from strength to strength. What's been their secret? They just knew how to adapt. You've got to look after the common people, but you've got to look after the local mandarins as well. If your ideas came into general fashion and the shire or district man-darins were strictly forbidden to take even the tiniest squeeze, why, nothing would *ever* get done in the provinces!

'You keep things respectable on the outside, and leave all the inside work to me. I'll manage things so you don't have to be personally involved. I am only trying to be helpful, sir. It's the least I owe you after being with you all these years.'

Jia Zheng hesitated. 'I suppose I too must look to my own sur-vival,' he said in the end. 'Do whatever you must. But I will play no part in it.'

He walked stiffly back into his private chambers.

Li Ten now came into his own and began to implement his plans with a vengeance. He had soon organized, behind Jia Zheng's back, an elaborate squeeze operation involving yamen staff and local mandarins. On the surface, day-to-day business in the yamen began running smoothly again, so smoothly that Jia Zheng allowed himself to set his mind at rest and, far from suspecting that anything was amiss, put absolute faith in Li. Any irregularities reported to his superiors were discounted by them in view of Jia Zheng's record for scrupulous honesty. His private secretaries had a shrewder idea of what was going on and tried to caution him. When he refused to listen, some of them resigned, others decided to stay on for friendship's sake. Thus it was that the tax-grain for that year was eventually collected and shipped to the capital without any apparent mishap.

*

One day, in one of his free moments, Jia Zheng was sitting in his study reading, when the chief clerk sent in a letter. It bore an official seal and the superscription:

From the Commandant of Haimen and surrounding Coastal Region
To the Yamen of the Kiangsi Grain Intendant
By Express Delivery

Jia Zheng opened the envelope and examined its contents:

Honoured Sir,
Last year when duty called me to the capital, I was privileged, on the strength of our common Nanking origin, to enjoy your hospitality on a number of occasions. At that time you graciously favoured my suggestion that the connection between our two families be further strengthened by a matrimonial alliance. I have since then had this constantly in the forefront of my mind, but was reluctant to press the matter after my transfer to maritime defence in this remote region. That circumstances should have put such an obstacle in the way of our plans has been a source of great regret to me. Now that the light of your noble presence illumines these southern skies, however, that obstacle has been removed. I had been thinking to write and send you my felicitations, when I received your letter.
From his bivouac an old soldier raises his hand in humble salute! Even on these distant shores, I feel myself basking in the genial warmth of your benevolence.
Dare I hope for your consent if I now propose this alliance once more? My son was favoured, I recall, with your gracious approval, and we have long anticipated the great joy that your daughter's charming presence would bring to our household.

If you are kind enough to confirm your acceptance, I shall despatch a go-between without delay. Though the journey is a long one for your daughter, it can be accomplished by boat. And though I cannot offer much in the way of pomp and ceremony, I can at least send a suitably furnished barge to receive her.

This brief missive carries my most sincere congratulations on your new appointment. In eager anticipation of your favourable response, believe me to be, honoured sir, your most humble and respectful servant,

Zhou Qiong.

'Fate seems indeed to play a decisive role in affairs of matrimony,' reflected Jia Zheng to himself after perusing the letter. 'I do remember suggesting this betrothal last year. There seemed to be several factors in its favour: Zhou was taking up an appointment in the capital, he and I were old friends and both from Nanking families, and his son was a good-looking enough young man. It was only a casual suggestion, and I never mentioned it at home. Afterwards he was transferred to Maritime Defence and the matter was dropped. And yet now an unforeseeable stroke of fate has sent me here to the provinces, and Zhou has broached the subject once more. Theirs seems a suitable family, and I think it would be a good match for Tan-chun. But I am here on my own, and I shall have to write home to consult them first.'

He was still deliberating, when one of the gate-attendants came in with an official despatch summoning him to a conference with the Viceroy, and he had to set out at once for the Viceroy's seat. After his arrival there, he was awaiting further instructions and sitting in his temporary lodgings, idly leafing through a pile of *Peking Gazettes* that lay on the table, when his eye was caught by a report from the Board of Punishments:

'In the case of Xue Pan, travelling on business, registered domicile Nanking . . .'

'Good heavens!' exclaimed Jia Zheng in some alarm. 'Have they memorialized already?'

He read on more carefully. The gist of the report was that Xue Pan, having killed Zhang San 'in an affray', had connived with the relatives of the deceased and other eyewitnesses to get himself off on a charge of 'accidental homicide'. Jia Zheng brought his hand down with a thump on the table.

'He's done for!'

He read the report through to the end:

The Metropolitan Governor has forwarded the following abstract of the case:

Xue Pan of Nanking, while travelling through the town of Tai-ping, stayed at Li's Inn. One of the waiters employed by Gaffer Li the proprietor was a certain Zhang San, with whom Xue was not previously acquainted. On the ___ day of the ___ month of the year ___, Xue Pan placed an order with the proprietor for some wine, as he had invited Wu Liang (a native of Tai-ping) to drink with him. When his guest came, he sent the waiter Zhang San to bring them the wine. The wine was sour, and Xue Pan told him to replace it with something better. Zhang San argued that since that particular wine had been ordered, it was impossible to change it. Xue Pan considered Zhang's behaviour insolent and raised his cup to throw the wine in his face. Unfortunately he exerted too much force and the cup slipped from his hand just as Zhang lowered his head to retrieve a chopstick from the ground. The cup struck Zhang on the top of the head, there was a substantial loss of blood, and he died shortly afterwards. Gaffer Li hurried to the scene but was too late to be of any help. He informed Mrs Zhang, née Wang, the deceased's mother, who came to the inn only to find her son already dead. She called out the beadle and brought a plaint at the local yamen. The then acting magistrate held an inquest and the coroner completed the usual certificate. Two crucial facts were, however, omitted: first, that the bregmatic fracture was one and one-third inches long; and second, that Zhang had also sustained injuries *in the small of the back*. The case was then sent up to the prefectural yamen, where it was confirmed that Xue Pan had only intended to throw the wine, that the cup had slipped from his hand, and that he had therefore accidentally caused the death of Zhang San. He was dealt with according to the law relating to Accidental Homicide, and permitted to pay a fine in commutation.

The Board has investigated the evidence given by the accused, by the various eyewitnesses and by the relatives of the deceased, and has found it to be inconsistent. It has also consulted the detailed provisions of the code relating to homicide, wherein a fight is defined as a 'struggle between two persons', and an affray as a 'struggle in which the parties strike one another'. There must be no evidence of such a fight or struggle if the offence is to be classified as accidental homicide. The case was therefore handed back to the office of the Metropolitan Governor to establish the exact facts, on the basis of which a final recommendation for sentence could be reached.

This is the substance of the Governor's final findings: Xue Pan was already intoxicated when Zhang San refused to replace the wine. Seizing Zhang by the right hand, *he struck him in the small of the back*. Whereupon Zhang began to abuse Xue Pan, who then *hurled his wine cup at him*, inflicting a severe wound on his skull. The bone was fractured, causing damage to the brain and immediate death. In other words, Zhang's death was directly caused by the force with which Xue Pan threw the cup. Xue Pan should therefore pay for this crime with his life. In accordance with the code relating to Homicide by Blows, he should be kept in custody until the Assizes, and then executed by strangulation. Wu Liang should be flogged and sentenced to penal servitude.

The Prefectural, Shire and District Magistrates implicated in this miscarriage of Justice should be dealt with as follows . . .

The report broke off at this point with the note 'To be continued'.

Jia Zheng reflected that it was he who, at Aunt Xue's request, had brought pressure to bear on the local magistrate to reverse the verdict in Xue Pan's case. If that magistrate had now been cashiered, and an enquiry had been held, he could be implicated himself. It was very worrying. He read through the next issue of the *Gazette*, but there was no further mention of the case. He searched through all the remaining issues without being able to find the conclusion of the report. He began to feel more and more uneasy, and was deep in thought when Li Ten came in and said:

'Will you please proceed to the yamen to attend on the Viceroy, sir? His attendants have already beaten the drum twice.'

Jia Zheng was miles away and heard none of this. Li had to repeat himself.

'What can I do?' muttered Jia Zheng to himself.

'Is something the matter, sir?' asked Li.

Jia Zheng confided to Li his anxiety about the report in the *Gazette*.

'Don't you worry too much about that, sir,' said Li. 'In fact, if you ask me, Mr Xue was quite lucky. Back in the capital I heard that he invited a lot of women along to that very inn and that they were all there together getting drunk and causing quite a rumpus on the very evening when he beat this waiter to death. And I heard that the local mandarin was not the only one to do the family a favour. Apparently Mr Lian spent a small fortune on the case, and sent bribes to every yamen concerned, to try to get Mr Pan off. It's funny the Board hasn't mentioned that in its report. I suppose in one way it's only to be expected. Now this affair has come to light, the people involved must all be busy covering up for each other. They're trying to sweep the whole thing under the carpet. They want to make it seem like a minor case of negligence. Then the worst that can happen to them is that they'll lose their jobs. They'd never want to admit to bribes being taken. Much too serious. Don't you worry about this one, sir, I'll get hold of the inside story. We'd best not keep the Viceroy waiting any longer . . .'

'You don't understand,' said Jia Zheng. 'It's the local magistrate I feel sorry for. For doing us this favour, he has forfeited his job. And that may not even be the end of it for him.'

'It won't do any good worrying about him, sir,' said Li. 'Your attendants have been waiting for a long time. You'd best be going in to see the Viceroy now, sir.'

To learn what it was the Viceroy wanted of Jia Zheng, please read the next chapter.

CHAPTER 100

Caltrop disturbs an elaborate seduction
and inspires bitter resentment
Bao-yu learns of a distressing betrothal
and laments an imminent departure

Jia Zheng was with the Viceroy for a long time, and outside the yamen speculation mounted as to the reason for the summons. Li Ten, in the absence of any information, assumed that his master was wanted in connection with this latest trouble in the *Gazette*, and feared the worst. At last the interview was over, and Li hurried forward to meet Jia Zheng and accompany him home. He was too impatient to wait until their return, and as soon as they were alone he asked Jia Zheng:

'What kept you so long, sir? Something of great importance, I suppose?'

Jia Zheng smiled.

'Not really. It turns out that the Commandant of the Haimen region, who has offered his son's hand in marriage to my daughter, is himself related to the Viceroy, and has written asking him to take a special interest in my well-being. The Viceroy was most affable, and even went so far as to say to me: "Now we are related too!" '

Li rejoiced inwardly, seeing in this new turn of events cause to be bolder still in his own schemes. He encouraged Jia Zheng enthusiastically to proceed with the marriage.

Communications between Kiangsi and the capital were slow, and it was hard for Jia Zheng to know whether or not he was personally implicated in Xue Pan's troubles. At such a great distance it would be difficult for him to influence the course of events in Xue Pan's favour. When he returned to his own yamen, he despatched a family servant to the capital to ascertain exactly what had happened, and at the same time to carry a message to Grandmother Jia, informing her of the marriage proposal. If she agreed, he suggested that Tan-chun should be sent straight away to join him, in preparation for the wedding. The servant set off with all speed for the capital. He reported first to Lady Wang, and then went to the Board of Civil Office, where his enquiries revealed that the only person to have suffered in the Xue Pan affair was the acting magistrate of Tai-ping, who had lost his job, and that Jia Zheng was not in any way implicated. The servant sent back a reassuring report to Jia Zheng, himself remaining behind to await further developments.

*

It will be remembered to what lengths Aunt Xue had gone, and with what large sums of money she had bribed the various courts involved, to bring in a verdict of 'accidental homicide' in the earlier stages of Xue Pan's case. She had been proposing to raise the money for his fine by selling the family pawnshop business. Now when she heard of the new verdict brought by the Board of Punishments, she sent still more bribes, but to no avail. The sentence was confirmed – death by strangulation after the Autumn Assizes. Day and night she wept tears of grief and rage.

Bao-chai visited her several times and tried to offer consolation:

'Brother Pan must have been born under an unlucky star, Mama! With the fortune that Grandpa left, he should have been able to lead a quiet and comfortable life. But instead it's been one disaster after another. First came Nanking and that disgraceful business over Caltrop. He was entirely to blame for that poor young man's death, and it was just lucky for him that we still had plenty of pull and money in those days, and were able to get him off.

'You'd have thought a scrape like that would have been enough to make him mend his ways. You'd have thought he might have taken life a bit more seriously after that and devoted more time to looking after his own mother. But no, as soon as we arrived here, it was the same story all over again. I hate to think how much you've suffered on his account, Mama, how many tears you've shed. Then he got married, and at last we thought life might quieten down a bit for all of us. But fate evidently had something else in mind. Eventually that dreadful woman drove him away with her insufferable carryings-on.

'And even *that* was not the end of it. As the saying goes: "Fate moves in a narrow lane, and collisions are hard to avoid!" It was only a few days before he was mixed up in this new murder case! You and Cousin Ke have done everything you possibly could. Apart from all the money you've spent, you've never stopped asking for help and thinking of ways to get him out. You can't go on struggling with fate. He'll have to pay the price for his own misdeeds.

'Most parents look to their children for support in their old age, and even in poor families a man will do his best to earn his mother a bowl of rice. But what has Pan done? Squandered a ready-made fortune, and made your life a misery. I know I shouldn't say this, but the truth is, he's the bane of your life, an affliction sent to test you, not a real son to you. You refuse to accept the truth, and wear yourself out like this, weeping at all hours of the day and night. You've got quite enough to cope with already, what with Jin-gui and her tantrums. It worries me so, seeing you in this state. I only wish I could be here with you all the time, and help keep the peace. But I can't. Bao-yu would never let me come back, however half-witted he may be.

'The other day Sir Zheng sent a message home to say how shocked he was to read the report in the *Gazette*. He has already sent one of his men to try to intervene on Pan's behalf. So you see – there are so many people trying to help Pan out of this mess he's made. And thank goodness I'm at least close by. I think if I were living a long way off and heard that this had happened, I'd simply die worrying about you. Please, Mama, give yourself a moment's respite. Be thankful that Pan is still alive. Use this opportunity to take stock. Ask one of the older men in the firm to find out what we owe and what we are owed, and see exactly how much we have left.'

'Dear girl,' said Aunt Xue tearfully, 'the past few days I have been so preoccupied with your brother I simply haven't had time to tell you of our own troubles. Whenever you've come to see me it's either been you trying to cheer me up or me giving you the latest news from the yamen. I haven't told you the worst. We have been struck off the register of court purveyors. Two of our pawnshops have been sold and we have already spent the money from the sale, while the manager of the other pawnshop has run off with thousands of taels and we're involved in another court case over that. Your cousin Ke has been out every day trying to collect some of the money owing to us. Our liabilities here will probably amount to several tens of thousands of taels, and we shall have to sell our share of the Nanking joint-stock business and some property as well, in order to meet our obligations. Two days ago I even heard a rumour that the pawnbroking side of the Nanking business has gone bankrupt and been closed down! If that turns out to be true, I really have come to the end of the road!'

Aunt Xue began weeping hysterically. Bao-chai was also in tears by now, but tried to comfort her:

'There's no sense in your distressing yourself about the finances, Mama. Let Cousin Ke take care of that. Though I must say it *is* distressing to see our employees abandon us and turn against us the moment we're down on our luck. I can understand them wanting to save their own skins; but I know that some of them are actually encouraging outsiders to cheat us out of our money. As for Pan's friends, it's a waste of time expecting any help from them. The only thing they're any good for is parties. The first sign of trouble and they're off.

'If you love me, Mama, please listen to my words of advice. At your age it's time you took more care of yourself and worried about others less. Remember, even if the worst comes to the worst, you'll manage somehow or other. Forget about the clothes and furniture. Let Jin-gui have them. Not many of the servants or serving-women will want to stay on, so you may as well let most of them go too. I feel sorry for Caltrop. After everything she's been through, I think you should keep her on with you. If you ever run short of anything, I can always help out, provided we've got it at home. I'm sure *he* wouldn't mind. And Aroma is a decent sort of girl. She knows about our troubles; in fact the slightest mention of your name brings tears to her eyes. *He* doesn't know that anything's the matter, so he hasn't been particularly worried. If he were to learn the truth, I think the shock might be too much for him.'

'Dear girl,' said Aunt Xue, not waiting for her to finish, 'whatever you do, don't tell him. He nearly died on account of Miss Lin. He's a little better now. If he were to have a sudden relapse, it would be such a trial for you! And then if you had to spend all your time nursing him, I should be robbed of my last source of comfort.'

'I've thought of that,' replied Bao-chai. 'That's why I haven't told him.'

At that very moment Xue Pan's wife Jin-gui came running into the outer room, screaming:

'What's the good of being alive? My man's done for now anyway.

It's no use pretending! The least we can do is march along to the execution ground and put up a fight! We've got nothing to lose!'

With this she began banging her head against the wooden partition, till her hair came undone and fell in disorder about her shoulders. Aunt Xue could only stare at her in speechless rage, while Bao-chai tried to reason with her 'dear sister-in-law', her 'good sister-in-law', all to no avail.

'*Dear* Mrs Bao!' retorted Jin-gui. 'We all know how well you've done for yourself. You and your *dear* Mr Bao will live happily ever after, I dare say! But I'm all on my own. I'm long past caring about appearances!'

She announced her intention of returning to her mother's, and made a dash for the street. Luckily there were enough people present to stop her, and eventually they managed to calm her down. Bao-qin, who was at this time still staying with Aunt Xue, in preparation for her own wedding, was so horrified by Jin-gui's behaviour that she resolved to keep well out of her way from then on.

*

Whenever Xue Ke was at home, Jin-gui would select one of her more provocative gowns and issue forth, her cheeks heavily powdered and rouged, her eyebrows pencilled, her hair dressed in its most alluring style. She would contrive to walk past his apartment, where she would give an artificial-sounding cough, or ask innocently who was inside. If she encountered him in person, she would at once waylay him and attempt to beguile him with seductive small-talk, simpering, pouting and purring by turns, displaying for his benefit the full range of her feminine charms. When the maids saw what she was up to, they beat a hasty retreat. Jin-gui carried on regardless, intent on executing Moonbeam's plan for the conquest of Xue Ke. He for his part avoided her if he could, and if he could not, endeavoured to be civil, out of a fear that she might otherwise cause worse trouble for him.

But Jin-gui's infatuation blinded her to the truth, so that Xue Ke's courteous manner only fanned the flames of her desire. The one thing she could not help noticing, however, the one detail that marred the illusion, was the way in which the object of her passion entrusted every smallest thing of his to Caltrop. The sorting, mending and washing of his clothes, all were given to her. And if she, Jin-gui, entered the room while the two of them were talking, she noticed how they hurriedly went their separate ways, as if she had intruded on some intimate tête-à-tête. All of this inflamed her jealousy. She could not, however, bring herself to confront Xue Ke directly about it, for fear that any move against Caltrop might set Xue Ke against herself. Instead she decided to bide her time, and continued to accumulate a deep and bitter store of resentment towards her rival.

One day Moonbeam came into her room and tittered:

'Mrs Pan, have you seen Master Ke?'

Jin-gui: 'I have not.'

Moonbeam: 'I told you he was fooling us with all that strait-laced talk of his. When *we* sent him some wine, he said he didn't drink; but just now I saw him at Mrs Xue's, quite tipsy and red in the face. If you don't believe me, why, go and wait for him in the doorway. He'll be coming this way. Stop him and ask him. See what he says.'

Jin-gui (annoyed): 'I'm sure he won't be coming out just yet. Anyway, he's such a cold fish. Words are wasted on him.'

Moonbeam: 'You're just being silly again, ma'am. Why not give it a try? If he plays, we can play too. If not, we'll just have to think of another way.'

Perhaps she's right after all, Jin-gui thought to herself. She posted Moonbeam outside to keep watch for Xue Ke, and went in once more to her dressing-table. She opened her mirror and looked herself up and down. A little more lipstick, a flowery handkerchief, and she was ready for the fray. Or almost ready: she still felt there was something missing, but before she could think what it was that she needed to add that final touch, she heard Moonbeam's voice outside:

'You seem in high spirits today, Master Ke! Been drinking somewhere, have you?'

This was her cue. Jin-gui raised the *portière* and stepped out just in time to hear Xue Ke's reply:

'Our manager Mr Zhang is celebrating his birthday today, and I was pressed into drinking half a cup. My face is still burning from it.'

Before he had finished, Jin-gui moved into the attack:

'Other people's wine has more flavour than ours, I dare say . . .'

Xue Ke felt the sting of her remark and blushed a deeper shade of red. He took a step towards her and said with a polite smile:

'Of course not, sister-in-law.'

Now that the conversation was launched, Moonbeam disappeared inside and left them to it. Jin-gui had intended to feign anger with her darling, but there was something so appealingly boyish about the flush on his cheeks and the slightly befuddled innocence in his eyes, that her heart melted and her feigned hostility fled to the distant land of Java. She smiled.

'You mean, you have to be led to water . . .'

'Precisely. I'm really no drinker.'

'I'm glad to hear it. Better than your cousin, anyway, forever boozing his way into trouble. At least *your* wife won't be left to sleep in an empty bed . . .'

She narrowed her eyes at him suggestively, and her cheeks began to glow. Xue Ke saw serious danger ahead, and decided to make a dash for it while he still could. But he was too slow. Jin-gui was not going to let him slip through her fingers now! In a second she was on him and had him in her clutches.

'Sister-in-law!' cried Xue Ke in consternation. 'This is most undignified!'

He was trembling all over. Jin-gui threw caution to the winds.

'Come in here with me. There's something important I have to tell you.'

Things had reached this critical juncture when a voice behind her called:

'Mrs Pan! It's Caltrop. She's coming this way!'

Jin-gui glanced wildly behind her. Moonbeam had lifted the *portière* to observe the course the interview was taking; and then when she caught sight of Caltrop coming from the other direction, had hastened to warn Jin-gui. Jin-gui in her panic relaxed her grip, and Xue Ke seized his chance of escape. Caltrop herself had noticed nothing and had been walking innocently on her way until Moonbeam called out, when she looked round and to her horror saw Jin-gui dragging Xue Ke into her boudoir. Caltrop immediately turned about and, heart thumping, began walking back in the direction she had come from. Jin-gui stood there a while, and stared in angry dismay after the vanishing form of Xue Ke. Then she gave a snort of exasperation and withdrew to her apartment, smarting with thwarted desire. Caltrop, who had come through the side gate and was making her way to Bao-qin's when she stumbled upon them, hurried back to her room.

Resentment towards Caltrop now festered within Jin-gui's bosom, and the poison worked its way into the very marrow of her being.

*

Later that same day, Bao-chai was in Grandmother Jia's apartment, and heard Lady Wang speaking of the betrothal Jia Zheng had proposed for Tan-chun.

'I'm glad the boy's from a Nanking family,' said Grandmother Jia. 'But if he came here once before, I can't understand why Zheng has never mentioned it.'

'We knew nothing about it either,' said Lady Wang.

'I can see advantages in the match,' said Grandmother Jia. 'The only objection is the dreadful distance involved. I know that Zheng is posted there at present. But supposing he is transferred later on, poor Tan will be so isolated.'

'With official families, there's no telling where they may be posted,' replied Lady Wang. 'The boy's father may also be recalled to the capital. Even if he isn't, one way or another "the falling leaf returns to the root", as they say: they're bound to come home sooner or later. Besides, Zheng's superior is in favour of the match, and it would be very difficult for him to refuse. I think he has more or less made up his mind already, and has only written to you for your formal approval, Mother.'

'If you are both in favour of it,' said Grandmother Jia, 'then well and good. It grieves me, though, to think how long it may be before Tan is able to come back and visit us. If it is more than a year or two, I fear I may no longer be alive to see her.'

She wept as she spoke.

'Marriage is something that happens to every girl once she grows up,' said Lady Wang, 'and even if the husband's family is a local one, you can never be sure that the two of them will stay in the district. He may always be posted away from home. That's one of the hazards of official life. The most important thing is that they should be happy together. Take Ying-chun's case. Her husband lives nearby. But that has not meant happiness for her. They never seem to stop fighting, and now he won't even feed her properly, and forbids her to touch any of the things we send. And from what I hear, things are getting worse. He won't allow her to come and visit us, and when the two of them quarrel, he pointedly reminds her that we owe his family money. Poor child! The future looks very bleak for her. The other day I was worried on her account and sent some of my women to call at the Sun home. Ying-chun was hiding in a side-room and wouldn't come out to see them. They insisted on going in, and found her freezing to death, poor thing, with nothing on but some threadbare old clothes. And it was a bitterly cold day! She broke down in front of them and begged them not to reveal her miserable plight to us at home. "It's my fate to suffer like this," she said. And we're not to send her any more clothes or food or anything. They never reach her, and her husband will only accuse her of complaining again and give her another beating. So you see, Mother, Ying may be close at hand, but the very closeness only makes her suffering harder for us to bear. Her mother turns a blind eye, and her father has refused to intervene at all. She is worse off than one of our lowest-grade maids!

'Although Tan is not my own daughter, I'm sure Zheng wants to do the best for her. He has obviously seen the boy and must approve of him or he wouldn't be in favour of the match. So I hope you'll agree, and then we can choose a lucky day for her to make the journey and send a proper escort to accompany her to Zheng's official residence. I am sure Zheng will see to it at his end that everything is done in a fitting manner.'

'Very well then,' Grandmother Jia concurred. 'I'll go along with Zheng's idea, and I leave it to you to make the necessary arrangements. Choose a suitable day in the almanac for travelling. There, the matter is settled now.'

'Yes, Mother.'

Bao-chai heard all this clearly, and although she did not breathe a word of protest, she thought to herself sadly:

'Tan is one of the very best of us. And now she is being married as well and sent away. One by one our numbers are dwindling.'

Seeing that Lady Wang had risen and was taking her leave, Bao-chai accompanied her out of the room and then returned immediately to her own apartment. She said nothing to Bao-yu of Tan-chun's engagement, but told Aroma later, when she found her sewing on her own. Aroma too was very unhappy at the news.

Aunt Zhao, on the other hand, was positively delighted.

'The girl's shown me nothing but disrespect,' she thought to herself. 'No one would ever have guessed that I was her mother! I receive worse treatment at her hands than one of her maids! She's always trying to better herself, and sides with anyone rather than her own mother or brother. With her in the way, Huan would never have been able to get anywhere. If her father has sent for her, then good riddance! I've given up hoping for any respect from her. I hope she's as miserable as Ying is. I'd be glad to see it happen.'

She hurried over to Tan-chun's apartment to offer her 'congratulations'.

'You certainly are on your way up in the world, my dear!' she crowed. 'I'm sure life at your new home will be even more to your liking than it is here. You must be pleased. Now remember, I *am* your mother, for all the good it's ever done me. So don't think of me as *all* bad. And don't forget about me altogether when you're gone.'

Tan-chun refused to respond to this display of spite and kept her head bent silently over her needlework. Aunt Zhao was effectively snubbed and left the room in a state of high dudgeon.

Tan-chun could see the ridiculous side of her mother's behaviour, but none the less it left her feeling both angry and wounded, and she sat for some time weeping quietly to herself. Eventually she walked out in a weary and dejected frame of mind, thinking she would like to drop in on Bao-yu.

'Tell me, Tan,' he said, the moment she entered his apartment, 'I know that you were with Cousin Lin when she died, and that you heard music in the distance. Do you think there was some unexplained mystery behind it? Do you think Cousin Lin was really a fairy, and that at her death she was merely returning to her heavenly abode?'

Tan-chun smiled.

'That sounds like another of your fancies. It was a strange night, though, that's certainly true; and the music was unlike any that I've ever heard before. Who knows, you may even be right.'

Bao-yu took this as confirmation of his hypothesis. He also recalled the words of the man he had encountered in his strange dream of a few months before, who had said that Dai-yu was 'no ordinary mortal and no ordinary shade, but a visitor from some immortal realm'. This mingled in his mind with another vivid memory, that of the Moon Goddess in the play he had seen the previous year. The Goddess and Dai-yu possessed the same ethereal beauty, the same otherworldly charm . . . After a while, when Tan-chun had gone, he felt a sudden and overwhelming urge to have

Nightingale close at hand, and asked Grandmother Jia to send her over to his apartment.

Nightingale was unwilling, on this as on previous occasions, to comply with Bao-yu's request; but she could hardly disobey an order emanating from Grandmother Jia and Lady Wang. Whenever she was in Bao-yu's presence, she did nothing but sigh, in a way that seemed to express both grief (for her mistress) and disapproval (of Bao-yu). When they were alone together, and Bao-yu took her by the hand and asked her very tenderly to speak to him about Dai-yu, she always refused to confide in him. Bao-chai observed this attitude of hers, and far from being cross, commended her to others for her loyalty to her mistress. As for Snowgoose, although it was she who had come forward to assist at the wedding, Bao-chai thought her rather a silly sort of girl and asked Grandmother Jia and Lady Wang to marry her off to one of the pages and set them up on their own somewhere. Nannie Wang had been retained to escort Dai-yu's coffin to the South at a later date, while Dai-yu's junior maids were transferred to Grandmother Jia's apartment.

Bao-yu's grief for Dai-yu and his general state of gloom were further compounded when he considered this dispersal of the remaining occupants of the Naiad's House. Then suddenly her death struck him in a new light: Dai-yu had been (or so Tan-chun had told him) perfectly lucid at her moment of death; this lucidity, when combined with the strange music, constituted conclusive proof that she had left this world to return to a higher one; and *that* surely was cause for joy! His new-found joy was short-lived, however, for presently he overheard Bao-chai and Aroma in the next room discussing the impending marriage of Tan-chun. With a cry of dismay, he fell back weeping on the kang. Bao-chai and Aroma came hurrying in to support him, with cries of 'What's the matter?', but he was too distraught to reply. After a while he composed himself sufficiently to speak:

'This is the final blow! One by one all my sisters and cousins have been taken away from me! Cousin Lin has joined the ranks of the fairies; my eldest sister has died – though it's true that even in her lifetime we had little enough chance to be together; Ying is coupled with that brute; now Tan is being sent to the ends of the earth to be married, and I shall never set eyes on her again! As for Xiang-yun, who knows where she will end up? Bao-qin is engaged to be married and won't be with us much longer. Will no one be spared? Am I to be left here all on my own?'

Aroma was ready with words of comfort, but Bao-chai silenced her with a wave of her hand:

'Don't humour him. Let me ask him a question instead.'

She turned to Bao-yu.

'What is it that you want exactly? Do you expect all your cousins to stay here and grow up into old maids, just in order to keep you company in your dotage? Don't they have your gracious permission to marry and lead their own lives? Tan is the first of your sisters to be sent such a long way from home, and since it's Father's decision there's no going against it. As for the others, has it never occurred to you that they might have plans of their own? You're not the only person in the world with feelings of brotherly love, you know. But if everyone with those feelings adopted your attitude, for a start, I wouldn't be living with you now, I'd still be at home.

'Honestly! Reading books is supposed to improve the mind and foster a more sensible approach to life. But *your* wits seem more addled than ever! If that's what you really think, Aroma and I may as well go and live somewhere else. Then you can go ahead and invite all the others to move in and look after you.'

Bao-yu took both of them by the hand:

'I know you're right. But why must it happen so soon? Couldn't they wait till I am dust and ashes!'

Aroma put her hand over his mouth:

'There you go! More nonsense! You've only just begun to recover, and Mrs Bao's getting her appetite back again at last. If you make another scene I shall wash my hands of you altogether!'

Bao-yu knew that they were talking sense. But in his heart he couldn't find a way to their sensible point of view. 'What you are saying is obviously right,' he moaned. 'But what can I do? I feel so utterly wretched.'

Bao-chai said nothing more but secretly despatched Aroma to fetch him a sedative. They did their best to calm him down, and Aroma suggested to Bao-chai that they should ask Tan-chun to refrain from calling on Bao-yu before her departure.

'There's no need to worry,' said Bao-chai. 'In a day or two, when he's in a more reasonable frame of mind, it would actually be a good thing for them to have a long talk. Tan is an extremely intelligent person, and not the type to pander to the sensibilities of others. I'm sure she'll give him some sound advice, and help to cure him from thinking in this way.'

Meanwhile Faithful arrived with a message from Grandmother Jia who had just learned of Bao-yu's relapse. Aroma was to comfort him and on no account to allow him to fret. Aroma assured Faithful that she would follow Grandmother Jia's instructions, and after sitting with them for a short while Faithful returned.

Grandmother Jia was also concerned about the preparations for Tan-chun's departure. Although Tan-chun would not be travelling with a complete trousseau, they should nevertheless provide her with all the personal effects she might need. Grandmother Jia sent for Xi-feng, told her of Jia Zheng's decision and placed these arrangements in her hands. Xi-feng undertook this responsibility, but to learn how she managed you must turn to the next chapter.

CHAPTER 101

*In Prospect Garden a moonlit apparition
repeats an ancient warning
And at Scattered Flowers Convent
the fortune-sticks provide a strange omen*

Xi-feng returned to her apartment and, seeing that Jia Lian had not yet come home, began supervising the preparation of Tan-chun's baggage and trousseau.

Later that evening, as dusk was giving way to night, she suddenly conceived the idea of going to visit Tan-chun. She told Felicity and a couple of other maids to accompany her, and sent one of them on ahead with a lantern. As they walked out, a brilliant moon had already risen, and Xi-feng told the maid carrying the lantern that she would not be needed and could go home. Then, as they passed the window of the tea-room frequented by the domestics, she heard the sound of chattering coming from within. An animated discussion of some sort seemed to be in progress, punctuated by an occasional sob or burst of laughter. It must be some of the older serving-women gathered for a gossip, thought Xi-feng; curious, and not a little apprehensive, she told Crimson to go in and mingle with them.

'Listen carefully,' she said. 'Lead them on, and find out what it is they're talking about.'

'Yes, ma'am,' said Crimson, and went on her errand.

Xi-feng continued towards the Garden, accompanied now only by Felicity. The gate had been left ajar and mistress and maid were able to push it lightly open and walk in. Within the Garden the moonlight seemed even brighter, and the trees cast deep pools of shadow. The intense silence created an atmosphere of extreme solitude and desolation. They were about to take the path to Autumn Studio when a gust of wind blew through the trees, releasing a shower of falling leaves and soughing through the branches with a doleful sound that startled the crows and other nesting birds into flight. Xi-feng had drunk a little wine earlier in the evening, and the wind, when it blew upon her, set her trembling.

'How cold it is!' said Felicity from behind, huddling up to try to keep warm. The cold was even too much for Xi-feng.

'You'd better go home straight away and fetch me my ermine-lined sleeveless jacket. I shall wait for you at Miss Tan's.'

Felicity was glad of a chance to put on some warmer clothes herself, and needed no second bidding.

'Yes, ma'am,' she replied, turning about at once and heading for home at a run.

Xi-feng had not walked much further when she thought she heard something behind her, a strange sound, like that of an animal snuffling. Her hair stood on end, and looking back she caught sight of something black and shiny, a nose, pointed, sniffing in her direction, and two eyes that glowed like lanterns. She was beside herself with terror and gave a cry of alarm, only to see the creature – for it was now recognizable as some sort of large dog – pad away from her, trailing a bushy tail. It went bounding up to the top of a mound of earth, stood stock-still, and then turned back towards her, raising its front paws in the air in a grotesque salutation.

Xi-feng – now in a state of abject panic and shaking hysterically – hurried on as fast as she could towards Autumn Studio. She had almost reached her destination and was turning past a large rock when she caught a fleeting glimpse of a figure in the shadows ahead of her. After a moment's hesitation she guessed it to be a maid from one of the apartments in the Garden, and called out:

'Who's there?'

Xi-feng repeated the question, but no one came forward. She was already beginning to feel quite faint, and in her confusion she thought she heard a voice behind her murmuring:

'Auntie, don't you even recognize me?'

She spun round and saw the figure of a lady standing there before her. There was something strangely familiar about her, the beauty of her features, the elegance of her attire; and yet somehow Xi-feng could not think for the moment whose young wife it could be.

'Auntie,' the lady continued, 'I see that the enjoyment of splendour and wealth is still your only concern, and that my warning to you years ago, to "plan for the hard times to come", has gone completely unheeded.'

Xi-feng lowered her head to try to think for a moment, but still could recall neither the person's identity, nor the occasion to which she was referring. The old lady gave a rueful laugh.

'How you loved me once! Has all memory of me been utterly erased from your mind?'

Suddenly Xi-feng knew. It was Jia Rong's first wife, Qin Ke-qing.

'*Aiyo!*' she cried. 'But you died long ago! What are you doing here?'

She spat at the ghost and fled. But as she did so she tripped on a stone, and the shock of the fall gave her senses a jolt, as if waking them from a dream. Although her whole body had broken out in a sweat and she was still shivering with fright, she now felt alert and clear-headed and could distinguish the forms of Crimson and Felicity walking in her direction. Anxious lest her disarray provoke unfavourable comment, she hurriedly raised herself from the ground.

'What have you two been doing?' she scolded them. 'You've been an age. Hurry up and bring me my jacket.'

Felicity came forward and helped her into the jacket, while Crimson supported her, ready to walk on to Autumn Studio.

'I've already been there,' said Xi-feng untruthfully. 'They are all asleep. Let's go home now.'

She set off in great haste with the two maids. She arrived to find Jia Lian already at home, and could tell from the expression on his face that he was in a worse humour than usual. Although she wanted to ask what the matter was, she reflected that she would only be scolded for her pains, and so went straight to bed.

Next morning Jia Lian rose at dawn, intending to pay an early call on Qiu Shi-an, Eunuch Superintendent of the Inner Palace, to seek his help in connection with some personal matter. He had a little time to spare before setting off, and began glancing through the copies of the *Gazette* that had been delivered the day before and were lying on his table. The first item he happened to read was a routine report from the Board of Civil Office, in which the Board requested an expedited appointment to the vacant position of Senior Secretary, and received imperial authorization to proceed according to precedent. The next report was from the Board of Punishments, and communicated a memorial from the Governor of Yunnan Province, Wang Zhong, concerning the arrest of a gang engaged in smuggling firearms and gunpowder. There were eighteen members of the gang in all, the ringleader being one Bao Yin, a domestic in the

employment of Grand Preceptor Jia Hua, Duke of Zhen-guo. Jia Lian
paused and appeared to be turning this last item of news over in his
mind for a moment. Then he read on to the next item, an impeachment
brought by Li Xiao, the magistrate of Soochow. The charge in this
case was that a certain mandarin had indulged his household servants
and allowed them to abuse their position in the maltreatment of
soldiers and civilians. It referred in particular to the attempted rape
and subsequent murder of an innocent married woman, and two other
members of her family, committed by one Shi Fu, who claimed to be a
servant in the household of Jia Fan, hereditary noble of the third degree.

Jia Lian seemed especially troubled by this last report. He would
have liked to read the sequel, but was anxious not to miss his appointment with the eunuch. Changing into formal attire and dispensing
with breakfast (though he did find time to take a couple of sips of the
tea that Patience had just brought him), he left the house, mounted
his horse and set off.

Patience put away his clothes and went in to wait on Xi-feng, who
was still in bed.

'I heard you tossing and turning last night, ma'am. You can hardly
have slept a wink. Why don't I give you a rub, and then maybe you'll
be able to have a little nap?'

Xi-feng made no reply, and Patience, interpreting this as consent,
climbed up onto the kang, sat down next to her and started to
administer a gentle massage. Xi-feng was on the point of falling
asleep when she heard Qiao-jie crying in the next room and opened
her eyes again. Patience called out:

'Nannie Li, what are you doing? Qiao-jie's crying. Go and pat her
on the back, you lazy old so-and-so!'

Nannie Li was rudely awakened from her slumbers, and vented
her ill humour on Qiao-jie by giving her a few hefty spanks, muttering to herself:

'Confound you, you wretched little brat! You've not long to live
anyway – so just shut up and go to sleep, instead of carrying on as if
your mother was dead, bawling at this ungodly hour!'

She gnashed her teeth and gave the child a pinch for good measure.
Qiao-jie began bawling again at once.

'For heaven's sake! Just listen to that!' exclaimed Xi-feng. 'She's
torturing my little girl! You go and give her the thrashing of her life,
the evil old strumpet! And bring Qiao-jie in here to me.'

'Don't be too cross, ma'am,' said Patience with a placatory smile. 'Nannie Li would never dream of doing Qiao-jie any harm. It must have been an accident. If we beat her, there will be no end to the gossip. I can just hear it: "Beating the servants before the day's even dawned!" '

After a long silence, Xi-feng heaved a deep sigh:

'See what they get up to while I'm still alive and kicking! When I die – which won't be long now – I dread to think what will become of my poor Qiao-jie!'

'How can you speak like that, ma'am?' said Patience, trying to smile again. 'Don't start the day off on such a gloomy note!'

Xi-feng smiled bitterly:

'What makes you so optimistic? I won't last much longer. I've known it for some time. When I look back over my twenty-five years, I really can't complain. I've seen things and tasted things most people have never so much as set eyes on. I've had more than my share of comfort and luxury. I've been able to indulge my every whim, no one's ever managed to get the better of me in anything. If I am fated to die young, why, that's something I shall simply have to accept.'

Tears were welling in Patience's eyes. Xi-feng laughed:

'Don't pretend to feel sorry for me! You'll be only too pleased to have me dead and out of the way. Then you'll all be able to lead happy and peaceful lives, rid of this "thorn in your flesh". There is only one thing I beg of you: whatever else happens, don't forget my little girl!'

Patience was by now in floods of tears. Xi-feng laughed again:

'Pull yourself together, for heaven's sake! I'm not going to die for a little while yet. It's too soon to start crying. Unless you want to send me to my grave before time?'

Patience dried her tears:

'I just found what you were saying so upsetting, ma'am.'

She carried on rubbing her back, and eventually Xi-feng dozed off.

Patience had no sooner climbed down from the kang than she heard footsteps outside. It was Jia Lian. He had ended up late for his appointment, and by the time he arrived Eunuch Qiu had already left for court. So he had been obliged to return home without having achieved anything, and was clearly in the blackest of moods. His first words when he saw Patience were:

'Aren't the others up yet?'

'No, sir.'

He flung aside the *portière* and walked into the inner room, exclaiming sarcastically:

'Marvellous! Still in bed at this hour! Feet up and twiddling their thumbs at a time of family crisis!'

He called impatiently for tea and Patience hastened to pour him a cup. Earlier that morning, after Jia Lian's departure, the maids and serving-women had all gone back to sleep, and as none of them had expected him back so early the household was still in a state of complete disorder. There was no fresh tea, and the best Patience could produce was a cup of cold tea warmed up. When Jia Lian discovered this, he was furious and hurled his cup to the ground. The sound of smashing china woke Xi-feng again, and she sat up in a cold sweat, crying out in alarm and staring wide-eyed around her. She saw her husband sitting beside the kang in a fuming rage, and Patience stooping to retrieve the fragments of broken cup.

'Why are you back so soon?' she asked. After a long interval in which no answer was forthcoming, she repeated the question, and finally he shouted at her:

'Would you rather I hadn't come back at all? Do you wish I'd dropped down dead somewhere?'

'That's a little unnecessary, isn't it?' said Xi-feng, smiling uneasily. 'I just wondered why you were back so early today, that's all. It's nothing to lose your temper about.'

'I failed to see the man again, so there was nothing to be gained by *not* coming home.' His voice was still raised.

'In that case,' said Xi-feng, still attempting a wan smile, 'you'll just have to be patient and wait till tomorrow. Go a bit earlier next time, and you'll be sure to see him.'

'Here I am,' shouted Jia Lian, 'up to my eyes in work of my own, with no one to lend me a hand, and I have to waste my time like this chasing another man's game! I've been tearing around days on end, and heaven alone knows why, when the person really involved is sitting at home and having a good time! He doesn't seem the least bit bothered. On the contrary, he's even had the nerve to throw a birthday party, with plays and all sorts of fun and games – while *I'm* still running around in circles trying to sort out his mess!'

He spat on the ground, and then proceeded to give Patience a thorough ticking-off for good measure. Xi-feng was choking with indignation. Her first impulse was to argue it out with him. But after a moment's reflection she thought it advisable to contain herself and still struggled to keep a smile on her face:

'But why work yourself up into such a rage about it? And why come ranting at me at this hour of the day? Did I ever say you had to do anyone this favour? If you've promised to, then be patient and go through with it for their sake. Anyway, it's inconceivable that someone in serious trouble could feel in the mood for parties and plays.'

Jia Lian: 'Precisely! Perhaps you'd like to go and ask him about it yourself tomorrow!'

Xi-feng (surprised): 'Ask whom?'

Jia Lian: 'Your brother.'

Xi-feng: '*Him?*'

Jia Lian: 'Of course! Who else?'

Xi-feng (concerned): 'But why does *he* need your help?'

Jia Lian: 'You're so well informed, you might as well be stuck at the bottom of a pickle-jar!'

Xi-feng: 'But I had no idea he was in any kind of trouble! How extraordinary!'

Jia Lian: 'Of course you didn't. Even Aunt Wang and Aunt Xue don't know about it. I didn't want to worry them. And you're always telling me how ill you are, so I decided to try to keep the whole thing from you as well. The very mention of it is enough to put me in a rage. Even today I wouldn't have told you, if you hadn't pressed me. No doubt you think that brother of yours is a marvellous fellow! But do you know what people call him?'

Xi-feng: 'What?'

Jia Lian: '*Wang Ren.*'

Xi-feng let out a puzzled little laugh.

'Well, that's his name, isn't it?'

Jia Lian: 'That's what *you* think. It's not *that* "Wang Ren"; it's the one meaning "Blind to all forms of human decency"!'

Xi-feng: 'Why, that's an insult! Who'd ever say such a thing?'

Jia Lian: 'It's no less than he deserves! I may as well tell you the truth, so that you can see for yourself what sort of a brother you really have. What about this birthday party he's giving for Uncle Zi-sheng?'

Xi-feng thought for a moment, then exclaimed:

'*Aiyo!* Why yes, now that you mention it, that's something I meant to ask you about: surely Uncle Zi-sheng's birthday falls during the winter? Bao-yu used to go every year. How strange! I remember quite clearly. When Uncle Zheng was promoted and Uncle Zi-sheng sent those players over, I made a mental note to myself. It seemed so out of character for him to do a thing like that. Uncle Zi-sheng has always been the mean one, not at all like Uncle Zi-teng. In fact the two brothers were always at daggers drawn. You only have to look at the casual way Uncle Zi-sheng behaved when Uncle Zi-teng died. You'd never have thought they were even related.

'I remember saying that when his next birthday came round we should be sure to send him some players as a return gesture, so as not to be beholden to him. But surely it's much too early in the year for him to be celebrating his birthday now? What's going on?'

Jia Lian: 'You still haven't got the faintest idea, have you? The very first thing your precious brother Ren did when he got back to the capital was to profit from Uncle Zi-teng's death by holding a memorial service. He was afraid we'd try to put a stop to it so he never told us. The funeral donations brought him in several thousand taels, I can tell you. Uncle Zi-sheng was furious with him afterwards for cornering the market. This put your brother in a bit of a spot. So for his next little project he picked Uncle Zi-sheng's birthday, the perfect opportunity to make some more money for himself, *and* placate old Zi-sheng into the bargain. He wasn't going to be held back by what the family or friends might say, or by the paltry fact that Uncle Zi-sheng doesn't really have a birthday until next winter. Let people think what they like, he doesn't care! He doesn't know the meaning of the word "pride"!

'Now, on top of all this, let me tell you why I got up so early this morning. Recently there's been a memorial from the Censorate. It's in some way connected with the recent disturbances on the coast. The wording refers to "the deficit left by Wang Zi-teng after his term of office" and asks that this deficit be "made good by his younger brother Wang Zi-sheng and by his nephew Wang Ren". The two of them got the wind up and asked me to try to pull a few strings for them. I agreed to do it for them. They seemed so pathetic and scared, and anyway I was afraid it might eventually affect you and Aunt Wang. I hoped old Qiu in the Inner Palace might see to it for me, perhaps get Uncle Zi-teng's successor to cook the books somehow. But I was late, damn it, he'd already left for court. So there I was, up at dawn, tearing around for nothing, while *they* put on plays and hold a party! If that isn't enough to make a man's blood boil, tell me what is!'

Xi-feng still felt she must put some sort of a case for her brother, partly out of her constitutional need never to admit defeat, and partly out of loyalty to her own family:

'However badly he may have behaved, he's still your brother-in-law. If you help him, you'll be doing a good turn for both of my uncles, for the living and the dead. Our family honour is at stake; so I implore you to help. Otherwise you know what will happen: I shall be held responsible for your wrath, and they'll blacken my name for ever.'

Xi-feng burst into tears. Sitting up in bed, she began to comb her hair, and to throw on some clothes.

'There's no need for you to react like that,' said Jia Lian. 'It's your brother who's behaved so abominably; I've said nothing against you. And the servants – when I had to go out this morning, I knew you were not well, so I didn't disturb you. But they just went on sleeping. Our parents never tolerated such behaviour. You've grown too slack. You want to please everybody, that's your trouble. And the moment I say anything critical, you start hauling yourself out of bed in protest. If I give the servants a piece of my mind, I suppose you'll stick up for them next. It's too absurd!'

Xi-feng dried her eyes.

'It's late,' she said. 'I ought to be getting up anyway.' After a pause, she continued: 'Even if that's how you feel, please try to do what you can for my family, for my sake. And you know how grateful Aunt Wang will be.'

'All right, all right,' grumbled Jia Lian. 'Stop teaching your grand-mother to suck eggs.'

'Why are you getting up, ma'am?' put in Patience. 'It's too early yet. And I don't see what *you* have to work yourself into such a terrible temper for, sir! Why take it all out on us? Hasn't Mrs Lian gone to enough trouble for you in the past? The number of times she's borne the brunt on your behalf! Perhaps I shouldn't say this, but in view of all that she's done for you, it doesn't seem very fair to make such a big fuss about this one favour, especially when you

think how many other people are involved. Do you have no consideration for her feelings? Why should she take all the blame anyway?
We were late getting up, and you're entitled to be angry with us –
we're only servants after all. But when you think how she has worked
herself into the ground and ruined her health, it seems so unkind of
you to pick a quarrel with her now!'

Patience's eyes filled with tears. Jia Lian's original ill humour,
strong though it had undoubtedly been, could not withstand the
combined opposition of both his womenfolk – at once so appealing
and so sharp-tongued.

'All right, forget it,' he said, with a bitter smile. 'She's hard enough
to cope with on her own, without you leaping to her defence. I know
I'm just an outsider here anyway, and you're both itching to have me
dead and out of the way.'

'Don't speak like that,' said Xi-feng. 'Who knows what will happen
to any of us? Very probably I shall die before you. The sooner I do,
the sooner my heart will be at rest.'

She began to weep again, and Patience tried to comfort her. It was
now broad daylight, and the sun was shining in at the window. Jia
Lian, who saw little prospect of steering the conversation out of this
impasse, took his leave.

Xi-feng was about to finish her toilet when one of Lady Wang's
junior maids came in:

'Her Ladyship says, will you be visiting your uncle today, ma'am,
and if so would you take Mrs Bao with you?'

Xi-feng had found the recent scene thoroughly depressing. It was
deeply mortifying that her own family should let her down so badly,
on top of which she was still suffering from the shock of her encounter in the Garden the previous evening, and felt in no mood for
an excursion.

'Tell Her Ladyship that I still have one or two things to see to,
and won't be able to go today. Anyway the party they're holding is
not what I would call a genuine occasion. If Mrs Bao wants to go,
she can go on her own.'

'Yes, ma'am.'

The maid returned with this message to Lady Wang's apartment.

When she had completed her toilet and dressed herself, Xi-feng
reflected that even if she didn't attend the party, she ought at least to
send a note. Besides, Bao-chai had not been married long, and would

probably feel rather nervous about going by herself. She decided she should visit her, if only to offer moral support, and after a brief call on Lady Wang she excused herself on some pretext and made her way to Bao-yu's apartment. He was reclining fully dressed on the kang, staring in a trance-like manner at Bao-chai, who was busy combing her hair. Xi-feng stood in the doorway for a while watching them. Bao-chai presently turned round and seeing her standing there promptly rose to her feet and asked her to be seated. Bao-yu also climbed down from the kang, as Xi-feng seated herself, with a playful smile on her face. Bao-chai scolded Musk:

'Why didn't you say that Mrs Lian was here?'

Musk laughed:

'When Mrs Lian came in, she gave us a sign to be silent.'

Xi-feng turned to Bao-yu:

'Well, what are you waiting for? Off you go! Honestly, I've never set eyes on such a great big baby. A lady wants to do her toilet in private, and you have to climb up beside her and sit there staring! Heavens above, you're man and wife now, you've all day to gawp at her. And what about the maids? Don't you care if they make fun of you?'

Xi-feng giggled and eyed Bao-yu, clicking her tongue in mock-disapproval. Her words seemed to have little effect on him other than making him feel rather uncomfortable. Bao-chai, however, blushed a fierce crimson, ashamed at having to listen but too embarrassed to reply. Aroma came in with some tea and Bao-chai endeavoured to conceal her embarrassment by offering Xi-feng a pipe of tobacco. Xi-feng rose to her feet and smilingly accepted.

'Cousin Chai, take no notice of us. Hadn't you better hurry and get dressed?'

Bao-yu meanwhile had begun shambling around, searching for something one moment, fiddling with something else the next.

'Off with you then!' said Xi-feng. 'Who ever heard of a husband waiting for his wife to go out?'

'These clothes aren't right,' said Bao-yu. 'That peacock cape Grannie gave me to wear last time I went to Uncle Zi-sheng's was so much nicer.'

'Well, go ahead and wear it this time then,' said Xi-feng teasingly.

'How can I? It's too early in the year.'

Xi-feng realized that she had inadvertently drawn attention to the incorrect 'timing' (and therefore fraudulent nature) of her uncle's party. It didn't matter so much about Bao-chai, who was herself related to the Wangs. But she felt embarrassed to have thus risked discrediting her own family in front of the maids. Aroma, whose mind was running along very different lines, hastened to add her explanation of Bao-yu's words:

'I don't think you understand, ma'am. He wouldn't wear that cape even if it were the right season.'

'Why ever not?' asked Xi-feng.

'I should explain, ma'am,' replied Aroma. 'Mr Bao's ways are sometimes so very strange. Her Old Ladyship gave him the cape to wear to his uncle Wang's party two years ago. He had an accident and burnt a hole in it. My mother was seriously ill at the time and I was at home looking after her. Skybright was still with us then, though she was already ill, and I was told when I got back that she had stayed up all night darning the cape for him. The mend was so neat that Her Old Ladyship didn't even notice it the next day. One day last year, when it was particularly cold, I told Tealeaf to take the cape to school in case Bao-yu needed something warmer to put on. But the sight of it reminded Bao-yu of Skybright and he said he never wanted to wear it again. He told me to put it away for good.'

'Poor Skybright!' put in Xi-feng before Aroma had finished speaking. 'Such a pretty girl! And so clever with her hands! If only she hadn't been quite so quick-tongued. Someone must have gone gossiping to Lady Wang, or she would never have dealt with the poor girl so harshly and driven her to such an early death.

'Which reminds me. Not so very long ago I saw Cook Liu's daughter – Fivey I think her name is – and couldn't help noticing that she's the spitting image of Skybright. I thought of bringing her in to work for me, and her mother seemed agreeable to the idea. Then I thought what a good replacement she'd make for Crimson in Bao-yu's apartment. But Patience told me it was Lady Wang's policy not to take on any more pretty maids like Skybright for Bao-yu. So I dropped the idea. Now that he's married I'm sure there can be no objection. I'll tell Fivey to start work here straight away. How would that be, Bao? Then if you ever find yourself missing Skybright, all you need to do is look at Fivey instead.'

Bao-yu had been about to leave the room, but at Xi-feng's mention of Fivey had stood there bemused. Aroma spoke for him:

'Of course he'd be pleased. He's wanted her as a maid for a long while, but knew that Her Ladyship was against the idea.'

'Very well then, I'll tell her to come tomorrow,' said Xi-feng. 'And I'll square your mother myself.'

Bao-yu's delight knew no bounds and he set off in high spirits for Grandmother Jia's apartment, leaving Bao-chai to finish her toilet.

Xi-feng had found the contrast between the way in which Bao-yu and Bao-chai clung to each other, and her own recent conflict with Jia Lian, somewhat depressing, and she was now anxious to leave. She rose and said to Bao-chai with a smile:

'Shall we go and see Aunt Wang now?'

Still smiling she walked out of the room, and Bao-chai accompanied her. They went first to Grandmother Jia's apartment, where they found Bao-yu informing the old lady of the proposed expedition to Uncle Wang Zi-sheng's. Grandmother Jia nodded:

'Off you go then. But don't drink too much, and be sure to come home early. Don't forget you're only just beginning to get well again.'

'Yes, Grannie,' said Bao-yu.

He had no sooner reached the courtyard than he turned round and re-entered the room, walking over to Bao-chai and whispering something in her ear. She smiled:

'Yes of course. Now be off with you!'

She hurried him on his way once more.

Grandmother Jia, Xi-feng and Bao-chai settled down to a conversation, but had barely exchanged three sentences when Ripple appeared:

'The Young Master has sent Tealeaf back with a message for Mrs Bao.'

Bao-chai: 'What's he forgotten now?'

Ripple: 'I told one of the junior maids to ask Tealeaf. The message is this: "The Young Master forgot to tell Mrs Bao something. She should not be too long if she *is* coming; and if she *isn't*, then she should take care not to stand in a draught".'

Grandmother Jia, Xi-feng and the entire assembly of old servingwomen and maidservants burst out laughing. Bao-chai blushed fiercely and said to Ripple with a scornful 'pfui':

'Silly creature! Is *that* worth running back in such a fluster for?'

Ripple giggled and sent a junior maid to scold Tealeaf, who raced back to Bao-yu, calling to the maid over his shoulder:

'The Young Master insisted on my dismounting to go on this fool's errand. If I *hadn't* delivered his message I'd have been in trouble with him, and now that I *have* I get it in the neck from *them*!'

The maid laughed and went running back to repeat this to the ladies. Grandmother Jia turned to Bao-chai:

'You'd better go, my dear, or he'll never stop fretting.'

What with this and Xi-feng's merciless teasing, Bao-chai felt too embarrassed to stay any longer.

*

When Bao-chai had taken her leave, Perfecta, one of the nuns from the Convent of the Scattered Flowers, came to call on Grandmother Jia. She greeted Xi-feng also, and sat down to take tea.

'Why haven't you been to see us for such a long while?' asked Grandmother Jia.

'These past few days we have had so many services at the Convent,' replied Perfecta, 'and so many grand ladies coming to make their devotions; I just haven't had a moment to call my own. Today I have a special reason for visiting Your Old Ladyship. We have a private service tomorrow which I thought you might possibly be interested in attending.'

'What kind of service is it?' asked Grandmother Jia.

'Last month,' replied Perfecta, 'the household of the late Excellency Wang was afflicted with a possession of spirits. Her Ladyship even saw her husband's departed spirit during the night. She came to tell me about it yesterday at the Convent, and pledged herself to an act of devotion at the shrine of our Bodhisattva of the Scattered Flowers. It's to be a forty-nine-day Solemn Mass for Purification of All Souls on Land and Sea, for the Preservation and Peace of All Members of the Family, for the Ascension into the Celestial Regions of All Departed Souls, and for the Well-Being in This Life of All the Living. I've been extremely busy with the preparations, and this is the first opportunity I've had to come and pay my respects.'

Xi-feng had always scorned all forms of superstition. But her encounter with Qin Ke-qing's spirit the night before had begun to undermine her scepticism, and Perfecta's words now struck a new chord in her. She could almost feel herself being converted to a belief in the efficacy of such rituals.

'Who is this Bodhisattva of the Scattered Flowers?' she asked the nun. 'How is it that he has the power to avert misfortune and keep evil spirits at bay?'

Perfecta could sense that a seed had been sown.

'Since you have asked, dear lady,' she replied, 'allow me to tell you a little about this Saint of ours. His story is an ancient and well-attested one, full of miraculous events. Born in the Land of Giant Trees in the Western Paradise, of humble parents who hewed wood for a living, the Bodhisattva came into the world with three horns on his head and four eyes in his forehead. He was three feet tall at birth, with arms so long that his hands reached the ground. His parents thought him to be the incarnation of some monstrous spirit, and abandoned him on an icy mountainside. But, unbeknown to them, this mountain was the haunt of a magic monkey, who used to come there hunting for food. On one of his excursions he discovered the child and noticed that from the tip of his head there emanated a white aura that streamed up towards Heaven, causing tigers and wolves to keep their distance.

'The monkey realized that this was someone very special indeed, and he carried the Bodhisattva-child home to his cave and reared him. The boy, so the monkey soon discovered, was endowed with prodigious innate powers of Perception, and with an intuitive ability to expound the Mysteries of Zen. He would engage the monkey in daily philosophical discussions and the two of them would practise meditation together. So wonderful were his words that at the sound of them the sky would be filled with an abundance of scattered flowers. After a thousand years had passed, he ascended into Heaven. The spot where he expounded the sutras, the Precinct of the Scattered Flowers, as it is called, can be seen on the hillside to this very day. Every prayer uttered there has proved efficacious. Many a miracle has been performed, many a soul delivered from its afflictions. In due time men built a temple there, and fashioned a statue of the Saint, before which they make offerings.'

'But what proof is there that any of this is true?' asked Xi-feng.

'Still sceptical, ma'am? What proof of that sort *can* there be, of a Living Buddha? But consider: if it were all a mere fabrication, it might have fooled one or two, but it could hardly have fooled the multitudes of intelligent men and women who have put their faith in him over the ages. The unbroken incense-offerings of believers, and the miracles wrought, testify to the enduring power of our religion and serve continually to inspire our faith.'

Xi-feng was almost convinced.

'In that case I shall visit you tomorrow and test it for myself. Do you have fortune-sticks at the temple? I should like to consult them. If they give me a plausible answer to my question, I shall embrace your faith.'

'Our fortune-sticks are particularly efficacious, ma'am,' said Perfecta. 'Try them tomorrow and see for yourself.'

'Why not wait until the day after?' put in Grandmother Jia. 'That will be the first of the month. Better to try then.'

Perfecta drank her tea and went on to visit Lady Wang, before returning to her Convent.

Xi-feng managed to struggle through the rest of that day and the next, and early in the morning of the first of the month she had her carriage made ready, and set out for the Convent of the Scattered Flowers, accompanied by Patience and a bevy of serving-women. Perfecta and the other nuns welcomed her, ushered her in and offered her tea, and then after she had washed her hands they all proceeded to the main hall of worship to burn incense. Xi-feng would not look up at the statues, but otherwise conducted herself like a devout believer, kowtowing and taking the tube of fortune-sticks from the altar. She prayed in silence, describing her encounter with the spirit and her chronic state of ill health, then shook the tube three times. There was a 'whoosh!' and one of the bamboo sticks shot out of the tube. Xi-feng kowtowed again and picked it up. It bore the inscription: 'No. 33. Supreme Good Fortune.' Perfecta promptly consulted the Divination Book and found under entry No. 33 the following line of verse, which she read aloud:

'Wang Xi-feng comes home to rest, in finery arrayed.'

Xi-feng was astounded to hear her own name, and asked the nun:

'Is there some historical person by the name of Wang Xi-feng?'

'Surely, ma'am,' replied Perfecta, 'a lady of your wide knowledge has encountered the story of Wang Xi-feng of the Later Han dynasty and what befell him on his way to the examination?'

Zhou Rui's wife was standing at Xi-feng's side and added with a smile:

'Why, that was the story the lady storyteller told at the Lantern Festival a couple of years ago. We asked her not to use your name as it was impolite.'

'Of course,' said Xi-feng with a laugh. 'I forgot.'

She went on to read the rest of the text:

> 'When twenty years away from home have passed,
> In silks the wanderer returns at last.
> The bee culls nectar from a hundred flowers;
> Honey for some, but for himself a thankless task.
>
> A traveller arrives.
>
> News is delayed.
>
> In litigation, success.
>
> In matrimony, reconsideration.'

Xi-feng could not make much sense of it, and Perfecta hastened to expound:

'My congratulations, ma'am! What an uncannily apt response on the part of the oracle! Since you have grown up here in the capital, you have never had a chance to visit your old home in Nanking. But now that Sir Zheng has received this provincial posting, he may well send for his family to join him and then, surely, you will "come home to rest, in finery arrayed"!'

As she spoke Perfecta copied down the text and gave it to one of the maids. Xi-feng was still only half-convinced by her interpretation. Perfecta set a vegetarian meal before her guest, but Xi-feng seemed loath to eat, and after a mouthful put down her chopsticks and rose to leave. She gave Perfecta a contribution 'for incense', and the nun, realizing that she could not persuade her to stay any longer, saw her out of the Convent.

When Xi-feng returned home, Grandmother Jia, Lady Wang and the others insisted on having a full report. She told one of the maids to recite the words of the divination, complete with the interpretation. The ladies were delighted:

'Perhaps Sir Zheng *is* planning to send for us all! What a nice trip that would be!'

Any doubts Xi-feng still harboured about the favourable reading of the omen were dispelled by their unanimous acceptance of it.

*

Our story now turns to Bao-yu. On the day in question, after waking from his midday nap, he noticed that Bao-chai was out and was beginning to wonder where she might be, when he saw her come back into the room.

'Where have you been?' he asked. 'You've been out a long time.'

'I've been looking at Cousin Feng's divination.'

Bao-yu was keen to hear the whole story. Bao-chai obliged; and when she had finished reciting the divination verse for him, she commented:

'Everyone else says it's a lucky omen, but personally I think there's more to the words than meets the eye. "Comes home to rest, in finery arrayed." Hm . . . We shall have to wait and see.'

'There you go, sceptical as ever,' quipped Bao-yu. 'Forever seeking strange meanings. It must be a lucky saying; anyone can tell that. You *would* have some pet theory of your own. So what do *you* think it means?'

Bao-chai was about to elaborate, when a maid arrived to inform her that her presence was required at Lady Wang's. To learn the reason for this summons, please read the next chapter.

CHAPTER 102

Illness descends upon the Jia family
in Ning-guo House
And charms and holy water are used
to exorcize Prospect Garden

Bao-chai went immediately to Lady Wang's apartment.

'As you know, Tan-chun is getting married,' began Lady Wang, when Bao-chai had paid her respects. 'You and Li Wan must have a word with her before she leaves, and try to cheer her up. She is your own cousin after all. She's such a sensible girl, and I know how well the two of you get along together. I understand that Bao-yu was most upset and started crying when he heard the news. You must talk him round too.

'I've been too poorly recently to be able to do much myself, and Feng spends half her days laid up in bed. You're a clever girl. From now on you're going to have to accept a greater share of the family responsibilities. Don't feel you must hold back all the time for fear of causing offence. In time the weight of this entire household will rest on your shoulders.'

'Yes, Mother.'

Lady Wang continued:

'There's another thing. Feng came here with Cook Liu's daughter yesterday and said she wanted her to fill the vacancy in your apartment.'

'Yes, Mother. Patience brought her over to start today,' said Bao-chai. 'She said that you and Cousin Feng were in agreement about it.'

'Yes. As a matter of fact it was Feng's idea. I decided it was not worth making an issue of it and going against her wishes. But I feel I should warn you all the same, the girl doesn't look altogether reliable to me. She could make trouble. A while ago I had one or two of Bao-yu's more flirtatious maids dismissed – I'm sure you knew about the affair; it led to your going home to live with your mother. Now that you and Bao-yu are married, things are different of course. But I still feel I ought to mention it, so that you can keep an eye on her. Remember, Aroma is the only dependable maid in your apartment.'

'Yes, Mother.'

Bao-chai stayed a little longer and then left. After dinner she visited Tan-chun and talked with her at some length, offering what comfort and advice she could. We need not describe their conversation in any detail.

The next day was Tan-chun's day of departure and she came once more to bid a final farewell to Bao-yu. He found the parting a painful one, as was only to be expected. But when she spoke to him calmly and philosophically of her 'obligations in life', although at first he hung his head in silence, in the end he began to look a little more cheerful. Tan-chun was relieved that he seemed able to view her future in a less tragic and more enlightened manner; and after saying goodbye to the rest of the family, she climbed into her sedan and set off on the long journey that would take her by land and water to the South.

*

Prospect Garden, once home to such a distinguished little society of young ladies, had since the death of the Imperial Concubine been left to fall into gradual ruin. With Bao-yu's marriage, Dai-yu's death and the departure of Xiang-yun and Bao-qin, the number of residents was already sadly depleted. Then, when the cold weather set in, Li Wan, her cousins Li Qi and Li Wen, Xi-chun and Tan-chun had all moved out to their previous abodes and had only ever gathered together in the Garden to enjoy themselves on particularly fine days or moonlit nights. With Tan-chun no longer at home and Bao-yu still convalescing and confined indoors, there was scarcely anyone left to enjoy the Garden's delights. It became a desolate place, its paths frequented only by the handful of caretakers whom duty still obliged to live there.

On the day of Tan-chun's departure, You-shi had come across to Rong-guo House to see her off. It was getting late by the time she left for home, and she decided to save herself the trouble of taking a carriage by returning through the Garden, using the side gate that communicated with Ning-guo House. As she walked through the grounds she was forcibly struck by the aura of desolation that pervaded the place. The buildings were unchanged, but she noticed that a strip of land along the inside of the Garden wall had already been converted into some sort of vegetable plot. A deep sense of melancholy oppressed her spirit. When she reached home she immediately developed a fever, and though she fought it off for a couple of days eventually she had to retire to bed. During the daytime the fever was not unduly severe, but at night it became almost insupportable and she grew delirious and started babbling to herself. Cousin Zhen sent for a doctor at once, who pronounced that she had caught a chill, which had developed complications and had entered into the *yang-ming* stomach meridian. This accounted for her delirious babbling and hallucinations. She would recover once she had opened her bowels.

You-shi took two doses of the medicine the doctor prescribed, but showed no sign of improvement. If anything she became more deranged than before. Cousin Zhen was now seriously concerned and sent for Jia Rong:

'Get hold of the names of some good doctors in town and send for one immediately. We must have a second opinion.'

'But the doctor who came the other day is extremely well thought of,' objected Jia Rong. 'It seems to me that in Mother's case medicine is of little use.'

'How can you talk like that!' exclaimed Cousin Zhen. 'If we don't give her medicine, what are we supposed to do? Just let her fade away?'

'I didn't say she couldn't be cured,' said Jia Rong. 'What was going through my mind was this: when Mother went over to Rong-guo House the other day, she came back through the Garden. And the fever began as soon as she reached home. It could be that she encountered some evil spirit on the way and is now possessed. I happen to know of an excellent fortune-teller in town, by the name of Half-Immortal Mao. He hails from the South, and is something of a specialist in *The Book of Changes*. I think we should ask him for a consultation first. See if he can shed any light on the matter. If that gets us nowhere, then let's by all means look for another doctor.'

Cousin Zhen agreed, and they sent for the fortune-teller at once. When he arrived, he and Jia Rong sat down together in the study and after drinking his tea Half-Immortal Mao began the consultation proper:

'On what matter does my esteemed client wish me to consult the *Changes*?'

'It concerns my mother,' said Jia Rong. 'She has fallen ill. Could you please seek some illumination from the *Changes* on her behalf?'

'Very well,' replied Mao. 'First I shall require some clean water with which to wash my hands. Then, will you be so good as to light some incense, and to set up a small altar? And I shall proceed with the divination.'

The servants carried out these instructions, and Mao extracted the divining cylinder from within his gown, approached the altar, and after making a profound reverence began shaking the cylinder, intoning the following prayer:

'In the name of the Supreme Ultimate, of the Yin and of the Yang, and of the Generative Powers of the Cosmos; in the name of the Holy Signs made manifest in the Great River, which embody the Myriad Transformations of the Universe, and of the Saints who in their wisdom leave no sincere request unheeded: here, in good faith, Mr Jia, on the occasion of his mother's illness, devoutly beseeches the Four Sages, Fu Xi, King Wen, the Duke of Zhou and Confucius, to look down from above and vouchsafe an efficacious response to this his earnest supplication. If evil lies hidden, then bring the evil to light; if good, then show the good. First we ask to be told the Three Lines of the Lower Trigram.'

He turned the cylinder upside down and the coins fell onto the tray.

'Ah! Most efficacious: for the Prime we have a Moving Yin.'

The second throw gave a Yang At Rest, the third another Moving Yin. $\frac{-X-}{-X-}$. Picking up the coins, Half-Immortal Mao said:

'The Lower Trigram has been communicated. Now let us ask to receive the Three Lines of the Upper Trigram, and thus complete the Hexagram.'

These fell as follows: Yang At Rest, Yin At Rest, Yang At Rest. $\frac{\quad}{-\ -}$. Half-Immortal Mao replaced the cylinder and coins inside his gown, and sat down.

'Pray be seated,' he said. 'Let us consider this in greater detail. We have here the sixty-fourth Hexagram, "Before Completion": $\frac{\overline{-\ -}}{-X-}$.

The Line of most significance to you and to your generation is the Tertian, with Fire at the Seventh Branch *Wu*, and the Signature "Ruin". This certainly indicates that Dire Misfortune lies in store. You have asked me to consult the *Changes* concerning your mother's illness, and great attention should therefore be paid to the parental Prime, which contains the Signature "Spectre", as does the Quintal. It would seem that your mother is indeed seriously afflicted. But all will still be for the best. The present misfortune is concatenated with Water at the First Branch *Zi* and at the Twelfth Branch *Hai*; but when this element wanes, with the Third Branch *Yin* comes Wood and thence Fire. The Signature "Offspring" at the Tertian also counteracts the Spectral influence, and with the regenerative effect of the continuing revolution of both the solar and lunar bodies, in two days the "Spectre" originally concatenated with Water at the First Branch *Zi* should be rendered void, and by the day *Xu* all will be well. But I see that the parental Prime contains further Spectral permutations. I fear your father may himself be afflicted. And your own personal Line has a severe concentration of "Ruin". When Water reaches its zenith and Earth its nadir, be prepared for misfortune to strike.'

Mao sat back, thrusting his beard forward, as if to emphasize the authenticity of his prognosis.

At the beginning of this rigmarole it was all Jia Rong could do to keep a straight face. But gradually Mao impressed him as a man who knew what he was talking about, and when he went on to predict misfortune for Cousin Zhen, Jia Rong began to take him rather more seriously.

'Your exposition is certainly very learned,' he commented. 'But could you, I wonder, be more precise as to the nature of the illness that is afflicting my mother?'

'In the Hexagram,' replied Mao, 'Fire at the Seventh Branch *Wu* in the Prime changes to Water and is thus controlled. This would indicate some inner congestion in which both cold and heat are combined. But I am afraid a precise diagnosis lies beyond the limitations of even a more elaborate milfoil reading of the *Changes*. For that, you would have to cast a Six Cardinal horoscope.'

'Is that branch of divination one with which you are also conversant?' asked Jia Rong.

'To a certain extent,' replied Mao.

Jia Rong asked him to cast the horoscope, and wrote down the relevant Stems and Branches. Mao proceeded to adjust his Diviner's Compass, setting the co-ordinates for the Heavenly Generals. The reading obtained was: 'White Tiger' at the Eleventh Branch *Xu*.

'This Configuration,' said Mao, 'is known as "Dissolution of the

Soul". The "White Tiger" is inauspicious, but is contained and prevented from doing injury when it occurs at a zenith of fortune. In this case, however, it is enveloped in a Mephitic Aura, and occurs at a seasonal passage where Confinement and Death predominate; it is therefore a hungry tiger and sure to do harm. The effect is similar to the spiritual dispersion consequent upon extreme shock. Hence the name of the configuration, which represents a state of acute physical and mental alarm, of profound melancholy; in illness it foresees death, in litigation misfortune. The Tiger is seen approaching at sunset, which means the illness must have been contracted in the evening. The wording reads: "In this configuration, a Tiger lies hidden in some old building, making mischief, or manifests itself in some more palpable way."

'You are enquiring specifically about your parents. In a Yang or daylight environment, the Tiger afflicts the male, while in a Yin or night-time environment it afflicts the female. This configuration therefore bodes ill for both of your parents.'

Jia Rong was stunned by this, and turned ashen pale.

'It all sounds very convincing,' he said, before Mao could continue. 'But it doesn't exactly tally with the Hexagram in *The Book of Changes*. How dangerous is the situation, do you think?'

'Do not panic,' said Mao. 'Let me look into this a little more carefully.'

He lowered his head in thought and mumbled to himself for a few moments. Then:

'All is well! We are saved! My Compass reveals a "Delivering Spirit" at the Sixth Branch *Si*. In other words, what we have here is a "Dissolution of the Soul" leading to a "Restoration of the Spirit", or Sorrow turning to Joy. There is therefore no real cause for concern. You should just exercise a little caution.'

Jia Rong handed him his fee and saw him off the premises, before returning to report to his father:

'The fortune-teller says that Mother's illness was contracted to-wards evening in an old building, and was caused by an encounter with a White Tiger spirit emanating from a corpse.'

'Didn't you say that she came back through the Garden the other evening?' said Cousin Zhen. 'It must have been there that she ran into this thing. And didn't your aunt Feng go walking in the Garden too, and fall ill afterwards? She denied having encountered anything out of the ordinary, but the maids and serving-women all told a different story. They said she'd seen a hairy monster up on a hill, with eyes as big as lanterns, and that she'd even heard it talk. It gave your aunt Feng such a fright that she went running home, and immediately fell ill and took to her bed.'

'Of course!' exclaimed Jia Rong. 'I remember! And I heard Bao-yu's boy Tealeaf say that Skybright had turned into a Hibiscus Fairy. So she must be haunting the Garden, for a start. And when Cousin Lin died, music was heard in the air, so *she's* probably there somewhere too, looking after some other flower. Ugh! It makes your flesh creep, to think of all the sprites and fairies there must be cooped up in there! It used to be perfectly safe when there were plenty of people living there and the place had a feeling of life about it. But now it's so dashed lonely! When Mother went through, she probably trod on one of the flowers, or bumped into one of the fairies. It sounds as if Mao's Hexagram was on the mark all right.'

'Did he talk of any real danger?' asked Cousin Zhen.

'According to him, by the day *Xu* all will be well. I must say, though, I hope his calculations don't turn out to be too accurate . . .'

'What do you mean?' asked Cousin Zhen.

'Well, if he's right, then there could be some trouble in store for you too, Father.'

As they were talking, there came a cry from one of the serving-women in the inner apartments:

'Mrs Zhen insists on getting up and going to the Garden! The maids can't hold her down!'

Cousin Zhen and Jia Rong went in to pacify You-shi.

'The one in red is coming to get me!' she screamed deliriously. 'The one in green is after me!'

The servants found her behaviour at once funny and frightening. Cousin Zhen despatched one of them to buy paper money, and burn it in the Garden. That night You-shi came out in a sweat and calmed down considerably, and by the day *Xu* she gradually started to recover.

Word soon spread that Prospect Garden was haunted, and the caretakers became too frightened to carry out their duties. Plants were left untended, trees unpruned, and all the flower-beds un-watered. No one dared walk around after dark, and as a result the resident wildlife began to make it their own domain. Things eventually got so bad that even in broad daylight the servants would enter the Garden only accompanied and armed with cudgels.

After a few days, Cousin Zhen fell ill as predicted. He did not send for a doctor. Whenever the illness permitted, he went to the Garden to pray and burn paper money; whenever it became severe, he uttered feverish prayers in his chamber. He recovered, and then it was Jia Rong's turn to go down; and after Jia Rong, the others, one by one. This continued for several months, and both households lived in constant fear. Even the slightest rustle or cry of a bird was suspect, and every plant or tree was feared to harbour a malicious spirit. Now that the Garden was abandoned and no longer productive, extra funds were needed again for the various apartments of the household, and this added to the already crushing deficit of Rong-guo House. The Garden's caretakers saw nothing to be gained by staying. They all wanted to leave the place, and invented a whole series of incidents to substantiate the presence of diabolical tree-imps and flower sprites. Eventually they achieved their goal: they were all evacuated, the garden gate was securely locked, and no one dared go in at all. Fine halls, lofty pavilions, elegant rooms and terraces became nothing more than nesting-places for birds and lairs for wild beasts.

*

Skybright's cousin, Wu Gui, lived, it will be remembered, opposite the rear gate-house of the Garden. It had reached the ears of Wu Gui's wife that Skybright, after her death, had become a flower fairy, and from then on she took the precaution of staying indoors every evening. One day Wu Gui went shopping and stayed out later than usual. His wife had caught a slight cold and during the day took the wrong medicine, with the result that when Wu Gui returned that evening he found her lying dead on the kang. Because of her reputation for promiscuity, other members of the household staff concluded that a sprite must have climbed over the Garden wall, enjoyed her at inordinate length, and finally 'sucked the sap' out of her.

This incident put Grandmother Jia in a great tizzy. She increased the guard around Bao-yu's apartment and had it constantly watched and patrolled. Some of the younger maids subsequently claimed to have seen weird red-faced creatures lurking in the vicinity, while others testified to the presence of a strange female apparition of great beauty. Such rumours soon multiplied, and Bao-yu lived in mortal terror. Bao-chai was less easily taken in, and warned the maids that any more fear-mongering would bring them a good hiding. Although this quietened things down a bit, there was still an atmosphere of great apprehension throughout both mansions, and more watchmen were taken on, which was an additional expense.

Jia She was the only one not to believe a word of it.

'There's nothing the matter with the Garden, for heaven's sake! Haunted! What an absurd notion!'

He waited for a warm day when there was a mild breeze, and went to inspect the Garden himself, accompanied by a large number of armed servants. They all advised him against going, but he would not listen. When they entered the Garden, the atmosphere was so dark and sinister, so oppressively Yin, that they could almost touch it. Jia She refused to turn back, and his servants reluctantly followed him in, with many a furtive and shrinking sideways glance. One young lad among them, already scared to death, heard a sudden 'whoosh!', and turning to look saw something brightly coloured go flashing past. He uttered a terrified *'Aiyo!'*, went instantly weak at the knees and collapsed on the ground. When Jia She looked back and stopped to question him, he replied breathlessly:

'I saw it with my own eyes! I did! A monster with a yellow face and a red beard, all dressed in green! It went up there, into that grotto behind those trees!'

Jia She was somewhat shaken himself.

'Did anyone else see this thing?'

Some of the servants decided to take advantage of the situation and replied:

'Clear as daylight, sir. You were up in front and we didn't want to alarm you, sir. So we tried to keep a grip on ourselves, and act as if nothing had happened.'

Jia She now lacked the courage to go any further. He turned back and went home as quickly as possible, telling the boys who had accompanied him not to say anything about what had happened, but merely to let it be known that they had had an uneventful tour of the Garden. He himself needed no further convincing that the Garden was haunted, and began to think it might be advisable to apply to the Taoist Pontificate for priests to perform an exorcism. His servants, meanwhile, who were by nature fond of making trouble, saw how frightened their master was, and far from concealing the episode, retailed it with a great deal of gusto and embellishment, creating quite a sensation and eliciting a good deal of open-mouthed astonishment.

In the end Jia She decided that there was no other recourse than to go ahead and hold a formal ceremony of exorcism. A suitable day in the almanac was chosen, and an altar was constructed in the Garden, on a dais in the main hall of the Reunion Palace. Images of the Three Pure Ones were set up, flanked by figures of the spirits presiding over each of the Twenty-Eight Constellations, and of the Four Great Commanders – Ma, Zhao, Wen and Zhou. Further down the hall, the sacred precinct was made complete with a diagrammatic representation of the Thirty-Six Heavenly Generals. The air was heavy with flowers and incense, the hall blazed with lanterns and candles. Bells, drums, liturgical instruments and other paraphernalia were arrayed along both sides of the hall, and emblematic banners were hoisted at each of the Five Cardinal Points (the Four Corners and the Centre). The Taoist Pontiff had delegated Forty-Nine Deacons for the ceremony, and they began by spending a whole day purifying the altar. Then three priests went the rounds of the hall, waving smoking bundles of joss-sticks and sprinkling holy water, and when this was done the great Drum of the Dharma thundered forth. The priests now donned their Seven Star Mitres and robed themselves in their chasubles emblazoned with the Nine Heavenly Mansions and the Eight Trigrams. Wearing Cloud-Mounting Pattens on their feet and holding ivory tablets in their hands, they addressed themselves in reverent supplication to the sages. For a full day they chanted the *Arcanum Primordii*, a text renowned for its efficacy in the dispelling of misfortune, the exorcizing of evil spirits and the general enhancement of propitious vibrations. Then they produced the Spirit Roll, which called on the Heavenly Generals to be present. It was inscribed with the following large characters:

A SUMMONS
IN THE NAME
OF THE
THREE REALMS,
THE ULTIMATE, THE PRIMORDIAL, AND THE PURE;
IN THE NAME
OF THE
SUPREME PONTIFF

AND THE
TALISMANIC POWER VESTED IN HIM;
ALL BENEVOLENT SPIRITS OF THE REGION
ARE HEREBY CALLED TO THIS ALTAR
TO DO SERVICE

The menfolk of both Rong-guo and Ning-guo House had taken courage from the presence of the priests, and were gathered in the Garden to watch the demon-hunt.

'Most impressive!' they all agreed. 'All those benevolent spirits and powers are bound to strike fear into the heart of even the most obdurate demon!'

They crowded in front of the altar to watch the rest of the proceedings. The young banner-bearing Deacons took up their positions in the hall, one group at each of the Five Cardinal Points, North, East, South, West and Centre, and awaited their orders. The three priests stood on the lower steps of the altar: one held the Magic Sword and the Holy Water, one the black Seven Star Banner, and one the peach-wood Demon Whip. The music ceased. The gong sounded thrice, the monks intoned a prayer, and the cohorts of banner-bearers began performing circular gyrations. The priests then descended from the altar and instructed the Jia menfolk to conduct them to every storeyed building, studio, hall, pavilion, chamber, cottage or covered walk, every hillside and water's edge in the Garden. In each place they sprinkled the Holy Water and brandished the Magic Sword. On their return, the gong rang out again, the Seven Star Banner was raised aloft and consecrated, and as it descended the Deacons formed a phalanx around it with their lesser banners, and the Demon Whip was cracked three times in the air.

This, thought the Jias, must be the climactic moment; now at last the entire company of evil spirits would be routed and captured. They thronged forward to be in at the finish. But nothing seemed to happen. No apparition, no sound; only the voice of one of the priests, ordering the Deacons to 'bring on the jars'. These receptacles were duly 'brought on', and in them the priests proceeded to 'confine' the invisible spirits, sealing them afterwards with official seals. The Abbot inscribed some magical characters in vermilion, and put the jars to one side, giving orders that they should be taken back to the temple. There they were to be placed beneath a pagoda, whose geomantic location would ensure that they and their contents were safely 'contained'. The temporary altar was dismantled and thanks given to the Heavenly Powers. Jia She made a solemn kowtow of gratitude to the Abbot.

Afterwards Jia Rong and the younger men of the family had a good laugh about it all in private:

'All that pantomime to catch the evil spirits! They might at least have let us have a look! What a farce! They probably didn't manage to catch a single one!'

'Fools!' snapped Cousin Zhen, when he heard this. 'Evil spirits don't behave like that at all. At certain times they condense into crude matter, at others they dissolve into the ether. With so many benevolent spirits present of course they wouldn't dare take on material form. It's their etheric form that's in question here. *That* is what Their Holinesses have taken hold of; by so doing they have rendered the spirits harmless. *That* is how the magic works.'

The younger generation were only half-convinced, and reserved their judgement until such time as they could observe a more visible diminution in demonic activity; the servants, who were told quite firmly that the spirits had now been caught, became less apprehensive as a result, and no further incidents or sightings were reported; while Cousin Zhen and the other invalids made a complete recovery (which *they* had no hesitation in attributing to the efficacy of the monks' spells).

There was, however, one page-boy who continued to find the whole episode highly amusing, and who shared his amusement with the others:

'I don't know what the earlier business was about, but that day we were in the Garden with Sir She, it was nothing more than a big pheasant that took off out of the undergrowth and went flying past us. Old Ropey got the fright of his life and thought he'd seen a ghost or something. He made a great song and dance about it afterwards. Most of the others believed him and backed him up, and Sir She swallowed the whole thing. Oh well, at least they put on a nice bit of mumbo-jumbo for us!'

But no one was convinced by his version of the story. And certainly no one was willing to live in the Garden again.

*

Some days later, when things had quietened down somewhat, Jia She thought he might discreetly move a few servants back into the Garden as caretakers, to make sure that no undesirable characters tried to sneak their way in there at night. He was about to issue instructions to this effect when Jia Lian came in.

'I have just been to visit Uncle Wang Zi-teng's family,' he said, after paying his respects, 'and while I was there I heard the most devastating piece of news. Uncle Zheng has apparently been impeached by the Viceroy! The charge against him is that he failed to control his subordinates and was responsible for the requisitioning of extortionate quantities of tax-grain. The Viceroy has asked for his dismissal.'

Jia She was stunned:

'This must surely be some idle rumour. Why, there was a letter from your uncle Zheng only the other day. Full of good news. He wrote that Tan-chun had arrived safely, and that he had chosen a suitable day to escort her to her future husband's family on the coast. The journey had passed off without mishap. Absolutely no cause for concern. What's more, the Viceroy is supposed to be related to Tan-chun's husband, and even gave a party to celebrate the wedding. How could the man impeach his own relative? Well, it's no use speculating like this: you'd better go and see the Civil Office people. Find out what you can, and report straight back to me.'

Jia Lian departed at once, and returned a few hours later.

'It's as I feared, Father. Uncle Zheng *has* been impeached. However, as an act of Imperial clemency his case did not go through the normal channels, but was dealt with directly by His Majesty. I have the exact wording of the Imperial Rescript:

On account of Jia Zheng's failure to control subordinate officials, and on account of the extortionate levying of tax-grain and cruel exploitation of the common people perpetrated under his administration, he deserves to be dismissed altogether. But because this is his first provincial posting, and because he is inexperienced as an administrator and has in this matter been deceived by his own subordinates, he is only to be demoted three grades, and by a special dispensation will be reinstated as Under-Secretary in the Board of Works. He is to return at once to the capital.

'This news is official. While I was at the Board of Civil Office a county magistrate from Kiangsi came for an audience. He said he was indebted to Uncle Zheng in many ways and had a high opinion of him, but considered him an inept manager of people. His servants got up to all sorts of skulduggery behind his back, and were squeezing the local officials for all they were worth. Uncle's reputation was already ruined. The Viceroy had known about it for some time, and he too was of the opinion that Uncle Zheng was basically a good man. I don't know quite why he brought the impeachment in the end. Perhaps he was afraid that things had got out of hand and that more serious trouble might lie ahead. In using this relatively minor charge as grounds for impeachment, maybe he was really trying to save Uncle Zheng from an even worse fate.'

Jia She interrupted Jia Lian:

'Go and tell your aunt Wang about this straight away. But don't trouble your grandmother at present.'

So Jia Lian went to report to Lady Wang. For the sequel, please turn to the next chapter.

CHAPTER 103

*Jin-gui dies by her own hand, caught
in a web of her own weaving
Yu-cun encounters an old friend in vain, blind
to the higher truths of Zen*

Jia Lian gave Lady Wang a full account of Jia Zheng's misfortune. The next day he paid another call at the Board of Civil Office, and on his return reported once more to Lady Wang, assuring her that he had done his utmost to put in a word for Jia Zheng in the right quarters.

'So you're sure the news is genuine?' she asked. 'Well, I dare say your Uncle Zheng will be none too displeased. In fact it will come as something of a relief to us all. He was never really suited to a provincial posting, and if he had not come home now I'm afraid those rascals would one day have ruined him altogether!'

'How is it that you are so well informed in this matter?' asked Jia Lian.

'Ever since your uncle Zheng has been at this post,' replied Lady Wang, 'not a penny has been remitted. On the contrary. He has been secretly sending here for considerable sums. You have only to look at the way the servants' wives are already decking themselves out in all sorts of fancy gold and silver ornaments to know what's been going on. It's obvious that their husbands have been making money behind your uncle Zheng's back. He just lets them get away with it. If it had gone any further, not only would he have lost his job but the inherited family rank might have been forfeited as well!'

'You're quite right, Aunt,' said Jia Lian. 'I confess that I was very shocked when I first heard the news. But now that I know the full facts of the case I feel considerably easier about it. It will be much better for Uncle Zheng this way. He will be able to work here in the capital in peace and quiet for a few years, without endangering his reputation any further. I think even Grandmother will be quite relieved when she hears the whole story. But I feel you should break it gently to her all the same.'

'I will,' said Lady Wang. 'You had better go now and see what else you can find out.'

Jia Lian was on his way out when one of Aunt Xue's old serving-women came running past in a great lather. She went directly into Lady Wang's apartment and without any preliminary courtesies burst straight out with: 'Our Madam says I'm to tell Your Ladyship there's terrible trouble at home again! Things have come to a pretty pass this time and no mistake!'

'What sort of trouble?' asked Lady Wang.

'Oh, something terrible! Just *terrible*!'

'You stupid old creature!' exclaimed Lady Wang with a snort of exasperation. 'If something serious has happened, for goodness' sake try to tell me what it is!'

'Master Ke's away and we haven't got a man in the house! It's a crisis and we just don't know what to do! Please will Your Ladyship send one or two of the Masters over to sort it out for us!'

Lady Wang still had not the slightest idea what she was talking about.

'Sort out *what* in heaven's name?' she asked impatiently.

'It's Mrs Pan! She's dead!' blurted out the old woman at last.

'*Pfui!*' exclaimed Lady Wang when she heard this. 'So that baggage is dead! Is *that* what all the fuss is about?'

'But it wasn't reg'lar, Your Ladyship. I mean, the way she died. Such a to-do! Please, Your Ladyship, send someone over right away!'

She set off back to the Xue compound. Lady Wang was both annoyed and amused:

'Honestly, what a hopeless old woman! Lian, go and have a look will you? It's a complete waste of time trying to make head or tail of anything that old creature says.'

The first part, about 'going and having a look', failed to reach the old woman's ears. She only caught the words 'a complete waste of time' and went running home in a great huff to Aunt Xue, who was anxiously awaiting her return:

'Well, who is Lady Wang going to send?'

The old woman sighed demonstratively:

'Fat lot of use family are at a time of crisis, I must say! Her Ladyship wouldn't lift a finger for us! All she did was call me a stupid creature!'

This seemed to make Aunt Xue angry, and she became rather flustered:

'If Her Ladyship wouldn't help, what about our own Mrs Bao?'

'I didn't even bother to tell her,' replied the old woman. 'How could she be expected to stand up for us if Her Ladyship wouldn't?'

Aunt Xue spat at her, and cried indignantly:

'Are you out of your mind? Her Ladyship is one of the Jias; but Bao-chai is my own child. She wouldn't let me down!'

The distinction suddenly seemed to dawn on the old woman.

'Lawks! I'd better go back and find her right away!'

As they were speaking, Jia Lian came in. He paid his respects to Aunt Xue, and after expressing his condolences went on to explain to her:

'When Aunt Wang heard that Mrs Pan was dead, she questioned your serving-woman but was unable to extract any sense from her at all. Aunt was very worried and sent me to find out what was going on and to give you a hand. If anything needs doing, Aunt Xue, just let me know and I'll do what I can.'

Aunt Xue had been working herself into a state of great indignation with the old woman, and had become so distraught she could do nothing but weep. On hearing Jia Lian's words she became articulate once more:

'I'm most obliged to you, Lian. I was sure my sister would stand by me. I'm afraid this old woman completely misunderstood you, and gave me a totally misleading impression. Now, please sit down and let me tell you the whole story.'

After a slight pause she continued: 'How shall I put it . . .? Well, in a nutshell, my daughter-in-law did not die a natural death.'

'I suppose it was suicide?' ventured Jia Lian. 'Was it despondency at Cousin Pan's imprisonment that drove her to take her own life?'

'If only it had been! Alas, no. Let me explain. For several months she'd been rampaging about the whole time, barefoot and with her hair in a terrible state. When she heard that Pan was facing a death sentence, after an initial fit of weeping she began painting herself up dreadfully with rouge and powder. Any remonstrations on my part would only have led to more atrocious scenes, so I tried to turn a blind eye. Then suddenly one day, for some reason unknown to me, she came and asked me if she could have Caltrop to keep her company. I said to her: "You've already got Moonbeam. Do you really need Caltrop as well? You've never liked her, so why go asking for trouble?' But she insisted, and I had no choice but to send Caltrop over to her room. The poor girl didn't dare disobey my orders and she went, ill though she was.

'Funnily enough, my daughter-in-law treated her very well. I was delighted; and although Chai suspected some ulterior motive, I was prepared to give her the benefit of the doubt. Anyway, a few days ago, Caltrop fell ill again, and Jin-gui cooked her some soup. She even made a point of serving it to her with her own hands. Poor Caltrop! There was the most unfortunate accident. Jin-gui dropped the soup just as she was coming up to the bedside, scalded herself and broke the bowl as well. I would have expected her to have blamed Caltrop; but no, she wasn't in the least angry, just went off at once to fetch a broom, swept up the pieces and gave the floor a good clean. Afterwards the two of them still seemed on friendly terms.

'Then yesterday evening she told Moonbeam to go and make two bowls of soup, which she said she would drink with Caltrop. It was a little later that we heard this terrific hullabaloo coming from her apartment. First Moonbeam started screaming her head off, then Caltrop screamed too and staggered out, leaning on the wall for support and calling for help. I went in at once and found Jin-gui writhing on the floor, with blood streaming from her nose and eyes; she was clutching feverishly at her stomach with both hands, and kicking both feet in the air. I was scared out of my wits. I asked her to tell me what had happened, but she was too far gone to answer, and after a few more minutes of agony she died. It looked very much like a case of poisoning to me.

'Then Moonbeam started wailing again and laid hold of Caltrop, claiming that it was her doing. But I hardly think Caltrop is that sort of person. Besides, she was almost too ill to get out of bed; how could she have had the strength to do such a thing? Moonbeam insisted, however, and still insists, that Caltrop is the culprit. My dear Lian! What was I to do? In the circumstances I had no choice but to tell the old women to bind Caltrop, to hand her over to Moonbeam and to lock them both in the room. Bao-qin and I have been up all night keeping watch, and we sent word to you the moment the gates were opened this morning. Lian, you know about such things. What's the proper course of action for me to take?'

'Do Jin-gui's family know yet?' asked Jia Lian.

'I thought it better to try to disentangle the whole affair ourselves before letting *anyone* know.'

'I would advise you to report what's happened to the authorities first and let them reach their own conclusions. It's only natural that we should suspect Moonbeam, but they might ask what Moonbeam would have stood to gain by poisoning her own mistress. And in a way it might almost seem more plausible to them that Caltrop should have done it.'

As they were speaking, some serving-women from Rong-guo House came in to announce the arrival of Bao-chai. Jia Lian decided that, although strictly speaking she was his younger cousin's wife, he need not withdraw; after all, she was also his cousin and he had known her from childhood. She greeted her mother and Jia Lian, and went in to sit with Bao-qin in the inner room. Aunt Xue joined her there and told her the story.

'Surely, by binding Caltrop we are virtually admitting her guilt?' was Bao-chai's immediate response. 'If Moonbeam made the soup, then *she* should be bound. And we must let the Xia family know, and report the death to the authorities.'

This seemed logical enough to Aunt Xue. She asked Jia Lian for his opinion:

'Chai is absolutely right. I'd better go and have a word with someone at the Board of Punishment, to make sure there's no trouble at the inquest. But I think it will be a bit hard to justify releasing Caltrop if we then bind Moonbeam instead.'

'I never wanted to bind Caltrop in the first place,' said Aunt Xue, 'but I was afraid that this unjust accusation, coming on top of her illness, might drive her to desperate measures. She might try to commit suicide, and then we'd have another death on our hands. It was for her own safety that I tied her up and handed her over to Moonbeam.'

'Quite,' said Jia Lian. 'But still, we have rather played into Moonbeam's hands. I think our principle now must be that, if one of them is bound, both must be bound; if one is set free, both must be set free. They were both present at the time of Jin-gui's death. Meanwhile we must send someone to comfort Caltrop.'

Aunt Xue told her serving-woman to open the door of Jin-gui's apartment and go in, while Bao-chai ordered some of her own women to accompany them and help them tie up Moonbeam. When they arrived they found Caltrop sobbing her heart out and Moonbeam gloating over her. Moonbeam fought back tooth and nail when they laid hands on her, but the women were too strong. After much shouting from Moonbeam they tied her up, and left the door open so that the two suspects could be more conveniently watched over.

Word had already been sent to Jin-gui's family. The Xias had originally lived outside the capital, but recently their circumstances had become much reduced, and partly for this reason, partly to be near Jin-gui, they had moved into town. Jin-gui's father was already dead, and the only surviving members of her family were her mother and her newly adopted brother, Xia San, a ne'er-do-well who had succeeded in squandering what remained of the family's resources. Now that they were living in town, he became a frequent visitor at the Xue household. Jin-gui was a fickle creature, little suited to the role of the faithful, pining wife. Her failure to entrap Xue Ke had left her ravenous for the slightest morsel, and now even this adopted brother of hers seemed an acceptable means of assuaging her desire. Xia San, however, was a trifle on the slow side, and although he sensed her intentions soon enough, held back from steering his craft directly into her capacious harbour. Jin-gui paid more and more frequent visits to her family, taking with her presents of money to pave the way for Xia San's eventual capitulation.

On the day in question, the day after Jin-gui's sudden death, he was eagerly awaiting one of these visits, and when the Xue servants arrived, he assumed that they had been sent by his sister to deliver one of her little parcels. When they told him instead that she was dead, and that it was, by all accounts, a case of poisoning, he flew into a storm and began ranting and raving at them. Mrs Xia, when she heard the news, wept volubly:

'She was doing quite nicely for herself there! What could she possibly want to go and take poison for? It must have been one of them that did it!'

Still weeping and protesting loudly, she called Xia San to accompany her, and set off at once on foot, without waiting to send for a carriage. The Xias were originally business-people with little breeding, and now that they were poor had no residual concern for appearances. Xia San went ahead, and his adoptive mother followed him out of the gate, weeping and wailing all the while, accompanied by a lame old serving-woman. She eventually hailed a rickety old cart that was passing in the street, and it carried them at full speed to the Xue compound, where she went in without a word of greeting, sobbing, 'My child! My darling!'

Jia Lian had gone to enlist support at the Board of Punishment, and Aunt Xue, Bao-chai and Bao-qin were holding the fort on their own. Mrs Xia's dramatic entry quite nonplussed them, and at first they were too frightened to say anything. Bao-chai and Bao-qin withdrew to the inner room. When Aunt Xue tried to reason with the intruders, Mrs Xia completely ignored her.

'What good has my daughter ever had from this family of yours?' she cried. 'Day and night she's had to put up with beatings and abuse. In the end you decided to separate her from her husband come what may, and even managed to get my son-in-law locked up in prison. You and *your* daughter were comfortable enough, thanks to all those important relatives of yours, but *my* daughter's very existence was still a thorn in your flesh, so you wanted to get rid of her for good and finally found someone to poison her. Poisoned herself indeed!'

She lunged at Aunt Xue, who backed out of her way, exclaiming:

'Mrs Xia! Kindly go and examine your daughter for yourself and speak to Moonbeam first, before making such wild accusations!'

As Xia San was still there in the room, lurking in the background, Bao-chai and Bao-qin were unable to come to Aunt Xue's defence and could only remain anxiously closeted in the inner room. By a fortunate coincidence, however, Lady Wang had just sent Zhou Rui's wife over to see how things were. When she came in and saw this elderly woman abusing and threatening Aunt Xue, she deduced that it must be Jin-gui's mother and approached her at once:

'Would you be Mrs Xia, ma'am? I suppose you know that Mrs Pan took poison? That's how she died, and it has nothing whatever to do with Mrs Xue. There is really no call for you to slander her in this way!'

'And who might you be?' asked Jin-gui's mother.

Aunt Xue, her confidence a little restored by the arrival of reinforcements, answered for Mrs Zhou:

'This good woman works for our relations the Jias.'

'Oh! Does she now?' sneered Mrs Xia. 'We all know about your wonderful relations! No doubt it's thanks to them that you managed to get your own son locked up in gaol. And now I suppose you are hoping to get away scot-free with the murder of my daughter too!'

She seized Aunt Xue.

'Out with it!' she cried. 'How *did* you do it? Let me see the body.'

Zhou Rui's wife attempted to pacify her:

'By all means. Go and have a look. But kindly take your hands off Mrs Xue!'

She finally succeeded in pulling Mrs Xia away from Aunt Xue. Xia San now emerged from the shadows to leap to his mother's rescue:

'Think you can attack my mother like this and get away with it just because you're one of *their* servants?'

He threw a chair at Mrs Zhou, which luckily missed. The servants who were with Bao-chai in the inner room heard this rumpus break out and came hurrying in to see what was happening. Fearing that Mrs Zhou might come off worst in the fray, they all surged forward and tried to calm the combatants down. Their threats and cajolements were in vain: mother and son merely grew more strident in their protestations and more desperate in their actions.

'We don't need reminding how powerful your Rong-guo relations are! What do we care! Now that Jin-gui's gone, we might as well fight it out to the death!'

Mrs Xia charged at Aunt Xue again with all her might. Despite their numbers, the servants could not withstand her. As the saying goes:

> If a man stakes all on his attack,
> Ten thousand men won't hold him back.

It was at this moment of crisis that Jia Lian returned, accompanied by seven or eight servants. Seeing how things stood, he ordered his men to drag Xia San outside, and told the ladies to stop fighting at once:

'Surely you can settle your differences in a more civilized fashion? Now, tidy the place up. The officers from the Board of Punishments will be here any minute to conduct the inquest.'

Mrs Xia had been in full spate when Jia Lian made his entrance. She was somewhat overawed by this strange gentleman with his retinue of servants, some of whom were already barking orders while others stood respectfully to attention, and she wondered which member of the Jia family it could be. Then she saw her adopted son taken away, and heard that the Board of Punishments had been informed and would shortly be holding an inquest, which ruined all her plans. She had originally intended to inspect her daughter's corpse, create a terrific fuss and go crying for justice; but now they had beaten her to it, and the wind was quite taken out of her sails. Aunt Xue for her part was too frightened to do anything. It was Mrs Zhou who said to Jia Lian:

'These people barged in, and without so much as a look at Mrs Pan this lady began to slander Mrs Xue. We tried to talk some sense into her, but then this ruffian butted in, and started using the most dreadful language in front of the young ladies. What a shocking way to carry on!'

'There's no point arguing with him now,' replied Jia Lian. 'It would only be a waste of time. When they question him under torture, he'll remember soon enough that the inner apartments are strictly reserved for women and that he has no right to be in here. His mother could surely have come to inspect her daughter's corpse by herself. It will look extremely suspicious to the authorities, very much as if *he* had come to rob the place.'

Jia Lian's men managed by one means or another to keep Xia San under control outside, while Mrs Zhou, emboldened by the presence of so many Jia supporters, began denouncing Mrs Xia in earnest:

'Really, madam, you should know better. You should have found out the facts when you arrived. Your daughter *must* have poisoned herself. The only other person it could have been is Moonbeam. Why go slandering without bothering to find out the truth and without so much as seeing the corpse for yourself? Do you think ours is the kind of family to stand by and let a daughter-in-law die without discovering the cause of her death?

'Moonbeam and Caltrop have both been bound. Your daughter had asked for Caltrop to move into her room earlier, because she said she wanted to keep an eye on her illness. That's why Caltrop was also there at the time of Mrs Pan's death. We were hoping that you could be present at the inquest and hear the officer establish the truth of the matter.'

Jin-gui's mother knew that she was beaten, and she followed Zhou Rui's wife into Jin-gui's apartment. She saw her daughter's corpse lying stiff on the kang, the face caked in dry blood, and at once broke down and began sobbing. Moonbeam, seeing someone from 'her side', cried out:

'Madam was so kind to Caltrop! She even shared her own room with her! But Caltrop grabbed the first chance that came along of poisoning her!'

The Xue family and servants raised a cry of protest:

'Nonsense! Who was it cooked the soup that Mrs Pan drank before she died? You!'

'I cooked it and served it,' said Moonbeam, 'but then I had to go out on an errand. Caltrop must have got up and put poison in the soup while I was out.'

Before Moonbeam could finish speaking Jin-gui's mother lunged at Caltrop and could only be restrained by the concerted efforts of the servants. Aunt Xue spoke next:

'This looks very much like a case of arsenic poisoning to me. We certainly don't keep any arsenic in the house. Whoever it was that did this must have commissioned someone else to buy the poison in town. The truth will come out at the inquest. Well, we'd best tidy her up and lay her out properly now in readiness for the officer from the Board of Punishments.'

The old serving-women came forward, lifted Jin-gui up and laid her out.

'With so many men about,' said Bao-chai, 'you had better clear away all those women's knick-knacks.'

As they were tidying up, a little crumpled paper package came to light beneath the mattress on the kang. Jin-gui's mother spotted it and picked it up to inspect it more closely. It was empty and she threw it down again. Moonbeam saw it, however, and cried out:

'Look! There's evidence! I recognize that package. A few days ago we were having a lot of trouble with mice, and when Mrs Pan went on one of her trips home, she asked her brother to buy some poison. It was in that package. I remember her putting it away in one of her jewellery boxes when she got back. Caltrop must have seen it there and used it to poison Mrs Pan. If you don't believe me, have a look in the jewellery box and see if there's any left.'

Jin-gui's mother did this. She opened the jewellery box, which was empty save for a few silver hairpins.

'What has become of all her jewellery?' said Aunt Xue in surprise.

Bao-chai told the servants to open the trunks and cupboards. All were empty.

'Who could have taken all these things?' she asked. 'We had better question Moonbeam.'

Jin-gui's mother seemed to become very apprehensive all of a sudden.

'Why should Moonbeam know about my daughter's things?' she protested.

'Come, ma'am,' put in Zhou Rui's wife, 'that's hardly a very sensible question. Miss Moonbeam was with Mrs Pan all the time. Of course she'd know.'

Moonbeam could see she was cornered, and would have to tell the truth:

'Madam used to take things with her whenever she went home. There was nothing I could do about it.'

A roar of indignation burst from the Xue camp:

'So that's it! Really, Mrs Xia! A fine mother you are! You talk your daughter into stealing our things; and then when the supply runs out, you force her to commit suicide so that you can blackmail us! They'll be *very* interested to hear *that* at the inquest!'

'Go outside,' said Bao-chai, 'and tell Mr Lian that the Xias must on no account be allowed to leave.'

Jin-gui's mother was now in a state of extreme trepidation, and cursed Moonbeam roundly:

'You little hussy! You scandal-monger! When did my daughter ever steal any of their things?'

'Stealing's nothing,' retorted Moonbeam coolly, 'compared to murder; and I don't mean to let myself be called a murderer in order to cover up for a thief.'

'If we can find the missing things, we'll know who the murderer is,' said Bao-qin. 'Someone quickly go and find Lian. He can ask that Xia fellow about the buying of the arsenic. They'll want to know about that at the inquest.'

Jin-gui's mother began to panic:

'Moonbeam must be possessed to speak such nonsense! When did my daughter ever buy arsenic? If you ask me, it was Moonbeam herself!'

'That's going too far!' cried Moonbeam wildly. 'I'm not taking that – not from you! Why, it was the two of you who were always telling Mrs Pan to stand up for her rights! It was you who advised her to make life unbearable for Mr Pan's family, and then, when they were ruined, to walk off with every last button in the house and find herself a decent husband! Do you deny that?'

Before Jin-gui's mother could reply, Zhou Rui's wife cried with glee:

'Denounced by one of your own servants! Well, what have you got to say for yourself now?'

Jin-gui's mother cursed Moonbeam again, and gnashing her teeth said bitterly:

'Haven't I treated you well? Are you trying to drive me to the grave? At the inquest, I shall testify that it was *you* who did it!'

Moonbeam glared at her angrily and then turned to Mrs Xue:

'Please release Caltrop, ma'am. There's no sense in harming an innocent person like this. I shall tell the whole truth at the inquest.'

Bao-chai immediately instructed the servants to release Moonbeam instead, and said:

'Come on, Moonbeam, you've always been a straightforward girl. Don't let yourself get involved in underhand dealings. You'll only suffer for it. If you've something to say, then go ahead and say it. Tell us the truth, and the whole affair can be cleared up once and for all.'

Moonbeam was terrified of being tortured at the inquest, and finally gave in:

'Every day Mrs Pan used to complain about the way life had treated her. "Why was I born to such a stupid mother?" she'd say. "Instead of showing me some sense and marrying me to Master Ke, she went and chose his half-baked booby of a cousin! I'd gladly die if I could only spend one day with Master Ke!" And then she'd always say how she hated Caltrop. I didn't pay much attention at first, and later when I began to notice how friendly she was being to Caltrop I supposed that Caltrop must have somehow earned her way back into her good books. I thought Mrs Pan made the soup for her as a kind gesture. Then I discovered that she had something quite different in mind! Something horrible!'

'That makes no sense at all!' interrupted Jin-gui's mother. 'If you are implying that she intended to do away with Caltrop, then how do you account for the fact that she ended up swallowing the poison herself?'

Bao-chai turned to Caltrop:

'You tell us what happened yesterday, Caltrop. Did you drink any of the soup?'

'A few days ago,' began Caltrop, 'when I was so ill that I could hardly lift my head, Mrs Pan offered to bring me some soup. I didn't dare refuse, and I was struggling to sit up when she had an accident on the way and spilt the soup all over the floor. It was a lot of trouble for her, cleaning it all up, and I felt very bad to have been the cause of it. Then yesterday she offered me some soup again, and though I didn't think I'd ever be able to swallow any of it, I decided I ought to try. I was just getting ready to drink some when I started feeling dizzy. I vaguely remember seeing Moonbeam clear the soup away, and thinking to myself what a relief it was not to have to drink any. But then, just as I was dozing off again, Mrs Pan came over and asked me to try some after all. She was drinking a bowl herself. I tried my hardest and managed to swallow a few mouthfuls.'

'There you are!' cried Moonbeam, hardly giving Caltrop time to finish. 'Now let me complete the picture for you. Yesterday Mrs Pan told me to make two bowls of soup, one for her and one for Caltrop. I was pretty fed up, that Caltrop should be thought important enough for me to have to wait on her. So I deliberately put an extra dollop of salt in one of the bowls, and made a secret mark on the side, intending to give that bowl to Caltrop. As soon as I had brought the soup in, Mrs Pan told me to go and send the boys for a carriage, as she was planning to go home on a visit. I went out, and when I'd done my errand I came back to find Mrs Pan sitting with the salty bowl in front of her. I was afraid that if she tasted how salty it was she would be very cross with me. I was wondering what to do, when luckily Mrs Pan left the room for a moment to relieve herself, and I was able to change the bowls round. It must have been fated that I should do so. When Mrs Pan came back, she took the salty soup to Caltrop's bedside and begged her to try some, drinking some from her own bowl (the one originally intended by her for Caltrop) at the same time. Caltrop didn't seem to notice the salt, and they both finished their bowls. I was laughing to myself, thinking what a rough palate Caltrop must have. I didn't realize then that Mrs Pan had plotted to poison Caltrop and had sprinkled arsenic in her soup while I was out of the room. And then later while *she* was outside, I changed the bowls round. And she never noticed. As the saying goes:

> It all fell out as Providence planned;
> The sinner died by her own hand!'

They pondered the details of Moonbeam's story, and it impressed them as both plausible and consistent. Caltrop was duly released, and they helped her back into bed.

Jin-gui's mother, meanwhile, growing more and more fearful with every minute, was racking her brains for some way of rebutting Moonbeam's accusations. After a good deal of discussion Aunt Xue and the other members of the family concluded that under the circumstances Xia San was the one who should be held responsible, as Jin-gui's accomplice. They were still debating heatedly how to deal with the matter when they heard Jia Lian call from outside:

'No more chatter! Get the place looking decent. The officer from the Board is on his way.'

Mrs Xia and her son were frantic. It seemed inevitable that they would come out badly at the inquest. At last Mrs Xia begged Aunt Xue:

'Please accept my humble apologies. It seems my daughter was misguided in her ways, and that she has met the end she deserved. If there is an inquest, it will look bad for your family too. I beg you to let the matter drop!'

'That is out of the question!' objected Bao-chai. 'It has already been reported. We can't let it drop now.'

Mrs Zhou offered her services as a mediator:

'The only way the matter could be dropped would be if Mrs Xia herself were to go forward and ask them to dispense with the inquest. In that case we wouldn't raise any objections.'

Xia San, who was being held outside, agreed after a certain amount of intimidation from Jia Lian to intercept the officer and make a written request for suspension of the inquest. The others all approved this course of action. Aunt Xue gave orders for a coffin to be purchased and for all the other funeral arrangements to be seen to. But at this point our narrative turns elsewhere.

*

Jia Yu-cun had recently been promoted to the post of Mayor of the Metropolitan Prefecture, with additional duties as Collector of Taxes. He went out one day on a tour of inspection of the agricultural area newly brought under cultivation, and his route took him through the shire of Innsite. When he came to the riverside hamlet of Rushford Hythe, he halted his sedan at the water's edge and waited for his servants to catch up with him, when they would all take the ferry to

the other side. He noticed a small broken-down temple on the out-
skirts of the village, with a few gnarled old pine-trees poking their
branches up through the ruins. Stepping down from his sedan, he
wandered over at a leisurely pace and strolled into the temple. The
gilt was peeling from the statues, and the courtyard was in a state of
extreme dilapidation. At one side stood a broken stone tablet with a
worn and barely legible inscription. Yu-cun was crossing the rear
courtyard towards the back hall of the temple when he saw, in the
shade of a cypress tree, a lean-to shed with a thatched roof, and
inside the shed a Taoist monk, seated with his eyes closed, deep in
meditation. Going closer and gazing into the man's face, Yu-cun was
struck by a strange familiarity, a feeling of having seen him somewhere before – though where he could not for the moment recall.
His attendants were about to wake the Taoist rudely from his
meditations, but Yu-cun stopped them and, advancing respectfully,
addressed him with the words:

'Venerable Master!'

The Taoist opened both eyes a slit and gave a faint smile.

'What brings you here, sir?'

'A tour of inspection has led me to these parts,' replied Yu-cun.
'Seeing your reverence so rapt in meditation, and deducing from this
the profundity of your spiritual attainments, I most humbly crave
from you some words of truth.'

'There is ever a whence, and always a whither.'

Yu-cun sensed something very mysterious about the old man.
Making a deep bow, he enquired:

'From which monastery does your reverence hail? What is the
name of this temple where you have made your hermitage? How
many live here? If it is a life of pure contemplation that you seek,
surely one of the sacred mountains would be a more conducive
dwelling place? And if it is good works that you wish to perform,
would not the busy thoroughfare be more appropriate?'

'A bottle-gourd is ample for my needs,' replied the Taoist. 'Why
build my hut on some famous mountain? As for this temple, only a
crumbling tablet of stone remains to point to its long-forgotten
origins. And why should I strive to do good works, when body and
shadow suffice? I am no "jewel in the casket" biding "till one should
come to buy", no "jade-pin in the drawer hid, waiting its time to fly".'

Yu-cun had always been a smart fellow. The reference to 'the bottle-gourd' and to his own couplet (written when he had been a poor lodger at the Bottle-gourd Temple in Soochow) at once brought to mind his neighbour from days gone by, old Zhen Shi-yin. Scrutinizing the Taoist again, he recognized him and saw that his old benefactor's face had not changed. He dismissed his attendants.

'Tell me the truth, sir,' he enquired confidentially, when they were alone. 'Are you not old Mr Zhen?'

A faint smile crossed the old man's face.

'What is truth, and what fiction? You must understand that truth is fiction, and fiction truth.'

Yu-cun's certainty was increased by the fact that the old man's words contained a pun on their names, Zhen being homophonous with 'truth', and Jia with 'fiction'. He bowed afresh and said:

'When your great generosity enabled me to travel to the capital, I enjoyed good fortune, and thanks to your blessing obtained the highest distinction in my examinations and was appointed to the very district to which you yourself had moved. That was where I first learned that you had achieved enlightenment and had renounced the world, to soar in the realm of the immortals. Although I sought anxiously to trace your whereabouts, in the end I came to the conclusion that a common layman such as myself, soiled with the dust of this mortal world, would never be granted another chance to behold your holy face. How blessed I am indeed to have encountered you again! I beg you, holy sir, to relieve my benighted ignorance. If you deign to accede to my request, allow me to provide for you and accommodate you in my humble abode close by in the capital, that I may derive daily benefit from your wisdom.'

The Taoist rose to his feet and returned the bow.

'Beyond my prayer-mat,' he replied, 'I know nothing. Of what Your Honour has just spoken I have understood not a single word.'

He resumed his sitting position. Yu-cun began to have misgivings.

'But surely,' he thought to himself, 'it must be him? The face, the voice are so familiar! After these nineteen years his complexion is quite unchanged. It must be that he has achieved a high degree of spiritual cultivation, and is therefore reluctant to reveal his former identity. He considers himself a new man. But he is my benefactor. Now that I have found him again, I must think of some way to show my gratitude. If material things cannot move him, still less I suppose will any mention of his wife and child.'

After reflecting thus, Yu-cun spoke:

'Venerable Sir, I understand that you are reluctant to reveal your former condition. But can you not vouchsafe your disciple some sign of recognition?'

He was about to prostrate himself when his attendants came to announce that it was getting late and he should cross the river at once. Yu-cun was hesitating, when the Taoist spoke to him again:

'Cross with all speed to the other side, Your Honour. We will meet again. Delay now, and a storm may arise. If you really deign to come again, I look forward to seeing you here by the ford another day.'

He closed his eyes and was lost once more in his meditations. Yu-cun, with some reluctance, bade him farewell and made his way out of the temple. He had reached the bank of the river and was preparing to board the ferry and make the crossing, when he saw a man running towards him at full pelt.

To learn who it was, please turn to the next chapter.

CHAPTER 104

Drunken Dime at large again –
a small fish whips up a mighty storm
Our Besotted Hero in agony once more –
a chance thrust quickens a numbed heart

'The temple you visited has just caught fire, sir!'

Jia Yu-cun turned round, to see flames leaping from the ground and a cloud of whirling ashes darkening the sky.

'How extraordinary!' he thought to himself. 'I left the place only minutes ago, and have walked but this little distance. How could such a fire have started? What if old Mr Zhen has perished in it?'

To return and investigate would almost certainly make him late for the ferry. On the other hand he felt a little uneasy about not going back at all. After a moment's thought, he asked the man:

'Did you notice whether the old Taoist managed to escape or not?'

'I was not far behind you, sir. I had a stomach-ache, and went for a bit of a stroll. That was when I looked back. When I saw the blaze and realized it was the temple that was on fire, I came here as fast as I could to let you know. I certainly didn't see anyone coming out of the flames.'

His twinge of conscience notwithstanding, Yu-cun was at heart a man who put his career first, and he felt insufficient concern to involve (and inconvenience) himself any further.

'Wait here until the fire has died down,' he told the servant. 'Then go back and see if you can find any trace of the old man. Report to me directly.'

'Yes, sir.' Reluctantly the man stayed behind to carry out these instructions.

Jia Yu-cun crossed the river and continued his tour of inspection, putting up for the night, a few stops later, at the official lodgings provided. Next morning, his duties were completed and he was greeted at one of the city gates by the usual throng of runners, who then escorted him through the streets with a great deal of noise and pomp. On the way, he heard from within his sedan one of the criers having some kind of altercation in the street, and asked what the trouble was. A man was dragged forward and deposited kneeling at the foot of the sedan. The crier himself then fell to his knees and gave the following account of the incident:

'This drunkard, instead of keeping out of Your Honour's way, came lurching right in front of your chair, sir. I told him to get off the road, but he answered back in a drunken and insolent manner, threw himself down on the ground in the middle of the street, and accused me of hitting him.'

Jia Yu-cun addressed the offender directly:

'This entire district, as you know, is in my charge, and every one of its residents falls under my jurisdiction. You, sir, must have known this only too well, and must also have been aware of my presence in these parts. In your drunken state the very least you could have done was to keep out of my way. But instead you have polluted the highway with your obnoxious person, and have then had the effrontery to slander one of my men! Explain yourself!'

'Paid fir the wine meself, din I?' grumbled the man. 'An' the ground's 'is Majesty's, innit? 'is Majesty never said I couldn't sleep on it if I'd adda few! Can't see what it's gorra do with you, yerroner!'

'Why, this fellow seems to consider himself completely above the law!' snapped Jia Yu-cun angrily. 'What's his name?'

'Ni Er,' replied the man. 'But they calls me the Drunken Diamond.'

Jia Yu-cun was not amused.

'Give this precious rogue a good thrashing,' he ordered grimly, adding by way of a vicious pun: 'That should soon cut him down to size!'

His attendants pinned Ni Er to the ground and administered a few hefty cracks of the whip. The pain soon cleared Dime's head, and he began begging abjectly for mercy. Yu-cun laughed loudly at him from his chair:

'Diamond, indeed! All right, leave him alone for the present. Take him back to the yamen. We can question him at leisure there.'

There was a cry from the runners, who immediately bound Dime and dragged him along behind the chair, ignoring his continued pleas for mercy.

Yu-cun went first to the Palace to report on his tour, and then returned to his yamen, where daily business soon engulfed him. He was too busy to give Dime another thought. But the bystanders who had witnessed the flogging in the street lost no time in telling the story to their friends, and the news soon spread that Ni Er the swank, Ni Er the drunken bully, had fallen foul of Mayor Jia and landed himself in deep water. Rumour of it eventually reached the ears of his wife and daughter, and that night when he failed to come home his daughter, fearing the worst, went to all the gambling-dens in search of him. His cronies only confirmed the story, and Dime's daughter was reduced to tears at the thought of what might have happened to her father.

'Don't take it to heart so, miss!' they said. 'That Mayor Jia's related to the Rong-guo Jias. And isn't young Jia Yun a buddy of your dad's? Why don't you and your mum go and ask *him* to put in a word for Dime? That should fix it.'

Dime's daughter thought this over to herself:

'They're right. Father has often said how friendly he is with young Mr Jia Yun next door. Perhaps I should go and see him.'

She hurried home and told her mother, and the following morning the two of them went to call on Jia Yun. He happened to be at home that day, and invited them both in, while his mother told the little maid to serve them tea. They related the story of Dime's arrest, and begged Jia Yun to help them secure his release.

'Of course!' agreed Jia Yun without the slightest hesitation. 'No trouble at all. I'll drop in at Rong-guo House, mention it to them, and the matter will soon be settled. This Mayor Jia owes everything to his connection with the Rong-guo Jias. One word from them and Dime will be a free man again!'

Dime's wife and daughter returned home in high spirits and with great expectations. They went to visit Dime in the yamen where he was being held prisoner, and told him the good news, that thanks to the intervention of Jia Yun and the Jia family he would shortly be set free. Dime was greatly relieved.

Unfortunately Jia Yun, having had his previous overtures rebuffed by Xi-feng, had been too cowed to visit her again, and since that day had hardly set foot inside Rong-guo House. The men on the Rong-guo gate treated callers strictly according to their standing with the family. If the family were known to have received a person with cordiality and respect, that person was welcomed and announced immediately; if, on the other hand, a person had once been cold-shouldered, the servants were quick to take their cue. If such a person called again, even if he were a relative, they would refuse to report his arrival and would send him away without more ado. So, when Jia Yun turned up and asked to pay his respects to Jia Lian, he got a very cool reception at the gate:

'Mr Lian is not in. When he comes home, we will inform him that you called.'

Jia Yun would have persisted and asked to see Mrs Lian, but he was afraid to provoke the gatemen any further, and with some reluctance turned about and went home. He had to face renewed importuning from Dime's wife and daughter the next day:

'But Mr Yun! We thought you said the Jias could get anything they wanted out of anyone! You're one of the family, and this isn't a big thing to ask. You can't have failed! You can't let us down like this!'

Jia Yun felt thoroughly humiliated, and tried to bluff his way out:

'Yesterday my relatives were too busy to send anyone. But I'm sure they will do something about it today, and then Dime will be set free. There's really no need to worry.'

Dime's wife and daughter waited to see how things would turn out. Jia Yun, having failed to gain access by the front entrance of Rong-guo House, now tried the back, thinking he might be able to get in touch with Bao-yu in the Garden. To his surprise he found the garden gate locked, and was obliged to return home once more, dejected and crestfallen.

'It was only a few years ago that Dime lent me that money,' he thought to himself. 'I used it to buy Mrs Lian a present of camphor and musk, and as a result she gave me the tree-planting job. But this time, just because I can't afford presents, I get the brush-off. She's got nothing to be proud of, lending out money – money that's been handed down in the family – while poor householders like us can't even borrow a tael when we need it. I suppose she thinks she's being clever, that this is a nice little nest-egg, a clever way to protect her own future. She doesn't know what a stinking reputation she's earned for herself. If I keep my mouth shut, well and good; but if I tell people what I know, she'll have more than one life to answer for in court!'

He found Dime's wife and daughter waiting for him when he got back, and this time he had to admit, albeit in a modified form, that his mission had not borne fruit:

'The Jias did send someone to put in a word for Dime, but I'm afraid Mayor Jia won't set him free. You might have more luck if you try Mr Leng Zi-xing. He's related to Mrs Zhou, and she works for the Jias.'

'What earthly good will a servant be,' complained Dime's family, 'when a respectable member of the family such as yourself can do nothing for us!'

Jia Yun found this highly mortifying. 'What you don't seem to realize,' he protested indignantly, 'is that nowadays servants can have more pull than their masters!'

Dime's wife and daughter could see that they were wasting their time with him.

'We're much obliged to you for all the trouble you've gone to, Mr Yun,' they muttered sarcastically. 'When Father gets out he's sure to want to thank you himself . . .'

They went their way. Eventually they found somebody else to assist in the extrication of Dime, who was duly acquitted and released, having suffered no more by way of punishment than a few strokes of the rod.

Upon his return to the family hearth, his womenfolk related to Dime how the Jias had failed to intervene on his behalf. Dime had already broached his first bottle, and angrily announced his intention of seeking out Jia Yun and teaching him a lesson:

'Lousy bastard! Ungrateful, sneaky little sod! When he had an empty belly and needed a job, who did it, who gave him a helping hand? Right first time: yours truly. 'Course, now I'm in a bit of a spot meself, he doesn't want to know, does he! Bloody marvellous I call it! I'm tellin' you, if I want to, I can take those Jias and rub their snotty little noses in the mud where they belong!'

The women tried anxiously to forestall any more of his grandiose threats:

'Drunk again, Dad! You're out of your mind! The bottle was your undoing a couple of days ago, and you got a good hiding for it. And now hark at you! At it again, before your bruises have even had a chance to heal!'

'Think a licking's going to scare me, do you?' bragged Dime. 'All I needed was a lead. It was all I needed. And now I've got one. Now I can nail 'em! Oh yes, I got pally with some fellers while I was inside, and I learnt a thing or two. Accordin' to them, this country's crawling with Jias of one breed or another, and a few days back there was a fair number of Jia servants taken in. I was pretty surprised to hear that. I mean, I knew the younger Jias and *their* servants were a bad lot, but I'd always thought the older ones were all right. How come *they*'d got into trouble?

'In the end, turns out that these Jias they were talking about were all from out of town – course, they're still related to the ones in town. Anyway, there's been some sort of hoo-ha, so these servants have been sent here for trying. So now I've got my lead! I'm laughing! That little Yun's an ungrateful beggar, that's what he is! My mates and I can spread the word on his family's carry-on, the cheating and bullying, the lending money at wicked rates, the wife-snatching . . . Oh, if *that* gets to the top, some heads'll roll all right then! That'll learn 'em who Dime is!'

'Go to sleep, you drunken old pisspot!' cried Dime's missus. 'Snatching *whose* wife, in the name of heaven? I never heard anything so ridiculous in all my life!'

'Fat lot you'd know, stuck at home all day!' retorted Dime. 'Coupla years back, I was having a throw in one of the dens, met this young feller, name of Zhang, and he told me how his woman was taken off of him by the Jias. Asked me for some advice. I just told him to forget it. Dunno where he is now, haven't seen him these two or three years. Next time I bump into that Zhang feller, I'll know what to tell him. Roast that little Yun alive! Make him crawl on his knees! Got my lead now . . .'

Dime promptly collapsed onto his bed in a stupor, mumbling incoherently to himself, and was soon soundly asleep. His wife and daughter dismissed his threats as the ravings of a drunkard, and early the next morning Dime set off once more for his gambling haunts, where we must leave him.

*

We return to Jia Yu-cun: the morning after his return home, refreshed by a good night's sleep, he told his wife (who, it will be remembered, had once been in service with the Zhen family in Soochow) of his encounter with Zhen Shi-yin. She reproached him for his heartlessness:

'Why did you not go back to look for him? If he has been burnt to death, we will be guilty forever of having done him a great wrong!'

She began to weep, and Jia Yu-cun tried to justify himself:

'How could I have intervened? A being like that lives on a different plane from people like us. He would only have resented the interference.'

At that moment a message was brought in for Yu-cun:

'The runner sent by Your Honour yesterday to investigate the fire at the temple has come to deliver his report.'

Yu-cun strolled out to receive the runner, who dropped one knee to the ground and said:

'I went back as you told me to, sir. I braved the flames and went into the temple to see if I could find the Taoist. His hut was completely razed to the ground, even the wall behind it had collapsed, and there was no trace of the old man. He must have been roasted alive . . . All that was left was his prayer-mat, and drinking-gourd; somehow they both seemed to have survived intact. I looked all over the place for any human remains, but there was not so much as a bone to be seen. I was going to bring you the prayer-mat and gourd, to show you, in case you didn't believe me, sir; but when I picked them up they just turned to ashes in my hands.'

Yu-cun deduced from this account that Zhen Shi-yin's departure from the scene of the fire had been no ordinary death, but rather some miraculous process of etherealization. He dismissed the runner, and went in again to his private apartment, where he made no mention to his wife of Shi-yin's metamorphosis by fire, thinking she would fail to understand and would only be distressed; instead he simply told her that no trace of the old man had been found, and that he had most probably escaped alive.

Leaving his private apartment, Yu-cun went to his study, and was sitting there pondering the few words Zhen Shi-yin had spoken during their brief encounter, when one of his attendants came in to convey an Imperial summons to the Palace, to peruse certain state papers. Yu-cun hurriedly took a sedan-chair to the Palace. As he arrived he overheard someone say:

'The Kiangsi Grain Intendant, Jia Zheng, has been impeached, and is at court to plead for clemency!'

Yu-cun pressed on into the Cabinet Office and greeted the various Ministers of State gathered there. He first performed his duty and glanced through the state papers (which spelled out His Majesty's displeasure with the state of the coastal defences), and then left the

Cabinet Office at once to find Jia Zheng and to commiserate with him on his impeachment, expressing his relief that it was not too serious a charge, and asking if his journey to the capital had been a comfortable one. Jia Zheng replied with a detailed account of his misfortunes.

'Has your plea for clemency been presented to the throne yet?' asked Yu-cun.

'It has,' replied Jia Zheng. 'I am expecting to receive the Rescript when His Majesty returns from lunch.'

Even as they were speaking, Jia Zheng was summoned to the Imperial presence, and hurried in. Those senior ministers who were connected with him waited anxiously in one of the antechambers; and when, after a lengthy audience, he finally emerged again, his face beaded with sweat, they all pressed forward to greet him.

'Well?' they asked. 'How did it go?'

'Frightened the life out of me!' gasped Jia Zheng, his tongue popping out of his mouth. 'I must thank you all, gentlemen, for your concern. I am relieved to inform you that I have come out of this business relatively unscathed.'

'On what subjects did His Majesty question you?'

'His first question concerned the smuggling of firearms in Yunnan Province. The original memorial on the case identified the ringleader as a member of the household of Jia Hua, the former Grand Preceptor. His Majesty thought he remembered the name as that of my father's cousin, and asked me if it was indeed the same man. I kowtowed at once and reminded him that my father's cousin was Jia *Dai*-hua. His Majesty laughed. Then he went on to ask me if there was not another relative of mine named Jia Hua, who had once been President of the Board of War, but had subsequently been demoted and then appointed Mayor.'

Jia Yu-cun was among those present. His more formal personal name was indeed Hua, Yu-cun being merely a commonly used sobriquet, and he nearly jumped out of his skin when he heard this.

'And how did you reply to this, sir?' he asked Jia Zheng.

'I replied most deliberately that the former Grand Preceptor Jia Hua hailed from Yunnan, whereas the Jia who was at present Mayor of the Metropolitan Prefecture was a Chekiang man.

'His Majesty's second question concerned the Jia Fan recently impeached by the Soochow censor. He asked me if this man also belonged to my family. I kowtowed and replied that he did. A cloud seemed to pass over His Majesty's countenance, and he said: "A disgraceful affair, for a man to let his own household servants run riot and lay their hands on the wives of innocent citizens!" I did not dare utter a word. "What relation of yours is this Jia Fan?" "A distant one, Your Majesty," I hastily replied. His Majesty gave a sound of disapproval and told me to withdraw. Altogether, I think you will agree, a most alarming experience!'

'Certainly an astonishing coincidence that these two other cases should have come up at the same time as yours,' concurred the others.

'The cases in themselves are not so very remarkable,' replied Jia Zheng. 'But the fact that both the gentlemen concerned belong to the Jia clan certainly bodes ill for us. I suppose in a way it's only to be expected: our clan is, after all, a large one, and over the centuries has spread itself throughout the entire Empire.

'There may be no scandal at present involving our branch of the family directly, but I fear that after this the name Jia will be very much in the forefront of His Majesty's mind. Not a prospect I view with relish, I must say.'

'Come, you have nothing to fear,' the others reassured him. 'Remember, the truth will always prevail.'

'I should dearly like to retire from public life altogether,' said Jia Zheng. 'But alas, I can hardly plead old age, and the hereditary family titles are an obligation that neither branch of the family can relinquish.'

'Now that you are reinstated at the Board of Works, sir,' put in Jia Yu-cun, 'I think you will find life a great deal less fraught with difficulty.'

'Metropolitan posts may be less troublesome in principle,' replied Jia Zheng, 'but since I have now served twice in the provinces, there's no saying what unpleasantness may still lie in store for me.'

'We all hold your integrity in the highest esteem,' the others reassured him again. 'And your brother's character is beyond reproach. However, you could perhaps be a little stricter with your nephew and the younger generation.'

'It is true, I have spent far too little time at home,' said Jia Zheng. 'And I have not kept a sufficiently careful watch on my nephew's behaviour. It is something I have been uneasy about myself. Since you have raised this issue, and since I know you to be well disposed towards my family, I would be obliged if you could be a little more specific. Tell me, for example, have you heard of any irregularities in my nephew Zhen's family at Ning-guo House?'

'We have only heard,' they replied, 'that he has somehow managed to fall foul of several Vice-Presidents, not to mention a few eunuch chamberlains at the Palace. It is nothing to worry about unduly as yet, but you should perhaps warn him to be a little more circumspect in future.'

When the conversation was over, the ministers saluted Jia Zheng and took their leave. Jia Zheng returned home, and was welcomed at the main gate by a full turn-out of the younger male Jias. He enquired first after Grandmother Jia, and then they each greeted him in turn, dropping one knee to the ground, and followed him into the mansion. Lady Wang and the other ladies had assembled for a formal welcome in the Hall of Exalted Felicity, after which Jia Zheng went to pay his respects to Grandmother Jia in her private apartment. He told her all his news, and when she asked about Tan-chun, gave her a detailed account of the wedding.

'I had to leave at short notice, and was unable to celebrate the Double Ninth festival with her. But although I did not see her then myself, some of her husband's family came to visit me and told me that she was getting on very well there. Her father-in-law and mother-in-law both send you their regards. They said that they might be moving to the capital this winter or next spring, which would certainly be most welcome. But since these recent coastal disturbances, I very much doubt if they will be able to move so soon.'

Grandmother Jia had at first been most upset by the news of Jia Zheng's demotion and return to the capital: apart from anything else it would mean that Tan-chun, who was living so far away from home, would be even more isolated from the family. But when Jia Zheng explained the favourable outcome of his audience with the Emperor, and set her mind at rest about Tan-chun, she cheered up considerably, and a smile could be seen on her face when she told him he could leave. Jia Zheng went next to see his brother, and then the younger men, and it was agreed that they would worship at the family ancestral shrine first thing the following day.

These duties performed, Jia Zheng retreated to his private apartment, where he spoke with Lady Wang and his other womenfolk, and then with Bao-yu, Jia Lan and Jia Huan. To his relief he observed a considerable improvement in Bao-yu, who seemed plumper and healthier than at the time of his departure for Kiangsi. He still knew nothing of the boy's mental derangement, and this discernible outward improvement was a source of some satisfaction to him and a welcome antidote to his own anxieties. He dismissed any reservations he still had about the way in which Grandmother Jia had handled the wedding. Bao-chai too, he noticed, seemed more mature and poised than ever, while young Lan was growing into a fine, cultured young man. Jia Zheng was visibly pleased by what he saw. The only blot on the landscape was Jia Huan. *He* did not seem to have changed in the slightest, and still failed to arouse in his father any flicker of paternal affection or pride.

After a silence lasting several minutes Jia Zheng suddenly seemed to think of something.

'There seems to be one person missing.'

Lady Wang knew he must be thinking of Dai-yu, whose death she had refrained from mentioning in any of her letters; and as she did not wish to spoil the pleasure of his homecoming by breaking the news to him now, she replied that illness had prevented Dai-yu from being present. This act of deception cut Bao-yu to the quick, but he did his utmost to appear composed, out of respect for his father.

Lady Wang invited all the children and grandchildren to the welcoming feast, and they drank to the Master's return. Xi-feng, although she was strictly the daughter-in-law of Jia She and Lady Xing, was also present by virtue of her role as manageress of the household, helping Bao-chai to pour the wine. Jia Zheng cut the party short, saying that after one more round they should all retire. The servants were also dismissed, with instructions to call on him the next day, after the ancestral sacrifice.

Jia Zheng and Lady Wang were at last alone and able to talk together. Lady Wang was still reluctant to broach any serious topic; when Jia Zheng referred to her brother Wang Zi-teng's death, she did her best not to appear too distressed; and when he mentioned Xue Pan's fresh calamities, her only comment was that he had brought them upon himself. At an opportune moment however she broke the news of Dai-yu's death, which seemed to come as a great shock to Jia Zheng, and to affect him deeply. Tears stole down his cheeks, and he sighed several times. Lady Wang herself could no longer contain her tears. Suncloud and her other maids who were standing close by gave her dress a discreet tug, and she quickly composed herself and steered the conversation towards a more cheerful subject. Soon afterwards they went to bed.

Early next morning, a ceremony was performed in the ancestral shrine, in the presence of all the young male members of the family, and afterwards Jia Zheng received Cousin Zhen and Jia Lian in the gallery at the side of the shrine, where he asked them for a report of the household accounts, which Cousin Zhen supplied, albeit in a highly selective form.

'As I have only just returned home,' commented Jia Zheng, 'I do not intend to subject you to an inquisition now, Zhen. But let me say this: while I have been away, I have heard it said that you have been allowing standards to slip. You must exercise the utmost diligence and caution. You are older than the other members of your generation, and should set an example to the younger ones. There must be no offence caused to people outside. And that applies to you too, Lian. This is no routine homecoming homily. I have my reasons for warning you. There are things I have heard. I repeat: you must both be more careful in future.'

Cousin Zhen and Jia Lian were by now bright red in the face, and all they could muster was a feeble, 'Yes, sir.' Jia Zheng did not pursue the matter any further, but went in to his own reception hall, where all the menservants were waiting for him; thence he proceeded to the inner apartments, to be welcomed by all the maids and serving-women. But we will not describe these events in any great detail.

*

Our story returns to Bao-yu, and to the occasion on the previous day when he had been secretly so upset to hear Lady Wang speak of Dai-yu's 'illness'. Jia Zheng had finally granted him permission to leave the family gathering, and he returned to his apartment. He arrived, having cried most of the way there, to find Bao-chai and Aroma chatting together, and went off at once into an outer room to be on his own and nurse his grief in private. Bao-chai told Aroma to take him some tea, and then decided to go out herself and join him, surmising that he was nervous of an impending confrontation with his father, when his failure to make any progress in his studies would be discovered (and no doubt punished). It was therefore her duty to offer him some comfort. Bao-yu turned the misunderstanding to his advantage:

'It's all right. You can go to bed. I just need some time to concentrate and collect my thoughts. Lately my memory has been so poor, and there will be trouble if I make a fool of myself in front of Father. You go to sleep. Aroma can sit up and keep me company for a bit.'

Bao-chai thought it advisable to humour him, and nodded her assent. As soon as she was out of the way, Bao-yu went to find Aroma, and whispered in her ear:

'Please will you ask Nightingale to come and see me? There's something I need to speak to her about. You must explain to her how things really are. Maybe then she'll stop being so angry with me.'

Aroma: 'I thought I heard you say you wanted time to concentrate and collect your thoughts. But now look at you! What kind of concentration is this? Whatever you want to ask her can wait till tomorrow, surely?'

Bao-yu: 'But I have this evening free. Tomorrow who knows what may happen? I may be sent for by Father, and then I won't have a moment to myself. Dear Aroma! Go and do as I say, please!'

Aroma: 'You know perfectly well she won't come unless Mrs Bao sends for her.'

Bao-yu: 'She might do, if *you* were to explain things to her first.'

Aroma: 'But what do you want me to say?'

Bao-yu: 'Surely by now you know what my feelings are, and why Nightingale has turned against me. It's all because of Dai-yu. It's all a big misunderstanding. You must convince Nightingale that I'm not the faithless monster she takes me for, that it's you and the others who have made me seem like one to her!'

As he said this, he glanced towards the inner room, and pointing in that direction, continued:

'I never wanted to marry *her*. It was forced on me by Grandmother and the rest. It was all a trick. It was they who drove Dai-yu to her death. They were to blame. If only I could have seen her once before she died and been able to tell her the truth! Instead, she died thinking that I had betrayed her! You heard yourself what Cousin Tan said; with her dying breath Dai-yu spoke of me with bitterness and resentment. That's why Nightingale has set herself so violently against me – out of loyalty to her mistress.

'Do *you* think I'm heartless? Think back to Skybright's death. Skybright was only my maid, and not as dear to me as Dai-yu; but even so, when she died I wrote a funeral ode for her and made an offering to her spirit – there's no need to keep it a secret from you any longer. Dai-yu witnessed it with her own eyes. Now she herself is dead; and is she to be ranked lower than Skybright? But I haven't been able to make her an offering of any kind. Won't her spirit see this as further proof of my heartlessness? Won't she feel greater bitterness towards me than ever?'

Aroma: 'I don't understand. If you want to write an ode and make an offering, then go ahead. Who's stopping you?'

Bao-yu: 'I've wanted to ever since I've been better. But somehow I seem to have lost all inspiration. For another person I might have been content with something uninspired. But for Dai-yu nothing but the very purest and the very best will do. That's why I must see Nightingale. I want to ask her what she can tell me of her mistress's feelings; I want to find out exactly how she came by that knowledge. I can remember what it was like before I fell ill. I can remember Dai-yu's feelings towards me then. But from that time onwards, everything becomes a blur in my mind. Didn't you tell me that her health had improved? Then why did death come so quickly? What did she say when I didn't visit her, while she was still well? And then when I fell ill, did she ever say why she never came to see me? I managed to get her belongings brought over here, but Mrs Bao won't let me touch them. I don't understand why.'

Aroma: 'Because she's afraid it will only upset you. Why else?'

Bao-yu: 'I don't believe that. There must be more to it. Then again, if Dai-yu cared about me, or missed me, why did she burn her poems before she died? Surely she would have left them for me as a memento? It's all so confusing. And what about the music that was heard in the air when she died? She must have become a fairy, or risen to heaven in the form of an immortal. If it comes to that, I don't even know if she's really dead. I've only seen the coffin; how can I be sure that she is still inside it?'

Aroma: 'Honestly! You get more ridiculous with every word! Are you trying to suggest that she could have been put in the coffin while she was still alive, and then somehow climbed out of it?'

Bao-yu: 'No. I meant something quite different. You see, if humans achieve immortality, there are two ways in which they can depart from this world: either they go in the flesh, in their earthly form, or they may discard their bodies, and their etheric body is then magically transported to another realm. Oh, Aroma, please help me! Tell Nightingale to come!'

Aroma: 'You'll have to wait till I've had a chance to explain all this to her properly. Then, if she agrees to come, well and good. If not, I can see I shall have to try again and have another long talk with her, and even after that, supposing she does come, she probably won't be prepared to say much to you. If you want my advice, you should at least wait till tomorrow. In the morning when Mrs Bao goes in to see Her Old Ladyship I'll have a word with Nightingale. We might get somewhere that way. I'll come back as soon as I've spoken to her and tell you how it went.'

Bao-yu: 'I suppose you're right. But you don't know how impatient I feel.'

At this point, Musk appeared:

'Mrs Bao says, it's already well past midnight, and will you go in to bed now, Mr Bao. Aroma must have got carried away chatting to you, and forgotten the time . . .'

'Goodness, it *is* late!' exclaimed Aroma. 'Time to go to sleep. If there's anything else, it can wait till the morning.'

Bao-yu rose reluctantly to go in to the bedroom, whispering in Aroma's ear as he passed by:

'Be sure not to forget tomorrow, whatever you do!'

'Of course I won't!' said Aroma with a smile.

'You two at it again!' said Musk, touching her cheek at Aroma in a saucy fashion. Then, to Bao-yu: 'Why don't you just go straight to Mrs Bao and tell her that you'd like to sleep with Aroma? Then the two of you can carry on "talking" till dawn. None of us will interfere, you needn't worry.'

Bao-yu raised his hand:

'That is quite uncalled for, Musk!'

'Little hussy!' said Aroma heatedly. 'Always having your little dig! You'd better look out! One of these days I'll rip that nasty little tongue of yours out of your mouth for good!' Turning to Bao-yu, she continued:

'Now see what you've done! This is all your fault. Keeping me up talking like this till one o'clock in the morning . . .'

She escorted him into his room and then went her separate way to bed.

Bao-yu was unable to sleep that night, and in the morning was still preoccupied with the same gloomy thoughts.

The new day began with an announcement from outside:

'The Master's family and friends have expressed a wish to hold a theatre-party to welcome him home. The Master however is insistent that plays would be inappropriate on this occasion; instead he will give a simple party at home, to which all family and friends are invited. The date has been set fot the day after tomorrow. This is the preliminary announcement.'

To learn who was invited, please read the next chapter.

CHAPTER 105

The Embroidered Jackets raid
Ning-guo House
And Censor Li impeaches
the Prefect of Ping-an

The day of the reception arrived. Jia Zheng was busily entertaining his guests in the Hall of Exalted Felicity, when Lai Da the steward hurried in to report that a Commissioner Zhao was outside, with a detachment of the Embroidered Jackets, the Imperial secret police:

'He says he is making a social call, and when I asked for his visiting card he told me there was no need for any such formality, as he was on the best of terms with you, sir. Then he got down from his carriage and started walking straight in. I beg you, sir, to go out with the young masters and receive him at once.'

'I've never had anything to do with this Zhao,' mused Jia Zheng. 'I wonder what can have brought him here? And at such an inconvenient hour. I can hardly abandon my guests to entertain him; and yet if I do not invite him in it will seem uncivil . . .'

He stood there thinking the matter over to himself, and Jia Lian urged him to hurry: 'If you wait much longer, Uncle, they will be upon us.'

Even as he said these words, a servant entered to announce that Commissioner Zhao had indeed already passed through the inner gate, and Jia Zheng hurried out into the courtyard to receive him. Zhao soon came into sight, smiling but silent, and walked straight on and up into the hall. He was followed by five or six of his aides, some of whom were known to Jia Zheng, but although Jia Zheng greeted them, none of them said a word in reply. Jia Zheng could only follow them helplessly back into the hall and ask them to be seated. Some of the guests were acquainted with Zhao, but he passed them by with his head in the air and ignored everyone except Jia Zheng, whom he eventually took by the hand and engaged in vague small-talk, smiling inscrutably all the while. The guests scented trouble in the air, and either sneaked out into the private apartments at the back of the mansion, or stood stock-still where they were, in an attitude of apprehensive respect.

Jia Zheng managed to maintain an anxious smile, and was about to attempt a response to one of Zhao's pleasantries when a flustered servant entered the hall and announced:

'His Highness the Prince of Xi-ping!'

Jia Zheng hurried out once again, to find the prince already entering the courtyard. Commissioner Zhao moved smartly forward ahead of Jia Zheng to salute the prince, and then gave his own aides their orders:

'His Royal Highness has now arrived; take your men and post yourselves at the front and rear gates of the mansion.'

Zhao's aides went off to do his bidding, while Jia Zheng and the other menfolk, filled with foreboding by this sinister turn of events, fell to their knees and kowtowed before the Prince of Xi-ping. The prince raised Jia Zheng with both hands and said with a reassuring smile:

'I would not intrude on you at such a time did I not have special reasons: I am entrusted with an Imperial Edict for your brother, Sir She. But I see that we have come upon you in the midst of a private gathering, and as it would hardly be fitting to proceed while your friends and relatives are still present, I would ask them to leave. Only the members of your own household need remain behind.'

'A most gracious gesture, I am sure,' interposed Commissioner Zhao sharply. 'But His Highness supervising operations at Ning-guo House is, I believe, taking this matter a little more seriously, and has already ordered every gate to be sealed.'

The guests learned from this that both mansions were in some sort of trouble, and began to fear that they themselves were trapped as well. The prince, however, seemed unperturbed, and announced smilingly:

'Gentlemen, please consider yourselves free to leave. Send for some of my men to escort them out,' he continued, addressing Zhao, 'and tell your own officers that these are all guests and are not to be hindered or subjected to any kind of search, but are to be let through without delay.'

As soon as they heard this, the guests vanished like a puff of smoke, leaving only Jia She, Jia Zheng and the immediate family, who stood there trembling and pale with fear. Shortly afterwards, constables swarmed in and stationed themselves at every doorway, thereby denying freedom of movement to masters and servants alike. Zhao turned to the prince, his face positively venomous:

'Will Your Highness be so good as to read the Edict, so that we can proceed with our task?'

The constables hitched up their robes, rolled up their sleeves, and stood smartly to attention to hear the Edict. The prince began his preamble with great deliberation:

'I am hereby instructed by His Majesty to proceed with Commissioner Zhao Quan of the Embroidered Jackets and to search, and take a complete inventory of, the property of Jia She.'

Jia She cowered prostrate on the ground as the prince mounted the terrace and, facing south, began the proclamation of the Edict proper:

'"Hearken! Inasmuch as Our subject Jia She has connived with a provincial official and has used his influence to persecute a defenceless citizen, he has shown himself unworthy of Our favour, has disgraced his ancestors, and is to be deprived of his hereditary rank. By Imperial Decree."'

'Arrest him!' barked Zhao. 'Take the others away and put them under close guard!'

This referred to the other Jia menfolk present – Jia Zheng, Jia Lian, Cousin Zhen, Jia Rong, Jia Qiang, Jia Zhi and Jia Lan. Bao-yu had somehow managed to slip out to Grandmother Jia's apartment earlier, on the pretext of some indisposition or other, while Jia Huan hardly ever put in an appearance at such social gatherings.

Zhao also told his aides to issue the junior officers and constables with their orders at once: they were to divide up and search the mansion room by room, taking a detailed inventory as they went along. These orders, and the brisk matter-of-fact efficiency with which they were delivered, had a devastating impact on the morale of the Jia family, young and old alike. They looked at one another in terror as they were led away, while Zhao's constables and personal lackeys began rubbing their hands in gleeful anticipation.

'I understand,' said the Prince of Xi-ping, 'that Sir Zheng and Sir She maintain separate establishments. Since the Edict only empowers us to search Sir She's property, the other apartments should be locked and sealed, until such time as I have received further instructions from His Majesty.'

Zhao rose to his feet.

'Your Highness, I should inform you that in point of fact Jia She and Jia Zheng do *not* maintain separate establishments. On the contrary, I am given to understand that the affairs of both branches of Rong-guo House are managed by one person, Jia Lian, who is the son of Sir She and the nephew of Sir Zheng. It is therefore imperative that we search the entire mansion.'

The prince was silent, and Zhao continued:

'In view of this, I shall personally direct the search of the residences of both Jia She and Jia Lian.'

'There is no hurry,' said the prince. 'Send word to the inner apartments first, and give the ladies time to withdraw. A few minutes' delay is neither here nor there.'

But even as he was speaking, Zhao's men, who had already led away the Jia menfolk, were dividing up into search parties and had begun their work, each taking one of the Jia servants to act as guide.

'Let there be no rowdy behaviour now!' cried the prince. 'I shall be along presently to supervise the proceedings myself.'

He rose to his feet in a dignified manner, and addressed his own attendants:

'Not one of you is to move. Wait here, and later we shall inspect the inventory together.'

Almost immediately one of Zhao's men returned from the search and knelt before him:

'Your Highness, restricted garments and skirts for palace use, and many other prohibited items, have been found in the inner apartments. I have given orders that these are not to be moved, pending Your Highness's instructions.'

Presently another search party returned and pressed before the prince:

'Two chests of property deeds found in the eastern side-compound, and one chest of promissory notes – all bearing illegal rates of interest!'

'Usurers!' hissed Zhao. 'They deserve to lose everything. Take a seat, Your Highness, and allow me to order the immediate confiscation of the entire contents of the mansion. We can report to the throne for the necessary authorization afterwards.'

At that moment an aide-de-camp came in to speak to the prince:

'The soldiers at the gate have sent word that the Prince of Bei-jing is here, as the special emissary of His Majesty, and will deliver a second Edict. You are requested to go out and receive him.'

Zhao welcomed this news.

'It was just my luck,' he thought to himself, 'to have been lumbered with this first prince! Now he's being replaced, and I should be able to get down to business!'

He went out to the front courtyard, to find the Prince of Bei-jing already facing south, and delivering the new Edict.

' "For the Edification of Zhao Quan, Commissioner of the Embroidered Jackets. Hearken! The men under Zhao's command are to arrest no one, with the exception of Jia She, who is to be held for questioning. The Prince of Xi-ping will supervise all other aspects of the investigation according to Our Instructions." '

The Prince of Xi-ping was delighted. He sat down with the Prince of Bei-jing, and told Zhao to take Jia She with him and return to his yamen. The search parties, having learned of the arrival of the new prince, had all congregated once more in the courtyard. They were most disappointed to hear that Zhao was being removed from the scene, and stood around, disconsolately waiting for their new orders. The Prince of Bei-jing selected two of the more honest-looking officers and a dozen or so of the older constables to stay behind, and dismissed all the others.

'I was just beginning to get extremely annoyed with old Zhao,' said the Prince of Xi-ping. 'You arrived with that second Edict in the nick of time. If you'd been much later, I'm afraid it would have gone badly for the Jias.'

'I heard at court,' replied the Prince of Bei-jing, 'that you had been entrusted with the original Edict, and that the investigation was in your hands, and I must say I was greatly relieved. I knew I could depend on you to see that things did not get out of hand. But I hadn't bargained on that old rogue Zhao. Tell me, where are Sir Zheng and young Bao-yu? I do hope these men have not been creating too much havoc.'

'Jia Zheng and the other gentlemen are being held under guard in the servants' quarters,' he was informed by the officers. 'The men have turned the entire house upside-down in the course of their search.'

The Prince of Bei-jing turned to one of them:

'Bring Sir Zheng here at once. I wish to speak to him.'

Jia Zheng was brought in, and fell to his knees, tearfully pleading for mercy. The Prince of Bei-jing stood up, took him by both hands and said:

'My friend, set your mind at rest.'

When the prince went on to inform him of the new Edict, Jia Zheng wept with emotion, and faced in a northerly direction to kowtow his thanks to the throne. Then he came forward again to receive any further instructions. It was the Prince of Xi-ping who continued:

'My friend, when Commissioner Zhao was here just now, his constables reported having found prohibited items of clothing, and promissory notes bearing excessive rates of interest. It will be hard to gloss all this over. The clothes were no doubt intended for Her Grace's use – that I can state quite plausibly in my report. But these promissory notes – what are we to say about *them*? I think you, Zheng, had better go now with one of the officers and give him a complete account of all Sir She's property. It is essential that you conceal nothing, or you will only make things worse for yourself.'

'How could I dare to conceal anything!' replied Jia Zheng. 'But I beg to inform Your Highness that our family estate has never been formally divided between my brother and myself; individually we own only whatever we happen to have in our apartments.'

'Very well,' said the princes. 'Proceed on that basis, and declare whatever is in Sir She's compound.'

The officers were instructed to execute this task in an orderly and civilized fashion, and departed with Jia Zheng.

*

Let us return to Grandmother Jia's apartments, where the ladies had been holding a party of their own that day. Bao-yu had come to join them, and Lady Wang asked him if he ought not to be with the men, for fear of angering his father. Xi-feng was also present, despite her illness, and she replied somewhat croakily on Bao-yu's behalf:

'I'm sure Bao-yu wasn't afraid of the company, Aunt Wang, and I'm sure he wasn't shirking his responsibilities. He just thought there were plenty of men to wait on the guests outside, and that he would be better employed helping us here – which is reasonable enough. If Uncle Zheng needs an extra hand, you can always send Bao-yu over later.'

Grandmother Jia laughed:

'Fengie may be ill, but she still has a tongue in her head!'

The party was warming up and the conversation becoming quite merry, when suddenly one of Lady Xing's maidservants came running in, screeching:

'Your Old Ladyship! Your Ladyships! The most terr . . . terrible thing has happened! Hundreds of bandits in big boots and hats have broken into the house, turned all the trunks and boxes upside down and started stealing our things!'

The ladies stared at her dumbfounded. Next, Patience hurried into the room, her hair dishevelled, dragging Qiao-jie by the hand and sobbing hysterically:

'Lord have mercy on us! I was having my meal with Qiao-jie when Brightie was brought in, his hands tied behind his back. "Hurry, miss," he told me, "go inside and tell Their Ladyships to hide. The prince is on his way in to search the house!" I nearly died of fright. I went into our apartment to rescue a few of the more important things, and ran into a gang of ruffians who pushed me out of their way. You'd better hurry and collect together all the clothes and things you'll need before it's too late.'

Lady Xing and Lady Wang were utterly flabbergasted; Xi-feng listened wide-eyed as Patience told her tale, and then slumped onto the floor with her head thrown back; Grandmother Jia burst into floods of tears before Patience had even finished, and was too distraught to utter a word. The whole room was in this state of total disarray, and the servants were falling over each other in their panic, when suddenly more cries were heard from outside:

'Ladies to withdraw! His Highness the Prince is approaching!'

Bao-chai and Bao-yu stood watching helplessly, as the maids and old nannies scrambled in every direction. The next they knew, Jia Lian came running in, panting:

'All is well! The prince has saved the day!'

They wanted to ask him what had happened, but Jia Lian was himself too infected by the general hysteria to be of any service as an informant. First he caught sight of Xi-feng lying unconscious on the floor, and cried out in alarm; then he saw that Grandmother Jia had also fainted from shock, and feared the worst for her. Patience succeeded in bringing Xi-feng round, and with the help of one of the maids helped her up onto her feet; while Grandmother Jia, when she finally regained consciousness, lay down sobbing on the kang, struggling for breath, as though she might faint again at any moment. Li Wan did her best to comfort her, and Jia Lian himself was at last sufficiently composed to tell them of the events that had taken place, and of the kindness shown them by the two princes – though he withheld the news of Jia She's arrest, which he was afraid might prove too great a shock for Grandmother Jia and Lady Xing. He then went to examine the condition of his own apartment, and found chests and cupboards broken open and ransacked. There was almost nothing left. He stared around him aghast, and tears sprang to his eyes. He heard his name called outside, and went out to find Jia Zheng with the two princes and the officer taking the inventory. The items were being called out one by one:

> One Longevity Buddha in aloeswood
> One Goddess of Mercy, ditto
> One Buddha plinth
> Rosary-beads in aloeswood, two strings
> Golden Buddhas, one set
> Nine gold-plated bronze mirrors
> Jade Buddhas, three
> Longevity and the Eight Immortals, a set of jade figurines
> Four Ru-yi sceptres – two in gold and jade, two in aloeswood
> Antique porcelain vases and jars, seventeen
> Fourteen chests containing antique *objets d'art* and mounted scrolls
> One large jade jar
> Two small ditto
> Large jade circular dishes, two pairs
> Two large glass folding-screens
> Two small kang screens
> Four large dishes in glass
> Four jade dishes
> Two agate ditto
> Four large dishes in solid gold
> Gold bowls, six pairs
> Eight bowls with pattern in gold inlay
> Gold spoons, forty
> Large silver bowls, sixty
> Silver dishes, sixty
> Ivory chopsticks with triple gold inlay, four bundles
> Gold-plated jugs with handles, twelve
> Small spittoons, three pairs

Two saucers
Silver cups and saucers, one hundred and sixty
Black fox-furs, eighteen
Sables, fifty-six
Russet fox-furs, forty-four
White ditto, forty-four
Mongolian lynx-skins, twelve
Partly tailored Yunnan fox-skins, twenty-five
Sea-otter skins, twenty-six
Seal-skins, three
Tiger-skins, six
Brown-and-black striped fox-furs, three
Otter-skins, twenty-eight
Red astrakhan-skins, forty
Black astrakhan-skins sixty-three
Partly tailored musquash-skins, twenty
Mongolian suslik, twenty-four squares
'Swansdown' velvet, four rolls
Grey squirrel-skins, two hundred and sixty-three
Japanese damask silk, thirty-two lengths
Imported worsted, thirty lengths
Serge, thirty-three lengths
Velveteen, forty lengths
Plain satin, one hundred and thirty bolts
Gauze silk, one hundred and eighty bolts
Corded silk-crêpe, thirty-two bolts
Bombasine and camlets, twenty-two rolls each
Tibetan yak's serge, thirty bolts
Dragon-robe satin, eighteen bolts
Cottons, assorted colours, thirty bundles
Sundry fur garments, one hundred and thirty-two
Various garments, padded, lined, unlined, gauze and silk – three
    hundred and forty
Nine pairs of belt-buckles
Items in brass and pewter, over five hundred
Clocks and watches, eighteen
Court chaplets, nine strings of one hundred and eight bands
Pearls, thirteen strings
Gold head-dresses, complete with jewels and precious stones, one
    hundred and twenty-three
Cushion covers and arm-rest covers in Imperial yellow satin, three
    sets

Palace dresses and skirts, eight sets
Two girdles in 'mutton-fat' white jade
Yellow satin, twelve bolts
Substandard silver, seven thousand taels
Pure gold, one hundred and fifty-two taels
Copper cash, seven thousand five hundred strings

All the furniture and properties bestowed by Imperial favour on the Rong-guo branch of the family had been itemized in a similar fashion, while property deeds and bonds for household servants had been put into separate covers and sealed.

Jia Lian followed this recital in detail, and was greatly puzzled to hear no mention of any of his own belongings. Presently one of the princes put an end to his bewilderment by asking Jia Zheng:

'Among the items confiscated earlier, there were promissory notes bearing exorbitant rates of interest – who is responsible for these? You must tell the truth, Zheng.'

Jia Zheng knelt, kowtowed and said:

'I have, alas, been insufficiently diligent in supervising my household. I was completely unaware of these activities. My nephew Jia Lian can doubtless answer your questions.'

Jia Lian hurried forward and fell to his knees.

'Since the chest containing these documents was found in my apartment, how dare I disclaim knowledge of them? I can only beg Your Highnesses' mercy. My uncle was quite unaware of their existence.'

'Your father has already been arrested,' said the princes to Jia Lian. 'This offence can be dealt with at the same time as his. We commend you for having made a clean breast of it.' They turned to their men: 'Jia Lian must be detained. The others may be released, but are to be kept within the confines of the mansion.' Finally they addressed Jia Zheng: 'You, Zheng, must be more circumspect in future. Stay here and await His Majesty's final Edict. We will now return to make our report to the throne, and in the meantime will leave guards here to keep watch over the house.'

They climbed into their princely sedans and were carried out of the mansion. Jia Zheng escorted them as far as the inner gate, where he knelt to see them off, and the Prince of Bei-jing stretched out a hand towards him as he passed, urging him to set his mind at ease. There was genuine concern written on the prince's face.

After their departure Jia Zheng managed to compose himself somewhat, though he was still suffering from a deep sense of shock. When Jia Lian came and asked him to call on Grandmother Jia, informing him that she was indisposed, he roused himself at once and went in. At every doorway he encountered frantic maids and serving-women, all wondering what turn events would take next. Too preoccupied to stop and question them, he hurried on to Grandmother Jia's apartment, and arrived to find Lady Wang, Bao-yu and the others gathered around Grandmother Jia, their faces wet with tears; there was silence in the room, broken only by the occasional fit of convulsive wailing from Lady Xing. The appearance of Jia Zheng brought cries of 'Heaven be praised!' and they hastened to reassure the old lady:

'The Master is safe and sound! He's here with us! Please don't fret any more, Grannie!'

Grandmother Jia gave a faint little gasp and opened her eyes a slit:

'Oh my son! I thought I'd never see you again!'

As she spoke, she burst out sobbing, and everyone in the room immediately followed suit. Jia Zheng was afraid that all this emotion might injure the old lady's health and checked his own tears:

'Please calm yourself, Mother. I cannot deny the gravity of what has happened. But thanks to the Emperor's generosity and the gracious favour of the two princes, we have been treated with great compassion. Brother She has only been taken for questioning, and when his case has been investigated I am sure His Majesty will deal with him leniently also. And so far, not a thing has been removed from the house.'

When Grandmother Jia learned that her elder son had been taken away, she broke down again, and it was a while before Jia Zheng could finally calm her spirits.

The first person to venture out of the room was Lady Xing. She went to inspect her own apartment, and found all the doors sealed with strips of paper and padlocked, and her maids and serving-women held prisoner inside. There was nowhere for her to take refuge, and she let out a great howl of despair. Finally she made her way to Xi-feng's apartment. Xi-feng's side-rooms were sealed in a similar fashion, but the door leading into the main hall was still open, and from inside she could hear the sound of sobbing. She went in, and saw Xi-feng lying on her couch with eyes closed, her face ashen-pale; Patience stood by her side, quietly weeping. Lady Xing thought Xi-feng must be already dead and broke down again. Patience came up to her:

'Please, Your Ladyship, don't cry! We carried Mrs Lian back and she looked as good as dead. She had a sleep and then she woke up again and started crying. Now she's more settled. Please try to be calm, Your Ladyship. How is Her Old Ladyship taking it?'

Lady Xing did not answer her question, but returned to Grandmother Jia's apartment. There she was surrounded by Jia Zheng's family. She reflected on her wretched fate: her husband and son were under arrest, her daughter-in-law was at death's door, her newly married daughter was suffering maltreatment, and now she herself had nowhere to turn. Her whole world seemed to be collapsing around her. The others took pity on her distress and did what they could to comfort her; Li Wan sent a servant to prepare temporary accommodation while Lady Wang deputed some of her own maids and serving-women to wait on her.

Jia Zheng meanwhile had returned to his outer study and was sitting there, stroking his beard and nervously rubbing his hands together, waiting in a state of great trepidation for the outcome of the princes' report to the throne. He heard one of the guards shouting outside:

'Which part of the house *do* you belong to, for goodness' sake? Since you've turned up here, we'll have to enter you in our book. Bind him and hand him over to the Jackets.'

Jia Zheng went out to the gate and found that the man in question was Big Jiao, the 'trusty old retainer' from Ning-guo House.

'What the devil brings you here?' he asked.

Stomping furiously on the ground and calling heaven to be his witness, Big Jiao cried:

'Hadn't I warned these good-for-naught masters time after time – and they always said I was agin them! But you, sir, *you* know the wounds I had at my master's side! And now look what we've come to! Mr Zhen and Master Rong both put in chains by some prince or other; the ladies manhandled and locked up in an empty room by some men from the whatsit guards; the slaves all penned up together, sir, like the worthless pigs that they are! Everything taken out for inventory and pushed to one side, lovely old furniture broken up, china smashed to smithereens ... And now they want to get their hands on me! In my more than four score years I've tied men aplenty for my master: but let 'em do it to me – never! I gave 'em the slip at first and said I was from Rong-guo House; but they wouldn't believe it and dragged me in. And now I find things are just as bad here. Nothing left worth living for. Whole place gone to the dogs. Well, I'm damned if I'll knuckle under now. I might as well go down fighting!'

He charged head-first at the guards, who, out of respect for his age, and not wishing to contravene the princes' orders, handled him with restraint.

'Calm down, old man. We're here to carry out an Imperial Edict. Now just take it easy and wait to see what His Majesty commands.'

Throughout this Jia Zheng said nothing, though he was cut to the quick by the old man's words.

'So it has come to this!' he finally exclaimed to himself. 'We are finished! I never thought we should be brought so low!'

He returned to his study and a little later was still sitting there, anxiously awaiting news from the Palace, when he heard Xue Ke come running into the courtyard and call out breathlessly:

'I got through by the skin of my teeth! Where's Uncle Zheng?'

Jia Zheng stepped out to greet him:

'I am so glad you were able to reach us. How did you persuade them to let you in?'

'I just begged and begged for all I was worth, and promised them money, and in the end they let me pass.'

Jia Zheng told him of the raid and asked him to try to find out on their behalf what was going on:

'We can't communicate with our friends and relatives. It would be too dangerous. You are the very person to carry word through for us.'

'I had heard of the charges brought against Ning-guo House,' said Xue Ke, 'but I had no idea things were so bad on this side too.'

'But what *are* the charges?' asked Jia Zheng.

'Earlier today,' replied Xue Ke, 'I was at the Board of Punishments on business of my own. I was enquiring about Cousin Pan's sentence, but while I was there I happened to hear of the indictments brought by two censors against Cousin Zhen. One was for corrupting the sons of noble families, encouraging them to gamble and that sort of thing. That was the lesser of the charges: the other was for forcefully taking as a concubine the fiancée of an innocent man; when she resisted, or so the indictment reads, he subjected her to physical violence and drove her to her death. To corroborate the charges, the censor concerned has arrested a servant of ours named Bao Er and has also brought as witness a certain Mr Zhang. Even the Chief Censorate may be in trouble, as this fellow Zhang originally appealed to them some time ago and had his appeal quashed.'

Jia Zheng stamped his foot before Xue Ke had finished speaking.

'What have things come to! This is truly the end!'

He sighed, and his cheeks were wet with tears. Xue Ke tried to console him, and then went out again to gather more news.

'Things look bad,' he reported later that day. 'At the Board of Punishments, I could discover nothing about the two princes and their report to the throne. But I did learn something else. Early this morning a censor named Li presented an impeachment against the magistrate of Ping-an, accusing him of toadying to a metropolitan official, of pandering to his superiors and of oppressing the common people – together with a whole string of serious related offences.'

'What has that to do with us?' replied Jia Zheng somewhat impatiently. 'What about our own people?'

'The two cases are connected,' said Xue Ke. 'The metropolitan official referred to in Censor Li's impeachment is in fact Uncle She: which means that he is implicated in a miscarriage of justice – which is a serious offence. His friends at court want to keep their hands clean if they possibly can, and there is no one even willing to keep us informed. It's the same with the guests who fled from the party just now – they have either gone home, or found some other hiding place in which to lie low until the storm blows over. A few members of the clan are even publicly asking who will be the lucky one to get the title now that the family has been disgraced. They all have an eye on it . . .'

Jia Zheng stamped his foot and interrupted him again:

'This is all the consequence of my elder brother's folly! And of the disgraceful ways into which Ning-guo House had fallen! But enough of this. Who knows if Lady Jia and Lian's wife are even still alive! You had best return and continue your enquiries, while I go and see how Lady Jia is. If you have any news, bring it as quickly as you can.'

As they were speaking, a confused cry was heard from within:

'Her Old Ladyship is sinking!'

Jia Zheng hurried away in great alarm. To learn if she lived, you must turn to the next chapter.

CHAPTER 106

*Wang Xi-feng feels remorse for the consequences
of her past misdeeds
And Grandmother Jia prays for the family's deliverance
from further calamity*

Jia Zheng hurried straight in to Grandmother Jia's apartment. The shock of the day's events had finally taken its toll, and she was unconscious again and breathing fitfully. Lady Wang, with the help of Faithful and the other maids, eventually brought her round. They persuaded her to swallow one of her combined dispersant and sedative boluses, which brought some slight relief. But she remained tearful and distraught. Jia Zheng stood by her side and tried to comfort her and rally her spirits:

'It is Brother She and I who have brought this misfortune on the family and caused you all this distress, Mother. Please try to take heart a little. We will do our utmost to set things to rights. If you should suffer in any way, our burden of guilt will be unbearable!'

'I am over eighty now,' replied the old lady, 'and ever since the day I came here as a girl and was married to your father, I have led a sheltered life. I have been blessed and protected by the family ancestors. I've never even heard of such terrible goings-on as these. I am too old for it all. I couldn't bear to see you punished. I'd rather die, and be spared the ordeal.'

She burst into tears once again, and Jia Zheng grew more and more agitated about her condition. Suddenly a voice was heard outside calling:

'News from court for the Master!'

Jia Zheng hurried out. The Prince of Bei-jing's aide-de-camp was waiting for him in the main reception hall, and greeted him with the words:

'Excellent news, sir!'

Jia Zheng thanked the aide for coming and begged him to be seated.

'What are my instructions from His Highness?' he asked.

'My master and His Highness the Prince of Xi-ping presented a joint report to His Majesty, and spoke at some length on your behalf, sir, stressing your penitence and your great appreciation of the clemency shown to you by the throne. His Majesty was most sympathetic, and mindful of the recent demise of Her Grace, he has resolved not to punish you, but instead to restore you to your former post as Under-Secretary at the Board of Works. Of the family property held under restraint, only that portion belonging to Sir She is to be confiscated. The rest will all be returned to you. His Majesty urges you to resume your official duties with diligence.

'The matter of the promissory notes will be investigated personally by my master. Any such notes referring to loans made at usurious rates of interest will be confiscated outright according to the relevant statute; notes negotiated at permissible rates, together with title-deeds of houses and land, will all be returned. Jia Lian is to be deprived of his position and rank, but otherwise will be exempted from further punishment and released.'

Jia Zheng rose from his seat and kowtowed in the appropriate direction for this act of Imperial clemency. He also bowed to the aide to express his profound gratitude for the prince's intervention on his behalf.

'Be so good as to convey my thanks to His Highness. Tomorrow I shall attend court in order to express my gratitude to His Majesty in person, and shall also present myself at His Highness's palace to make my kowtow.'

The prince's aide took his leave. Shortly afterwards a court official arrived to proclaim the Edict, followed by the officers entrusted with its execution, who supervised the proceedings scrupulously, confiscating only what had been specified, and restoring everything else to its owner. Jia Lian was released, while Jia She's domestic staff, men and women alike, were all taken away into public service.

Jia Lian's position was not to be envied. Some of the promissory notes and documents were returned, and none of his other property had been officially confiscated, but his apartment had been ransacked and nothing but the bare furniture had been left in place. His initial relief at being set free and escaping the punishment he feared soon gave way to a profound sense of loss, when he beheld his own and Xi-feng's possessions of a lifetime – altogether about sixty thousand taels' worth – gone in a morning's work. His father's imprisonment,

Xi-feng's critical state of health: the strain was almost more than he could bear. And now he had to face Jia Zheng, who summoned him and berated him, barely suppressing a sob:

'I have, alas, been too busy of late with my official duties, and have paid insufficient attention to family matters. I thought I could rely on you and your wife. I can hardly remonstrate with your father for his misconduct; but this usury that has come to light – who in heaven's name is responsible for that? Families like ours simply do not dabble in such things. The documents have been confiscated, and both principal and interest are forfeit: but it's not the money, it's the appalling blow this will deal to our reputation!'

Jia Lian fell to his knees:

'In managing our family's affairs, Uncle, I have never acted with a view to private gain. All the accounts have been kept by the stewards – Lai Da, Wu Xin-deng, Dai Liang and the others. Please summon them and hear the truth from their lips. These past few years, our expenditure has far exceeded our income, and there have been deficits in the accounts that I have simply been unable to make good, despite the numerous unsecured debts I have had to negotiate. Aunt Wang will be able to tell you all about it. As for the money loaned out, even I have no idea where that has come from. You'd better ask Zhou Rui and Brightie.'

'So, you are telling me you don't even know what goes on in your own apartment, let alone the rest of the household! I shall not pursue this matter any further with you at present. Consider yourself extremely lucky to have been let off so lightly. Now you'd better stir yourself and find out what's happening to your father and Cousin Zhen.'

Jia Lian felt very hard done by, but swallowed his tears and departed in obedience to his uncle's instructions.

Left alone, Jia Zheng ruminated on the family's misfortunes, heaving many a heartfelt sigh:

'It was in vain that my grandfather and my great-uncle served the throne so loyally, winning the family great honour and two hereditary titles. Now both our houses have been disgraced, both titles have been stripped from us. And if I look further ahead, I can see no respite, no rising star in the younger generation capable of stemming this tide of degeneration! Great Heaven! That our noble line should have come to this! Thanks to an act of exceptional clemency on His

Majesty's part, *I* have been spared, and *my* property has been restored. But both households must now look to me for their daily sustenance, and how can I hope to support them all? This latest revelation of Lian's is another grievous blow; not only have we no reserves, we are seriously in debt. We have evidently been living under false pretences for years! And I have only my own stupidity to blame! How can I have been so blind? If only my eldest son were still alive! In Zhu I might at least have had some support. But Bao-yu, for all that he is my son, and now a grown man, can offer me no help whatsoever.'

Throughout this silent soliloquy Jia Zheng had been weeping despite himself, and the collar of his gown was damp with tears.

'As for Mother – so far from supporting her in her old age, we have nearly driven her to her death. Whom can I blame for this calamitous state of affairs but myself?'

He was brooding like this, sunk in the deepest gloom and self-reproach, when a servant entered to announce the arrival of various friends and relations. Jia Zheng received them, thanking them each individually for their concern.

'These misfortunes of ours,' he said to them, by way of apology, 'are the direct consequence of my own failure to inculcate proper standards in the younger generation.'

'We beg to differ,' replied one of them. 'We have long considered Sir She's conduct questionable. And Mr Zhen has been even more arrogant and dissolute in his ways. Now their misdemeanours have come to light and have brought them public censure. The fault lies entirely with them. It is most regrettable that their misdeeds should have rebounded on you, sir.'

'I have known many cases of similar conduct,' commented another, 'but none of them involved an indictment like this. Mr Zhen must have somehow caused offence . . .'

'The intervention of the censor in this case can be easily explained,' countered another. 'It appears that one of your own household servants and some of his less respectable friends have been spreading unpleasant rumours, and that these reached the censor's ears. He wished to substantiate them before proceeding any further, and persuaded this same servant of yours to go along and give information. Knowing how generously you treat your staff, I find it hard to believe that such a thing could have happened.'

'That's the way with servants,' remarked another. 'They take advantage of their masters' generosity. Since we are among friends here, I think I may be permitted to speak my mind. I know what an incorruptible man you are, sir; but while you were in Kiangsi, your reputation was somehow tarnished. That was your servants' doing. You will have to be more cautious in future. Although you have escaped with your own property intact this time, if His Majesty should ever have occasion to question your integrity again, it might be considerably less pleasant for you.'

Jia Zheng seemed greatly perturbed by this.

'What do you mean? In what way was my reputation tarnished?'

'There is of course no shred of material evidence,' came the reply, 'but we have heard others say that during your time as Grain Intendant you instructed your servants to practise extortion.'

'As Heaven is my witness,' exclaimed Jia Zheng, 'no such thought even entered my head! My men were cheating and bullying behind my back. Any more of this sort of gossip and I shall be finished!'

'It's no use fretting about the past,' commented one of the company. 'But you should examine your present staff carefully. Weed out any refractory elements among them and deal with them severely.'

At that moment one of the janitors entered the room:

'Sir She's son-in-law, Mr Sun, has sent a servant with a message, sir. His master is too busy to come in person. This man is instructed to inform you that the Suns are expecting you to discharge Sir She's debts.'

Jia Zheng looked gloomy and harassed, and gave a perfunctory acknowledgement. His friends laughed contemptuously:

'This Mr Sun has a bad reputation; and it certainly seems well founded. When his father-in-law has his home raided and his property confiscated, so far from offering assistance, he comes hounding him for money. It's preposterous!'

'Let's not talk of him,' replied Jia Zheng. 'That whole match was a blunder on my elder brother's part. I should have thought my poor niece had suffered enough at this young man's hands, without his having to torment me as well.'

As he was speaking, Xue Ke appeared.

'I have learned,' he reported to Jia Zheng, 'that Commissioner Zhao is insisting on pursuing every detail of the indictment. I am afraid that Uncle She and Cousin Zhen will have a hard time of it.'

'You must seek the prince's help in this matter,' Jia Zheng's friends advised him. 'Without his intervention, you may all be ruined.'

Jia Zheng thanked his visitors for their advice, which he said he would be sure to follow, and they all took their leave.

It was already lighting-up time, and Jia Zheng went to pay his evening respects to Grandmother Jia, who seemed slightly recovered. He returned to his apartment, and sat once more silently brooding over Jia Lian and Xi-feng's reckless behaviour. Their usury, now that it had come to light, would damage the whole family and he blamed them bitterly for it. But he reflected also that Xi-feng was gravely ill, and had lost everything in the raid, which was sure to have been a great additional blow to her, and decided not to criticize her for the time being, but to contain his anger and say nothing. The rest of that night passed without further event.

Early next morning Jia Zheng went to the Palace to give thanks for the Emperor's clemency, and afterwards to the palaces of the Prince of Bei-jing and the Prince of Xi-ping, where he kowtowed to them and begged them to intervene on behalf of Jia She and Cousin Zhen. The princes spoke reassuringly in reply. Jia Zheng went on to visit other friends and colleagues to enlist their support.

*

Our narrative turns to Jia Lian. He ascertained, from his enquiries in official quarters, that his father and Cousin Zhen were indeed facing a serious charge; and seeing that there was nothing he could do to help, returned despondently home. In his apartment, Patience sat weeping and watching by Xi-feng's bedside, while Autumn could be heard in the side-room grumbling to herself. When Jia Lian came close to Xi-feng and saw how feeble she was, he could not bring himself to vent his resentment on her. Patience said to him with tears in her eyes:

'Everything's gone! We'll never get any of it back. And look at Mrs Lian, sir. You must send for a doctor.'

'Psh!' spat Lian bitterly. '*I'm* only alive by the skin of my teeth; do you expect me to bother on her behalf?'

These words did not escape Xi-feng, and she opened her eyes and looked at Jia Lian in silence. Tears began to trickle down her cheeks. Jia Lian walked out of the room, and Xi-feng said to Patience:

'You must be more realistic! Now things have come to this, you must put me out of your mind. I only wish I could die today and have done with it! If I still mean anything to you, then the one thing I beg of you is to look after little Qiao-jie when I'm gone. Do that for me, and my soul will thank yours in the next world.'

Patience burst into tears.

'Come on,' said Xi-feng, 'you're no fool! They may not have come here and said so to my face, but I know they blame me for what's happened. It's not true. It was others outside who started it. But I admit I was foolish to lend money and create trouble for myself. All my plans and schemes have come to nothing. My lifetime of striving has been in vain. I'm broken, I'm the lowest of the low. Cousin Zhen took Mr Zhang's fiancée as a concubine and drove her to her death – that's one of the charges, isn't it? Well you know who *he* is, this Mr Zhang, don't you? If You Er-jie's story ever comes to light, Mr Lian will be disgraced. And then how will I ever face the world? I wish I could put an end to everything! But how? I can't bring myself to swallow gold or take poison. And you talk of sending for a doctor! That's not showing your love for me; that's just prolonging my agony!'

Patience grew more and more distraught with every word of Xi-feng's. She felt deeply for her, and resolved to keep a closer watch on her, for fear she might give in to despair.

Luckily Grandmother Jia knew nothing of such harrowing scenes as these. Her own recovery and peace of mind were much aided by the knowledge of Jia Zheng's reinstatement, and by the constant presence of Bao-yu and Bao-chai at her side. She had always had a soft spot for Xi-feng, and now she called Faithful to her and said:

'Take these things of mine over to Mrs Lian. And give Patience some money, so that she can look after her properly. When she is well again, I shall go through the rest of my belongings carefully and see what else I can find for her.'

She also told Lady Wang to see to Lady Xing's needs. The entire Ning-guo estate, including all their property and servants, had been inventoried and impounded. Grandmother Jia gave orders for a carriage to be sent to fetch You-shi and Jia Rong's wife. These two forlorn ladies and Cousin Zhen's two concubines, Lovey and Dove, were the only people left in the once luxurious apartments of Ning-guo House. Not a single servant had been spared. Grandmother Jia set aside an apartment for them next to Xi-chun's, designated four old serving-ladies and two maids to wait on them, and ordered that their food and other daily requirements should be provided from the main kitchens. She also sent them clothes and other necessities, and instructed the accounts office to issue them the same monthly allowance as members of the Rong-guo branch.

But it was out of the question to squeeze money from accounts to cover the expenses (mainly bribes) now incurred in gaol by Jia She, Cousin Zhen and Jia Rong. Xi-feng was penniless and Jia Lian deeply in debt; while Jia Zheng, in his characteristically ineffectual fashion, could only say:

'I have had a word with various friends, and am confident they will do whatever they can.'

Jia Lian could think of no way of raising the money. It was no use turning to Xi-feng's side of the family; the Xues were bankrupt, her elder uncle Wang Zi-teng was dead, and the other Wangs were in no position to help. In the end, in desperation, he secretly sent a man to the Rong-guo country estates with orders to effect an urgent sale of one thousand silver taels' worth of land. This money he used to provide for the family members in prison. When the servants saw their masters reduced to such measures, some decided to take advantage of the situation and themselves invented excuses for borrowing against the rent due from the family's eastern estates. But we anticipate a later part of the story.

*

Grandmother Jia saw the family stripped of its hereditary titles; she saw one of her sons and the two other men in gaol awaiting trial; she heard the incessant lamentations of Lady Xing and You-shi, and knew that Xi-feng was gravely ill. Bao-yu and Bao-chai were some comfort to her, but they could not relieve her of the sorrow and grief that constantly gnawed at her heart. One day towards evening, she sent Bao-yu back to his apartment, and struggling up unaided from her couch instructed Faithful and the other maids to go round the mansion and light incense before every statue of the Buddha. Finally she gave orders for a large bushel-shaped bundle of joss-sticks to be lit in the open, and leaning on her stick walked out into her courtyard. Amber knew that she must be intending to pray, and placed a crimson felt hassock for her to kneel upon. The old lady made her offering of incense, knelt and kowtowed several times. She chanted the name of Buddha, and with tears in her eyes began to pray:

'Almighty Lord Buddha! I your humble servant, born into the family of Shi, and married into the house of Jia, earnestly beseech you to show your compassion. For many generations we have done no wrong, we have not trodden in the ways of violence or arrogance. I have done my humble and inadequate best to stay in the paths of righteousness, to support my husband and to assist my sons. But the younger generation have acted with wanton recklessness, they have incurred the wrath of providence, and now our home has been raided and our property taken from us. My son and two of the younger men are held in prison and must expect the worst. The blame for all of these misfortunes must rest on my shoulders, for having failed to teach the younger generation the true principles of conduct. Now I kowtow and beg Almighty Heaven to protect us. May those in prison see their sorrow turned to joy, may the ailing swiftly recover their health. May I alone be permitted to carry the whole family's burden of guilt! And may the sons and grandsons be forgiven! Have pity on me, Almighty Heaven, and heed my devout supplication; send me an early death that I may atone for the sins of my children and grandchildren!'

As this mumbled prayer came to an end, Grandmother Jia broke down and began sobbing so pitifully that she all but choked. Faithful and Amber consoled her, helped her to her feet and escorted her back into the house.

Lady Wang came in shortly afterwards with Bao-yu and Bao-chai to pay their evening respects. Grandmother Jia's tearful state moved them greatly, and they all three began crying aloud. Bao-chai had her own cause for grief. Her brother's future was very precarious; no one knew whether his sentence would be reduced or whether he would be released from gaol. As for herself, although Jia Zheng and Lady Wang were not directly affected by recent events, Bao-chai could see that the Jia family was nevertheless crumbling around her, while her own husband continued to behave in as moronic and helpless a fashion as ever. As she contemplated her own plight, her sobs became more heart-rending even than those of Grandmother Jia and Lady Wang.

Bao-yu himself succumbed to despair.

'Grandmother is crippled with care in her old age, Mother and

Father are weighed down with sorrow. My sisters and cousins are gone, scattered like clouds on the four winds, and every day leaves me more alone, with nothing to sustain me but memories of past happiness, of the golden days of the poetry club in the Garden. Ever since Cousin Lin's death, there's been nothing I can do to shake off this lethargy and depression, and I only keep myself from perpetual weeping so as not to upset Chai, who worries herself about her brother and grieves for her mother, and rarely so much as lets a smile cross her face.'

Bao-chai's inconsolable weeping affected him so deeply that finally he began wailing desperately himself, which in its turn upset Faithful, Suncloud, Oriole and Aroma, and soon all of them, each for their separate reasons, were sobbing profusely. Eventually this incapacitating wave of grief spread to the other maids and there was no one left to play the part of comforter. A chorus of lamentation filled the room and reached the ears of the serving-women on night-duty outside, who sent urgent word to Jia Zheng.

Jia Zheng was sitting brooding in his study (as had become his wont) when the news reached him. He sprang up in alarm and hurried towards Grandmother Jia's apartment. On his way he heard the sound of many voices wailing in the distance and feared the worst for the old lady. His heart sank as he hurried on into her apartment. He found her, however, to his great relief, sobbing but alive and well.

He turned to the assembled family and reproached them:

'At a time like this, you should be comforting Lady Jia, not making matters worse with all this crying.'

There was a sudden silence, during which they all looked round at each other in amazement. Jia Zheng said a few soothing words to Grandmother Jia, then spoke to the others again before leaving.

'We came here to cheer Lady Jia up,' they were thinking to themselves. 'We meant to comfort her. How could we forget ourselves like this and make matters worse!'

They were still in this state of bewilderment, when an old serving-woman arrived with two women from the Shi household. Having curtseyed to Grandmother Jia and greeted all the others present, they delivered their message:

'Our Master the Marquis, Her Grace the Marchioness and Miss Shi have sent us with this message: they have heard your news and want to assure you that this will be nothing more than a temporary setback. They were concerned that Sir Zheng and Their Ladyships might be unduly distressed, and asked us particularly to say that Sir Zheng should set his mind at ease. He himself is in no danger. Miss Shi would have come herself, but she is being married in a few days' time.'

Grandmother Jia felt a little awkward about expressing her gratitude to these serving-women.

'When you return,' she said, 'please convey my regards to your Master and Mistress. What our family has suffered was decreed by fate. Another day I shall call in person to thank the Marquis and Marchioness for their concern. As for Xiang-yun's marriage, I'm sure they must have found her a fine young man for a husband. I should be so pleased to know a little about his family.'

'His family is not a particularly wealthy one,' replied the women. 'But he is a very nice young man, and has such a gentle nature. We have seen him quite a few times, and he closely resembles your Master Bao. He also has considerable literary talent.'

Grandmother Jia was very pleased with this description.

'It sounds most suitable I must say. Xiang-yun is a lucky girl. Her family and ours have always abided by the old Southern marriage customs, and that is why none of us have set eyes on the groom to this day. Only recently I was thinking about my own family, and particularly about Xiang-yun. She has always been my favourite. She used to spend over half the year with me when she was a little girl. I had meant to find a nice husband for her myself when she grew up, but with her uncle away from home I could hardly be the one to take the initiative. Well, fortune has smiled on her, and she has found a good match, so now I can set my mind at rest. I know that they'll be married within the month, and I would have so liked to drink a cup of wine at the reception – but even that's out of the question I'm afraid. This latest upheaval has quite taken my strength away. Please give them my regards when you return, and say that we all send our very best wishes. And tell Miss Shi she is not to worry on my account. I'm over eighty now, and if I die I shall have no cause to complain. I have had more than my share of blessings. My only prayer is that she and her husband may live happily together to a ripe old age. Then I shall rest content.'

As she spoke, Grandmother Jia could not help weeping. One of the Shi serving-women replied:

'Please do not distress yourself, Lady Jia. Once Miss Shi is married and has celebrated her Ninth Day, I'm sure she and her husband will come here to pay you their respects. Then you will be able to see them yourself, and that will make you happy.'

Grandmother Jia nodded.

The women left. Bao-yu seemed to be the only person at all affected by the news of Xiang-yun's impending marriage. He looked somewhat bemused, and thought to himself:

'Why is it that girls have to get married as soon as they grow up? Once they're married, they're bound to change. Even dear Yun has to obey her uncle's will. Now if we meet again, it will never be the same. She is bound to be distant towards me. What is the point of living, if I am to be forever shunned like this?'

He felt himself becoming tearful again. But for Grandmother Jia's sake he endeavoured not to weep and instead sat there brooding silently to himself.

Jia Zheng was still concerned for Grandmother Jia's health, and presently he came in to see how she was. Finding her somewhat improved he went out again and summoned the steward Lai Da, ordering him to bring the complete register of household servants employed in responsible positions. He went over this register with him entry by entry. Apart from Jia She's servants, who had been taken away, there were more than thirty families on the register, with a total of two hundred and twelve male and female servants. Jia Zheng sent for the forty-one male servants at present employed in the mansion and interrogated them all about the accounts for the past years – checking with them the totals for income and expenditure in their various departments. The chief steward presented the ledgers for inspection, and Jia Zheng could see at a glance that none of the figures balanced. Expenditure outweighed income by far, and additional expenses had been incurred over several years in connection with Her Grace the Imperial Concubine. There were several entries revealing irregular loans raised outside. When he looked at the rents from the family estates in the Eastern provinces, he could see that in recent years income had shrunk to less than half what it had been in his grandfather's time, while the family's expenses were ten times as great. This palpable evidence of mismanagement came as a great shock to him, and he stamped his foot angrily:

'This is monstrous! I thought Lian was competent to handle these things! And now I find that we have been mortgaging ourselves up to the hilt in order to keep up an empty show! We've been living far beyond our means. This recklessness was bound to lead to ruin. And it is too late now for me to start introducing economies!'

He paced up and down with his hands behind his back, unable to devise a remedy for the family's deep-seated economic infirmity. His servants knew that their master had no head for business, and that he would only agitate himself to no avail on this score.

'It's no use worrying, sir,' they advised him. 'Every household is the same. Even princes of the realm! If you could but see *their* accounts, you'd find that they fail to balance their books too. They just keep up appearances and muddle along from day to day as best they can. You should think how lucky you've been. The Emperor's been kind and allowed you to keep your part of the family property. Mind you, even if everything had been confiscated, you would still have been able to get by somehow or other!'

'What nonsense you talk!' cried Jia Zheng angrily. 'You servants are worthless rogues, every last one of you! When your masters prosper, you spend their money as you please; and when there's nothing left to spend, you beat a retreat at the first opportunity. What is it to you if we live or die? You say we are lucky not to have had everything confiscated – but what do you know? Do you realize that with our reputation as it stands at present, we'll be hard put to it to avoid bankruptcy. And with you putting on airs, acting as if you were rich, talking as if you were important, swindling people left right and centre, we don't stand a chance. When calamity strikes, you are quite content to see us take all the consequences. I am informed that it was one of your number, a servant by the name of Bao Er, who spread the very rumours that have incriminated my brother and Mr Zhen. Why is his name nowhere to be seen on this register?'

'Bao Er isn't officially on our books, sir,' came the reply. 'He was originally on the Ning-guo register. Then he caught Mr Lian's eye as a trustworthy sort of person, and both he and his wife were taken on by Mr Lian. His wife died, and after that he went back to Ning-guo House. Once when you were busy at the Board, sir, and Her Old Ladyship and Their Ladyships and the other young masters were all away mourning at the mausoleum, Mr Zhen came over to inspect things on this side, and brought Bao Er with him. Bao Er went back with him to Ning-guo House again afterwards. It is so many years since you were involved in matters of this nature, sir, and it is hardly surprising if such details slip your mind. You probably think his is the only name not entered on the register. The fact is that every man has several dependants – even servants have servants of their own!'

'Preposterous!' exclaimed Jia Zheng.

An immediate solution to these economic ills still failed to present itself to Jia Zheng's mind, and he sent the servants away. He had already resolved what general course of action to follow, but decided to wait first to see the nature of the sentence passed on Jia She and Cousin Zhen.

A day or so later, he was in his study puzzling his head over some figures, when a servant came hurrying in to inform him that his presence was immediately required at court. Jia Zheng set off at once, in a state of extreme trepidation. To learn whether the outcome was favourable or otherwise, please turn to the next chapter.

CHAPTER 107

Impelled by family devotion, Grandmother Jia
distributes her personal possessions
Favoured with an Imperial dispensation, Jia Zheng
receives his brother's hereditary rank

Jia Zheng arrived at the Palace, and greeted the various princes and ministers of the Privy Council assembled there to meet him.

'His Majesty has instructed us to send for you,' said the Prince of Bei-jing. 'He would like us to ask you one or two questions.'

Jia Zheng fell hastily to his knees, and the inquisition proceeded:

'Were you aware that your elder brother had connived with a provincial official for personal gain? That he had abused his influence and bullied a defenceless citizen? That he had permitted his son to indulge in gambling and loose living, and that this same son forcefully took to his bed the fiancée of an innocent person and drove her to her death when she would not gratify his desires? Were you aware of all this?'

Jia Zhen replied as best he could:

'Upon the expiry of my term of office as Education Commissioner, an appointment I owed to the gracious favour of His Majesty, I was engaged at first in supervising relief measures, and then on my return home at the end of last winter I was deputed by my superiors to inspect reconstruction work and was subsequently appointed Grain Intendant for Kiangsi Province. From this last post I returned to the capital under impeachment, and have now resumed my former position at the Board of Works. I have truly endeavoured to be diligent in the performance of all these official duties, but I fear that I have completely neglected to keep my own household in order. For this inexcusable shortcoming on my part, for my abject failure to instruct my sons and nephews in the true principles of conduct, for my base ingratitude to the throne, I can only beg that His Majesty will punish me with fitting severity.'

The Prince of Bei-jing went in to communicate this to the Emperor, and after a short while returned with the Imperial Edict, which he declaimed to the assembled company:

'We have received an indictment from the Censorate stating that Jia She connived with a provincial official and abused his own personal influence to bully a defenceless citizen. The provincial official named by the censor was the prefect of Ping-an. Jia She, so the impeachment reads, was in communication with this prefect with a view to perverting the true course of justice. When closely interrogated, however, Jia She testified that the prefect was in fact a relation of his by marriage and that their connection was a purely personal one. The censor has therefore been unable to substantiate this part of the charge. Another part, however, has been verified, namely that Jia She abused his personal influence in coercing the man named Stony to part with a set of antique fans. These fans were none the less trifles, and the case must therefore be distinguished from serious cases of extortion. Stony's subsequent suicide can also be ascribed to his own eccentricity, and he cannot be strictly considered to have been "driven to his death". We see fit to show leniency to Jia She, and hereby sentence him to penal service at a military post on the Mongolian border, where he shall redeem himself by diligent service.

'With reference to the first charge brought against Jia Zhen, that he forcefully took to his bed the betrothed of an innocent citizen and drove her to her death when she would not gratify his desires: upon consulting the original records at the Censorate, We find that the lady in question, a certain Miss You Er-jie, was betrothed to a certain Zhang Hua when both were still in their mothers' wombs. The marriage was never solemnized, indeed Zhang himself wished to annul it on the grounds of his own poverty. The lady's mother was also quite willing for her daughter to be taken as a concubine, not by Jia Zhen himself but by his younger cousin. So clearly this was not a case of forceful appropriation. Then the case of Miss You San-jie: the charge here is that following her suicide she was buried secretly and the facts of her death were concealed from the authorities. On further investigation it has been found that this Miss You San-jie was the younger sister of Jia Zhen's wife, and that it was his original intention to arrange a marriage for her. The widespread and malicious rumours circulating about her character, her own subsequent feelings of shame and remorse and the insistence of her fiancé that she should return his betrothal gifts were the cause of her suicide, not any direct maltreatment or coercion on the part of Jia Zhen. As the holder of a hereditary rank, however, Jia Zhen deserves to be severely punished for his ignorance of the law and for his failure to report the burial of a deceased person. In view of the fact that he is a descendant of a loyal and distinguished subject, We cannot bring ourselves to impose the heavy penalty strictly required by law, but choose to exercise Our discretion, hereby sentencing him to be stripped of his hereditary rank and sent to a maritime frontier region, there to redeem himself by diligent service. Jia Rong, who is too young to have been involved in these affairs, is acquitted. Jia Zheng has for many years held provincial posts in which he has served conscientiously and prudently, and he is absolved from the consequences of his failure to govern his household correctly.'

Jia Zheng responded to the Edict with tears of gratitude, and hastily kowtowed, first in the direction of the Imperial throne, then towards the prince, whom he begged to convey to the Emperor a humble plea of devotion.

'A simple kowtow will suffice,' said the prince. 'There is no need of anything further.'

'My gratitude to His Majesty, for so graciously absolving me of blame, and for restoring my portion of the family property, knows no bounds,' said Jia Zheng. 'I feel a great sense of inner remorse. Please allow me to donate to the Imperial purse all my hereditary emoluments and accumulated property.'

'His Majesty is indeed humane and compassionate towards His subjects,' replied the prince. 'He is wise and discriminating in his judgements, and never errs, whether it be in recompensing virtue or in punishing vice. In having your property thus restored, you have been blessed with his exceptional favour. There is really no call for any further gesture on your part.'

The other gentlemen present concurred.

So Jia Zheng kowtowed again, first towards the Emperor and then to the prince, and left the Palace, hurrying home to bear the news to Grandmother Jia, knowing the anxious suspense in which she would be awaiting his return. The entire Jia household, menfolk and womenfolk, were waiting anxiously at the entrance of Rong-guo House to learn the outcome of his interview, and breathed a huge sigh of relief when they saw him return safely home. None dared to question him as he hurried past them and on into Grandmother Jia's apartment. He recounted to her the details of the latest Edict; and Grandmother Jia, though pleased that some of the charges had been dropped, was understandably distressed to learn that the two titles were lost to the family and that both Jia She and Cousin Zhen were sentenced to penal servitude. Lady Xing and You-shi simply broke down when they heard the news.

'You must not distress yourself, Mother,' pleaded Jia Zheng. 'Although Brother She will have to work at the Mongolian frontier post, he will still be serving the nation, and will not be maltreated. If he acquits himself creditably, he may be fully reinstated. As for Zhen, he is still a young man and a bit of hard work certainly won't do him any harm. This is a lesson we would have had to learn sooner or later. We cannot rest for ever on the laurels of our forefathers.'

He added a few more words of this kind, which comforted Grandmother Jia. After all, she had never been particularly fond of Jia She, and Cousin Zhen was not her own grandson. But Lady Xing and You-shi were inconsolable.

'We are ruined!' thought Lady Xing to herself. 'With my husband sent into exile in his old age, who can I turn to? Lian is supposed to be my son, but he has always attached himself more to his uncle Zheng than to his own father. Now that we are all dependent on Zheng, Lian and Xi-feng are bound to lean even more towards that side of the family. I shall be completely abandoned; I have nothing to look forward to but loneliness and misery for the rest of my days.'

You-shi had always been in charge of Ning-guo House, and apart from Cousin Zhen she was the only one of the family to have earned the respect of the domestic staff. She and Cousin Zhen had a happy marriage moreover. Now he was to be sent away in disgrace, everything they had was confiscated, and they would be obliged to look to the Rong-guo branch for support. Grandmother Jia loved her well enough, but still, she would be the recipient of charity, and she would have to bring Lovey and Dove along with her, not to mention young Rong and his wife, who were still too young to be independent.

'It was really Lian's fault that my sisters came to such a wretched end,' she reflected. 'And yet he and Xi-feng have survived unscathed, while we are reduced to this desperate state of affairs.'

Grandmother Jia was greatly affected by You-shi's disconsolate sobbing, and she turned to Jia Zheng and asked him:

'Now that their sentence has been pronounced, will your brother She and young Zhen be allowed to come home to say goodbye? Rong has been acquitted, so I assume that *he* will be set free.'

'In the normal course of events such a visit would not be allowed,' replied Jia Zheng. 'But I have already asked if as a personal favour Brother She and Cousin Zhen could be allowed home to make preparations for their departure, and the Board of Punishments has most graciously agreed to make this concession. I assume that Rong will be set free and will accompany them. Now, please don't you worry, Mother. I shall do all I can for them.'

'I'm growing old and senile,' said Grandmother Jia. 'It's years since I last enquired about the family's finances. The Ning-guo side has had everything confiscated, I know, and that of course includes the house itself. On our side, your brother She and Lian have had their things taken too. Now, you'd better tell me: how much money do we have left? And what are our estates in the Eastern provinces worth? When those two have to go, we must give them a few thousand taels of silver to take with them.'

Jia Zheng saw himself caught.

'If I tell the truth,' he thought to himself, 'I fear it will come as a great blow. But if I conceal it, heaven alone knows how we will be able to pay for our present needs, let alone manage in the future.'

'Had you not asked, Mother,' he began, 'I would never have bothered you with this. But since you have asked, and since Lian is present, I am bound to say that yesterday I examined the family accounts, and discovered the truth. Which is this: our exchequer has for a long time been completely empty – in fact, more than empty. There are substantial debts. I must somehow find money, and without delay, to mollify the officials involved in Brother She's case. Without such intervention I fear they will both suffer, despite His Majesty's generous concern. I am still not certain how this money can be raised. The Eastern estates cannot be depended on for anything. The rents for the forthcoming year have long been borrowed against. Our only recourse will be to sell what clothes and jewellery they are lucky enough to have left in their possession, and to let Brother She and Cousin Zhen take the proceeds of that sale with them. How we ourselves will manage afterwards is another matter altogether.'

Grandmother Jia was once more reduced to floods of tears.

'Is it really so desperate? Can we have fallen so low? I've never experienced anything like this. I can remember my own family in the old days; they were ten times as grand as us, yet they managed to live beyond their means for years. And even in the end, no such calamity as this ever befell them. It was more gradual. It must have been a year or two before they were finished. But you seem to be saying that we may not even last another year!'

'If only we still had the two hereditary state emoluments to fall back on,' said Jia Zheng. 'Then we might be able to procure a loan. But as things stand, no one is going to lend us a penny.'

Even his cheeks were now streaming with tears.

'It's certainly no use turning to our own relatives for help,' he continued. 'The ones that owe us a favour are penniless, and the ones that don't are unlikely to come forward and help us now. I did not examine the accounts in any detail yesterday, but I did glance at the register of household staff. We can barely afford to keep ourselves alive, let alone such a host of servants.'

These final details in Jia Zheng's tale of financial woe plunged Grandmother Jia in still deeper gloom. Presently Jia She, Cousin Zhen and Jia Rong arrived and paid her their respects. The sight of them somehow brought home to her the true horror of their predicament. She took Jia She by one hand, Cousin Zhen by the other and burst out sobbing. The two men hung their heads in shame and, when she began weeping, fell to their knees and cried:

'We have dishonoured the family! We have forfeited the glory won by our forefathers! We have brought you grief! We are not even worthy to be buried when we die!'

At this a chorus of wailing filled the room.

'Come on now,' urged Jia Zheng. 'We must lose no time in thinking of a way to provide them with funds. They can stay with us only a day or two at the most.'

Grandmother Jia did her best to contain her grief.

'Go now, both of you,' she said, holding back her tears, 'and speak with your wives.' She turned to Jia Zheng: 'There must be no delay, and I can see it would be futile trying to borrow. We have so little time. I shall have to do something myself. Oh dear, this is all so dreadfully confusing! Things mustn't be allowed to go on like this!'

She called Faithful to her and sent her off with some secret instructions.

Jia She and Cousin Zhen meanwhile left the room and conversed tearfully with Jia Zheng outside, expressing their remorse for their past waywardness and anticipating with gloom the bitter exile that lay ahead. Then they went over and lamented with their wives. Jia She was growing old, and the prospect of separation was less harrowing for him and Lady Xing than it was for Cousin Zhen and You-shi.

Jia Lian and Jia Rong held their fathers' hands and wept at their side. Frontier service was a less severe punishment than military exile, but it would still be a long and painful ordeal. They could only try to steel themselves to it as best they could.

Grandmother Jia told Lady Xing, Lady Wang, Faithful and a bevy of maids to look through every one of her trunks and boxes, and to take out all the personal belongings she had stored away over the years of her marriage. Then she summoned Jia She, Jia Zheng, Cousin Zhen and all the other menfolk to attend while she made a distribution. She began by giving Jia She three thousand taels of silver.

'You are to take two thousand with you,' she said, 'for the journey and for any expenses afterwards, and leave one thousand here for your wife. This three thousand is for you, Zhen. You must take one thousand with you, and leave two thousand for your wife. In this way, although they will be living with us, they will still be independent and able to make separate catering arrangements. I shall provide for Xi-chun's marriage when the time comes. Now Xi-feng; I feel sorry for her, she tried so hard for so long, and has ended up with nothing. She too shall have three thousand taels, and she is to keep all of it for her own use and not give a penny to Lian. I know she is much too ill now, and in no fit state to come and receive it herself, so Patience can take it to her.

'Here are some robes that once belonged to my husband, and some of the gowns and jewellery that I used to wear when I was young – I don't need them any more. The men's clothing can be divided between She, Zhen, Lian and Rong. Their wives can share the ladies' things. This five hundred taels of silver is for Lian to pay for transporting Miss Lin's coffin to the South next year.'

When this distribution was complete, she turned to Jia Zheng:

'The debts you mentioned must be honoured at once. Take this gold and use it for that purpose. Their misdeeds have driven me to these drastic measures, but don't think I have forgotten that you too are my son. In due time you will receive your fair share. Bao-yu is married and can have what is left here – gold and silver worth several thousand taels. And Li Wan: she has always been such a dutiful granddaughter-in-law to me, and little Lan is such a sweet child. Here's some for them too. There, I've finished.'

Jia Zheng was moved to tears to see how clearly she had worked everything out.

'We have failed you, Mother!' he sobbed, falling to his knees. 'We have not done our filial duty towards you in your old age; and yet you shower us with such bounty! How can we ever outlive our shame!'

'Oh poppycock!' exclaimed Grandmother Jia. 'Don't you worry, if it weren't for this crisis I should certainly have kept it all for myself! But let's be serious: our staff is much too large. You are the only one left with an official post, Zheng, so we don't need more than a few servants. Tell the stewards to call the staff together and make the necessary arrangements. Each establishment must make do with as few servants as possible. We would have had to manage with none at all if our household had been confiscated. The same goes for the ladies' apartments. We must find husbands for some of the maids, and give others back their freedom. And although our property has not been taken, I still think it would be best if you handed over the Garden. Lian should be given the job of sorting out the country estates. Some can be sold, some kept on, as seems most appropriate. Above all there must be no more pomp in future, no more empty show. We must be realistic. And another thing I should mention. We still have some money belonging to the Zhen family of Nanking. It's in safe keeping with your wife, Zheng. Someone should be sent to take it back to them straight away. If anything else should happen to us, we'd only involve them in a lot more trouble, push them out of the frying-pan and into the fire.'

Jia Zheng, who was painfully aware of his own incompetence in such matters, mumbled a contrite 'Yes, Mother' to all of these eminently practical instructions, thinking to himself:

'What a flair she has for organization! And what worthless bunglers we all are by comparison!'

He could see that Grandmother Jia was tired, and begged her to lie down and rest.

'The little you see here is all I have left,' she said. 'When I die, you can use some of it to pay for my funeral, and give the remainder to my maids.'

They found this mention of her death greatly upsetting, and all fell to their knees once more.

'Please set your mind at ease, Mother. In time to come, if we enjoy your blessing and can once more regain His Majesty's favour, then we shall do our utmost to atone for past errors, to restore the family fortune and to support you into your hundredth year.'

'If you can only somehow make amends,' said Grandmother Jia, 'then perhaps I shall be able to face our ancestors with pride when I die. Don't think that I know only how to enjoy a comfortable life, and that I have no stomach for poverty! That's not it at all. It's just that I am rather shocked by all this. During the past few years you have seemed so prosperous, and I was only too glad not to interfere; to jolly along and mind my own business. I never for one moment imagined that we were in such a precarious state. I've always known that we were living beyond our means, of course, but I thought somehow we'd manage to muddle through. I suppose we were "dulled by habit"; we couldn't adjust, we were too used to things as they were. Well now we must use this opportunity to economize and set things to rights, or else our family will be the laughing-stock of the world. You may think it's the poverty that appals me. But it's not. What I have always cared about more than anything is our family tradition, our family honour. Every day of my life has been lived in the hope that this generation would outshine our ancestors. But I would have been content just to maintain our position as it was. I had no idea of the disgraceful jiggery-pokery those two were up to behind my back!'

Grandmother Jia was ruminating aloud in this fashion when Felicity came hurrying into the room and ran over to Lady Wang in a great fluster:

'Oh Your Ladyship! Mrs Lian heard the news from court this morning, and she's cried such a lot that now she seems quite faint. Patience sent me over to let you know.'

'How *is* Mrs Lian?' Grandmother Jia asked her before she'd finished speaking. 'Not at all well today,' replied Lady Wang on Felicity's behalf.

'*Ai!*' exclaimed the old lady, rising wearily to her feet. 'These young people are the bane of my life! I can see they want to drive me into my grave!'

She asked her maids to assist her and announced her intention of paying Xi-feng a visit herself. Jia Zheng hastened to detain her, and endeavoured to calm her down:

'This has all been so distressing for you, Mother. You have already exerted yourself so much in finding a solution to our problems. You really must give yourself a bit of a rest. I am sure my wife can go over and see to Xi-feng. There is no need for you to expose yourself to any further upsets. If anything serious were to happen to you, how should I ever forgive myself.'

'You may all leave now,' ordered Lady Jia. 'Come back a little later. There are still a few things I want to say.'

Jia Zheng, his attempt at filial consolation having been thus peremptorily crushed, did not venture to say any more. He went out to superintend the practical arrangements for the convicts' departure and instructed Jia Lian to choose some servants to accompany them.

Faithful assembled a group of serving-women to carry Xi-feng's presents and to escort Grandmother Jia over to Xi-feng's apartment. Xi-feng was very weak and almost unconscious, while Patience's eyes were red and swollen from crying. When she heard that Lady Jia and Lady Wang, accompanied by Bao-yu and Bao-chai, were on their way, Patience hurried out anxiously to greet them.

'How is she now?' asked Grandmother Jia the moment she saw Patience.

Patience was afraid of frightening the old lady.

'A little better, ma'am.'

She escorted the party inside and hurrying over to Xi-feng's bed lightly drew aside the bed curtains. Xi-feng opened her eyes and, when she saw Grandmother Jia enter the room, was filled with shame. Earlier she had come to the conclusion that the whole family had turned against her, that no one cared for her any more, that they were all indifferent whether she lived or died. And yet now Grandmother Jia had come to visit her personally. Her spirits were immediately restored, and she even struggled to sit up; but Grandmother Jia ordered Patience to settle her down again.

'Don't you move, dear,' she said to Xi-feng. 'Are you feeling a little better now?'

'Oh yes, Grannie, I am. A lot better,' replied Xi-feng, holding back her tears. 'But it grieves me when I think how you and Mother and Aunt Wang have loved me, ever since I came here as a young bride, and how little I have been able to return that love. How cruelly fate has possessed me, driving me quite out of my mind, making me fail in my duty to you and Aunt Wang, preventing me from ever winning your praise . . . Yet still you trusted me, still you allowed me to play my part. And all I've ever done is ruin things for everyone! How can I look you and Auntie in the face again? This visit is more than I deserve. I'm afraid Heaven will punish me for it, by taking away most of the few days I may have left to live . . .

She sobbed violently.

'This whole nonsense was started by the men,' Grandmother Jia consoled her. 'It was nothing to do with you. I know some of your belongings have been taken, but don't you worry: I've brought you all sorts of presents – take a look and see.'

She instructed one of the serving-women to bring the presents forward and exhibit them. Possessions had always meant a great deal to Xi-feng, and the sudden loss of all of her worldly goods had dealt a severe blow to her morale. She had also been tormenting herself with the thought that everyone in the family secretly blamed her for what had happened, and as a consequence she had all but lost her will to live. This new evidence of Grandmother Jia's affection was a much-needed tonic; and it seemed that Lady Wang was not really so cross with her either, to judge from the fact that she had accompanied Grandmother Jia. And had Jia Lian not been acquitted, after all? Xi-feng kowtowed to Grandmother Jia from her pillow:

'Please don't worry on my behalf, Grannie. If I can continue to enjoy your blessing, and if I recover my health, I'll gladly be your lowliest maidservant and do any menial task, devote myself heart and soul for the rest of my life to serving you and Aunt Wang.'

This abject gratitude was too pitiful a sight for Grandmother Jia, and she broke down and wept. Bao-yu immediately followed suit. He had never witnessed anything resembling a family crisis. His life till recently had consisted for the most part of peaceful and pleasant pursuits, and he had been protected from too close an acquaintance with real suffering. But now wherever he turned he saw anguish and weeping. It had the effect of accentuating his imbecility; and if he saw anyone else crying, he instantly responded by doing likewise.

Seeing what low spirits her visitors were in, Xi-feng did her best to muster a few cheerful words, and then begged Grandmother Jia and Lady Wang to return to their apartments, promising to come and kowtow to them as soon as she was well enough. She raised her head feebly from the pillow as she spoke.

'Look after her well now,' Grandmother Jia enjoined Patience. 'And if you're short of anything, be sure to come and let me know.'

She took Lady Wang back with her to her own apartment. On the way, she could hear the sound of weeping coming from every quarter. It was more than she could bear. She sent Lady Wang away and told Bao-yu to bid his Uncle She and Cousin Zhen farewell and to return immediately afterwards.

Left on her own, she sank onto her couch in tears. Faithful tried every way she knew of consoling her, and finally Grandmother Jia dozed off.

Understandably Jia She and Cousin Zhen viewed the prospect of their exile with little relish. The men chosen to accompany them were equally reluctant to go, and complained bitterly of their lot. To be parted in life is in truth more painful than to be parted by death, and the witnessing of such a parting often more distressing than the parting itself. Rong-guo House, once a scene of such brilliance and distinction, now echoed with the sounds of wailing and lamentation.

Jia Zheng had always been a great stickler for formalities, and despite everything he continued to observe towards Jia She the solemn respect prescribed towards an elder brother. The two brothers shook hands at home, and Jia Zheng then rode out ahead to beyond the city walls and there waited to drink the ritual farewell cup of wine. He exhorted Jia She to remember the compassion the state had shown him on his ancestors' account, and to prove himself worthy of it. Jia She and Cousin Zhen wiped the tears from their eyes, and set off for their different destinations.

Jia Zheng returned home with Bao-yu. As they neared the gateway of Rong-guo House they saw a crowd gathered outside and heard a confused hubbub of voices:

'An Imperial Edict issued today! The Rong-guo hereditary rank and title to be passed on to Sir Zheng!'

The men in the crowd were demanding their statutory tip for bringing this good news, but the janitors were resisting vigorously:

'The title belonged to the family in the first place, and was inherited by our masters. That's not worth a tip!'

'Come on!' came the indignant reply. 'Think of the glory! A title like that is the most glorious thing there is – and your Sir She could never hope to get it back, not after what he's done. Now His Majesty, in his wisdom and mercy, greater than the sky is broad, has passed it on to Sir Zheng; why, that's nothing less than a miracle for your family! Definitely worth a tip!'

Jia Zheng entered the house and received a full report on the matter from the janitors. His pleasure was inevitably mingled with shame that his own good fortune had been made possible only by his elder brother's disgrace. He was momentarily overwhelmed and wept tears of emotion. Then he hurried in to convey the news to Grandmother Jia, who took him delightedly by the hand and urged him to show himself worthy of this signal honour. Lady Wang was also present, anxious that Grandmother Jia might be *souffrante* and in need of consolation, and she too was delighted to hear Jia Zheng's news. Only Lady Xing and You-shi felt their own misfortune the more keenly, an emotion they took pains to conceal.

*

The family's sponging friends and relatives, who had kept well clear while times were hard, learned that Jia Zheng had now been given his brother's title and – deducing from this that the Emperor must still view the Jias with a favourable eye – flocked to Rong-guo House to offer their felicitations. But Jia Zheng's feelings were running along very different lines. He was by nature a man of such soul-searching integrity that, so far from congratulating himself on his good luck, he was greatly troubled at heart, and wondered how he would ever be able to show his gratitude sufficiently. The following day he went to the Palace to make a formal expression of thanks, and this time went so far as to submit a memorial begging that his restored residence, together with Prospect Garden, be accepted as a gift by the Emperor. An Edict was issued in reply to this request, dismissing it as quite superfluous; and Jia Zheng, his conscience a little placated, returned home and applied himself with devotion and zeal to his official duties.

The family's finances were still as precarious as ever. Income continued to fall far short of expenditure. Entertaining, making connections with the right people and winning favours were not Jia Zheng's strong point. The servants knew how incorrigibly upright he was, while Xi-feng was still sick and unable to apply her experience to the solving of the present crisis. The debts Jia Lian was forced to incur were mounting daily, and it seemed almost inevitable that he would have to mortgage still more property and sell still more land. The servants could see it coming. Some of them were quite wealthy themselves and were worried that Jia Lian might come to them for money. Some tried to keep out of harm's way by feigning poverty, some asked for leave of absence and went looking for other employment.

One exception was Bao Yong. Though he was a newcomer and had arrived only a short while before the crisis, he proved to be a most industrious and loyal servant, and was appalled by the way the other servants were taking advantage of their masters. He had insufficient status among the domestic staff to dare voice his feelings to the offenders, and could only eat his evening meal and take his indignation to bed. The others disliked him for not going along with them, and complained about him to Jia Zheng, calling him an incompetent, a drunkard and a troublemaker.

'Let him be,' was Jia Zheng's response. 'He was recommended to me by the Zhens, and we cannot be too hard on him. After all, we may be poor, but we can surely afford to feed one extra mouth.'

When they failed in their attempts to have him sacked by the master, the servants turned next to Jia Lian with their complaints; but Jia Lian felt in no position to exert his authority, and in the end they had to let Bao Yong be.

One day Bao Yong was feeling particularly angry and, having drunk a few cups of wine to comfort himself, went for a stroll in the street outside the main entrance to Rong-guo House, where he happened to overhear the following conversation:

'See that great mansion in there?' said one of the two men, pointing to Rong-guo House. 'Wonder how they're managing after that raid the other day . . .'

'Oh *they*'ll be all right!' replied the other. 'I've heard that one of their daughters was a concubine of His Majesty's. She's dead now, but a connection like that doesn't die so quickly. And they're on hob-nobbing terms with all sorts of princes, dukes, marquises and earls. They'll never be short of friends. Take the present Mayor, who used to be Minister of War, he's from the same family. With people like that to look after them, they'll always be all right.'

'Hm!' replied the first. 'You may live locally, but I can see you're rather out of touch. I don't know about their other friends, but that

Mayor Jia you mentioned is a regular bounder! I'll tell you why I say that. I've seen him at Rong-guo House countless times, so I know he's had a lot to do with them in the past. When the censor brought that indictment against members of the Jia family, the Emperor asked him to look into the matter and establish the facts of the case. And what do you think he did? Because he owed both branches of the family big favours himself, and because he was afraid he'd be suspected of covering up for his own friends, he went to the other extreme. He said the most terrible things about them. *That's* what led to both houses being raided. It's shocking how people treat their friends nowadays, isn't it!'

This casual conversation happened to fall on the ears of one who understood only too clearly what it meant.

'That such a scoundrel should live and breathe on this earth!' thought Bao Yong secretly to himself. 'I wonder what relation of the Master's he is? If I so much as set eyes on him, I'll beat the innards out of him! To hell with the consequences!'

Wild (and somewhat befuddled) thoughts of revenge filled Bao Yong's loyal breast. Suddenly the cry of official runners could be heard clearing the way, and from where he was standing Bao Yong heard one of the bystanders whisper to the other:

'Why, here he comes now, the very Mayor Jia we were talking about!'

Bao Yong was seething with righteous indignation, and the wine lent him the final touch of inspiration and courage.

'Blackguard!' he yelled recklessly. 'Scurvy knave! Would you forget the kindness shown you by our masters the Jias?'

From within his sedan Jia Yu-cun heard the name 'Jia' and leaned forward to see what was going on. Just another drunken lout in the street, not worth bothering with. His sedan moved on, and Bao Yong swaggered home feeling very pleased with himself and far too drunk to be discreet. He made a few enquiries, and his fellow-servants confirmed that the Mayor did indeed owe his entire career to the patronage of the Jia family.

'Well he's an ungrateful scoundrel, and I've told him so!' boasted Bao Yong. 'After all they've done for him, to kick them in the teeth like that! I gave him a piece of my mind, and he didn't dare answer me back either . . .'

Until now, the other servants, who were united in their dislike of

Bao Yong, had been unable to persuade Jia Zheng to get rid of him. This was the very pretext they had been waiting for, and they seized their chance to report him to the Master for being drunk and disorderly and creating a disturbance in the street. Jia Zheng was extremely nervous of provoking the authorities any further, and was very angry when he heard of Bao Yong's riotous behaviour. He summoned him and gave him a thorough dressing-down. He still felt that in view of his connection with the Zhens it would be wrong to punish him too severely, and instead transferred him to caretaking duties in the Garden, with strict instructions not to go wandering outside again.

Bao Yong was a straightforward sort of fellow. Once he worked for a man, that man was his master, to serve and protect with every ounce of loyalty he had. He was greatly dismayed that Jia Zheng should have listened to tales and been misled into scolding him in this fashion. But he did not say a word in protest. He merely packed his bags and moved into the Garden to commence his new duties.

To learn what followed, please read the next chapter.

CHAPTER 108

A birthday party held for Sister Allspice necessitates
a false display of jollity
And ghostly weeping heard at the Naiad's House provokes
a fresh outburst of grief

We have already told how the Emperor rejected Jia Zheng's plea to donate both Rong-guo House and Prospect Garden to the throne. None of the Jia family lived in the Garden any longer, and its gates were permanently locked. You-shi and Xi-chun, whose temporary lodgings in Rong-guo House adjoined the Garden wall, found it an eerie and desolate place to be near, and it was partly for this reason that Bao Yong had been appointed caretaker.

Jia Zheng now applied himself in earnest to the practicalities of the household, and in accordance with Grandmother Jia's instructions endeavoured to implement a gradual reduction in the size of the staff, and a range of other economies. But he soon found the task too much for him, and turned for help to Xi-feng. Although Lady Wang had little affection left for her, Xi-feng was still a favourite of Grandmother Jia's, and Jia Zheng judged that one way or another, despite everything, she must have retained some of her flair for business. She accepted the responsibility with a good grace, only to discover that the depredations of the Embroidered Jackets and the financial after-effects of the raid had made it impossible to get anything done in Rong-guo House. The necessary funds were simply not forthcoming. The ladies and their maids, from the highest to the lowest, used as they were to a life of ease, and finding that in their new and greatly reduced circumstances many of their old everyday luxuries could no longer be afforded, did nothing but complain. Xi-feng did her utmost to fulfil her duties, and despite her illness tried to please Grandmother Jia as best she could.

Jia She and Cousin Zhen eventually arrived at their designated places of exile. Thanks to the sums of money they had taken with them, they were comfortable enough, for the present at any rate, and both wrote home that they were well and that the family was not to worry on their account. Grandmother Jia was much relieved, and the news brought a little comfort to their wives.

Some days later, Shi Xiang-yun, who was now married and had paid her Ninth Day visit to her own home, came to call on Grandmother Jia. The old lady said what a favourable report she had heard of her husband, while Xiang-yun confirmed that married life was turning out happily for her, and begged Grandmother Jia to set her mind at rest. At the mention of Dai-yu's death they both shed tears, and Grandmother Jia's distress was further increased by the thought of Ying-chun and her trials. Xiang-yun remained with her for a time, doing her best to cheer her up, then went to call on the others, and returned later in the day to Grandmother Jia's apartment to rest. The conversation that evening turned to the Xue family, and Xiang-yun learned from Grandmother Jia how as the result of Pan's escapade the Xues were now facing total ruin. Pan's death sentence had, it is true, been suspended, and he was still alive in gaol; but there was no telling whether or not they would be able to save his life by having the sentence commuted the following year.

'And you still haven't heard about Pan's wife,' Grandmother Jia went on. 'She came to a very nasty end, and there was nearly the most dreadful scandal. But Lord Buddha in his all-seeing wisdom caused her own maid to come forward and tell us the whole story. Mrs Xia for all her antics could do nothing in the face of the truth, and ended up asking herself for the inquest to be waived. Your aunt Xue gave Pan's wife a makeshift burial. She has young Ke living with her now. What a wonderful lad he is. Such a strong sense of duty! He feels he should postpone his own wedding until his cousin Pan is released from gaol and his murder case has been resolved. Of course that makes things rather hard meanwhile for poor Xiu-yan, who has to stay on with her aunt Xing. And it's not much better for Bao-qin, who can't marry her young Mr Mei until after his period of mourning for his father. Dear oh dear! What with one thing and another, our relations seem to be in much the same case as we are ourselves. Let me see now, what other news is there? In the Wang family, your aunt Wang's elder brother, your great-uncle Zi-teng, has passed away; Fengie's elder brother Ren has disgraced himself; and her second uncle Zi-sheng, your other great-uncle Wang, has turned out badly too. He couldn't settle his elder brother's debts, and had to come running to us to bale him out. We've had no news of the Zhens, ever since they too were raided and had their property confiscated.'

'Have you had any news from Tan since she left?' asked Xiang-yun.

'Since her marriage, your uncle Zheng has returned from his post and he tells me that Tan is very happy at her new home, even though of course it is *so* far away down there on the coast. We still haven't heard from her directly, and I do worry about her a great deal. We've had so many other troubles to contend with here, I simply haven't had time to do anything for her. And then there's Xi-chun. I still haven't been able to find a husband for *her*. The less said about young Huan the better. Oh, things have changed greatly since you were here, my dear — greatly for the worse, I'm afraid. Your poor cousin Chai has not had a day's peace ever since she married into our family. And Bao-yu is still as addle-pated as ever. Dear oh dearie me! We really *are* in a sorry state!'

'I grew up here,' said Xiang-yun, 'so of course I know everyone very well. I can see for myself how they've changed. At first I wondered if perhaps they were just being a little distant towards *me*, because I've been away so long. But then I thought it over and could see it wasn't that at all. They wanted to be their old cheerful selves with me, but somehow as soon as we started talking they got upset. That's why I didn't stay long and came back here to you, Grannie.'

'I'm old enough to take what's happened in my stride,' said Grand-mother Jia. 'But the young people seem to go to pieces. I wanted to find some way of cheering them all up for a day, but then I just couldn't summon up the energy.'

'I have an idea,' said Xiang-yun. 'Isn't it Bao-chai's birthday the day after tomorrow? Why don't I stay on to wish her a happy birthday — then we can all enjoy ourselves for a day. What do you say, Grannie?'

'Goodness! I *am* getting gaga!' exclaimed Grandmother Jia. 'If you hadn't mentioned it I should have forgotten altogether. Of course you're right! Tomorrow I'll give the cooks some money and we'll have a party. Before Chai married Bao-yu, we must have celebrated her birthday several times. But not since she's been part of the family. Bao-yu, poor child, who used to be such a bundle of mischief and fun, has been so badly affected by our troubles that he can hardly put two words together. I can still count on Wan. *She* never changes, whether times are good or bad. She and little Lan still spend their days quietly together. She's a marvel!'

'Xi-feng is the most changed,' said Xiang-yun. 'She *looks* so different for a start, and no longer speaks with her old zest. Tomorrow I must see if I can draw them out and cheer them all up. But I'm afraid that, although they won't say so, in their hearts they may resent me for being so lucky and for having . . .'

She stopped short and blushed fiercely. Grandmother Jia understood what she meant.

'There's no cause for you to worry on that score, my dear. You and your cousins grew up together as children. You used to play with each other, you were always chatting and laughing together. Don't think of them in that way. We should all learn to accept life's ups and downs. We should know how to enjoy prosperity while it lasts, and how to endure poverty with patience. Your cousin Chai has always taken a broad view of life. In the old days, when her family were so well off, she never used to put on airs; and since they've fallen on hard times she has been quite unshaken by it all. Now that she's part of our family, when Bao-yu is nice to her she is as quiet and content as ever, and if he leads her a bit of a song and dance occasionally, I've never seen her get ruffled. That girl seems blessed with the most wonderful disposition. Your cousin Dai-yu was so different – quick to criticize others and take offence herself. It was hardly surprising that she died so young, poor child. As for Feng, she's seen something of life, she should know better than to let little trials and tribulations get her down. It's a weakness in her character . . . Yes, I shall set aside a special sum of money for Chai's birthday, and we'll make a jolly little party of it and let her enjoy herself properly for once.'

'That does sound a good idea, Grandmother,' replied Xiang-yun. 'I'll go ahead then and invite all the girls, and we can have a real reunion!'

'Yes, you go ahead,' said Grandmother Jia. In her enthusiasm she called Faithful over and said:

'Take a hundred taels of silver and tell accounts that we want food and drink for a two-day party, starting tomorrow.'

Faithful gave the money to an old serving-woman to take out to the accounts office. The remainder of that evening and night passed without any further event.

The next day a servant was sent to fetch Ying-chun for the party. Aunt Xue and Bao-qin were invited, and were asked to bring Caltrop with them. Mrs Li was also invited, and later that day she arrived together with Li Wen and Li Qi.

These preparations were kept secret from Bao-chai. One of Grandmother Jia's maids simply came to tell her that her mother had called, and to invite her over to the old lady's apartment. Bao-chai was pleased to hear of her mother's arrival, and went dressed as she was to greet her. She found her cousin Bao-qin and Caltrop there, and Mrs Li with the Li sisters, and presumed that they had all come to call upon hearing that the family troubles were over. She greeted Mrs Li, then Grandmother Jia, then exchanged a few words with her mother and said hello to the Li sisters.

'Now, will the ladies please be seated,' said Xiang-yun from the side, 'and we can congratulate our cousin and wish her a long and happy life on this very special occasion.'

Bao-chi looked rather bewildered for a moment. Then she thought to herself, 'Of course! Tomorrow's my birthday!' 'It's quite right for you to come and visit Grandmother,' she protested. 'But you certainly shouldn't have gone to all this trouble on my account.'

Bao-yu heard this as he came in to greet Aunt Xue and Mrs Li. He had originally been thinking of organizing something for Bao-chai's birthday himself, but had said nothing to Grandmother Jia because of the general confusion of the past few weeks. He was delighted that Xiang-yun had taken the initiative.

'Yes, tomorrow's her birthday,' he said. 'I was meaning to remind you, Grannie.'

'Shame on you!' cried Xiang-yun with a playful laugh. 'As if Grannie needed you to remind her! Who do you think invited everyone here but Grannie?'

Bao-chai secretly doubted this. But then she heard Grandmother Jia say to her mother:

'Poor Chai – it's been more than a year since she married Bao-yu, and somehow with one thing after another, we've never celebrated her birthday. Today I wanted to do it properly, so I invited you and Mrs Li over. I thought it would be a nice opportunity for us all to have a chat.'

'You're only just starting to feel better, Lady Jia,' protested Aunt

Xue. 'It is my daughter who should be thinking how best to do her duty and show you her love and respect. You really shouldn't go to such lengths on young Chai's account.'

'Bao-yu is Grannie's favourite grandson,' said Xiang-yun, 'so of course Grannie has a soft spot for Chai as well! Anyway Chai deserves it!'

Bao-chai hung her head in modest silence.

Bao-yu meanwhile was marvelling to himself at Xiang-yun's forthrightness:

'I always imagined that Xiang-yun would change once she was married; that's why yesterday I was rather reserved with her. As a result I suppose she herself decided to keep her distance. But to hear her talk now, she seems quite the same as ever. Why has marriage made *my* wife more modest and bashful than before, more tongue-tied than ever?'

While these thoughts were passing through his mind, a junior maid came in to announce the arrival of Ying-chun. Shortly afterwards Li Wan and Xi-feng arrived, and they all exchanged greetings. Ying-chun referred to her father's departure:

'I wanted to come and see him before he left, but my husband wouldn't allow me to. He said he didn't want *his* family to be infected by our bad luck. He wouldn't listen to anything I said, and there was nothing I could do. I cried for two or three days.'

'Why did he let you come today then?' asked Xi-feng.

'This time he said that since Uncle Zheng had been given the title, there was no harm in renewing contact.'

She burst into tears.

'I've been feeling quite wretched myself,' Grandmother Jia upbraided her, 'and I asked you all here to celebrate my granddaughter-in-law's birthday and to have a bit of fun. I thought there'd be lots of laughter to cheer us up – and there you go mentioning this unhappy business of yours and upsetting me all over again.'

Ying-chun and the rest were silenced.

Xi-feng tried her hardest to put on a brave front for the occasion and to jolly the old lady along; but somehow she seemed to have lost the knack of making people laugh, and her efforts all fell flat. Grandmother Jia herself was anxious to make it a happy occasion for Bao-chai, and deliberately egged Xi-feng on.

'You're a lot more cheerful today, aren't you, Grannie?' said

Xi-feng, trying her best to oblige. 'Here we all are gathered together again after such a long time. It's quite a reunion!'

Even as she said the words, she looked around her, noticed the all too obvious absence of Lady Xing and You-shi, and fell silent. The word 'reunion' had also jolted Grandmother Jia's memory, and she sent word at once to invite the missing ladies. Lady Xing, You-shi and Xi-chun knew they must obey a summons from Grandmother Jia, even though a party was the very last thing they felt like. The mere fact that Grandmother Jia was celebrating Bao-chai's birthday in the midst of their misfortune was proof enough of where her affections lay. They came into the room looking a picture of misery. Grandmother Jia enquired after Xiu-yan, and Lady Xing concocted an illness that had prevented her niece from attending the party. Grandmother Jia herself knew quite well that Xiu-yan's absence was prompted by the presence at the party of Aunt Xue, the aunt of her husband-to-be.

Presently wine and sweetmeats were served.

'There's no need to send any out to the men,' said Grandmother Jia. 'Today can be ladies' day.'

Though Bao-yu was a married man, as Grannie's favourite he was allowed to join in the fun. He was placed not at a table with Xiang-yun and Bao-qin, but on a special chair next to Grandmother Jia. He went round with Bao-chai, pouring a cup of wine for each of the guests on her behalf.

'Sit down now both of you,' commanded Grandmother Jia, 'and let's all have a drink. Later in the evening you can do your duty to everyone. But if you start getting all formal now and make everyone stand on ceremony, you'll spoil my mood and take all the fun out of the party.'

They obeyed and sat down. Grandmother Jia turned to the others:

'For goodness' sake let's relax a bit. We only need one or two maids each to wait on us. Faithful, take Suncloud, Parrot, Aroma and Patience off to the back and have a cup of wine together.'

'But we still haven't kowtowed to Mrs Bao,' protested Faithful. 'How can we go and drink without having done that?'

'If I say so, then you can. Now, off with you!' ordered Grandmother Jia. 'We'll send for you later if we need you.'

Faithful and her fellow maids obeyed.

Grandmother Jia now pressed her guests to drink up. But she soon discovered that they were not at all their old party-going selves.

'What's the matter with you all?' she asked fretfully. 'Why can't everyone cheer up a bit?'

'We're eating and drinking,' replied Xiang-yun. 'What more do you expect of us?'

'When they were still children,' said Xi-feng, 'it was easy for them to be carefree and happy. Now that they're grown up, they're too self-conscious and well mannered to let themselves go. That's why they seem so dull.'

Bao-yu said confidentially to Grandmother Jia:

'It's best if we *don't* say anything, Grannie. If we so much as open our mouths we're bound to upset someone. Why don't you suggest a drinking game instead?'

Grandmother Jia had inclined her head to one side to listen to him.

'If it's to be a game,' she replied with a laugh, 'we'll have to call Faithful back!'

Bao-yu needed no second bidding, but went straight out to the rear of the apartment to find Faithful.

'Grandmother wants to play a game and needs your help.'

'Mr Bao, can't we relax and drink a cup of wine in peace? Do you *have* to invent ways of disturbing us?'

'It's nothing to do with *me*. Honestly. It's Grandmother. She sent me to fetch you.'

'Oh very well then,' said Faithful, resigning herself to her fate. 'You all stay here and drink your wine. I'll be back shortly.'

She set off to Grandmother Jia's apartment.

'There you are!' cried Grandmother Jia when she appeared. 'We're going to play a drinking game.'

'Mr Bao said you wanted me, Your Old Ladyship,' said Faithful, 'so I came straight away. What kind of game were you thinking of playing?'

'Well not one of those clever bookish ones, for a start. They're too boring. And not one of those rowdy ones either. Think of something new and entertaining for us.'

Faithful pondered for a moment:

'As Mrs Xue is one of our visitors, and seeing that she is an elderly lady and won't want to rack her brains too much, why don't we just get out the dice-bowl and throw for song-titles? The loser has to drink a cup of wine.'

'That sounds a good idea,' said Grandmother Jia. She told one of the maids to put the dice-bowl on the table.

'We'll throw four dice,' said Faithful. 'If the combination has no particular name, the thrower's forfeit is one cup of wine. If it does have a name, the number of cups the others have to drink will depend on the combination.'

'That sounds easy enough,' they replied. 'We'll follow your lead.'

Faithful threw two dice to determine who should start. They insisted that Faithful should drink a cup first herself, then counting from her they came to Aunt Xue, who threw, and came up with four 'ones'.

'That has a name,' said Faithful. '"The Four Old Hermits of Mount Shang". All senior guests must drink a cup.'

Grandmother Jia, Mrs Li, Lady Xing and Lady Wang complied.

Just as Grandmother Jia was raising her cup to her lips, Faithful said:

'Since that was Mrs Xue's throw, she must now think of a song-title to match it; and the person next to her must cap it with a line from "The Standard Poets". Forfeit for failure in either case is one cup.'

'This is a plot!' cried Aunt Xue. 'I don't stand a chance!'

'Go on,' Grandmother Jia encouraged her. 'Have a go. You'll spoil the fun if you back out. I'm next, and I'm sure to fail, so then we'll be in the same boat.'

Aunt Xue tried her hand:

'How's this: "Greybeard sporting in the Flowers"?'

Grandmother Jia nodded, and recited the line:

'"They deem it idle mimicry of youth . . ."'

The dice-bowl passed to Li Wen, who threw two 'fours' and two 'twos'.

'That has a name too,' said Faithful. '"Two Travellers Lost in the Tiantai Mountains".'

Li Wen proposed the song-title 'Two Scholars at Peach-blossom Spring', and Li Wan, who was sitting next to her, recited the line:

'"Searching for Peach-blossom Spring to flee the tyranny of Qin".'

Everyone had a drink, and the dice-bowl passed to Grandmother Jia, who threw two 'twos' and two 'threes'.

'I suppose I shall have to drink a forfeit.'

'No,' said Faithful. 'That has a name. "A Swallow over the River Guiding her Chicks". Everyone has to drink a cup.'

'Most of your chicks have flown the nest, haven't they, Grannie?' quipped Xi-feng.

They gave her a meaningful look, and she immediately fell silent.

'Now what shall I say for my song?' said Grandmother Jia. 'What about "The Sire Leading his Grandson"?'

Li Qi was next to her, and quoted the line:

' "Lazily watching the children catch willowfloss".'

Everyone applauded her choice.

Bao-yu was longing to have a go, but so far the dice-bowl had not reached him. Now at last it was his turn. He threw a 'two', two 'threes' and a 'one'.

'What's that?' he asked.

Faithful laughed.

'A dud! Drink a forfeit and throw again.'

Bao-yu did as he was told. This time he threw two 'threes' and two 'fours'.

'That's better,' said Faithful. 'That's "Zhang Chang Painting his Wife's Eyebrows".'

Bao-yu knew she was making fun of him, and Bao-chai blushed fiercely too. Xi-feng didn't seem to have noticed anything out of the ordinary, and told him to hurry up and think of a song.

'Then we'll see whose turn it is next.'

Bao-yu was too embarrassed:

'I'll pay the forfeit. And there's no one sitting next to me anyway.'

The bowl came next to Li Wan. She threw, and Faithful announced the name of the combination as 'The Twelve Beauties'. Bao-yu hurried over to Li Wan's side and studied the dice: the red and green pips were symmetrically paired.

'Doesn't that look pretty!' he exclaimed.

Suddenly he recalled his dream, and the registers of the Twelve Beauties of Jinling. He wandered back to his seat in a daze.

'In my dream they were twelve,' he mused. 'But of my fair cousins, most have been scattered to the four winds. Why have so few been spared?'

He gazed around him. Xiang-yun and Bao-chai were present that day, it was true; but the absence of Dai-yu struck him with a sudden and overwhelming force and he knew that he was about to burst into tears. Not wanting the others to witness his distress, he pretended to feel hot, and expressed a desire to go and change. He begged leave to 'hand in his tally' and left the party.

Xiang-yun noted his departure, and thought he was probably peeved by the fact that he had not had a good throw and had been outshone by the others. She herself began to feel rather bored and irritated by the game.

'I can't think of anything,' said Li Wan, who had thrown the 'Twelve Beauties'. 'We are missing one of the party now anyway. I'd better just drink my forfeit and be done with it.'

'This game is not turning out to be much fun,' said Grandmother Jia. 'Why don't we call it a day? Let Faithful have one last throw.'

A junior maid placed the bowl in front of Faithful, who did as Grandmother Jia told her and threw the dice. She had two 'twos' and a 'five'. As the last dice continued to rattle in the dice-bowl, Faithful cried out:

'Pray I don't get another "five"!'

Finally it came to rest; there it was, five pips as plain as could be.

'Oh dear!' exclaimed Faithful. 'I've lost.'

'Doesn't that have a name?' asked Grandmother Jia.

'It does,' said Faithful. 'But I'll never be able to think of a song to match it.'

'Well, you tell us the name, and I'll try to think of something.'

'This one's called "Waves Sweep the Floating Duckweed".'

'There's nothing particularly hard about that,' said Grandmother Jia. 'Here's a song for you: "Autumn Fish in a Den of Caltrops".'

Xiang-yun, who was sitting next to Faithful, proposed the line:

' "The white duckweed moans, as autumn descends on the southern river." '

'Very apt!' they all exclaimed.

'The game's finished,' announced Grandmother Jia. 'Let's all have two more cups of wine and then eat our dinner.'

She looked round and noticed that Bao-yu was still absent.

'Where's Bao-yu gone? Why isn't he back yet?'

'He went to change,' Faithful informed her.

'Who went with him?'

Oriole came forward:

'When I saw that Mr Bao was going out, I told Aroma to go with him.'

This set the ladies' minds at rest. They waited a little longer for him to return, and then, since there was still no sign of him, Lady Wang sent one of the junior maids out to look for him. The maid went to his new apartment, but the only person there was Fivey, setting out candles.

'Where's Mr Bao gone?' the maid asked her.

'He's over at Her Old Ladyship's for the party,' replied Fivey.

'No he's not. I've just come from there. Her Ladyship sent me to fetch him. She'd hardly do that if he was there in the first place.'

'Well, in that case, I don't know where he is. You'd better look somewhere else.'

The maid was obliged to return and on her way met Ripple.

'Did you see where Mr Bao went?'

'I'm looking for him too,' said Ripple. 'Her Ladyship and the others are waiting for him so that they can start dinner. Where *can* he have got to? You'd better hurry back and report to Her Old Ladyship. Don't say we can't find him, just say the wine didn't agree with him and he won't be having any dinner. Say he'll be over when he's had a little lie-down. Ask Her Old Ladyship and Their Ladyships to start without him.'

The junior maid carried Ripple's message to Pearl, who passed it on to Grandmother Jia.

'He doesn't usually eat much anyway,' commented the old lady. 'He may as well miss out on dinner then, and have a rest. Tell him he needn't come back at all today. His wife is here, and that will do.'

'Is that clear?' said Pearl to the junior maid.

'Yes, Miss Pearl,' said the maid, not daring to explain what had really happened. She went out and walked around for a bit, then returned, claiming to have conveyed the message to Bao-yu. No one took a great deal of notice. They ate their dinner and then sat chatting.

*

Our narrative leaves them and returns to Bao-yu. Overwhelmed by a sudden sense of grief, he had quit the party and was wandering aimlessly outside. Aroma hurried after him and asked what the matter was.

'Nothing really,' he replied. 'I just feel very miserable all of a sudden. Why don't we go for a little stroll over to the apartment where Cousin Zhen's wife is living, and leave them to their drinking?'

'But Mrs Zhen is at the party,' said Aroma. 'Who do you want to visit in her apartment?'

'No one,' replied Bao-yu. 'I just thought I might drop in on her for a second. I'd forgotten she was at the party. I'd still like to go and see what sort of an apartment it is that she is living in.'

Aroma went along with him, and the two of them talked as they went. They soon came to You-shi's apartment, and noticed that the small side gate next to it leading into the Garden was half-ajar. Bao-yu did not go into You-shi's apartment at all; instead he went up to the two old serving-women in charge of the side gate, who were sitting there on the threshold having a conversation, and asked them:

'Is this side gate kept open?'

'Not usually,' replied one of them. 'But today we were told that Her Old Ladyship might be wanting some fruit from the Garden, so it's to be kept open in case.'

Bao-yu walked slowly up to the gate and, having confirmed for himself that it was open, made as if to go in; but Aroma held him back anxiously.

'You mustn't go in there. The Garden is haunted. It's been empty for ages. You might bump into something nasty like the others did!'

Bao-yu was tipsy enough to feel a little daring, and replied:

'I'm not afraid of such things!'

Aroma tugged at him with all her might and wouldn't let go. The serving-woman came up:

'Nowadays the Garden is ever so quiet and peaceful. Since the priests came and drove away the evil spirits, we often go in on our own to pick flowers and fruit. If Mr Bao wants to have a look, we'll go in with him. With so many of us, there's surely nothing to be afraid of.'

Bao-yu was delighted; and Aroma was obliged to abandon her attempts to dissuade him, and followed them in herself.

As Bao-yu entered the Garden, a scene of utter desolation greeted his eyes whichever way he turned. The flowers and trees seemed every one to be wilting, to be more dead than alive, and the paint had long since started to peel from the walls of many of the buildings. In the distance he espied a thicket of bamboo, an isolated patch of brilliant green foliage.

Bao-yu contemplated the view for a moment.

'Ever since I fell ill and left the Garden,' he said, 'I've been living at Grannie's. It must be months since I've been here. What a wilderness it has become in that time! But look over there at that single clump of green bamboo that's doing so well – surely that's the Naiad's House?'

'You've been away too long,' said Aroma. 'You've lost your sense of direction. While we've been talking we've already walked past Green Delights. And look –' (she turned back and pointed) – *there's* the Naiad's House, over there!'

Bao-yu's eyes followed the direction of her pointing hand.

'If we've already passed it, then let's go back and have a look.'

'It's getting rather late now,' said Aroma. 'Her Old Ladyship will be waiting for you to start dinner. We'd better go back to the party.'

Bao-yu said nothing. He walked on, along the route he imagined he had trodden so many times in the past, and began making his way towards his 'Naiad's House'. Percipient Reader, it will no doubt have surprised you to hear that Bao-yu had lost his way in the Garden after an absence of less than a year. The truth of the matter is that Bao-yu was quite correct in his orientation; it was Aroma who, anticipating his reaction to the sight of the Naiad's House, had at first deliberately kept him occupied with conversation, and then when she saw him walking instinctively in that direction despite her efforts – heading, as she feared, straight into the arms of evil spirits – had tried to convince him that they had already walked past the place. Bao-yu's heart was fixed, however; his compass was firmly set, and he was not to be so easily diverted.

He pressed ahead, and reluctantly Aroma followed. Suddenly he stood still. He seemed to be listening and watching.

'What is it?' asked Aroma.

'Is there someone living there now?' he asked.

'I should hardly think so,' she replied.

'I could have sworn I heard someone weeping inside! There *must* be someone!'

'You're imagining things,' said Aroma. 'It's because you always used to come here and find Miss Lin crying.'

Bao-yu was unconvinced and still wanted to approach and listen from a closer distance. The old women hurried forward:

'It's getting rather late now, sir. Time to be getting back. We're not afraid of going anywhere else in the Garden, but just here the way is so dark and you never know . . . We've heard tell that since Miss Lin died they're always hearing sounds of weeping here. No one will come near the place.'

Bao-yu and Aroma both started when they heard this.

'You see! I told you!' cried Bao-yu, the tears springing to his eyes. 'Oh, Cousin Lin! Cousin Lin!' he sobbed. 'How could I have wounded you so! Please don't reproach me! Don't feel bitter towards me! It was my father and mother who made the choice. In my heart I was always true to you!'

With each word he became more and more distraught, and finally broke into a great wail of grief. Aroma was wondering what on earth to do, when she saw Ripple hurrying towards her with a cohort of serving-women.

'Are you quite out of your mind!' cried Ripple. 'Bringing Mr Bao here of all places! Her Old Ladyship and Her Ladyship are dreadfully worried and have sent everywhere to look for him. Just now the women on the side gate said they'd seen the two of you come in here. Their Ladyships had the fright of their lives when they heard! They scolded me and told me to form a search party and come straight here. Hurry up now, we'd better be quick!'

Bao-yu was still sobbing pitifully, but Aroma and Ripple dragged him away, wiping the tears from his eyes and chiding him with a description of the anxiety his grandmother was suffering on his account. In the end he gave in and followed them back.

Aroma could imagine only too vividly how worried Grandmother Jia would be and she took Bao-yu straight back to the old lady's apartment. None of the party had gone home; they were all there waiting for Bao-yu's return.

'Aroma!' cried Grandmother Jia severely. 'I thought you were a sensible girl. That's why I've always trusted you with Bao-yu. How *could* you take him into the Garden? He's only just beginning to get better, and a nasty experience might set him right back. And *then* where would we be?'

Aroma did not dare say a word in her own defence, but hung her head in shame. Bao-chai for her part was deeply shocked to see how pale Bao-yu seemed on his return. Bao-yu refused to watch Aroma take the blame, and spoke up on her behalf:

'When we went in it was broad daylight, and there was nothing to be afraid of. I haven't been for a walk in the Garden for such a long time, and today I'd had a little wine at the party and was feeling in the mood for a stroll. Why did you think I would have a nasty experience?'

At this last remark of his, Xi-feng, who had herself been so badly scared in the Garden, shuddered and said:

'Bao, you shouldn't be so reckless!'

'It's not recklessness,' countered Xiang-yun. 'It's devotion. He probably went there to find the Hibiscus Fairy. Or maybe it was some other sprite . . .'

Bao-yu made no reply. Lady Wang seemed too agitated to speak.

'So there wasn't anything frightening in the Garden then?' asked Grandmother Jia. 'Well, don't let's talk about it any more. But in future, if you want to go walking there, you must at least take more people with you. If it hadn't been for this little escapade of yours, our guests would have left long ago. Off you go now, all of you, and have a good night's sleep. Come back early in the morning. Tomorrow I shall make up for today and see that you enjoy yourselves properly. And this time we won't let *him* spoil things!'

They all said goodbye to Grandmother Jia and the party broke up. Aunt Xue stayed the night with Lady Wang, Xiang-yun with Grandmother Jia, while Ying-chun went to stay with Xi-chun. The others all returned to their respective apartments.

When Bao-yu reached home, he was still a picture of misery. Bao-chai knew the cause of his endless sighing, and deliberately turned a deaf ear to it. She was concerned however that if he continued like this he might fall into a serious depression and revert to his old idiocy. Going into the inner room she called Aroma aside and questioned her in detail about Bao-yu's excursion in the Garden. To learn of Aroma's response, you must read the next chapter.

CHAPTER 109

*Fivey shares a vigil, and receives
affection meant for another
Ying-chun pays her debt to fate, and returns
to the Realm of Primordial Truth*

Bao-chai, having extracted from Aroma a detailed account of what
had happened in the Garden, feared that a fresh bout of grief might
indeed cause Bao-yu to fall ill again. In an attempt to avert this she
deliberately alluded to Dai-yu's dying moments, in the course of an
apparently casual conversation with Aroma.

'Human beings have certain feelings towards each other while
they are alive,' she went on to say. 'But after death a person enters a
separate realm and becomes a different entity. Someone still alive
may continue to be infatuated, but the dead person, the object of that
feeling, will be quite oblivious of it. Besides, if Miss Lin has become
a fairy, she must take a very dim view of lesser mortals and would
hardly deign to mingle with them on this earthly plane. To start
imagining such things is to invite trouble and to lay oneself open to
possession by evil spirits.'

She was talking to Aroma, but her words were clearly intended for
Bao-yu's ears. Aroma realized this and replied in an appropriate vein:

'Of course she's not a fairy. It's out of the question. If Miss Lin's
spirit *were* haunting the Garden, why has she never once appeared to
me in a dream? She and I were good friends, after all . . .'

Bao-yu was listening from outside, and considered this idea of
Aroma's carefully:

'It *is* strange! Since I first learned of Cousin Lin's death, I've
thought of her constantly, every day. But why have I never once
seen her in my dreams? It must be because she's in Heaven, and
thinks me a dull earthling incapable of communicating on her exalted
level. I know what I'll do: tonight I'll sleep here in the outer room.
Perhaps since I've just returned from the Garden she will be more
aware of my feelings, and will condescend to visit me this once in a
dream. If she does, I must be sure to ask her where she has gone, so

that I can make offerings to her regularly. If on the other hand it turns out that she is too pure for even a single dream-visit, then I must try to put her out of my mind once and for all.'

Having made this resolution, he said aloud:

'I shall sleep out here tonight. You needn't be bothered on my account.'

Bao-chai did not try to oppose him directly, but cautioned him:

'Don't go having any foolish ideas. Didn't you see how worried Mother was when she heard that you'd been in the Garden? She could hardly speak for anxiety! You must be sensible and look after yourself. If you go and do something silly again and Grandmother finds out, it's us she'll blame for not taking proper care of you.'

'I wasn't being serious,' said Bao-yu. 'I'd just like to sit here for a while and then come in. You must be tired too. Go to sleep, don't wait up for me.'

Bao-chai thought he would probably come in later, and said with an air of affected nonchalance:

'Very well then. I'm going to sleep. Aroma can look after you.'

This was exactly what Bao-yu had been hoping for. He waited until Bao-chai had gone to bed and then told Aroma and Musk to lay out his bedding. He sent one or the other of them in at frequent intervals to see if 'Mrs Bao was asleep yet or not'. Bao-chai pretended to be asleep, although in fact she was wide awake and remained so the entire night. Bao-yu was quite taken in, and said to Aroma:

'You and Musk can both go and sleep now. I'm not upset any more. If you don't believe me, stay here with me until I fall asleep and then go in. But I don't want to be disturbed later on in the night.'

Aroma stayed for a while, saw him into bed and made him some tea. Then she closed the door and retired to the inner room, where after finishing a few odd jobs, she lay down. She too only feigned sleep, and lay awake, ready to jump up if Bao-yu needed her outside.

Bao-yu dismissed the two serving-women on night-watch; and when he was alone he sat up very quietly, said a silent prayer and then lay down again. At first sleep eluded him, but gradually his mind grew more peaceful and eventually he nodded off and slept soundly the whole night through. When he awoke it was already broad daylight. He rubbed his eyes, sat up in bed and reflected. He had had a dreamless sleep. Nothing whatsoever had occurred. He sighed.

'As the poet once said,' he mused out loud:

> Since death's parting, slow and sad the year has been;
> Even in my dreams, her soul has not been seen.'

Bao-chai, who in contrast to Bao-yu had not slept a wink all night, heard him recite these well-known lines from Bo Ju-yi's 'Song of Enduring Grief', and remarked:

'What a singularly inept quotation! If Cousin Lin were alive, she'd be cross with you again, for comparing *her* to Yang Gui-fei!'

Bao-yu was embarrassed that she had overheard him. He climbed out of bed and walked sheepishly into the inner room.

'I meant to come in last night,' he said. 'But somehow I lay down and fell fast asleep.'

'What difference does it make to me whether you came in or not?' said Bao-chai.

Aroma had not slept either, and hearing the two of them talking she hurried over at once to pour tea. At that moment a junior maid from Grandmother Jia's arrived.

'Did Mr Bao have a good night's sleep?' she asked. 'If so, then will he and Mrs Bao please call on Her Old Ladyship as soon as they have completed their toilet?'

'Please inform Her Old Ladyship,' replied Bao-chai, 'that Mr Bao slept extremely well and that we will both call presently.'

The maid departed with this message.

Bao-chai completed her toilet at once, and accompanied by Oriole and Aroma she went first to pay her respects to Grandmother Jia. Then she called politely on Lady Wang and Xi-feng, before returning once more to Grandmother Jia's. Her mother had by now arrived.

'How was Bao-yu last night?' was what everyone wanted to know.

'He went to sleep as soon as we got home,' Bao-chai informed them. 'He was fine.'

They were relieved to hear this and the conversation passed to various other topics. Presently a junior maid came in to say that Ying-chun was going home:

'Mr Sun sent someone to Lady Xing's to complain, and Her Ladyship sent word to Miss Xi-chun to say that Miss Ying-chun must not be detained, but should return at once. Miss Ying-chun is at Her Ladyship's now. She's very upset, and is crying. She will be coming over presently to say goodbye, ma'am.'

Grandmother Jia was greatly distressed.

'Why did fate have to bring together a sweet child like Ying and this monster Sun! She'll have to bear with it for the rest of her life. There's no way out for her, poor girl!'

As they were speaking, Ying-chun came in, her cheeks wet with tears. The family were still supposed to be celebrating Bao-chai's birthday, so she did her best not to cry as she made her farewells. Grandmother Jia knew that Ying-chun must not delay her departure and she did not try to detain her.

'You'd best be on your way,' she said. 'But please, however bad things are, try to look on the bright side! He's what he is and there is little you can do to change him. In a few days I'll send someone to invite you home again for another visit.'

'Oh Grannie!' sobbed Ying-chun. 'You've always loved me! But it's no good! I know I'll never come home again!'

She could contain herself no longer, and tears streamed down her cheeks.

'Come along now!'

They all did what they could to cheer her up: 'Of course you'll come again! You should be thankful you're not at the other end of the world, like poor Tan. She has almost no chance whatsoever of coming home.'

This mention of Tan-chun only brought more tears to the eyes of Grandmother Jia and the ladies. Once again, the fact that it was Bao-chai's birthday induced one of them to try and strike a more optimistic note:

'Who knows: if peace is restored on the coast, Tan's father-in-law may be transferred back to the capital, and then we shall be able to see her!'

'Of course!' everyone concurred.

Ying-chun had now to contain her grief as best she could and take her leave. They saw her out, and then returned to Grandmother Jia's, where the party continued for the rest of that day and into the evening. When they saw that the old lady was tired, they all went their separate ways home.

*

Aunt Xue, after bidding farewell to Grandmother Jia, went to have a talk with Bao-chai:

'Your brother has survived this year, and if he can only receive an Imperial pardon and have his sentence reduced, he may still be able to pay his fine and be set free. These past few years have been so unbearably lonely and wretched for me! I've been thinking, perhaps I should go ahead with your cousin Ke's wedding after all; what do you think?'

'You're anxious about it, aren't you, Mama?' replied Bao-chai. 'Pan's marriage turned out so badly, and you're worried that Ke's will be the same. Well, my advice is to go ahead. You know Xiu-yan's character, and have nothing to fear on that account. Life is very hard for her at present. Once she's married into our family, however poor we are, it's bound to be better for her than being totally dependent on others as she is now.'

'In that case,' said Aunt Xue, 'will you tell Lady Jia when you have a chance? I've no one at home, and I should like her to choose a lucky day for the wedding.'

'Just talk it over with Ke and choose a good day between you,' said Bao-chai. 'Then you can let Grandmother and Aunt Xing know, and go ahead with the wedding. I'm sure Aunt Xing will be only too glad to be rid of Xiu-yan.'

'I heard today that Xiang-yun is going home,' said Aunt Xue. 'Lady Jia wants Bao-qin to stay on here with you for a few days. She will be marrying too, quite soon, so you should take the chance of having a good chat with her.'

'I will, Mama.'

Aunt Xue remained with her daughter a little longer, and then after saying goodbye to the others, went home.

*

Let us return to Bao-yu. When he found himself in his apartment again that evening, he pondered his experience of the night before. There was no denying the fact that Dai-yu had failed to appear to him in a dream. That meant one of two things: either she had indeed already become a fairy, and was holding herself aloof from intercourse with as coarse a being as himself; or else *he* was just being too impatient. He decided to give this second alternative the benefit of the doubt, and resolved to prolong his experiment a little.

'Somehow last night,' he said to Bao-chai, 'when I fell asleep outside, I had a sounder night's sleep than I usually do in the inner room. I woke up feeling very calm and refreshed. I've been thinking, I should like to try it again for another couple of nights. But I suppose you and Aroma will object again . . .'

Early that morning when she had heard him reciting the poem, Bao-chai knew it was the memory of Dai-yu that had inspired it. She knew that this obsession of his was something mere words would never cure, and concluded that she might as well let him go ahead and spend the two nights outside, and thus be the agent of his own disenchantment. Anyway, the fact of the matter was that he *had* slept soundly the previous night. She had been awake herself, and knew.

'What nonsense!' she replied. 'Why should we object? If you want to sleep there, go ahead. Just don't have any foolish ideas. You'll only be laying yourself open to possession by evil spirits.'

Bao-yu laughed: 'Why ever should I do that?'

Aroma was opposed to the plan:

'I think you should sleep in the inner room. It's harder to look after you properly in the outer room. You might catch a chill or something.'

Before Bao-yu had time to reply, Bao-chai gave Aroma a meaningful look.

'Oh well,' said Aroma, taking the point, 'at least you should have someone with you to bring you a drink if you need one.'

Bao-yu laughed:

'Why not you?'

Aroma was embarrassed by this. She blushed fiercely and said nothing. Bao-chai knew that Aroma was too sensible nowadays for that sort of banter, and spoke on her behalf:

'Aroma is used to being with me now. I think she should stay here. Musk and Fivey can look after you. Besides, Aroma has spent all day traipsing about with me, and she's tired. She deserves a rest.'

Bao-yu smiled and walked out of the room.

Bao-chai told Musk and Fivey to make up his bed in the outer room.

'Sleep lightly,' she instructed them, 'and be ready to bring him a drink if he wants one.'

'We will, ma'am,' they replied, and went out, to find Bao-yu sitting bolt upright on the couch, eyes closed and palms together, like a monk in meditation. They did not dare say a word, but stood staring at him, with a smile on their faces. Bao-chai sent Aroma in to see if she was needed, and Aroma too found his posture highly comical.

'Time to sleep,' she whispered. 'What do you want to start meditating for at this hour of the night?'

Bao-yu opened his eyes and looked at her.

'You can all go to bed now,' he announced. 'I shall sit up for a little longer and then go to sleep.'

'Last night,' said Aroma, 'you kept Mrs Bao awake till morning. Surely you're not intending a repeat performance, are you?'

Bao-yu could see that if he did not go to sleep nobody else would either, and climbed into bed. Aroma gave Musk and Fivey a few final instructions, and then went back to the inner room to sleep, closing the door behind her.

Musk and Fivey sorted out their own bedding, and waited for Bao-yu to fall asleep before going to bed themselves. But he remained obstinately wide awake. Watching them make the beds, he found himself suddenly thinking of the time when Aroma had been away and Skybright and Musk had been left to look after him. It was on that occasion that Musk had gone out during the night and Skybright had tried to play a trick on her and give her a fright. She had been too lightly dressed, and had caught cold as a result; and it was this cold that eventually led to the illness from which she died. His mind was now completely taken up with memories of Skybright. Then suddenly he remembered how Xi-feng had once likened Fivey to Skybright – 'the spitting image' had been her words. Imperceptibly his old feelings towards Skybright began to transfer themselves to Fivey. He lay there pretending to be asleep, and furtively watching her. The more he watched her, the more the resemblance struck him, and the more he felt himself aroused. All was silent in the inner room; *they* must be asleep, he thought to himself. But he needed to discover if Musk was still awake. He called her name a couple of times, and there was no reply. Fivey heard, however:

'What do you want, Mr Bao?'

'I'd like to rinse my mouth.'

Fivey could see that Musk was asleep, so she hurriedly rose from her bed, trimmed the wick in the lamp again and took Bao-yu a cup of tea, carrying the spittoon in her other hand. She was in too much of a hurry to change, and had nothing but a little pink silk jacket over her pyjamas. Her hair was loosely coiled on top of her head.

Looking at her, Bao-yu could almost imagine Skybright come back from the dead. Suddenly he remembered Skybright's dying words: 'If I'd known in advance that it would be like this, I might have behaved rather differently . . .' He stared at Fivey in a besotted fashion, quite oblivious of the teacup in her outstretched hand.

Ever since the departure of Parfumée, Fivey had given up all idea of coming to serve at Green Delights; but then, when Xi-feng gave orders for her to be taken into Bao-yu's service, she was more excited about it than Bao-yu himself. To her surprise, after her arrival the generally distinguished and dignified manner in which Bao-chai and Aroma conducted themselves made a deep impression on her, and she found herself coming to respect and admire them greatly, whereas Bao-yu by contrast seemed to her to have degenerated into a complete idiot, and to be not half so handsome as he used to be. Besides she knew that Lady Wang had dismissed some of the maids for flirting with Bao-yu, and she therefore decided to dismiss any foolish and romantic notions she might previously have entertained concerning him. But now here *he* was, the simpleton, evidently taking a fancy to her (she knew nothing of the process by which his feelings for Skybright had been transferred to her).

Both her cheeks were burning. She did not dare say anything out loud, but whispered:

'Mr Bao, please go ahead and rinse your mouth!'

He smiled and took the cup in his hand. She could not tell whether he ever did rinse his mouth or not, as the next she knew he was giggling and asking her:

'Weren't you friends with Skybright?'

Fivey didn't understand what he was getting at.

'Of course. We were all of us on good terms.'

Bao-yu lowered his voice to a whisper:

'When Skybright was so very ill, I went to visit her. You were there, weren't you?'

Fivey smiled and nodded her head.

'Did you hear her say anything?' asked Bao-yu.

'No,' replied Fivey, shaking her head.

Bao-yu held Fivey's hand. He seemed to be completely carried away. She blushed fiercely and her heart missed a beat.

'Mr Bao!' she whispered. 'Whatever's on your mind, just go ahead and say it. But please stop behaving like this.'

Bao-yu let go of her hand.

' "If I'd known in advance that it would be like this, I might have behaved rather differently . . ." That's what Skybright said. Surely you must have heard?'

It seemed quite plain to Fivey what manner of 'different behaviour' he had in mind. She felt she must protest:

'If that's what she said, she should have been ashamed of herself! No decent girl would suggest a thing like that!'

'Don't you start preaching at me too!' snapped Bao-yu irritably. 'I was thinking how like Skybright you looked – that's the only reason I told you what she said. How dare you slander her!'

Fivey could no longer discern Bao-yu's true intentions.

'It's late,' she said. 'You really should go to sleep and not sit up like this. You might catch cold. Didn't you hear what Mrs Bao and Aroma said just now?'

'I'm not cold,' said Bao-yu. As he said this, it suddenly struck him that Fivey was most inadequately clad, and that *she* might catch a chill just as Skybright had done.

'Why aren't you wearing a proper robe?' he asked her.

'You called, and it sounded important,' she replied. 'I was hardly going to take time off to dress! I would have, mind you, if I'd known you were going to keep me talking this long.'

Bao-yu handed Fivey the pale blue silken padded jacket that was lying on the bed, and told her to put it on. But she refused.

'You keep it – I'm not cold. And anyway, I've a perfectly good robe of my own.'

She went across to her bed and put on a long robe. She listened out for a moment. Musk was sound asleep. She crossed slowly back to Bao-yu:

'I thought you were supposed to be having a quiet night?'

Bao-yu smiled.

'To tell you the truth, that was never my intention. Actually, I was hoping to meet a fairy . . .'

His words strengthened her suspicions.

'Who do you mean?'

'I'll tell you if you like,' he replied. 'But it's a long story. You'd better come up here and sit next to me . . .'

'But you're all tucked up in bed!' she protested, blushing again and smiling coyly. 'How can I possibly sit next to you?'

'Why not? One night a year or two ago, when the weather was cold and Skybright stayed up to play a trick on Musk, I was afraid she was going to catch a chill, so I tucked her under my quilt to keep her warm. What's wrong with it? People shouldn't be so prudish.'

Fivey thought he was merely putting ideas into her head. She did not know that he sincerely meant every word he said. She contemplated her dilemma. She could hardly escape; and yet if she remained, it would be equally awkward for her to remain standing or to sit down beside him. She gave him a little glance and her face puckered into a smile:

'Don't say such silly things! People might hear. No wonder you have such a reputation. How can you still need to go flirting, with two such beautiful ladies as Mrs Bao and Aroma by your side! Don't you ever suggest such a thing again, or I'll report you to Mrs Bao. And then you'll have cause to be ashamed!'

As she was speaking there was a sudden noise outside, which startled them both, and shortly afterwards Bao-chai could be heard coughing in the inner room. Bao-yu made a quick motion with his lips, and Fivey hurriedly extinguished the lamp and stole back to bed. In fact, earlier that evening, both Bao-chai and Aroma had gone straight to sleep, exhausted after their previous sleepless night and the day's exertions, and both of them had slept soundly through this conversation between Bao-yu and Fivey. It was the sudden noise in the courtyard that had woken them too. They listened for any further sound, but all was quiet. Bao-yu meanwhile lay down in bed again, and was thinking to himself:

'That noise must surely have been Cousin Lin! She came, and then, when she heard me talking with Fivey, she decided to give us both a fright.'

He lay there tossing and turning, a thousand wild fancies running through his head, and only nodded off some time after three in the morning.

Bao-yu's advances had left Fivey with a guilty conscience, and when Bao-chai coughed she feared that they had both been overheard, and lay awake worrying about it all night. Early the next morning she rose, and seeing Bao-yu still fast asleep, began quietly tidying the room. Musk was already awake.

'Why are you up so early?' she asked Fivey. 'Don't tell me you've been awake all night . . .'

This led Fivey to suspect that Musk had overheard them too. She smiled awkwardly and said nothing. Presently Bao-chai and Aroma got up, opened the door and came into the outer room, where they were greatly surprised to find Bao-yu still asleep. It puzzled them that he should have slept there so soundly on two consecutive nights.

When Bao-yu awoke and saw them all standing around him, he sat up at once and rubbed his eyes. He thought back over the night. No, there had still been no dream. He had met no one. He consoled himself with the words of the old saying:

> Fairies and mortals tread different paths,
> And ne'er the twain shall meet.

As he climbed slowly down from his bed, Fivey's words about Bao-chai and Aroma were still ringing in his ears: 'two such beautiful ladies'. Yes, she was right, he thought to himself, and proceeded to stare at Bao-chai. Bao-chai thought he was drifting into one of his brown studies, and felt certain it must be to do with Dai-yu again, though she still had not enquired whether his dream had been fruitful or not. She soon began to feel uncomfortable under his penetrating gaze, and finally asked:

'Well, did you meet a fairy last night or not?'

Bao-yu concluded from this that she must have overheard his tête-à-tête with Fivey. He gave a nervous little laugh and replied with feigned surprise:

'What do you mean?'

Fivey for her part was feeling more and more guilty and apprehensive, and silently observed Bao-chai's reaction. Bao-chai turned to her next and asked with a smile:

'Well, did Mr Bao talk in his sleep last night?'

At this Bao-yu, muttering some incoherent excuse, walked rather sheepishly from the room. Fivey blushed fiercely and replied as evasively as she could:

'He said something or other early in the night, but I didn't quite catch it. Something about "knowing in advance that things would be like this", and then something about "behaving rather differently". I couldn't understand what he was trying to say, so I just told him to go back to sleep. Then I fell asleep myself, and if he said any more I certainly didn't hear it.'

Bao-chai lowered her head in thought:

'Obviously something to do with Dai-yu. If I let him go on sleeping in the outer room he's bound to get more and more of these weird ideas into his head, and who knows what strange apparitions and flower fairies we'll have then. It is his weakness for our sex that has always been his vulnerable spot. How can I win him over myself? Until I can do that, this will never stop.'

A fierce and somewhat unmaidenly blush came to her cheeks, and she walked back into the inner room in something of a fluster to do her toilet.

*

During the two-day birthday festivities, Grandmother Jia had over-eaten, and on the second evening she was a little off colour. The following day she had a painfully bloated feeling in her stomach, which Faithful wanted to report to Jia Zheng. But Grandmother Jia forbade her:

'I've just been a bit greedy over the past couple of days. A fast will soon put me right. Don't you go making a fuss.'

Consequently Faithful told no one.

*

That evening, when Bao-yu returned to his apartment and saw Bao-chai come in from paying her respects to Grandmother Jia and Lady Wang, he recalled the incident in the morning and blushed with shame. His embarrassment was evident to Bao-chai. For someone subject to such extremities of feeling (she thought to herself) the only remedy lay in the manipulation of those very feelings themselves.

'Will you be sleeping outside again tonight?' she asked.

Bao-yu did not seem keen to pursue the matter:

'I really don't mind one way or the other.'

Bao-chai could think of no suitable retort.

'What's that supposed to mean?' protested Aroma. 'I don't believe you really slept so soundly out there . . .'

Fivey promptly leapt to Bao-yu's defence:

'Mr Bao had a very peaceful night, apart from talking in his sleep. I couldn't make head or tail of what he said, and it seemed best not to argue with him.'

'I shall sleep out there tonight,' announced Aroma, 'and we'll see if *I* talk in my sleep. You can go ahead and move Mr Bao's bedding back into the inner room.'

Bao-chai made no comment. Bao-yu was too full of remorse to object, and went along meekly with Aroma's plan. He was eager to make it up with Bao-chai, while her concern that too much introspection and grief would injure his health caused her to be especially tender towards him; she was quite deliberately trying to 'graft herself' on to the 'stem' of his affections, drawing him closer to her and usurping Dai-yu's place in his heart. When Aroma went to sleep in the outer room that evening, Bao-yu was in a frame of mind to exhibit his penitence, and Bao-chai naturally had no intention of rejecting him. As a result, their marriage was that night physically consummated for the first time, and they tasted to the full the joys of nuptial intercourse. From this union Bao-chai conceived a child. But that belongs to a later part of our story.

*

When Bao-chai and Bao-yu rose in the morning, Bao-yu performed his ablutions and went ahead to call on Grandmother Jia. She had that very morning had a sudden fancy to give something to her darling grandson and to her devoted granddaughter-in-law, and had told Faithful to open one of her trunks and take out an antique Han dynasty jade thumb-ring, a family heirloom of hers. She knew it could not compare with Bao-yu's original jade, but thought nevertheless that it would make rather an unusual pendant. Faithful found it and handed it to Grandmother Jia.

'I don't think I've ever seen this before. How could you remember so clearly where it was after all these years? You knew exactly which casket and which trunk. With your instructions I was able to find it straight away. What do you want it for, ma'am?'

'I wouldn't expect you to know about this ring,' replied Grandmother Jia. 'It was originally given to my father by my great-grandfather, and then when I was married my father sent for me and made me a present of it. He told me it was a very precious thumb-ring made in the Han dynasty, of the variety known as "broken circle". He wanted me to keep it as a memento. I was very young at the time and didn't think much of it; I just put it away in a trunk. And when I came to live here, and saw so many other treasures around me, it didn't seem so very special. I've never even worn it. It must have been lying in that trunk for over sixty years. I was thinking today what a good grandson Bao-yu is to me; and since he has lost his own jade, I thought I might give this to him, just as my father gave it to me.'

Presently Bao-yu arrived to pay his respects.

'Come here,' said Grandmother Jia with a twinkle in her eye. 'Come and have a look at something.'

Bao-yu walked over to the couch where she was lying, and Grandmother Jia handed him the jade thumb-ring. He took it in his hands and inspected it. It was about three inches in circumference, slightly elliptical in shape like an elongated melon, of a reddish hue. It was a very beautiful piece of workmanship. Bao-yu was most taken with it and enthused at some length.

'Do you like it?' said Grandmother Jia. 'This was handed down to me from my great-grandpa, and now I'm passing it on to you.'

Bao-yu smiled, and dropping one knee to the ground to express his thanks, said he would like to go and show the ring to his mother.

'When she sees it she will tell your father,' Grandmother Jia teased him, 'and then *he* will say that I love you more than I ever loved him. They have never even set eyes on it before.'

Bao-yu smiled and went out, leaving Bao-chai to stay for a while and chat with Grandmother Jia before taking her leave.

The old lady fasted for two days, but she still had a painfully bloated stomach, and began to cough and have dizzy spells. The ladies found her in good spirits when they paid their duty calls, but they sent a message to Jia Zheng that she was indisposed. He came immediately, and on leaving her apartment sent at once for a doctor to take her pulses and give a diagnosis. The doctor came presently and after a consultation pronounced that the condition was nothing unusual for a person of Grandmother Jia's age. Faulty diet had caused a slight chill, which a little dispersant medication would soon put right. He wrote out a prescription, and Jia Zheng, seeing that it contained nothing out of the ordinary, told one of the maids to brew the ingredients up and administer the decoction to Grandmother Jia.

Jia Zheng visited Grandmother Jia morning and evening. After three days, when there was still no sign of improvement, he said to Jia Lian:

'You must get in touch with a better doctor and ask him to come and look at your grandmother as soon as possible. I'm afraid none of our regular doctors is good enough.'

Jia Lian thought for a moment:

'I remember a while ago when Bao-yu was ill, we ended up calling in a doctor who was not strictly speaking a regular practitioner at all – and yet he was the one to put Bao-yu right. Why don't we send for him again?'

'Medicine is certainly a subtle art,' Jia Zheng mused aloud. 'And sometimes the ablest physicians are not recognized as such. By all means send someone to fetch this man.'

Jia Lian departed at once, only to return with the news that the doctor in question had recently left town to instruct his disciples and would not be coming back for another ten days. As the matter was urgent, Jia Lian had invited another, who was already on his way. Jia Zheng waited anxiously for this doctor's arrival.

During this illness, all the ladies were in constant attendance on Grandmother Jia. On one occasion, when there was quite a gathering of them in her apartment, one of the old women whose duty it was to watch the side gate of the Garden came in with a message.

'Sister Adamantina from Green Bower Hermitage in the Garden has heard that Her Old Ladyship is ill, and has come specially to call.'

'She so rarely visits,' they commented. 'Go and invite her in at once.'

Xi-feng went over to the bedside to tell Grandmother Jia, and Xiu-yan, Adamantina's old friend, went out to meet her. Adamantina was wearing the head-covering of an unshorn nun, and a pale blue plain silk gown with a patchwork full-length sleeveless jacket over it, bordered with black silk; she had gathered her gown with a russet-green woven sash, beneath which she wore a long white damask-silk skirt decorated with a pattern in grey. She drifted in with her usual otherworldly air, holding a fly whisk and fingering a rosary, and followed by one of her attendants. Xiu-yan greeted her:

'When I lived in the Garden too, I could come and see you often; but recently the Garden's become so deserted, and it's been difficult for me to go in there on my own. And anyway the side gate is usually closed. That's why I haven't been able to visit you for so long. How lovely it is to see you again!'

'You and the others were always too caught up in the hustle and bustle of life,' replied Adamatina. 'That's why even when you lived in the Garden I didn't visit very often. But I've heard of the recent troubles, and learned that Her Old Ladyship has fallen ill; I've been thinking of you and I wanted to see Bao-chai. What difference does it make to me if the gates are closed or not? I chose to come, and I came; if I hadn't chosen to come, it would have made no difference how much anybody wanted me to.'

Xiu-yan laughed.

'You haven't changed a bit, have you!'

By now they had entered Grandmother Jia's room. The ladies all welcomed Adamantina, and she went up to the bedside, enquired after the old lady's health and chatted with her for a while.

'You're a religious person,' said the old lady. 'Tell me: am I going to get better or not?'

'A person as charitable and virtuous as yourself, Lady Jia, will surely live to a ripe old age,' replied Adamantina. 'You've just caught a slight chill, and I'm sure a few doses of medicine will put it right. At your age the important thing is to relax and not worry so much.'

'But you know I'm not the worrying type,' said Grandmother Jia. 'I've always been one for my bit of fun. There's not much the matter with me, I just feel a little uncomfortable and have this bloated feeling in my stomach. The last doctor I saw said it was because I was letting myself get too overwrought. But you know perfectly well that no one dares to rub *me* up the wrong way! I don't think that doctor really knew what he was talking about. I told Lian the first doctor was right – I've just got an upset stomach and a cold. Lian should send for him again tomorrow.'

She called Faithful over:

'Tell the kitchen to prepare some vegetables so that Sister Adamantina can have something to eat while she's here.'

'I've already eaten,' said Adamantina. 'I won't have anything now.'

'Even if you are not going to eat,' said Lady Wang, 'stay and chat with us a little.'

'Very well. It's so long since I've been here. I wanted to see how you all were anyway.'

She talked with them a little longer, and then said she must be going. As she looked around she caught sight of Xi-chun.

'Why are you looking so thin, Xi?' she asked. 'You mustn't wear yourself out so with your painting.'

'I haven't painted for ages,' said Xi-chun. 'The room I'm living in now is not so light. And besides I don't feel like painting nowadays.'

'Where are you living now?' asked Adamantina.

'In a room to the east of the gate you've just come through,' replied Xi-chun. 'It's very close, if you ever feel like dropping in.'

'One day I will,' replied Adamantina. 'When I'm feeling in the right frame of mind.'

Xi-chun and the others saw her out, chatting as they went. By the time they returned, the maids informed them that the doctor was closeted with Grandmother Jia, and they all left and went their separate ways.

Contrary to everyone's cheerful prognostications, Grandmother Jia gradually deteriorated. None of the treatment she received had any beneficial effect, and she started suffering from diarrhoea. Jia Zheng realized that her condition was becoming critical, and grew extremely concerned. He sent a messenger to the Board to say that he would be taking leave and staying at home, and he and Lady Wang waited on the old lady day and night, personally preparing and administering her medicines. One day they had just watched her eat and drink a little and were feeling slightly more optimistic, when they saw an old serving-woman poke her head round the door. Lady Wang sent Suncloud out to see who it was, and she discovered it to be one of the women Ying-chun had taken with her on her marriage.

'What have you come for?' she asked.

'I've been waiting an age!' replied the old woman. 'I couldn't find a maid anywhere and I didn't want to come barging in. I've been worried silly!'

'What's the trouble?' asked Suncloud. 'Don't tell me Mr Sun has been bullying our Miss Ying again!'

'She's past hope!' said the old woman. 'He had one of his fits the day before yesterday, and she was crying all that night, and then yesterday she had a bad attack and could hardly breathe. They wouldn't send for a doctor, and today she's even worse!'

'Her Old Ladyship's ill herself!' said Suncloud. 'For goodness' sake don't go making a lot of noise!'

Lady Wang had heard this conversation from inside, and afraid that Grandmother Jia would react badly to this latest turn of events, she ordered Suncloud to take the serving-woman away and talk to her somewhere else. But Grandmother Jia still had her wits sufficiently about her to overhear and understand a great part of the conversation.

'Is Ying dying?' she cried.

'Certainly not,' protested Lady Wang. 'These women lose all sense of proportion. She's just been a little poorly these past few days and they were concerned for her and came here to ask for a doctor.'

'They'd better have mine,' said Grandmother Jia. 'Tell him to go and see her at once.'

Grandmother Jia began to grow very distressed.

'Of my three granddaughters,' she said, 'the eldest spent her share of good fortune and died; Tan, my third, is married and has gone to live at the other end of the world, and I shall never see her again; and now Ying – I knew life was hard for her, but somehow I thought she would live to see better days. Now she's going to die, and she's so dreadfully young! And I shall be left here, a useless old woman with no reason to be alive!'

Lady Wang and Faithful did what they could to console her. Bao-chai and Li Wan were not present that day, and Xi-feng had been too ill to attend for several days. Lady Wang was afraid that Grandmother Jia's illness would be aggravated by all this mental distress, and she sent at once for the other ladies, while she returned to her own apartment and called Suncloud to her.

'That stupid old serving-woman!' she grumbled. 'In future when I'm with Her Old Ladyship, you're not to disturb me, no matter what the trouble is!'

Suncloud promised to obey this injunction, and said no more. The old woman meanwhile had just reached Lady Xing's when the news arrived that Ying-chun had died. Lady Xing burst into tears. In Jia She's absence she had to send Jia Lian to the Suns to represent the family. Grandmother Jia was so ill that no one dared break the news to her.

Alas! What a cruel end for such a gentle creature, her flowerlike beauty crushed within a year of marriage!

None of the Jias could leave home with Grandmother Jia as she was, and the Suns gave Ying-chun a predictably makeshift funeral.

Grandmother Jia continued to deteriorate steadily, but still her only thought was for her granddaughters and great-nieces. On one occasion Xiang-yun was in the forefront of her mind, and she sent a maid to see how she was. The maid returned and tiptoed in to find

Faithful. Faithful was at the bedside, as were Lady Wang and the other ladies; and the maid, not wishing to disturb them, went round to the back to find Amber.

'Her Old Ladyship sent me to fetch news of Miss Xiang-yun,' she told Amber, 'and I found her crying her heart out! Her husband has suddenly been taken ill, and the doctors say there's no hope for him. At the best it will turn into a consumption and he may last another four or five years! You can imagine how badly Miss Xiang-yun has taken it! She's already heard about Her Old Ladyship's illness, but now she simply can't leave home. She told me not to mention her husband's illness to Her Old Ladyship. If she does ask after Miss Xiang-yun, you must think of some way to explain her absence.'

Amber heaved a deep sigh, and after a long silence dismissed the maid. She too thought it unwise to inform Grandmother Jia, and went to her bedside with the intention of telling Faithful to invent some story. She found Grandmother Jia deathly pale, and everyone in the room whispering among themselves:

'You can see she's going!'

Amber did not dare utter a word. Jia Zheng discreetly called Jia Lian over to whisper something in his ear, and Jia Lian tiptoed off to do his bidding. Outside he assembled the remaining household staff.

'Her Old Ladyship will soon be gone. You must make sure that everything is in order. First fetch out the coffin-boards for inspection, and measure them up for a lining. Go round all the apartments, take everyone's measurements, and give the tailor a complete list, with instructions to make everyone a set of mourning clothes. Arrange for the funeral awning to be constructed in the courtyard and for coffin-bearers to be hired. And have extra staff put on duty in the kitchen.'

'Mr Lian,' replied Lai Da, on behalf of the others. 'You don't need to worry about these things. We have already thought of everything. But where is the money coming from?'

'We won't need to borrow,' said Jia Lian. 'Her Old Ladyship has made provision herself. The Master told me just now that he wants no expense spared. It must be done in style; we must put on a good show.'

'Yes, sir.'

Lai Da and the others went about their business at once, and Jia Lian returned to his own apartment.

'How is Mrs Lian?' he asked Patience.

Patience shot her mouth out towards the inner room:

'Go and see for yourself.'

Jia Lian went in. Xi-feng was struggling to dress herself, but was too weak to do so. She had collapsed on the kang, and was leaning on the little kang-table.

'It's no good hoping to snatch some rest now!' exclaimed Jia Lian. 'Grandmother is sinking fast and you must be there. Hurry up and tell them to tidy things up in here. And pull yourself together! If the worst happens, we won't be able to get away for quite a while.'

'We've got nothing left to tidy up!' said Xi-feng bitterly. 'Only a few odds and ends, nothing worth bothering about. You go on ahead, Sir Zheng may want you. I'll come as soon as I'm properly dressed.'

Jia Lian returned to Grandmother Jia's apartment and reported discreetly to Jia Zheng that all had been seen to and the various duties assigned. Jia Zheng nodded. The Imperial Physician was announced, and Jia Lian went out to receive him. Grandmother Jia's pulses were taken and then the physician emerged to inform Jia Lian in hushed tones:

'Lady Jia's pulse-rate is very poor. You must be prepared for the worst.'

Jia Lian understood and passed the message on to Lady Wang and the others. Lady Wang beckoned Faithful with a meaningful glance and told her to prepare Grandmother Jia's funeral clothes. Faithful went to fetch them.

The old lady opened her eyes and asked for a drink of tea. Lady Xing brought her a cup of ginseng tea, and she put her lips to it.

'Not this!' she protested. 'Give me a proper cup of tea!'

They dared not deny her this request, and promptly brought her a cup of real tea. She took one gulp, and then another, and then announced that she wanted to sit up.

'Mother,' pleaded Jia Zheng on behalf of the others, 'whatever you want, you have only to tell us; but please don't exhaust yourself by trying to sit up.'

'I've had a drink and I feel a bit better now,' she replied. 'I'd like to sit up and chat for a bit.'

Pearl and the other maids gently supported her with their hands. She seemed momentarily revived. Whether she was to live or die will be told in the next chapter.

CHAPTER 110

*Lady Jia ends her days, and returns
to the land of shades
Wang Xi-feng exhausts her strength, and
forfeits the family's esteem*

Grandmother Jia sat up in bed and began to speak:

'I have been part of the Jia family for over sixty years. I have had a long life and enjoyed my full share of happiness. I think I can say that all my children and grandchildren from Zheng downwards have turned out well. As for Bao-yu: I have loved him so dearly and . . .'

Her eyes searched the room for Bao-yu, and Lady Wang pushed him towards the bed. Grandmother Jia extended one hand from beneath the bedcovers and took hold of him:

'My boy, you must promise to do your very best for the family!'

'Yes, Grandma,' choked Bao-yu, his eyes brimming with tears. He struggled to contain his weeping and stood listening to her, as she continued:

'I want to see one of my great-grandchildren, and then I think I can set my heart at rest. Where's my little Lan?'

Li Wan pushed Lan forwards. Grandmother Jia let go of Bao-yu and took Lan by the hand.

'You must be a good boy and always do your duty to your mother. And when you're grown up, you must win her honour and glory! Now, where's Fengie?'

Xi-feng was standing by the side of the bed and hurried round to face Grandmother Jia.

'Here I am, Grandma.'

'My child,' said Grandmother Jia, 'your trouble is that you're too clever! Try to be more charitable in future and to make your peace with fate. I know I'm not much of a one to talk; the most I've done in my life is try to be honest and to bear my misfortunes with patience. I've never been the sort for fasting or prayer. The only good work I ever did was to have those copies of the Diamond Sutra made a year or so ago. I wonder if they've all been distributed yet?'

Xi-feng informed her that the copies had not yet been distributed.

'The sooner that act of devotion is completed the better,' said the old lady. 'I know my elder son She and Cousin Zhen are detained in exile, and cannot be here: but how could that little devil Xiang-yun be so heartless? Why has she not come to see me?'

Faithful and her fellow maids knew the reason only too well, but said nothing.

Grandmother Jia looked next at Bao-chai. As she did so, she sighed and a flush began to spread across her face. Jia Zheng knew this to be a sign of imminent death. He came forward with the ginseng broth, but Grandmother Jia's teeth were already tightly clenched. She closed her eyes, then opened them once more and gazed round the entire room. Lady Wang and Bao-chai came forward and supported her gently, while Lady Xing and Xi-feng dressed her. The old serving-woman prepared the bed where she was to be laid out, and arranged the coverlet. There was a faint rattle in her throat, a smile stole across her face, and she was gone. She was eighty-two years old. The serving-women hurried forward to lay her on the bed.

Jia Zheng and the other menfolk knelt in the outer room, Lady Xing and the womenfolk knelt by the bed; from both rose the first chorus of lamentation. The servants outside had all made their preparations, and as soon as word came from the inner quarters, every gateway was thrown open, from the main entrance to the inner gate leading to the ladies' apartments, and white paper was pasted on every door. The funeral awning was raised over the courtyard, and a memorial archway erected outside the main entrance. Every member of the household immediately put on their mourning clothes.

Jia Zheng reported his bereavement and the commencement of his three-year period of mourning to the Board of Rites, who submitted a memorial requesting the Emperor's instructions in the matter. His Majesty, being a person of the profoundest compassion and kindliness, in consideration of the services rendered and distinctions obtained by previous generations of the family, and especially in view of the relationship of the deceased to the Imperial Jia Concubine, authorized a bounty of one thousand taels of silver and instructed officers from the Board of Rites to make offerings and do reverence before her coffin. Jia household servants were despatched to notify all relatives and family friends of Lady Jia's death, and they all came to condole; for while they knew that the Jias had come down in the world, they also saw that the family continued to enjoy the Emperor's favour. An auspicious day was chosen for the encoffinment and subsequent lying-in-state.

Since Jia She was away from home, Jia Zheng was acting head of the family. Two of Grandmother Jia's grandsons, Bao-yu and Jia Huan, and her great-grandson Jia Lan, all of whom were too young to take part in the reception, mourned by the coffin. Her other grandson, Jia Lian, was busy organizing the servants, with the help of Jia Rong and various male and female relatives. Ladies Xing and Wang, Li Wan, Xi-feng and Bao-chai were supposed to be chief mourners and therefore in constant attendance on the coffin. Strictly speaking, one of the other ladies had to be chosen to orchestrate the reception. There were three immediate possibilities: there was You-shi, who ever since Cousin Zhen's departure and her installation in Rong-guo House as a dependant had kept very much in the background, and was anyway unfamiliar with the workings of this side of the family; there was Jia Rong's new wife, who was even less confident of her abilities in this respect; and there was Xi-chun, who was still too young, and though she had grown up with the Rong-guo branch had remained totally ignorant of family practicalities. None of these was really a plausible candidate.

The only person for the job was Xi-feng. With Jia Lian in charge of the 'outside', it would make good sense for her to run the 'inside' and look after the lady guests. She had always had great confidence in herself in the past and had assumed that Grandmother Jia's funeral would be the culmination of her career, an opportunity for her to prove how indispensable she was. Ladies Xing and Wang remembered how well she had coped with Qin Ke-qing's funeral, and thought they could rely on her to repeat her success. When therefore they absolved her from her duties as a mourner and asked her to take over full responsibility as manageress once more, she could hardly refuse.

'After all,' she thought to herself, 'I've always been in charge here. The servants are used to taking orders from me. It was Lady Xing's servants and You-shi's who were hard to handle before, and they've all gone. It will be less convenient settling bills without tallies, but I shall have cash available from Grandmother's fund, so there should be no problem. It will help having Lian in charge of his side of the reception, too. Even though I'm not well, I think I should be able to

get by without discrediting myself. It's bound to be easier than Qin
Ke-qing's funeral.'

She waited until the morning after the Third Day, during which
ceremonies were held welcoming back the spirit of the deceased.
Then she told Zhou Rui's wife to summon a general assembly of the
staff and to bring the registers. When she scrutinized them, she
found that altogether there were only twenty-one men, nineteen
serving-women, and a dozen or so maids. It would not be enough.

'Why, we have fewer servants for Lady Jia's funeral than we had
for Qin Ke-qing's!' she thought to herself with dismay. Even after
calling in extra hands from the country estates, there would still be a
serious shortage.

She was turning this problem over in her mind when one of the
junior maids came in:

'Miss Faithful would like you to go over and see her, Mrs Lian.'

Somewhat reluctantly Xi-feng went over to Grandmother Jia's
apartment, where she found Faithful in floods of tears. The moment
she saw Xi-feng, she clutched hold of her and cried:

'Please be seated, Mrs Lian, and let me kowtow to you! I know
one shouldn't do such things during a period of mourning, but I
really *must*!'

Faithful fell to her knees, and Xi-feng held out her hands to
prevent her.

'Come on! What's the meaning of all this? If you've something on
your mind, then just go ahead and say it!'

Faithful insisted on kneeling, and Xi-feng continued her attempts
to pull her to her feet.

'Her Old Ladyship's funeral has been placed entirely in your hands
and Mr Lian's,' sobbed Faithful. 'Her Old Ladyship left a special
sum of money to pay for it. While she was alive, Her Old Ladyship
never wasted a penny on herself; now that the time has come for her
funeral, I beg you, ma'am, to do the right thing by her and give her a
proper send-off! Just now I heard the Master talking about it – "The
Book of Songs this", and "Confucius that" – I didn't understand a
word of what he said. I caught one sentence, though: "In funerals,
sincere grief is of more importance than outward show." I asked Mrs
Bao to explain what he meant, and she said that the Master wants to
keep the funeral a simple affair. He believes that heart-felt grief is the
truest form of devotion, and that there is no need for extravagant

display. But as I see it, for someone like Her Old Ladyship, things *ought* to be a bit grand. I know I'm only a servant, and have no right to speak in these matters, but I feel that Her Old Ladyship loved us both during her lifetime, ma'am, both you and me, and now that she's dead we *owe* it to her to send her off with a bit of style! I know how good you are at that sort of thing, ma'am, and I wanted to ask for your support, so that we could decide together what's best. I've been with Her Old Ladyship all my life, and death cannot part us! If I don't see this done properly, how am I ever to look her in the face again?'

Xi-feng found Faithful's way of talking rather odd.

'Don't you worry,' she replied. 'Of course everything will be done in proper style. Sir Zheng may talk of economy, but we have certain standards to maintain. We'll spend every penny of the money on Lady Jia, if need be.'

'Before she died,' said Faithful, 'Her Old Ladyship said that everything left over after the family distribution had been made was to be given to us. If there's not enough money for the funeral expenses, ma'am, then take our share of Her Old Ladyship's belongings and pawn them. Whatever the Master may say, he can hardly go against Her Old Ladyship's last wishes. He was here himself when she divided everything up.'

'You've always been such a sensible girl,' said Xi-feng. 'What's got into you today?'

'Nothing's got into me,' protested Faithful. 'I just know that Lady Xing doesn't care, and that the Master is being too cautious. It may be that you are of the same mind as the Master, ma'am. If you're afraid too, and think that a proper funeral will get us into trouble, then no one will dare to give Her Old Ladyship her due. That would be the most terrible thing! I'm only a maid, so of course it's no personal concern of mine. But think what a disgrace it would be for the family!'

'I hardly need reminding of that,' replied Xi-feng. 'Set your mind at rest. I shall take care of everything.'

Faithful once more entreated Xi-feng to do her utmost, and pledged her undying gratitude.

'What a strange creature!' thought Xi-feng to herself, as she left Grandmother Jia's apartment. 'I wonder what can be in her mind? Of course she's right: Grannie's funeral should be stylish. Oh dear! I can't pay too much attention to Faithful's complaints. I'd better just stick to the book and follow family precedent.'

She summoned Brightie's wife, and sent her with a message to Jia Lian, asking him to come and see her.

'What do you want me for?' he asked, when he arrived shortly afterwards. 'Just keep your end up on the "inside". There should be no problems. If you're in any doubt, stick to Uncle Zheng's instructions.'

'There you are,' said Xi-feng. 'What you say only bears out Faithful's fears.'

'What fears are they?'

Xi-feng repeated the substance of her interview with Faithful.

'Who cares what the maids say?' retorted Jia Lian. 'I've just been in to see Uncle Zheng, and this is what *he* said: "We'd like to lay on something grand for Mother's funeral, but although some people will understand that it's her money we're using, less well-informed observers may suspect us of secretly holding on to some of our own resources. They may think we still possess hidden wealth. Of course," Uncle Zheng went on to say to me, "if we don't spend all of Grandmother's money on the funeral, no one will want to appropriate what's left for their own personal use. In one way or another it should still be spent on Grandmother. Now she was a Southerner, and though we have ancestral burial-land in the South, there are no buildings on it. When her coffin has been transported to the South, with any money that's left over we can put up some buildings on the ancestral burial-ground, and buy a few hectares of land to provide for the sacrifices. If we ever return to the South ourselves, it will come in handy, and even if we don't, we can always let some of the poorer clan members live on it. They can keep up the seasonal offerings and sweep the graves at regular intervals." That was Uncle Zheng's proposal. Don't you think it a sound one? You're surely not suggesting that we spend the entire amount on the funeral, are you?'

'Has any of the money been issued yet?' asked Xi-feng.

'Not a penny of it,' replied Jia Lian. 'I heard that when Mother learned of this proposal of Uncle Zheng's, she sang its praises and did her utmost to encourage both him and Aunt Wang in their efforts to economize. So what can I do? I already have several hundred taels owing for the awning and the pall-bearers' fees, but the cash still hasn't been issued. If I go and ask for it, they'll all tell me the money's there but that I must get the work finished first and reckon up afterwards. There's no one we can borrow from: the servants with any money of their own have all disappeared. When I called a roll, some were "absent sick", others were "in the country", while the ones still here have stayed on only out of sheer necessity and are no use to us. They're interested only in making a profit for themselves.'

Xi-feng was lost in thought for a moment.

'How *are* we going to manage, then?' she said finally.

As she was speaking a maid came into the room:

'There's a message for you from Lady Xing, ma'am. Today is the third day of the ladies' reception, and the arrangements are still topsy-turvy. The guests should not have to be kept waiting for their food, after the funeral offering has been made! They had to ask for their meal several times before they were served. And even when the main dishes arrived, there was still no rice. Surely we can do better than that!'

Xi-feng hurried in to give the servants orders to serve lunch, and they managed to produce something passable. Unfortunately there was an unusually large crowd of guests that day and the staff were at their most sullen and apathetic. Xi-feng had to supervise them herself, then she hurried out and told Brightie's wife to call a general meeting of all the serving-women. She gave each one clear instructions, to which they replied with a surly, 'Yes, Mrs Lian,' and proceeded to do nothing during the afternoon.

'Look how late it is! Why haven't you served the evening offering and meal yet?' demanded Xi-feng.

'Serving the food would be no problem, ma'am,' came the reply, 'if we had the necessary utensils . . .'

'Fools!' exclaimed Xi-feng. 'This is your job! Of course you'll get whatever you need!'

The servants reluctantly applied themselves to their 'impossible' tasks, while Xi-feng went straight to the main apartment to seek Ladies Xing and Wang's permission for the necessary utensils. But there was still such a throng of guests around them that it was impossible for her to get a word in. Evening was drawing on, and in despair she went to see Faithful and asked her for the use of Grandmother Jia's spare dinner service.

'Why come asking *me* for it?' exclaimed Faithful. 'Mr Lian

pawned it a couple of years ago! You'd better ask him if he ever redeemed it.'

'I don't want the silver or gold,' said Xi-feng. 'The regular service will do.'

'What do you suppose Lady Xing and Mrs You have been using since they moved in?' asked Faithful pointedly.

Xi-feng knew she must be telling the truth, and left at once for Lady Wang's apartment, where she managed to talk Silver and Suncloud into lending her a service, had a quick inventory made by Sunshine, and told him to hand the things over to the servants.

Faithful saw Xi-feng in this state of disarray, and although she did not call her back to complain, she thought to herself:

'Why is Mrs Lian, who used to be so capable, bungling things so badly this time? The past couple of days have been a disgrace. It's poor gratitude for Her Old Ladyship's love!'

She was not aware that Lady Xing was deliberately starving Xi-feng of funds. Jia Zheng's views on economy coincided neatly with Lady Xing's own anxieties about the future, and she saw every tael saved on the funeral as a contribution not only to the family's reserves, but also to her own financial security. Her position in this was strengthened by the fact that strictly speaking it was Grandmother Jia's eldest son who should have been in charge of the funeral. Jia She was not at home, but Jia Zheng was an incorrigible stickler for convention, and whenever consulted would reply: 'Ask Lady Xing what she thinks.' Lady Xing considered Xi-feng extravagant and Jia Lian untrustworthy, and consequently held tightly on to every penny of the funeral funds. Faithful however took it for granted that the money for the funeral had already been issued, and ascribing the present crisis to a lack of zeal and loyalty on Xi-feng's part, she redoubled her wailing before the coffin of her dead mistress.

Lady Xing and Lady Wang knew only too well what Faithful was complaining about, but so far from acknowledging that the cause lay in their own refusal to equip Xi-feng properly for her task, they began criticizing Xi-feng out loud:

'Faithful is right: Feng is letting us down badly . . .'

In the evening, Lady Wang summoned Xi-feng and rebuked her:

'We may be living in somewhat straitened circumstances, but we must maintain our standards none the less. During the past two or three days I've noticed that the maids have not been looking after our guests properly. Clearly you have failed to give them adequate instructions. Please will you make more of an effort and show a little more family spirit.'

Xi-feng was speechless. She would have brought up the fact that she had not been issued with any money, but money was supposed to be Jia Lian's province, whereas Lady Wang was complaining about the 'inside' service. She dared not answer back.

'Strictly speaking,' said Lady Xing, who was standing to one side, 'your Aunt Wang and I, as Lady Jia's daughters-in-law, should be taking care of the reception, not a member of the junior generation; but we're very tied up with the mourning, and that is why we delegated the responsibility to you. You mustn't think you can be slack.'

Xi-feng blushed fiercely. She was about to say something in her own defence when she heard a drum begin outside: it was time for the dusk offering of paper money. A wail rose from the assembled mourners and her chance to speak had gone. She thought she would wait till later, but after the offering Lady Wang urged her to hurry about her duties.

'We can take care of things here. You go and see to it that everything is in order for tomorrow.'

Xi-feng did not dare utter a word, but went out, containing her chagrin and her tears as best she could. She called another meeting of the staff and reminded them once more of their duties:

'Ladies, dears, take pity on me I beg you! I am being blamed for everything by Their Ladyships, and it's all because you are not doing your jobs properly. You are making a laughing stock of us. I beseech you to make a special effort tomorrow.'

'But madam,' came the reply, 'this isn't the first time you've been in charge. You know us, we'd never dare disobey your orders. But this time the ladies are asking *too* much. Take this last meal: some wanted to eat here, others wanted to eat in their own rooms. We ask Lady So-and-so to come and take her meal, and then Mrs Somebody-else doesn't turn up . . . How can we possibly cope? We beg you, ma'am, to have a word with the maids and ask them not to be so fussy!'

'Her Old Ladyship's maids are very hard to please,' replied Xi-feng. 'And it's hard for me to give orders to Their Ladyships' maids. Who is there I *can* speak to?

'But Mrs Lian! When you managed the funeral for Ning-guo House, you had people beaten, you scolded them, you took a very strong line – and everyone obeyed you. Are you going to let your authority be challenged now by these *maids*?'

'On that occasion,' sighed Xi-feng. 'Their Ladyships were in no position to find fault with me. But this time it's not Ning-guo House; I'm on home territory, and open to public scrutiny. So everyone's finding fault with me. Besides, I'm not getting money when I ask for it from accounts. If something is needed at the reception, and I send out for it and nothing happens, what can I do?'

'But Mr Lian's in charge of that side of things. Surely he'll give you whatever money you need?'

'That's what *you* think!' replied Xi-feng. 'His hands are just as tied as mine. He has no control over the money. He has to ask for every penny himself. He's got no cash at all.'

'But isn't Her Old Ladyship's money his to use?'

'Ask the stewards,' said Xi-feng. 'They'll tell you.'

'No wonder the menservants outside are complaining! They keep saying what a big job it is, what hard work, and that there's no chance of making anything on the side. How can things possibly run smoothly when there's no money?'

'Enough talking,' said Xi-feng. 'All of you concentrate on your jobs and do them as best you can. If I hear any more complaints from Their Ladyships, I'll be after you.'

'We'll do whatever you tell us to do, ma'am, we'll not say a word. But with all their different ideas, it will be hard to satisfy every one of the ladies.'

Xi-feng implored them:

'My dears! Help me out tomorrow, please! Give me a chance to talk things over properly with the maids, and we'll discuss the matter again.'

The servants went about their business.

Xi-feng felt bitterly wronged, and the more she thought about the situation she was placed in, the more pent-up she became.

At first light, after a sleepless night, she had to report once more for duty to Ladies Xing and Wang. She would have liked to discipline the maids, but was afraid of arousing Lady Xing's resentment; she would have liked to confide in Lady Wang, but Lady Xing had already set Lady Wang against her. The maids, seeing that Their

Ladyships were not supporting Xi-feng, started to make life harder for her than ever. The only exception was Patience, who stood loyally by Xi-feng.

'Mrs Lian would like to do things properly,' she explained to the others, in an attempt to win them over. 'But Sir Zheng and Their Ladyships have given orders for strict economy to be observed, and there's nothing she can do about it.'

Buddhist sutras were read, Taoist masses were celebrated, there was an endless stream of ritual lamentations and sacrifices to the spirit of the departed; but somehow, in the prevailing climate of retrenchment, the mourners did not fully throw themselves into things, and the ritual had a rather perfunctory air about it. Each day saw the arrival of princely consorts and ladies of high rank, none of whom Xi-feng could receive in person as she was too busy trying to keep things going below-decks. She had no sooner mobilized one servant, when another was found to be missing; she lost her temper, she begged; she muddled through one session, and then had to cope with a fresh set of problems. By now Faithful was not the only one to see that things were awry. Even Xi-feng herself knew, to her great mortification, that the funeral reception was a shambles.

Though Lady Xing was wife of the elder son of the deceased, she was able to justify her own indifference towards the practical arrangements with the handy text: 'Grief is the Essence of Devotion.' Lady Wang followed suit, as did all the other ladies of the family – with the single exception of Li Wan. She saw the difficulties Xi-feng was having, and though she did not dare speak up on her behalf, she sighed to herself and thought:

'There's a popular saying: "The Peony owes much of its beauty to its leaves." Mother and Aunt Xing have always relied on Xi-feng; but how can she help them, when the servants no longer obey her? If Tan were at home, she could help. But as things are, even Xi-feng's own servants are running round in circles and muttering behind her back, complaining that there's no profit in it for them and that they're just making fools of themselves. Father is a great believer in filial piety; but he doesn't understand the practicalities. In something big like a funeral, you have to spend money if you want things done properly. Poor Feng! After all these years, who would have thought she would come to grief over Grandmother's funeral!'

When an opportunity presented itself, Li Wan spoke to her own servants:

'Now don't you go treating Mrs Lian disrespectfully just because everyone else is. Don't imagine it's enough for a funeral if people dress in mourning and keep the wake. Don't think a few days of muddling through like that will suffice. If you see the others in difficulties, you must lend a hand. This is a family concern. Everyone should do their best to help.'

Li Wan's trusted servants replied:

'You are quite right, ma'am. We wouldn't dream of going against Mrs Lian. But Faithful and the others seemed to be blaming her . . .'

'I've already spoken to Faithful,' said Li Wan. 'I've told her that it's not Mrs Lian's fault, Mrs Lian is doing all she can to give Her Old Ladyship a proper funeral. But she isn't getting the money. How can the cleverest daughter-in-law in the world make congee without rice? Faithful knows the truth now, and she doesn't hold Mrs Lian to blame any longer. Mind you, Faithful's behaving quite strangely, I must say, she's not at all her usual self. While Her Old Ladyship was still alive to love and protect her, she never put on airs, but now that Her Old Ladyship is dead and her support is gone, she seems to be acting in a most peculiar fashion. I felt sorry for her before. She should thank her lucky stars that Sir She is away from home, and that she's escaped *that* fate. If he were here, her future really would look grim.'

As she was speaking, Jia Lan came in.

'It's time you went to bed, Mama,' he said. 'The guests have been coming and going all day, and you must be worn out. It's time you had a rest. I haven't looked at my books at all these past few days. Today Grandmother said I can sleep at home. I'm so pleased, as it means I shall be able to do some work. Otherwise, by the time the mourning period is over, I shall have forgotten everything.'

'You're such a good boy!' said his mother. 'Of course you're right to study. But today you should rest too. Wait until the procession's over, then you can get down to your books again.'

'If you're going to sleep,' replied Jia Lan, 'I'll go to bed too, and do some revision in bed.'

The servants were loud in his praises:

'What a wonderful boy! So young, but so keen to make the most of the slightest opportunity to study! Not like his uncle. Mr Bao may be a married man, but he's still as childish as ever. To see him these last few days, kneeling down in there with Sir Zheng – so awkward and wretched, itching for Sir Zheng to get up so that *he* could dash off to find Mrs Bao and start whispering to her about goodness knows what. Mrs Bao wouldn't pay him any attention so he went and pestered Miss Bao-qin, and she avoided him, and Miss Xiu-yan wouldn't talk to him either, and in the end Miss Xi-luan and Miss Si-jie were the only ones who *would*. *They* hung on his every word. It seems Mr Bao still has only one interest in life: fooling about with the young ladies. There's not a shred of gratitude in him for the way Her Old Ladyship loved him all those years. He's not a patch on Master Lan! You certainly have no cause to worry for the future, Mrs Zhu!'

'He may be a good boy,' commented Li Wan, 'but he's still so young. By the time he's grown up, who knows what will have become of the family? Tell me, how has young Master Huan been behaving?'

'Oh, he's a regular disgrace!' replied one of the servants. 'A right little rascal, forever poking his nose into other people's affairs and sneaking around the place. Even when he is supposed to be mourning, the moment one of the young ladies arrives, he starts peeping out from behind the screens.'

'Huan's getting quite grown up now,' said Li Wan. 'The other day I heard something about his being engaged. But it had to be put off because of the funeral. Now, no more gossiping: in such a big family as ours, with so much going on, we'll never be able to set everything to rights. There was one other thing I wanted to ask you. Have carriages been arranged for the funeral procession the day after to-morrow?'

'Mrs Lian has been so busy these past few days,' came the reply. 'She's been in a terrible state. So far as we know, she hasn't given any instructions about carriages yet. Yesterday we heard one of the men saying that Mr Lian has put Mr Qiang in charge of that. Apparently we haven't enough carriages or drivers ourselves, and they're planning to borrow from relations.'

Li Wan smiled sadly:

'Are they sure our relations will agree to lend?'

'You must be joking, ma'am! Of course they'd lend us their carriages. The trouble is, they may all be using their own for the funeral, so it looks as if we may have to end up hiring all the same.'

'We can hire carriages for the servants. But will we be able to find decent white funeral carriages for Their Ladyships?' said Li Wan.

'Lady Xing and both Mrs You and Mrs Rong from Ning-guo House are all without carriages of their own. How are they going to come if we don't hire?'

Li Wan sighed.

'I remember the day when we thought it a joke to see one of our relatives riding in a hired carriage! Now they'll be laughing at us. Tomorrow you must tell your menfolk to make sure our carriages and horses are prepared well in advance. We don't want any last-minute panics.'

'Yes, ma'am.'

Li Wan's servants went about their business.

*

Our story now turns to Shi Xiang-yun. Earlier, because of her husband's illness, she had only been able to come once to mourn for Grandmother Jia. She calculated now that there were two days left before the funeral procession was due to set off; and since her husband's condition had been positively diagnosed as a consumption, and he was therefore in no immediate danger, she decided she must call once more. She came on the day before the final wake. She recalled all Grandmother Jia's love for her, and then her thoughts turned to her own fate, to have married such a fine husband, a man of such grace and talent, of such a gentle disposition, only to watch him being taken from her slowly and inexorably by an illness whose roots must surely lie in some previous lifetime. She wept with renewed grief for most of that night, despite the persistent efforts of Faithful and the other maids to console her.

Bao-yu was unbearably distressed by the sight of Xiang-yun's weeping, but could hardly go to comfort her in the midst of the ceremonial lamentations. The plain mourning-clothes she was wearing and the absence of any make-up seemed to make her even prettier than before her marriage. He looked round at Bao-qin and the other girls; they too were plainly dressed, with a minimum of ornamentation. The very simplicity lent a charm and grace to their appearance. His eyes rested on Bao-chai: how well mourning-clothes became her! She looked even more attractive than in her everyday attire.

'The men of old,' mused Bao-yu to himself, 'used to say that of all flowers none could rival the splendour of plum-blossom, not for its early blooming but for the incomparable purity of its whiteness, the unsurpassable freshness and delicacy of its scent. If only Cousin Lin were here now, and dressed in a simple mourning gown, how exquisitely beautiful *she* would look!'

He felt a pang of grief, tears rolled down his cheeks, and he began sobbing loudly and unrestrainedly. It was a funeral after all, and no one would think such behaviour out of place. The ladies were already busy rallying Xiang-yun when suddenly they heard another familiar voice break out wailing on the outside of the screen. They surmised that both cousins were overwhelmed by memories of Grandmother Jia's past love and kindness, and little guessed that Xiang-yun and Bao-yu each had private cause for grief. Their heart-felt lamentations soon brought tears to everyone's eyes, and it fell to Aunt Xue and old Mrs Li to offer comfort and counsel moderation.

The following day was the wake proper, and therefore busier than ever. Xi-feng was utterly exhausted, but there was nothing for it, she had to struggle on and muddle her way through the morning, even though she had by now lost her voice. By the afternoon, when the number of guests reached its peak and demands were being made on her from all quarters, she had reached breaking point and was searching in desperation for some second wind when a young maid came running in:

'*Here* you are, ma'am! No wonder Lady Xing is so cross! "So many guests," she said. "I can't possibly take care of them. Where's Mrs Lian? Hiding somewhere with her feet up, I'll be bound!" '

This unmerited rebuke provoked a sudden surge of indignation within Xi-feng. She struggled to control herself, but tears started to her eyes, and all went black before her. A sickly taste rose into her mouth and she began to vomit up quantities of bright red blood. The strength ebbed from her legs and she sank to the ground. Luckily Patience was at hand and hurried over to support her mistress as she crouched there, blood gushing from her mouth in an unstaunchable stream.

To learn if she survived this crisis or not, you must turn to the next chapter.

CHAPTER III

A devoted maid renders a final service, and accompanies
her mistress to the Great Void
A villainous slave takes his revenge, and betrays
his masters into the hands of thieves

Patience hurried forward, and with the help of another maid she
raised Xi-feng from the ground and gently escorted her to her room.
There she laid her down with great care on the kang and told Crimson
to bring a cup of hot water and hold it to her lips. Xi-feng drank a
sip of the water and then sank into a heavy sleep. Autumn came
briefly into the room, glanced at her lying there, and walked out
again. Patience did not ask her to stay, but turned instead to Felicity
who was standing at her side and said:

'Go and tell Their Ladyships at once.'

Felicity informed Ladies Xing and Wang that Xi-feng had vomited
blood and would be unable to continue with her duties. Lady Xing
suspected Xi-feng of malingering, but refrained from expressing her
suspicions in front of her female relatives.

'Tell Mrs Lian to go and lie down then,' she said.

No one made any further comment. That evening an endless stream
of family and friends came to call, and only thanks to the help of a
few close relations could a semblance of normality be maintained.
Xi-feng's absence was the cue for many of the staff to give up
working altogether, and little now stood between Rong-guo House
and total chaos.

At ten o'clock in the evening, when those guests who lived a long
way off had departed, the family began to prepare for the wake, and
a chorus of lamentation rose from the womenfolk gathered within
the funeral screen. Faithful wept herself into a faint, and had to be
propped up and given a vigorous pummelling. When she came round,
all she could say was:

'Her Old Ladyship was always so good to me! I want to go with
her!'

Her words were not taken seriously, but were considered a natural, if rather hyperbolic, expression of her grief. Later, when the time came for the wake proper, and over a hundred family and servants were gathered together for the ritual, Faithful was nowhere to be seen, and in the general flurry of activity no one bothered to check where she was. The turn came for Amber and Grandmother Jia's other maids to lament and make their offering, and they would have looked for Faithful then to join them, but thought she had probably worn herself out with weeping and gone to lie down somewhere, and decided to let her be.

When the ritual was over, Jia Zheng told Jia Lian to ensure that all was ready for the funeral cortège, and discussed with him who was to look after the house in the family's absence.

'I've told Yun to stay at home and take charge,' said Jia Lian. 'And Steward Lin and his family will stay behind as well and supervise the dismantling of the awning. I still don't know which of the ladies should be left in charge of the inner apartments.'

'I heard your mother say that Xi-feng was ill and wouldn't be going,' replied Jia Zheng. 'So she will be staying at home anyway. And Cousin Zhen's wife suggested that, as she is so seriously ill, Xi-feng should have Xi-chun and a few maids and serving-women to keep her company. Between them they can keep an eye on Grandmother's apartments.'

Jia Lian had his reservations about this proposal.

'You-shi doesn't like Xi-chun,' he thought to himself, 'and is deliberately preventing her from going on the procession. But Xi-chun can't take charge on her own. And Xi-feng is too sick to be of any help.'

'You should go and rest now, Uncle,' he said to Jia Zheng. 'I'll report back to you when I've had a word with Mother.'

Jia Zheng nodded, and Jia Lian went in to Lady Xing's apartment.

Earlier in the evening, Faithful had wandered off on her own, brooding tearfully to herself:

'All my life I've lived with Her Old Ladyship, and now that she's dead I've nowhere to turn. Sir She is not at home, that's something to be thankful for, but I don't like the way Lady Xing is behaving. Sir Zheng will never intervene on my behalf, and one way or another the future looks very bleak. The young masters will all be trying to get their way. We shall each of us be dealt with as they think fit, some kept for their beds, some married to their page-boys ... Well, I for one won't stand for it! I'd rather die! But *how*? That's the question ...'

She had made her way towards Grandmother Jia's inner room. From the threshold she detected a faint form in the dim lamplight within, a lady with a sash in her hand, poised as if in the very act of hanging herself from a beam. Faithful was not in the least frightened.

'Who can this be?' she asked herself. 'Someone bent on the same course as myself, but with greater resolve ...'

'Who are you?' she said aloud. 'We seem to have the same thought! Let us die together!'

There was no reply. Faithful walked a little closer and could see now that it was not one of the maids from Grandmother Jia's apartment. She looked more carefully. A chill breeze blew past her, and the lady's form vanished into thin air. Faithful stood there for a moment longer in a daze, then walked back into the outer room and sat down on the edge of the kang, lost in thought. Suddenly she exclaimed:

'Of course! That's who it was! Mr Rong's first wife, from Ningguo House. But she died long ago. What was she doing here? I suppose she must have come to fetch me. But why was she going through the motions of hanging herself?'

After a few moments' thought:

'That's it! She was showing me *how*!'

With this realization, the evil had entered the very marrow of her being, and her resolve was formed at last. She rose to her feet as if in a trance and went to her toilet box, opening it and weeping all the while. She took out the lock of hair that she had once cut from her head, and slipped it inside the bosom of her dress. She untied the sash from around her waist and looped one end of it over the beam where Qin Ke-qing had just stood. Then she gave herself up to one last fit of weeping. Hearing the guests leave in the distance, and fearing that someone might come in and surprise her before the deed was done, she quickly pulled the door to and fetched a footstool. Standing on the stool, she tied a slip-knot in the sash, put her head through the knot and kicked the stool away. Alas! The last breath was soon strangled from her throat, and her gentle soul fled its mortal frame.

The wandering soul was still uncertain whither to proceed when it saw once more the faint form of Qin Ke-qing standing before it. 'Mrs Rong!' it cried, advancing urgently towards the apparition. 'Wait for me!'

'I am not Mrs Rong,' came the reply. 'I am Disenchantment's younger sister, Ke-qing.'

'But you're most definitely Mrs Rong,' protested Faithful. 'How can you deny it?'

'Listen,' replied the other. 'I will tell you the true story of all this, and then you will surely understand. I once occupied the highest seat in Disenchantment's Tribunal of Love. My responsibility was the settlement of Debts of Passion. I went down into the human world, where naturally I was destined to become the world's foremost lover, my mission being to draw lovesick lads and lovelorn maidens with all speed back to the tribunal and the settlement of their debts. As part of this mission it was my Karma to hang myself. I have now seen through the illusion of mortal attachment, and have risen above the Sea of Passion to return to the Paradise of Love. This leaves a vacancy in the Land of Illusion, in the Department of Fond Infatuation. You have been chosen by Disenchantment to take my place, and I have been sent to guide you there.'

'But I am a most *un*passionate person!' protested Faithful. 'How can I be considered a lover?'

'You don't understand,' replied the other. 'Earthlings treat lust and love as one and the same thing. By this means they practise all manner of lechery and immorality, and pass it off as "harmless romance". They do not understand the true meaning of the word "love". Before the emotions of pleasure, anger, grief and joy stir within the human breast, there exists the "natural state" of love; the stirring of these emotions causes passion. *Our* kind of love, yours and mine, is the former, natural state. It is like a bud. Once open, it ceases to be true love.'

Faithful's soul signalled understanding with a nod, and followed Qin Ke-qing.

When the wake was over, Ladies Xing and Wang began giving instructions to those of the servants who were staying behind to look after the house, and Amber went in search of Faithful to ask her whether their carriages had been hired for the next day. She looked in vain in the outer room of Grandmother Jia's apartment, and then she noticed that the door to the inner room was on the latch, and putting her eye to the crack peered through into the half-lit interior. A flickering lamp filled the room with eerie shadows. No sound could be heard from inside and she retraced her steps, saying to herself:

'Where can the wretched girl have disappeared to?'

On her way out she bumped into Pearl.

'Have you seen Faithful?' she asked.

'No,' replied Pearl. 'I've been looking myself. Their Ladyships want to speak to her. Most probably she's fallen asleep in the inner room.'

'I've just had a look – she didn't *seem* to be there,' said Amber. 'The lamp needs trimming, and it's awfully dark and spooky inside. I didn't actually go inside. Shall we go in together and look properly?'

The two maids entered the room. First they trimmed the lamp.

'Who put this footstool here?' exclaimed Pearl. 'I nearly tripped over it.'

As she spoke she looked upwards and let out a horrified cry.

'*Aiyo!*' She fell back and collided with Amber, who looked up in turn, screamed and stood rooted to the spot. Their cries were soon heard, and other maids came running into the room. There were more shrieks of horror, and word was sent at once to Ladies Xing and Wang.

When Lady Wang and Bao-chai heard the news, they both burst into tears and set off to Grandmother Jia's apartment to see for themselves.

'I never thought Faithful had it in her to do this!' exclaimed Lady Xing. 'Send someone at once to inform Sir Zheng.'

Bao-yu stood dumbfounded, an expression of glazed horror in his eyes. Aroma and his other maids rallied him:

'Cry if you must, but don't bottle it up like this!'

Finally he managed to emit a piercing wail.

'What a rare girl Faithful was to choose such a death!' he had been thinking to himself. 'The purest essence of the universe is truly concentrated in her sex! She has found a fitting and noble death. We, Grandmother's own grandchildren, are despicable by comparison. We have shown ourselves less devoted than her maid.'

He found something strangely comforting in this thought, and by the time Bao-chai had come to his side to soothe his tears, he was smiling again.

'Oh dear!' cried Aroma. 'Mr Bao's going mad again!'

'It's nothing to worry about,' Bao-chai reassured her. 'No doubt he has his reasons.'

Bao-yu was pleased to hear Bao-chai say this.

'Perhaps she really *does* understand me,' he thought to himself. 'If so, she is the only one.'

He was drifting off into some other fantastic reverie when Jia Zheng arrived.

'Faithful is a commendable child!' exclaimed Jia Zheng with a sincere sigh of admiration. 'Lady Jia's love for her was not in vain!'

He turned to Jia Lian:

'Send someone to buy her a coffin, and lay her in it this very night. Tomorrow her remains can be conveyed together with Mother's, and her coffin can lie in state behind that of her mistress. In this way her noble act can be carried to a fitting conclusion.'

Jia Lian went out to execute these instructions, and gave orders for Faithful's body to be let down and laid out in Grandmother Jia's inner room.

When Patience heard the news of Faithful's suicide, she came with Oriole and a whole crowd of other maids and they all wept bitterly before Faithful's body. The occasion caused Nightingale to think of her own future and the precariousness of her present situation, and she regretted that she herself had not chosen Faithful's path and followed Dai-yu to the grave. By so doing she would at least have fulfilled her duty as a maid and died a noble death. In Bao-yu's apartment she was doing little more than marking time. Although he was very considerate and affectionate towards her, she knew that nothing would ever come of it. All these thoughts added a note of personal grief to her lamentations.

Lady Wang sent at once for Faithful's sister-in-law. She told her to supervise the encoffinment, and after consulting with Lady Xing, issued her an allowance of one hundred taels (from Grandmother Jia's fund). She also promised to sort out all Faithful's private effects and give them to her as soon as she had time. The sister-in-law kowtowed, and so far from exhibiting any signs of grief, seemed rather pleased.

'What wonderful courage Faithful showed!' she exclaimed. 'And what a lucky girl she is, to have won such glory, and such a splendid funeral into the bargain!'

One of the serving-women nearby rebuked her·

'That's quite enough from you! A hundred taels is a poor bargain for your own sister-in-law's life! Think how much *more* profit you'd have made out of her if you'd only managed to flog her earlier on to Sir She! Then you'd have had something to crow about!'

The words struck home, and Faithful's sister-in-law departed blushing. At the inner gate she met Steward Lin with a team of men carrying in the coffin and returned with them, helping them lay Faithful's corpse in the coffin, and herself putting on a show of mourning.

Since Faithful had died in the best Confucian tradition, 'out of devotion to her mistress', Jia Zheng sent for incense and himself lit three joss-sticks before her coffin.

'For her loyalty and devotion,' he said, having made a solemn bow, 'she deserves to be elevated above the rank of a mere maid. The younger generation must pay homage to her.'

Bao-yu's delight knew no bounds. He came forward and with almost exaggerated reverence performed a series of full-blown kowtows. Jia Lian also recalled Faithful's past kindnesses to him, and would have followed suit, but Lady Xing restrained him:

'One of the masters is quite enough. Too much of this might ruin her chances of being born again . . .'

Jia Lian desisted. But Bao-chai felt uneasy at Lady Xing's words. 'Strictly speaking, I shouldn't kowtow to her,' she said. 'But this is a special case. We are all of us too bound by our commitments to the living to give in to any extreme display of grief. But Faithful has acted for us. She has given the fullest expression to *our* devotion, and now we should ask her to continue serving Grandmother in the next world on our behalf. That would at least be a small token of our love!'

She walked forward on Oriole's arm and poured a libation of wine before Faithful's coffin, the tears streaming in profusion down her cheeks. When the libation was completed, she kowtowed several times in succession and sobbed emotionally. Some of the assembled company commented wryly that now Bao-yu and his wife were both demented; others protested that their conduct evinced a sincere grief; while some restricted themselves to observing that they had at least manifested a sense of what was right and proper. Jia Zheng, for his part, was pleased with them.

He had by now settled the caretaking arrangements, and it was agreed that Xi-feng and Xi-chun would stay behind, while all the other ladies would take part in the procession. No one slept a great deal that night.

At four in the morning, the cortège could be heard gathering outside, and by seven it was ready to move off, with Jia Zheng at the head, in full mourning attire and weeping profusely, as the rites demanded of a filial son. The street was lined with the funeral booths of countless families, which need not be described in detail here. At last they reached the Temple of the Iron Threshold and the coffins were set out, while the menfolk in mourning prepared to spend the night at the temple.

*

At home, Steward Lin supervised the dismantling of the funeral awning, carefully bolted the doors and put up the shutters on the windows, swept the courtyard and appointed wardens for the night-watch, to commence their duties that evening. It was a well-established rule at Rong-guo House that the innermost gate was closed at ten, and after that hour entrance to the inner apartments was strictly forbidden to males. Female domestics kept the watch inside. Xi-feng, despite a night's rest, had still not recovered from her attack, and although she seemed a little more composed, she was certainly not capable of getting about. Patience and Xi-chun therefore undertook a tour of inspection, and gave the women on night-watch their instructions before retiring to their separate apartments.

*

Our narrative turns at this point to Zhou Rui's foster-son, He San – who, it may be remembered, had been flogged and expelled from Rong-guo House by Cousin Zhen the previous year for fighting with his fellow-servant, Bao Er, and had since then spent most of his time in the gambling-dens. With Grandmother Jia's death, He San thought there might be a possibility of reinstatement, or at least a job of some kind in the offing for him, and he made enquiries at Rong-guo House several days in succession. Finally it became clear that he was engaged on a futile quest, and heaving many a disgruntled sigh he made his way back to one of his usual haunts, and slumped into a chair. His cronies noticed his depressed air and called out to him:

'San, old mate, why not have another fling? Who knows, your luck might turn.'

'I'd love to!' exclaimed He San bitterly. 'But I haven't a penny left to play with.'

'Come off it! After all the time you've been away at your old Pa Zhou's place? You must have fixed yourself up all right! Don't come the beggar on us!'

'That's what you think! Oh, they've got plenty – millions in fact – but they're keeping it all tucked away. They won't spend it. They'll hang on to it and hang on to it and in the end it will take a fire or a thief to make them let go!'

'You can't expect us to believe they're *that* rich, after what they had confiscated in that raid?'

'You don't realize,' replied He San. 'It was only what they couldn't hide that got taken. The old lady left behind a stash of her own when she died, and they won't part with a penny of it. It's all put away in her room. They're going to decide what to do with it after the funeral.'

These words seemed to make a particularly strong impression on one member of the company, who exclaimed after a few more throws of the dice:

'All I ever do is lose! I'll never break even. I'm off to bed.'

As he walked out, he took He San to one side and muttered:

'A word, old San.'

He San followed him out.

'I can't bear watching a clever fellow like you go skint, when there's no need . . .'

'It's my luck,' muttered He San. 'What can I do about it?'

'I thought just now you said Rong-guo House was stacked with money. Why not get some of it for yourself?'

'Wait a minute,' rejoined He San. 'It may be stacked with money, but that doesn't mean they'd give *us* a penny of it!'

The man laughed.

'Well, if they won't give it away, why don't we just help ourselves . . .'

He San began to catch his drift.

'And just how do you propose to do that?' he asked.

'Oh show some guts, man! Don't be so feeble!' was the reply. 'I'd have got my fingers on it long ago.'

'What sort of "guts" have *you* got then?'

The man's voice dropped to a whisper:

'If you want to make a lot of money out of this, all you have to do is show us the way in – I've got some friends in this line of business, first-class operators. They're just the ones for this job. And it so happens the Jias are all away at this funeral, and there's only a few women left at home. Mind you, a whole garrison of men wouldn't scare *my* friends . . . But maybe you're scared?'

'Me!' objected He San hotly. 'I'm not scared! Do you think I'm worried about old Zhou? Why, I only let him be my foster-dad because his missus asked me to. He's nothing. But it all sounds a bit dodgy to me. Could land us in a lot of trouble. The Jias have got connections with every yamen. Supposing we *do* manage to get the stuff out, it'll be hard to get rid of it.'

'This time you're in luck, old friend,' said the other. 'Some of my seafaring mates happen to be in the area at this very moment, waiting for a job like this to crop up. Once we've got our hands on the money, you and I would be wasting our time in these parts. We'd be far better off going to sea with my mates and spending our fortune there! Good idea, eh? Of course, if you can't bear the thought of parting from your old foster-mum, we'll just have to lug her along too. One big happy family, eh!'

'You're drunk!' exclaimed He San. 'You don't know what you're talking about. The whole idea's a crazy one.'

None the less, he took the man aside into an out-of-the-way alley, and the two of them stood there talking a while longer before going their separate ways. Our story must leave them for the time being.

*

We must return to Rong-guo House and to Bao Yong, the former Zhen family retainer now living with the Jias, who after a dressing-down from Jia Zheng had been demoted to caretaking duties in the Garden. In the general bustle of Grandmother Jia's funeral, no one thought of assigning him a task. He was unconcerned by this and continued to mind his own business, cooking for himself and leading a somewhat carefree and independent life. If he felt bored, he would take a nap, and on waking would practise with sword and stave in the Garden. On the day of Grandmother Jia's funeral procession, of which he was quite aware, although he had been given no part to play in it, he was taking a stroll in the Garden when he saw the figure of a nun accompanied by an old matron, making their way to the side gate, where they began knocking. He went up to them:

'Where would you be going, Reverend Mother?'

The old matron replied:

'We heard that Lady Jia's wake is over, and as we couldn't see Miss Xi-chun in the procession we thought she must have stayed at home. Sister thought she might be lonely and has come to call on her.'

'None of the family are at home,' said Bao Yong. 'I'm in charge of the Garden and I must ask you to return to your quarters. If you want to visit, please wait until they have come back from the procession.'

'And who do you think *you* are, you ruffian?' the matron protested indignantly. 'What business is it of yours *where* we go?'

'I don't like your type,' replied Bao Yong. 'I say you can't go, and that's final.'

'Why, this is downright mutiny!' the old matron retorted angrily and noisily. 'When Lady Jia was alive they never stopped us going anywhere. What kind of an upstart are you, to start throwing your weight around in this insolent manner? I don't care what you say, I *will* go out this way!'

She seized the door-knocker and struck it several times with all her might.

Adamantina was speechless with rage as she listened to this exchange. She was on the point of going home when the old women on the other side of the gate heard the sound of an argument and opened up to investigate. Deducing that Adamantina must have been offended by Bao Yong, and knowing that she was on intimate terms with the ladies of the house, especially Miss Xi-chun, the women feared that at some later date she might report them for not letting her through, and thereby get them into serious trouble. They hurried after her:

'We had no idea you were here, Your Reverence. Our apologies for being so slow in opening the gate. Miss Xi-chun is at home, and would be so pleased to see you. Please come on in. That stupid caretaker is new here. He doesn't know anything. We'll report him later to Her Ladyship and she'll have him beaten and get rid of him.'

At first Adamantina refused to change her mind. But the old

women kept on pestering her, begged her not to get them into trouble, were on the point of falling to their knees, until in the end she really had no choice but to turn back and follow them into the mansion. Bao Yong, seeing how things stood, understandably made no further attempts at obstruction but went back to his room, scowling and fuming to himself.

Adamantina went straight to Xi-chun's apartment. She offered her condolences and they chatted for a while.

'I still have a few more nights to last out before the others come home,' said Xi-chun. 'Xi-feng is sick, and I'm all on my own. It's so boring and lonely – and scaring! If only I had someone to keep me company! Now that you've come all this way, won't you stay the night? Please! We could play Go together and chat.'

At first Adamantina was reluctant. But she felt sorry for Xi-chun, and then at the mention of the game Go her eyes lit up and she agreed to stay, instructing the matron to return to the Hermitage and send one of the novices with her tea things, her clothes and her bedding. Xi-chun was delighted and for her part instructed Landscape to go and fetch some of the supply of the previous year's rainwater, which had been stored and put aside for making tea. She made a point of saying that Adamantina would not be needing a cup, as she had her own set. The novice presently arrived with Adamantina's things, Xi-chun made the tea, and the two of them were soon carried away in a spirited conversation that lasted until eight o'clock in the evening, when Landscape laid out the Go-board, and they settled down to play. Xi-chun lost the first two games, but then Adamantina gave her a handicap of four and she managed to win the next by half a point.

Before they knew, it was two o'clock in the morning. Outside, the night was breathlessly still.

'I must meditate at four,' said Adamantina. 'You go in now and rest. My own girl can wait on me.'

Xi-chun was reluctant to go, but complied out of respect for Adamantina's religious practice. She was about to go into her bedroom when suddenly she heard a great cry coming from the women on night-watch in Grandmother Jia's apartment, which was soon taken up by her own serving-women:

'Help! Help! Someone has broken in!'

Xi-chun, Landscape and the other maids were scared out of their wits. Next they heard shouting coming from the men on night-duty in the outer apartments.

'Dear oh dear!' exclaimed Adamantina. 'There must be burglars in the house!'

She hurriedly closed the door of the room and covered her lamp. Peeping through a hole in the window, she could see several men standing in the courtyard outside. Speechless at first with terror, she turned and crept quietly back into the room, gesturing with her hands and finally saying to the others:

'Heaven save us! What great burly fellows there are out there!'

As she spoke, there was a clatter on the roof-top above her head and she heard the night-watchmen bursting into the courtyard with cries of 'Stop thief!'

'Everything has been taken from Lady Jia's apartment! We must find the thief!' called one of them. 'The others have already gone to the east wing. We'll search the west.'

One of Xi-chun's old women, hearing familiar voices, called out from inside:

'Some of them have climbed up on our roof!'

'Look!' cried the night-watchmen. 'There they are! Up there!'

A confused hubbub ensued, several tiles came hurtling down from the roof, and none of the watchmen had the courage to climb in pursuit. They were all standing there rather helplessly when a fresh burst of noise came from the direction of the side gate to the Garden, followed by the sound of the gate itself being broken down, and in stormed a great hefty fellow with a wooden club in his hand. They all tried to hide, without any success.

'We must stop them all, every one of them!' bellowed the new arrival. 'Follow me!'

They stood there paralysed with fear, while the club-wielding man continued to harangue them. One of the more perspicacious among them finally identified him as Bao Yong, and gradually the others regained their nerve and began saying shakily:

'One of the thieves managed to escape altogether! But some of them are still up on the roof.'

The instant Bao Yong heard this, he vaulted up onto the roof and went in hot pursuit.

After the main part of their mission was accomplished, the thieves, knowing how unprotected the Jia mansion was, had been casually snooping around in Xi-chun's courtyard, and had caught a glimpse there of a very attractive young nun, which had put all sorts of mischievous ideas into their heads. They knew that the apartment was unguarded save by a handful of scared old women, and were about to kick the door in and put an abrupt end to Adamantina's meditations when they heard the sound of footsteps coming from outside and escaped onto the roof-top. They soon saw that they outnumbered their pursuers and had decided to fight it out when a man leapt up onto the roof and came after them.

He was on his own and they therefore moved into the attack with short swords, only to find themselves quickly outmatched. With a few powerful and deftly placed strokes of his club, Bao Yong had soon despatched one of them off the roof, while the rest fled over the wall into the Garden, where others of the gang had been stationed to receive the stolen goods. These now drew their swords in defence of the returning party, and seeing there was only one man following them, they closed in on him.

'Petty thieves!' stormed Bao Yong. 'Do you dare to do battle with me?'

'They knocked one of us down!' exclaimed one of the gang. 'He may not even be alive, but we'd better try to get him out!'

Bao Yong moved into the attack, and four or five of the thieves formed a ring around him, brandishing their swords in a confused mêlée, which finally broke up when some of the night-watchmen plucked up enough courage to come to Bao Yong's aid, and the outnumbered thieves made good their escape. Bao Yong, still in hot pursuit, tripped over some unseen obstacle lying on the roof, and when he clambered to his feet and saw that it was a chest, he deduced that the thieves had failed to take their loot with them, and therefore abandoned his pursuit. They must anyway be well ahead and beyond reach by now, he reflected. He told the servants to fetch lights. On closer inspection he discovered that there were several chests and that they were all empty. He gave orders for them to be removed and himself headed back to the main apartment. His lack of familiarity with the lay-out of the mansion caused him to wander into Xi-feng's apartment, where all the lights were ablaze.

'Have the thieves been here?' he asked.

'We haven't opened the doors,' came Patience's trembling voice from within. 'But we heard cries from the main apartments – you'd better go there.'

Bao Yong had no sense of direction, but he saw the other watchmen in the distance and followed them to the main apartment, where he found doors and windows thrown open and the women on night-duty sobbing.

Presently Jia Yun and Steward Lin arrived, appalled by the news of the burglary. They found Grandmother Jia's door wide open and could see by the lamplight that the lock had been wrenched open and the chests and cupboards inside had all been broken apart. There were curses for the women on night-duty:

'Are you all half-dead? Didn't you even know there were thieves in the house?'

'There's a roster for night-duty,' came the tearful reply, 'and we're on second and third watches. We never stopped on our rounds, we checked front and back. The thieves came during the fourth and fifth watches, just after we finished duty. We heard the shouting, but couldn't see anyone, and when we came to look, the things had already gone. Please, sirs, question the fourth and fifth watch, not us!'

'You deserve to die, the lot of you!' exclaimed Steward Lin. 'I'll talk to you later. First I must inspect the rest of the house.'

The night-watchmen led him to You-shi's apartment, which was securely closed. They heard voices crying from within:

'We nearly died of fright!'

'Has anything been taken from here?' asked Lin. The women finally opened the door.

'No, we've had nothing stolen.'

Next Lin led his men to Xi-chun's, where again they heard voices inside:

'Lord save us! Miss Xi-chun's died of fright! *Please* wake up, miss!'

Lin told them to open up, and asked them what had happened. An old woman appeared in the doorway:

'The thieves were fighting in our courtyard, and Miss Xi-chun was terribly frightened. Luckily Sister Adamantina and Miss Land-scape have brought her round. We've had nothing stolen.'

'What do you mean – fighting?' asked Lin.

One of the watchmen replied.

'It was young Bao Yong who saved the day, sir. He climbed onto the roof and chased them away. And I heard one got knocked down.'

'Yes,' put in Bao Yong. 'The body's over by the Garden gate. You'd better hurry over there and have a look.'

Jia Yun and company went to the Garden gate, and sure enough there lying on the ground was the dead body of a man, which on closer inspection was found to resemble very closely Zhou Rui's adopted son He San. They were all greatly taken aback by this discovery. One man was left to stand guard over the body and two were sent to keep a watch on the front and rear Garden gates, which were both found to have their locks intact. Lin now gave orders to open the main gate and to report the burglary to the police.

The police arrived straight away and began their investigation. The thieves, they concluded, had climbed up onto the roof-top from a back alley and had made their way across to Grandmother Jia's apartment, where broken tiles were found and more tracks leading straight to the Garden at the rear.

'They were armed!' cried all the servants on night-duty.

The police officer seemed somewhat put out by this:

'There is no evidence of torches or anything that would point to armed robbery. What grounds have you for this accusation?'

'When we chased them, they started throwing tiles at us from the roof and we couldn't get near them. But our Bao Yong managed to climb onto the roof, and he went after them and chased them as far as the Garden, where a whole lot more of them were waiting and put up a fight. But when they found they couldn't beat our Bao Yong, they fled!'

'You see,' exclaimed the officer. 'If they were really armed robbers, they would surely have been able to overpower a single opponent. Anyway, enough of that. Find out exactly what's been taken and provide us with an inventory. Then we can make a proper report on the matter.'

Jia Yun and the other men now went to the main apartment, where they found Xi-chun, and with her Xi-feng, who had dragged herself there despite her illness. Jia Yun enquired after Xi-feng's health, and greeted Xi-chun, and then they all set about the un-enviable task of determining what was missing. With Faithful dead, and Amber and the other maids away at the funeral, no one knew where to start. The stolen things were all Lady Jia's personal belongings and had always been kept stored away under lock and key. They had never been properly inventoried.

'The chests and cupboards were full of so many different things,' they said. 'And now they're all empty. The thieves must have had ample time to do their work. What were the women on night-duty doing, for heaven's sake? Since the dead body was He San's, and since he is the adopted son of the Zhous, they were probably all in on it together.'

Xi-feng was livid with rage when she heard this.

'Tie up all the women concerned,' she ordered, 'and hand them over to the police for questioning.'

There was a general outcry, pleas for mercy, women down on their knees begging. To learn what was done with them, and whether or not any of the stolen goods were found, please turn to the next chapter.

CHAPTER 112

Adamantina discharges a karmic debt and receives a blow
from the Hand of Providence
Aunt Zhao concludes a deadly feud and sets out
on the road to the Nether World

The women on night-duty went down on their knees and begged Xi-feng to spare them, but Steward Lin and Jia Yun told them they were wasting their breath:

'The Master left us to mind the house, and now that things have gone wrong, we must all take our share of the blame. You needn't think anyone's going to bale *you* out. If Zhou Rui's adopted son is involved, then everyone – from Her Ladyship downwards – men and women, masters and servants, is under suspicion.'

'Fate has brought this on us,' said Xi-feng, struggling for breath. 'Why waste words? Just take them away. As for the stolen things, you must be sure to tell the police that they all belonged to Her Old Ladyship. Only the masters know the details. When we've sent word to them and they come home, then of course we can make out a list and hand it in to the police. The same statement must be made to the civil authorities.'

'Yes, ma'am.' Jia Yun and Steward Lin went out to execute these instructions.

Xi-chun had said nothing throughout this, but now she began to whimper: 'I've never heard of anything so terrible in all my life! Why did it have to be *us*? When Uncle Zheng and Aunt Wang come home, how am I to face them? They'll say they left the house in our hands, they'll blame us for this disaster. I shall die of shame!'

Xi-feng: 'It's not our doing. The women on night-duty must take the blame.'

Xi-chun: 'It's all very well for you to say that. You were ill anyway. But I've got no excuse! It's exactly what my sister-in-law planned! She *wanted* me to come to grief! She deliberately talked Aunt Xing into giving me this responsibility. Now I'm quite disgraced!' She broke down, sobbing violently.

Xi-feng: 'You mustn't take it like that. We are all in disgrace. If you adopt such a silly attitude, how am *I* to hold my head up?'

As they were speaking they heard a man's voice shouting in the courtyard:

'I said we should have no truck with such women. They're witches and whores the lot of them! The Zhen family never allowed people like that in the house, and I didn't expect things to be so lax here! Her Old Ladyship's funeral procession was hardly through the front entrance yesterday when that nun from that Hermitage place came pestering to be let in. I told her straight out that she couldn't, but then the old women on the side gate turned round and gave *me* some cheek, and begged her to come in. So some of the time the side gate was closed, some of the time it was open – who could tell what was going on! I lay awake worrying about it till two in the morning, and then I heard shouts coming from the house here. So I called at the gate, but they wouldn't open up, and as the shouting was getting worse I broke the gate down and came in. I saw some men in the west courtyard, chased them and killed one of them. I only found out today that the place I was in was the courtyard of Miss Xi-chun's apartment. So the nun was there with her at the very time the burglary took place. She slipped out this morning before dawn. *She* must have been the one who let the burglars in. She's the traitor in our midst!'

'Who is that insolent fellow?' asked Patience. 'How dare he use such language with Mrs Lian and Miss Xi-chun here inside?'

'He mentioned the Zhen family,' said Xi-feng. 'It must be that vile servant they palmed off on us.'

Xi-chun had heard and understood Bao Yong only too clearly, and felt more wretched than ever as a consequence.

'Wasn't there something about a nun in his babblings?' Xi-feng continued, turning to Xi-chun. 'How did you come to have a nun staying with you? Where did she spring from?'

Xi-chun told her that Adamantina had visited her, and that she had stayed on to play Go and keep her company during the night.

'Oh, Adamantina!' exclaimed Xi-feng. 'How could she possibly have betrayed us! What a ridiculous idea! But still, it would be most unfortunate if this loathsome creature's accusations ever reached Sir Zheng's ears.'

The more Xi-chun thought about the possible consequences for Adamantina the more distressed she became. She rose to leave, but Xi-feng, though anxious herself to return to her own apartment, feared that Xi-chun might do something rash in her present state, and asked her to wait a little.

'Before we go, we must make sure they have sorted what's left of Grandmother's belongings; and we must set a watch.'

Patience: 'But nothing can be sorted before the authorities carry out their inspection. Till then we should leave everything as it is. Has anyone been sent to inform Sir Zheng?'

Xi-feng: 'You'd better send one of the serving-women to find out.'

Presently the reply came back:

'Steward Lin can't go himself. Most of the servants are needed to be in attendance for the inspection, and those that can be spared are incapable of explaining things clearly to the Master. So Young Master Yun has already gone.'

Xi-feng nodded, and sat down anxiously with Xi-chun to wait.

*

The gang, who had been brought together by He San and his friend for the express purpose of burgling Rong-guo House, succeeded in laying their hands on a fair amount of gold, silver and valuables and had already passed it out before they were discovered. Even then they were able to see at a glance that their pursuers were nothing to be afraid of, and therefore moved on to the west courtyard to investigate possibilities for burglary there. Through the window they spied two very attractive young ladies sitting together in the lamplight, one of whom was dressed in a nun's habit. Their baser instincts were immediately aroused, and they would have burst recklessly in had they not a moment later seen the figure of Bao Yong coming in hot pursuit. They then made a quick getaway, leaving the unfortunate He San behind to the fate we have already described, and reassembled afterwards in secret with their 'fence'. The next day they learned that He San had been stopped and killed, and that the police and civil authorities had been alerted. It was no longer safe for them in town, and after some discussion they decided to make their way back without delay to their headquarters on the coast and rejoin their pirate friends. A general warrant for their arrest would soon be issued, after which it would be impossible for them to pass through the inspection posts.

There was however one especially brazen character among them.

'It's all very well saying we ought to leave town,' he said. 'But I've still got my eye on that little nun. Beautiful little piece of work! I wonder which convent she's from, the luscious thing!'

'*Aiyo*!' exclaimed one of the others. 'I've just remembered. She must be that nun who lives right on the premises, in Prospect Garden, in that place they call Green Bower Hermitage. Wasn't there a story going round a year or two ago about her and their Master Bao? She fell head over heels in love with him and in the end they had to call in the doctor. She must be the one!'

'In that case,' said the first, 'let's lie low tonight and give the skipper time to buy the gear we need to pass as travelling merchants. Tomorrow at dawn bell you can start leaving town at intervals and wait for me at Seven Mile Bank.'

It was settled. They shared out the spoils and went their separate ways.

*

When Jia Zheng and the rest of the cortège had conveyed the coffins of Lady Jia and Faithful to the temple and had formally deposited them there until such time as they could be placed in a permanent grave, the various relatives and friends who had accompanied them took their leave. Jia Zheng installed himself in one of the outer wings of the temple as his 'mourning quarters', while the ladies stayed in the inner room where the coffins had been placed. There was continuous lamentation throughout the night.

The next morning they began the funeral offerings once more, and were in the act of setting out the sacrificial dishes when Jia Yun burst in. First he kowtowed before Grandmother Jia's coffin, then he hurried over to Jia Zheng, dropped one knee to the ground and proceeded to give a breathless account of the previous night's burglary and the loss of Grandmother Jia's belongings. He described how Bao Yong had given chase and had killed one of the robbers, and concluded by saying that the facts had already been laid before the police and civil authorities. Jia Zheng listened to all this aghast, while the ladies, who overheard with horror from the inner room, were also too shocked to speak and could only sob loudly. Eventually Jia Zheng composed himself sufficiently to ask:

'What sort of an inventory has been made of the stolen items?'

Jia Yun: 'None of the servants knew what was there, so the inventory has not been made yet.'

Jia Zheng: 'A good thing too. After the confiscation, if we were to include things of value in the inventory, we'd be guilty of a further infringement of the law. Tell Lian to come here at once.'

Jia Lian had gone with Bao-yu and some of the other young male Jias to make offerings in a different part of the temple, and hurried back on receiving Jia Zheng's summons. The news put him in a state of extreme agitation, and in front of Jia Zheng he began cursing and swearing at Jia Yun:

'Miserable wretch! I entrust you with an important responsibility, and expect you to organize the night-watch properly, and look what you have gone and done! Are you half-dead or something? I'm amazed you have the nerve to come here at all!'

He spat in his face. Jia Yun stood there with his hands hanging at his sides, not daring to breathe a word.

Jia Zheng (to Jia Lian): 'Swearing at him won't achieve anything.'

Jia Lian (falling to his knees): 'What are we to do?'

Jia Zheng: 'There's nothing we *can* do, except wait and hope that the authorities apprehend the thieves. The trouble is we never opened any of Grandmother's boxes. When you came to me for money, I thought it improper to start taking her silver when she'd only been dead a few days. I decided to wait until after the funeral and to settle all our accounts at once and invest any surplus in trust-estates here and in the South. So we don't even know exactly what she had left. Now the police want an inventory, and we can hardly include anything of value on it; but at the same time we'll never get away with "sundry quantities of gold and silver and various items of clothing and jewellery". Come on, what are you still kneeling down there for, you useless creature!'

Jia Lian did not dare say a word, but rose to his feet and began walking out of the room.

Jia Zheng: 'Where are you off to now?'

Jia Lian retraced his steps.

'I thought I should go home at once and try to sort this out properly.'

There was a 'hm' from Jia Zheng (signifying, 'I should think so too'), and Jia Lian hung his head abjectly.

Jia Zheng: 'Report first to your mother. When you go home, take one or two of Grandmother's maids with you. Tell them to think carefully, and produce something in the way of an inventory . . .'

Jia Lian knew that Faithful had been in charge of all Grandmother Jia's personal effects, and that now she was dead it would be useless to ask Pearl or the other maids to remember. But he hadn't the nerve to contradict Jia Zheng, and responding docilely to his instructions, he went to the inner room, where he had to endure the reproaches of Ladies Xing and Wang, and was then ordered to hurry home and bid the women on night-duty prepare themselves for their mistresses' wrath. Assuring his mother and aunt with a somewhat ill grace that he would do as they commanded, Jia Lian went out and ordered one of his men to hire a carriage for Amber and Grandmother Jia's other maids, while he himself mounted a mule and hastened home with a few of his pages. Jia Yun had no stomach for further confrontations with Jia Zheng, and he sneaked out in a sort of sideways slither, mounted horse and caught up with Jia Lian. Their ride into town passed uneventfully.

Jia Lian was greeted at Rong-guo House by Steward Lin, who led him into Grandmother Jia's apartment, where they found Xi-feng and Xi-chun waiting. Seething as he was with bitterness towards them both, Jia Lian restrained himself and turned to ask Lin:

'Have the authorities had a look yet?'

Lin (kneeling guiltily): 'Both the police and the civil authorities have made an inspection, sir. They discovered the burglars' tracks, and examined the corpse.'

Jia Lian (with considerable surprise): 'What corpse?'

Steward Lin told him how Bao Yong had killed one of the burglars, and that the dead man showed a strong resemblance to Zhou Rui's adopted son.

Jia Lian: 'Send for Jia Yun!'

When Jia Yun came in, he too fell to his knees before Jia Lian.

Jia Lian: 'Why didn't you tell Uncle Zheng about this, that one of the burglars was Zhou Rui's adopted son, and that he had been killed by Bao Yong?'

Jia Yun: 'The men on night-duty only said that it *looked* like him. I was afraid they might turn out to be wrong, so I didn't mention it.'

Jia Lian: 'Idiot! If you'd told me, I could have brought Zhou Rui with me to identify the corpse. That would have settled any doubt.'

Lin: 'The authorities have taken the corpse away and exhibited it in the market-place for identification.'

Jia Lian: 'That's pretty damned foolish of them! As if anyone would come forward for a man that's been killed escaping from a burglary!'

Lin: 'There's no need for identification anyway, sir. I recognized the man myself.'

Jia Lian pondered for a minute.

'Of course! Wasn't it Zhou Rui's adopted son that Mr Zhen wanted to have flogged a year or so ago?'

Lin: 'That's right, sir. He was caught fighting with Bao Er. You must have seen him at the time.'

Jia Lian was made angrier still by this revelation, and wanted to beat the man on night-duty, but Steward Lin pleaded with him to abate his wrath.

'They had their orders, sir, and I'm sure they did their duty. But it is a strict family regulation that men are not allowed beyond the inner gate. Even we are not allowed in unless expressly sent for. Master Yun and I did our rounds regularly in the outer apartments; the inner gate was firmly closed, and none of the outer gates was left open. The burglars broke in from a back alley.'

Jia Lian: 'Where are the women who were supposed to be on night-duty in the inner apartments?'

Lin informed him that on Xi-feng's instructions the women had all been detained and bound, and were waiting to be interrogated.

Jia Lian: 'And Bao Yong?'

Lin: 'He has gone back to the Garden.'

Jia Lian: 'Send for him.'

The pages went to fetch Bao Yong, and when he arrived Jia Lian praised him for his conduct:

'It's a good job you were here! Otherwise I dare say everything in the house would have been taken!'

Bao Yong said nothing. Xi-chun was terrified that he was going to open his mouth and start abusing Adamantina. Xi-feng maintained an apprehensive silence.

It was reported meanwhile that Amber and the other maids had arrived from the temple, and they entered and amid much weeping exchanged greetings with the rest of the household. On Jia Lian's orders the servants searched Grandmother Jia's apartment to see what if anything the burglars had left behind, and found nothing but clothes, a few lengths of fabric and some caskets of copper cash. Jia Lian was now more distraught than ever. The men working on the awning and the pall-bearers had not been paid, nor had the extra kitchen expenses for the funeral reception been met. Where was he to find the money now? He brooded morosely, while Amber and the other maids went into Grandmother Jia's inner rooms and broke into a renewed fit of sobbing as they surveyed the havoc. The boxes and cupboards were all flung open, and how could they possibly remember what had been in them? However, they eventually managed to concoct a list of sorts, which they handed to a servant to deliver to the authorities. Jia Lian issued instructions for that night's watch, and Xi-feng and Xi-chun went back to their rooms. Jia Lian thought it best not to spend the night at home, and did not even find time to reproach Xi-feng for her part in the affair. As soon as he could get away he mounted horse and galloped back to the temple. Xi-feng was still anxious that Xi-chun might be contemplating suicide, and sent Felicity over to comfort her.

*

At ten o'clock that night the gates were firmly barred – a somewhat superfluous precaution by now – and everyone lay in bed in a state of nervous wakefulness. But our narrative leaves Rong-guo House and returns to the nun-besotted burglar. He knew that the Hermitage occupied an isolated location in the Garden, and that the nun's only companions there were a few old matrons and novices, who would present no obstacle. He made his plans accordingly. At midnight, when all was quiet, equipped with a knife and a supply of potent narcotic incense, he scaled the Garden wall, and from his vantage point there he could see in the distance lamps burning in the Hermitage. He crept stealthily across and hid himself in an out-of-the-way corner.

By two o'clock, there was only a single night-light still burning. Adamantina was sitting cross-legged on her mat. She took a short break from her meditations, and after several gusty sighs reflected aloud to herself:

'When I came to the capital from my old home on Mount Xuanmu, I had hoped to make a name for myself. But then when the Jias invited me to stay here, I could hardly decline their invitation. And now I can't even do something as simple and innocent as paying a visit to Xi-chun without being heaped with abuse by some coarse creature. And later in the night I had such a fright! How nervous I've been all day, ever since my return. I simply can't settle down properly and meditate.'

She usually meditated alone, and even today had not asked the others to stay up with her. But suddenly at four o'clock she began to tremble with cold and was about to call out to one of her women when she heard a sound through the window. She thought immediately of what had happened the previous evening and gave a terrified cry for help! But it brought no answer. From where she sat she could detect a strange smell seeping right into her head, and she felt her limbs becoming gradually numb and incapable of movement, her mouth incapable of speech. Panic began to grip her. Helplessly she watched as a stranger entered her room, a man, with a knife glistening in his hand. Though she was paralysed, her mind was still clear, and thinking that she was about to be murdered she steeled herself mentally to her fate and found herself surprisingly free of fear. Then to her amazement the man slipped the knife back into the scabbard slung over his shoulder, came towards her and put both his arms softly round her. He fondled her briefly, then hoisted her up onto his back. By now Adamantina was too groggy to understand what was happening to her. The drugs had sent her into a profound stupor, and she surrendered her virginal body into the stranger's hands, to do with as he pleased.

With Adamantina on his back, the man made his way to the Garden wall, which he scaled with a rope-ladder, climbing down to where some of his accomplices were waiting with the getaway cart. They bundled her in and set off. The impressive-looking official titles inscribed on the carriage lanterns enabled them to pass through the district barricades, and by the time they reached the city gate it was opening time and the gatekeeper did not even bother to ask any questions, thinking they were on official business. Once out of the city, they pressed on to Seven Mile Bank, where they joined the rest of the gang and agreed to make their ways separately to the South coast.

It is not known what eventually became of Adamantina: whether she submitted willingly to her captor's desires, or whether she resisted and died in so doing. In the absence of conclusive evidence as to her ultimate fate, it would be futile for us to speculate on that subject. Instead, our narrative returns to the Hermitage. One of the old nuns who had her quarters to the rear of Adamantina's meditation chamber slept that night until four in the morning, when she was awakened by the sound of voices from the front room. Adamantina must be having a restless spell in her meditations, she concluded. But then afterwards she heard heavy (and unmistakably male) footsteps and the sound of doors and windows opening and closing. She would have risen to investigate, but her limbs had become quite weak and she could not so much as open her mouth to speak. No further sound came from Adamantina's room, and the old nun lay there till dawn in a stupor, with her eyes wide open. It was only then that her head began to clear; she threw on some clothes and told the old matrons to heat the water for Adamantina's morning tea. Then she went to the front room, but to her alarm found no trace of Adamantina, and door and windows open wide. She began to have suspicions about the sounds she had heard in the night.

'Where could she have gone so early in the morning?' she asked aloud.

Walking out into the Garden, she saw a rope-ladder hanging from the wall, and lying on the ground beneath it a scabbard and sash.

'Oh my goodness! It must have been a burglar last night! He must have put us all to sleep!'

She called the others to rise and make a search of the Hermitage. The main gate was still firmly closed.

'Oh dear, the fumes from the stove were terrible last night!' grumbled the old matrons and young novices alike when they were summoned. 'None of us felt like getting up this morning. What do you want us for at this ungodly hour?'

'Sister Adamantina has disappeared!' exclaimed the nun.

'She's probably in Our Lady Guan-yin's chapel meditating.'

'You're all still dreaming! Come and have a look.'

The women finally roused themselves in a flurry of alarm, opened the main gate of the Hermitage and searched throughout the Garden. Then it occurred to them that Adamantina might have gone to visit Xi-chun, and they went in a body to knock at the side gate, only to receive another round of abuse from Bao Yong.

'We don't know where Sister Adamantina went last night,' they said. 'We're looking for her. Open up, old fellow, and let us into the house. We just want to find out if she's been visiting there or not.'

'She was the one who let the burglars in!' cried Bao Yong. 'Now they've got what they came for, and she's gone off with them to enjoy it!'

'Holy name!' exclaimed one of the women. 'You'll have your tongue cut out in hell for such wicked talk!'

Bao Yong (vehemently): 'Rubbish! Any more trouble from you and I'll have to use force.'

Women (smiling obsequiously now and pleading): 'Please sir, we beseech you, open the gate. Just let us have a look. If she's not there, we'll never bother you again.'

Bao Yong: 'Very well. If you don't believe me, go in and look for yourselves. But if you don't find her, I shall want an explanation from you on your way back.'

He opened the gate and the women went in to Xi-chun's apartment.

Xi-chun was in very low spirits that morning, and was still brooding about what had happened the previous day:

'Adamantina went home so early yesterday. I wonder if she heard what that servant Bao Yong said. If he has offended her again, she'll never come and visit me; and then I shall have lost my only real friend in the world. With Mother and Father both dead and my own sister-in-law hating me the way she does, I find it so hard to face other people. Before there was always Granny Jia, I knew I could count on her for affection. Now that she's gone too, I'm utterly alone. What will become of me?'

She thought of the other girls and their various fates:

'Ying-chun driven to her death; Xiang-yun married to a consumptive; Tan-chun living at the other end of the world . . . Each one of them had her destiny, and each was powerless to change its course. Adamantina is the only free one among us, free as a wandering cloud or a wild crane. If I could only be like her, how happy I would be! But how *can* I hope to follow her example? I belong to a *wealthy family*! And now I've let even my family down, and I'm in complete disgrace. Neither Aunt Wang nor Aunt Xing understands how I feel. There's no telling how life will turn out for me!'

She was more resolved than ever to take the final, irrevocable step, to cut her hair and by so doing signal once and for all her entry into

the religious life. Landscape and the other maids heard the snip of
the scissors and hurried over, but they were too late. She had already
removed a good half of her hair.

'Before one disaster is over, here's another!' cried Landscape in
alarm. 'What are we to do now?'

This was the state of disarray that prevailed in Xi-chun's apartment
when Adamantina's old women arrived on their search. Landscape
enquired what their mission was and was shocked to hear of Adamantina's disappearance.

'She left us early yesterday morning and hasn't been back since,'
she informed them. Xi-chun overheard from inside and asked in
alarm:

'Where has Adamantina gone?'

One of the women told the tale, how they had heard sounds in the
night, had been put to sleep by the incense, had found Adamantina
missing in the morning and discovered the rope-ladder and scabbard
by the Garden wall. Xi-chun was both distressed and puzzled. She
recalled Bao Yong's accusations of the previous day, but dismissed
them at once from her mind, reflecting that most probably the burglars had spotted Adamantina and come back during the night to
carry her off. But she knew Adamantina; surely a person of such
chastity and pride would have died rather than submit to such
indignity?

'Didn't you hear anything?' she asked of the women.

'We heard,' they replied. 'But we couldn't do anything. We could
only lie there with our eyes wide open, unable to say a word. The
burglars must have put us to sleep by burning some sort of incense.
And Sister Adamantina must have been overcome with the fumes
too. That's why she couldn't speak either. Besides, there were
probably a lot of them, armed to the hilt, so she would have been too
scared to make a noise or cry out.'

Bao Yong could be heard yelling from the gate:

'Get those stupid old hags out of here and close the gate at once!'

Landscape, who was afraid of causing fresh trouble, told the
women to leave immediately and gave orders for the gate to be
closed.

Xi-chun was now more miserable than ever. Landscape and her
other maids repeatedly urged her to take a more reasonable view,
and persuaded her to put up the remaining portion of her hair.

'We mustn't spread the word about Adamantina,' they all agreed. 'Even if it is true, we must behave as if we know nothing until Sir Zheng and Lady Wang come home.'

From this day, Xi-chun's determination to renounce the world was immovable. But of this no more at present.

*

When Jia Lian returned to the Temple of the Iron Threshold, he reported to Jia Zheng that he had interrogated the men on night-duty and had seen to it that an inventory was prepared and delivered to the authorities.

'How did you manage with the inventory?' asked Jia Zheng.

Jia Lian showed him a copy of the list Amber had made up from memory, adding:

'All Grandmother's presents from Her Grace are clearly indicated. Any other unusual or conspicuous items have been left off the list. When my period of mourning is over, I shall instigate a search for those items and am confident we shall find them.'

Jia Zheng thought this course of action wise, and nodded his silent approval.

Jia Lian went in to see Ladies Xing and Wang, and begged them to urge Jia Zheng to return home as soon as possible. The longer they stayed away the greater the chaos would be when they got back.

'I quite agree,' said Lady Xing. 'So long as we stay here, we'll only be in this dreadful suspense anyway.'

'I would not dare suggest an early departure myself,' said Jia Lian. 'But if it came from you, Mother, I am sure Uncle Zheng would agree.'

Lady Xing discussed the matter with Lady Wang, and they both agreed that Lian's suggestion was a good one.

As it turned out, by the next morning Jia Zheng was himself anxious to return and sent Bao-yu in to the ladies with this message:

'I propose that we return today and resume our mourning here in two or three days' time. I have given the necessary instructions to those of my servants who are staying behind; would the ladies be so good as to do likewise?'

Lady Xing instructed Parrot and some of the other maids to stay as mourners, and left Zhou Rui's wife and a few of the older stewardesses in overall charge. Everyone else was to return home. There was an immediate bustle of activity as carriages were prepared and horses saddled, and Jia Zheng led the family in a final lamentation, bidding ceremonial farewell to Grandmother Jia's mortal remains.

They had all risen from their prostrations and were about to leave, when they noticed that Aunt Zhao was still down on her knees. Aunt Zhou thought she must still be weeping and came over to help her up. But something more than grief had incapacitated her; she was foaming at the mouth, her eyes were fixed in a glassy stare, her tongue protruded from her face. The sight gave everyone a nasty turn, and Jia Huan came up to his mother crying frantically, which seemed to bring her round momentarily.

'I won't go home!' she began babbling. 'I'm going back to the South with Lady Jia!'

'But why should Lady Jia need you to go with her?' they asked.

'I've been with her all my life. Sir She wanted to separate us and tried all manner of tricks to lay his hands on me. I thought old Mother Ma could help me get my own back but that was all money wasted: it didn't work, nobody died. Now if I go home, I'm afraid someone may try to take revenge!'

At first they thought she was possessed by the spirit of Faithful, but her subsequent reference to Mother Ma pointed to something quite different. The ladies said nothing, but Suncloud and some of the other maids interceded with the spirit on Aunt Zhao's behalf:

'Sister Faithful, your death was of your own choosing; what does it have to do with Mrs Zhao? Please set her free!'

With Lady Xing present they didn't dare say any more.

'I'm not Faithful!' protested Aunt Zhao. 'I've been sent for by King Yama of the Nether World. He wants to question me about Mother Ma and the black magic . . .'

She dropped her voice to a whisper, and continued:

'Oh Mrs Lian, put in a good word for me with Lord Yama! For all the bad that I've done, there must be some good! Dear Mrs Lian! Dearest Mrs Lian! I never meant to harm you! I was such a fool! I should never have listened to that old slut!'

While this extraordinary scene was taking place, Jia Zheng sent in a servant to fetch Jia Huan. One of the serving-women went out to inform the Master that Aunt Zhao was possessed by some evil spirit, and that Jia Huan was looking after her.

'What nonsense!' exclaimed Jia Zheng brusquely. 'We're leaving now anyway.'

So the men set off, while Aunt Zhao continued to rave deliriously and no one could bring her to her senses. Lady Xing was afraid she might say something even more indiscreet.

'Leave some women here to keep an eye on her,' she ordered. 'We really must be going. When we reach the city we'll send a doctor.'

Lady Wang had always disliked Aunt Zhao and was only too glad to abandon her. Bao-chai, on the other hand, was less ill-disposed towards her; she knew that Aunt Zhao had tried to harm Bao-yu, but could not help feeling sorry for her all the same and secretly asked Aunt Zhou to stay behind with her. Aunt Zhou was a good soul, and agreed to do so. Li Wan volunteered to stay as well, but was informed curtly by Lady Wang that her presence would be unnecessary.

They were now ready to leave.

'What about me?' asked Jia Huan in some alarm. 'Do I have to stay too?'

'You great booby!' retorted Lady Wang contemptuously (and not a little hypocritically). 'Would you forsake your own mother when she is at death's door?'

Jia Huan dared not utter another word.

'Dear brother,' said Bao-yu, 'you really ought to stay. As soon as we get to town, I'll send someone out to you.'

They climbed into their carriages and returned home, leaving Aunt Zhao with Aunt Zhou, Jia Huan and a few serving-women at the temple.

When they reached home, Jia Zheng, the ladies and the rest of the family went to Grandmother Jia's apartment and tearfully surveyed the scene. Steward Lin came in at the head of the domestic staff to pay their respects.

'Get out!' shouted Jia Zheng as they fell to their knees. 'I shall deal with you tomorrow!'

Xi-feng had already fainted several times that day, and was too weak to come out and welcome them home. The only person to receive them was Xi-chun, looking extremely ashamed of herself. Lady Xing ignored her entirely, Lady Wang was her reasonable self, while Li Wan and Bao-chai took her by the hand and spoke a few comforting words. You-shi predictably had a barbed comment to make:

'What a deal of trouble we have put you to these last few days, my dear!'

Xi-chun could say nothing in reply, but only blushed a deep crimson from ear to ear. Bao-chai took You-shi aside and gave her a meaningful look. The ladies went to their rooms.

Jia Zheng examined the extent of the damage, heaving many a silent sigh. He went into his study and, sitting on his mourning mat, sent for Jia Lian, Jia Rong and Jia Yun and gave the three of them a short homily. Bao-yu wanted to wait on him in the study, but Jia Zheng said it would not be necessary. Jia Lian went to his mother's room. That night passed uneventfully.

First thing next morning Steward Lin came into the study and knelt before Jia Zheng, who asked him for a full account of the calamity. Lin mentioned that Zhou Rui was involved:

'Mr Lian's servant Bao Er has been arrested, and some of the items on the inventory of stolen property have been found on his person. He is being interrogated, and they hope to trace the burglars through him.'

This piece of information threw Jia Zheng into a rage:

'That our servants should have the base ingratitude to betray us to thieves, that they steal from their own masters! It is sheer treason!'

He sent a man at once to the temple to bind Zhou Rui and deliver him to the authorities for questioning. Lin remained kneeling and did not dare rise to his feet.

'What are you still down there for?'

'I deserve to die, sir! I beg your forgiveness!'

Lai Da and some of the other stewards now came in to pay their respects and to present the various bills for funeral expenses.

'Give these to Mr Lian to deal with. He can report back to me afterwards.'

Jia Zheng bellowed at Lin to get up and leave the study. Jia Lian now knelt on one knee and whispered a suggestion in Jia Zheng's ear.

'Out of the question!' snapped Jia Zheng, glowering at Lian. 'Just because the money for Mother's funeral has been taken by thieves, does that mean we must stoop to fining our own servants?'

Jia Lian blushed and said nothing further. He stood up but dared not move.

'How is it with your wife?' asked Jia Zheng.

Jia Lian knelt again.

'I'm afraid she is near the end.'

Jia Zheng sighed.

'I never dreamt that our family would crumble as quickly as this! And now, to add to our misfortunes, Huan's mother has been taken ill at the temple, and we still don't know what's the matter with her. Do you know anything about this?'

Jia Lian did not dare breathe a word.

'Tell one of the servants,' said Jia Zheng, 'to take a doctor out there and have a look at her, will you?'

'Yes, Uncle.'

Jia Lian went out at once, and executed these instructions. To learn if Aunt Zhao survived or not, please turn to the next chapter.

CHAPTER 113

*Xi-feng repents of her former misdeeds, and entrusts
her child to a village dame
Nightingale softens a long-standing animosity,
and warms to her besotted master*

After the departure of most of the family from the temple, Aunt
Zhao grew more delirious than ever, and those who had remained
with her listened aghast. Two serving-women attempted to support
her where she knelt on the ground, one minute raving incoherently,
the next sobbing her heart out in anguish. Then she grovelled and
began begging for mercy:

'Oh Great Lord Red Beard! You're killing me! I'll never be so
wicked again!'

She wrung her hands and howled in agony. Her eyes bulged out
of their sockets, blood gushed from her mouth, her hair was wildly
dishevelled. She was a terrifying sight, and no one now dared go
near her.

By evening her voice began to grow hoarse and she sounded more
and more like a croaking harpy. None of the women could bear to be
in her presence, and they deputed some of the more courageous
menfolk to come in and keep watch on her. One minute she seemed
to be gone, then she came round again, and so it went on all night.
By the next morning she was incapable of speech, her face was
horribly contorted and she began rending her clothes and baring her
bosom, as if someone else was stripping her naked. She was now
totally inarticulate, and the torment she was undergoing was terrible
to behold.

She seemed to have reached a final crisis, when the doctor arrived.
He would not take her pulse, but gave orders at once for her last
things to be made ready and himself prepared to leave without further
ado. The servant who had brought him entreated him to stay and
take her pulse, so that he could at least return with a satisfactory
report to his master, and in the end the doctor relented. He felt her
pulse once, and pronounced that there was no sign of life. Hearing

this, Jia Huan burst out wailing, and immediately everyone's attention was turned to him and no one spared another thought for Aunt Zhao, lying dead on the kang, her feet bare, her hair in disarray. Only Aunt Zhou seemed affected.

'Such is the end of a concubine!' she thought morbidly to herself. 'And *she* even bore the Master a son. Who knows what sort of a death *mine* will be!'

The servant meanwhile hurried back to inform Jia Zheng, who sent a man to attend to Aunt Zhao's funeral arrangements and to stay on with Jia Huan at the temple for three days, after which they were both to return. The accepted version of Aunt Zhao's death was that she had been called before the Infernal Tribunal and tortured to death for her wilful attempt to injure the lives of others. A speedy end was also predicted for Xi-feng, since Aunt Zhao had named her as her own accuser in the Nether World.

When this last piece of gossip reached the ears of Patience, she was most distressed. Her mistress did indeed seem beyond hope of recovery, and to make matters worse, Jia Lian had recently made it plain that he had no scrap of affection left for his wife. He was now more preoccupied than ever, and appeared completely unconcerned by Xi-feng's illness. Patience did her best to be cheerful with Xi-feng; but Ladies Xing and Wang, although they had been back from the temple for several days, had neither of them paid her a personal visit, and had only sent a maid to enquire after her health. Their coldness intensified Xi-feng's misery, as did the fact that Jia Lian on his return had not so much as a kind word for her.

All Xi-feng wanted now was to die a quick death, and this made her a prey to all manner of evil spirits. On one occasion she saw the figure of You Er-jie slowly approaching her bed from the back of the room.

'It is so long since we last met, sister!' said the apparition. 'I've thought a great deal about you, but it's been impossible for me to come and see you. Now I've managed to do so at last, and I find you reduced to this extremity. Lian is too much of a fool to appreciate what you've done for him, and instead he complains how mean you are, and says that you're ruining his career and making him feel thoroughly ashamed. I can't bear to see you treated so!'

'I myself have come to regret my own small-mindedness,' mumbled Xi-feng in reply. 'Dear sister! It is so kind of you to visit me like this, and to put past grievances behind you!'

Patience was standing at her side and heard her speaking.

'What was that, ma'am?' she asked.

Xi-feng suddenly awoke and recalled at once that You Er-jie was dead. This must be her spirit seeking the life of her tormentor in vengeance. Now that Patience had woken her, she felt scared but at the same time reluctant to confess her fear. She tried somewhat shakily to compose herself.

'I'm just feeling a little unsettled,' she said to Patience. 'I think I must have been talking in my sleep. Will you come and give me a rub?'

Patience climbed up onto the kang and had just started pummelling her when a junior maid came in and announced that Grannie Liu had come, and was being brought in by the serving-women to pay her respects to Mrs Lian.

'Where is she?' asked Patience, getting down anxiously from the kang.

'She didn't presume to come straight in,' replied the maid. 'She is waiting for Mrs Lian's instructions.'

Patience nodded. She thought that Xi-feng would feel too weak to receive visitors, and said to the maid:

'Mrs Lian needs to have a rest. Tell Grannie Liu to wait a while. Did you ask her what she has come about?'

'They have already asked her,' replied the maid, 'and she said she has come on no particular business. She has only just learned of Her Old Ladyship's death. She would have come before if she had known sooner.'

Xi-feng had overheard them, and called Patience over:

'If someone has had the kindness to call, we must not appear rude or unappreciative. Go and ask Grannie Liu to come in. I should like to talk to her.'

Patience reluctantly complied, and went out herself to fetch Grannie Liu. As soon as she left the room, Xi-feng began to drift off to sleep again, and as her eyes closed she saw another apparition – this time a man and a woman walking towards the kang. It seemed they were about to climb up onto it, and she called out in alarm for Patience:

'There's a man coming towards me!'

Her cries brought Felicity and Crimson rushing to her bedside.

'What do you want, ma'am?'

Xi-feng opened her eyes. The figures had vanished. She knew they must be spectres come to haunt her, but again could not bring herself to say so in front of the maids.

'Where's that wretched Patience got to?' she asked.

'Didn't you send her to fetch Grannie Liu?'

Xi-feng lay still for a while in silence to recover her spirits. Presently Patience returned with Grannie Liu, who had brought a little girl with her and was asking:

'And where's our Mrs Lian?'

Patience led her up to the kang.

'Good day, ma'am,' said Grannie Liu.

Xi-feng opened her eyes, and as she looked at the old dame, she felt strangely moved.

'How are you, Grannie?' she asked. 'Why has it been so long since you last came to see us? How big your granddaughter has grown!'

Grannie Liu was most distressed to see the state Xi-feng was in – as thin as a stick, and evidently confused in her mind.

'Why, Mrs Lian!' she exclaimed. 'To think that in the few months since last I was here you could have fallen so ill! I'm a foolish old baggage and deserve to die for not having visited you sooner!'

She told little Qing-er to come up and pay her respects, but the girl only giggled. Xi-feng thought what a sweet child she was, and told Crimson to take charge of her.

'We country folk never fall ill,' pronounced Grannie Liu. 'If happen we should, then we pray to the gods and make our vows. We never take medicines and the like. I'm wondering now if you mightn't have fallen foul of some evil spirit, to have taken ill like this, ma'am?'

Patience was aware that Grannie Liu's rustic superstitions were ill-timed, and gave her a meaningful tug from the rear. The old dame interpreted this correctly and fell silent. But her words had in fact found an echo in Xi-feng's own thoughts.

'Grannie, dear,' she said, speaking with a great effort, 'you're a lady with years of experience, and what you say is true. Did you know that Aunt Zhao had died too? You met her when you were here, didn't you?'

'Holy Name!' exclaimed the old lady in the greatest surprise. 'Fancy *her* dying, just like that! She was such a sturdy body. And she'd a young son if I recall – what will become of him?'

'He'll be all right,' Patience consoled her. 'He still has the Master and Lady Wang to look after him.'

'That's as may be,' replied Grannie Liu gravely. 'But can you be so sure, miss? I mean, it's his own mother – however bad she may have been – as has died. Nobody can ever take a mother's place.'

This coincided with another of Xi-feng's keenest anxieties, and she broke down and began sobbing. They all rallied round to comfort her.

When Qiao-jie heard her mother in such distress, she came to the kang, held her hand and burst into tears herself.

'Have you said hello to Grannie Liu?' asked Xi-feng tearfully.

'No, Mama.'

'She gave you your name, and is like a foster-mother to you. Give her a curtsey now.'

Qiao-jie went across to Grannie Liu and was about to curtsey when Grannie Liu seized her and said:

'Holy Precious Name! Don't you go weighing me down with such honours – it'll carry me to my grave! Miss Qiao-jie, it's over a year since I last was here; do you still remember me?'

'Of course I do! That time when I saw you in the Garden I was still a very little girl. But I remember two years ago I asked you to bring me some big crickets. I can see you haven't brought me any. You must have forgotten.'

'Oh missie!' exclaimed Grannie Liu. 'What a silly old soul I am! If you want crickets we've enough and to spare at home. But you never come and visit us. If you came, you could bring home a cartload of crickets if you so wanted.'

'In that case,' put in Xi-feng, 'why not take her home with you for a visit?'

'How could I possibly, ma'am?' said Grannie Liu laughing. 'Such a fine gentle young lady that's grown up wrapped in silks and satins and used to dainty things to eat – why, what would I give her to play with at home? What would I feed her with? Would you have me die of shame?'

She cackled and went on:

'Mind you, I *could* act as a matchmaker for the young lady. Ours may only be a village, but we've wealthy folk there all the same, with land that spreads for thousands of acres around and hundreds of cattle and a fair bit of money too. Nothing to compare with the treasure you've got here, of course. In fact come to think of it you'd probably not so much as glance at such folk really, ma'am. But to us country people they're dwellers in heaven!'

'By all means go ahead and propose the match,' said Xi-feng. 'I should be only too pleased to give Qiao-jie in marriage to such a family.'

'Come, ma'am, you must be joking. Why, I dare say you'd be fussy about some great official family that lived in a big mansion, let alone simple country people. And even if you were willing, I hardly think Their Ladyships would be!'

Qiao-jie found the conversation embarrassing and had gone off somewhere to talk to Qing-er. The two girls were soon chatting away together, and gradually struck up a friendship.

Patience was worried that Grannie Liu's endless ramblings would wear Xi-feng out, and presently she took her aside and said:

'Speaking of Her Ladyship, you still haven't been to call on her. I'll find someone to take you over there. It would be a great pity not to see her now that you're here.'

Grannie Liu was about to set off, but Xi-feng called her back:

'What's the great hurry? Sit down, I want to talk to you. Tell me how things have been at home.'

Grannie Liu thanked Xi-feng profusely for her kind concern.

'If it weren't for your help, ma'am,' she began, pointing at Qing-er, 'her ma and pa would have starved to death by now. Life is still hard (how could it be otherwise for country folk?), but they've been able to scrape together an acre or two and put down a well and grow some vegetables and fruits and gourds. With the money they get every year for the produce, they manage to keep body and soul together. And what with the clothes and material you've been sending us so regularly these past two years, ma'am, we're thought of as among the more comfortably off in our village. Holy Name! I remember the day when Qing-er's father came into town and heard the news that your family had been raided by the Embroidered Jackets, ma'am. When he came home and told me, I nearly died of the shock! Then later someone else told me it wasn't *your* side of the family after all – I was so relieved! Afterwards I heard about Sir Zheng being promoted and was so pleased I wanted to come straight here to offer my congratulations. But we had so much to do on the land that I couldn't get away. And then yesterday I heard that Her Old Ladyship had passed away! I was bringing in the beans, and I was that shocked I couldn't go on, I just had to sit down on the ground and cry my heart out. I said to my son-in-law: "I don't care what you say, it may be true or it may just be a rumour, but either way I'm going into town to find out for myself!" They're not a bad sort, my daughter and her man, and they wet their eyes too when they heard the news. So this morning they saw me off and I left before first light and came here as quick as I could. There was no one to ask on the way and I couldn't get any news, so I came straight here to the back gate and when I saw the door-gods all pasted over with white I got the shock of my life. I tried finding Mrs Zhou, but there was no sign of her. Then I ran into a young lady who told me Mrs Zhou was in trouble and had been given the sack. I waited for ages before I saw someone I knew and was able to come in. I'd no idea you were so sick too, ma'am!'

Grannie Liu was in tears. The distressing effect she was having on Xi-feng made Patience anxious, and she drew her aside before she could say any more:

'Now, Grannie, after all this talking your mouth must be awfully dry. How about a nice cup of tea?'

She took her off into one of the maids' rooms, while Qing-er continued playing in Qiao-jie's room.

'I really don't want any tea,' protested Grannie Liu. 'Please, miss, can someone take me over to Her Ladyship's now? I'd like to pay my respects and mourn for Her Old Ladyship.'

'There's no hurry,' said Patience. 'It will be too late for you to leave this evening anyway. I was afraid you would upset Mrs Lian with all your talking. That's why I hurried you out. I hope you won't take offence.'

'Holy Name! How very thoughtful of you, miss! But how is Mrs Lian ever going to get better?'

'Does it look serious to you?' asked Patience.

'Maybe I shouldn't say this,' replied Grannie Liu, 'but to me it looks very nasty.'

They heard Xi-feng calling and Patience hurried to her bedside. Xi-feng said nothing further, however, and Patience was just asking Felicity what the trouble was when they were interrupted by the arrival of Jia Lian. He glanced at the kang where Xi-feng lay, then without a word stomped into the inner room, uttered a series of exasperated grunts and sat down. Autumn was the only one to follow him in. She poured his tea and waited on him attentively, whispering something in his ear. Jia Lian summoned Patience and asked her:

'Isn't Mrs Lian taking medicine?'

'What if she isn't?'

'Oh, how should I know? Bring me the key to the chest.'

The blackness of his mood was more evident than ever to Patience. She restrained herself from saying anything in reply, but went out and whispered in Xi-feng's ear. Xi-feng was silent. Patience fetched a casket, placed it by Jia Lian's side and walked away.

'Where are you off to in such a damned hurry?' snapped Jia Lian. 'Aren't you going to take the key out for me, now that you've dumped the thing there?'

Patience tried not to react. She opened the casket, took out the key and opened the chest with it. Then she asked:

'What do you want from it?'

'What have we got in there?'

Patience finally broke down. Half angrily, half tearfully she begged Jia Lian:

'Please, won't you tell us what the matter is? It's not fair to keep us in this dreadful suspense . . .'

'What is there to say? You're the ones who caused this trouble in the first place. Now we owe four or five thousand taels for Grandmother's funeral, and Uncle Zheng has told me to mortgage some family property to raise the money. Do you imagine we've anything left to mortgage? It's going to look pretty bad if we can't meet our debts. I never asked to do this. I shall just have to pawn the things Grandmother gave me. Well, what's the matter with you? Don't you agree?'

Patience did not say a word, but started taking everything out of the chest. Crimson came up to her:

'Come quickly! Mrs Lian has been taken bad!'

Patience hurried in, forgetting Jia Lian entirely, and found Xi-feng waving her arms wildly in the air. She tried to hold her down, calling out to her tearfully. Even Jia Lian now came in to have a look. He stamped his foot and cried:

'This will be the death of me!'

Tears started to his eyes. Felicity came in:

'You're wanted outside, sir.'

Jia Lian checked himself and went out.

Xi-feng was weakening with every minute, and Felicity and the other maids began wailing and sobbing. Qiao-jie heard and came running in, followed by Grandmother Liu, who hurried over to the kang and began muttering prayers to the Buddha and a lot of other mumbo-jumbo, which appeared to rally Xi-feng's spirits a little. Presently Lady Wang arrived, having heard the news from a maid; by this time Xi-feng was more peaceful, and Lady Wang saw no undue cause for concern. She greeted Grannie Liu and asked her how long she had been at Rong-guo House. Grannie Liu returned the greeting and immediately began talking at some length about Xi-feng's illness. After a while Suncloud appeared with a message that her mistress was wanted by Sir Zheng, whereupon Lady Wang gave Patience a few instructions and left.

After her bad spell, Xi-feng's mind seemed to grow clearer. She saw Grannie Liu in the room once more, and began to feel a growing faith in the efficacy of the old dame's prayers. She told Felicity and the others to leave them alone and, calling Grannie Liu over to the side of her bed, confided to her that she felt very troubled at heart and was constantly seeing spirits. Grannie Liu replied that in her home village there was a certain miraculous Bodhisattva, and a certain temple where prayers were always answered.

'I beseech you to pray for me,' said Xi-feng. 'If you need money for offerings, I can provide it for you.'

She slipped a golden bracelet off her wrist and gave it to Grannie Liu.

'There's no need of that,' said Grannie Liu. 'If we country-folk make a vow, we give a few hundred cash when we get better – no need for anything as grand as this. If I go and pray for you, that will be your vow, ma'am, and when you're better you can go yourself and give what you want.'

Xi-feng knew that Grannie Liu was sincere, and did not try to press the bracelet on her.

'My life is in your hands, Grannie!' she said. 'My little girl also is pursued by countless ailments and afflictions. I entrust her to you as well.'

Grannie Liu readily agreed.

'I really ought to be going if I'm to catch the gates,' she said. 'There's still just time. In a day or two, when you're better, you can come and offer thanks.'

Xi-feng's soul was beleaguered by the spirits of those she had harmed during her lifetime, and she was eager for the old lady to go and pray for her:

'Do your best for me. If I can only get some peaceful sleep, I shall be so grateful to you. You can leave your granddaughter here.'

'But she's only a country lass, and has no manners,' protested Grannie Liu. 'I'm afraid she'll only make trouble here. I'd better take her with me.'

'Don't you worry. She is one of the family, it will be quite all right. We may be hard up, but I think we can feed one extra mouth.'

Grannie Liu could tell that Xi-feng meant what she said, and for her part she was only too pleased to let Qing-er stay with the Jias a few days and save a little at home. The only problem was that Qing-er herself might not be willing. She decided to call her over and offer her the choice, and soon discovered that the two girls had become firm friends, that Qiao-jie was most reluctant to let Qing-er go, and that Qing-er herself was eager to stay. The old lady gave her grandchild a few parting words of advice, said goodbye to Patience and hurried out, anxious to reach the city gates before they closed. And there our narrative must leave her.

*

Green Bower Hermitage was built on Jia family land, and when Prospect Garden was created for the Visitation, the site of the Hermitage was included within the Garden's precincts. But as a religious establishment it had always been self-supporting, and had never been dependent on Jia family charity. The nuns in residence had reported Adamantina's calamity to the authorities and were waiting for them to apprehend the criminals. Meanwhile, since their community belonged to Adamantina, they resolved to stay where they were, and informed the Jias to this effect.

Although the household staff all knew of Adamantina's disappearance, they had not wanted to trouble Jia Zheng with such a matter at a time when he was in mourning and had a great deal else on his mind. In fact Xi-chun was the only one of the family to know about it at first, and was in a state of constant anxiety and suspense on Adamantina's behalf. Then the story, or rather two versions of it, reached Bao-yu's ears; according to one she had been kidnapped, according to the other she had succumbed to the temptations of the flesh and eloped of her own free will with a lover. 'She must have been kidnapped,' Bao-yu thought to himself in great perplexity. 'A person like her would never have acquiesced in such a thing. She would rather have died!' As time went by there was still no news of her whereabouts, however, and every day Bao-yu sighed sadly to himself, reluctant to believe that Adamantina of all people, the self-styled 'Dweller Beyond the Threshold' of this world, could have come to so worldly an end. His thoughts ran on to the happier days they had shared in the Garden and the more troubled times that had followed: 'Since Ying left home, some of my cousins have died, others have been married. Somehow I always thought that if there was one absolutely pure and incorruptible person among us, it was Adamantina. But now this sudden storm of calamity has blown up out of nowhere, and a death stranger than Dai-yu's has taken her away!' As he pursued this train of thought to its logical conclusion, a line from *Zhuang-zi* came into his mind: 'This life, this insubstantial tissue of vanity, floats like a cloud on the wind!' With this he burst into tears, and Aroma, who thought it was another of his fits, endeavoured to comfort him with tender words of affection.

At first Bao-chai could not imagine what had upset him, and she admonished him in her usual fashion. But when he continued depressed despite her efforts and remained in an apparent state of trance for days on end, she became greatly perplexed and eventually, after making persistent enquiries, discovered the truth. She was herself greatly distressed to learn of Adamantina's disappearance, but her concern for Bao-yu tempered her grief, and she rallied him again briskly:

'Look at young Lan now: I've heard that he's been hard at work ever since he returned from the funeral! He hasn't been going to school, but day and night he pores over his books at home on his own. And he's only Lady Jia's great-grandson! You're her grandson; she had such high hopes for you. And Father worries day and night about you. And yet you indulge yourself and ruin your health over some trifle, some silly piece of sentimentality. We depend on you. What will happen to all of us, if you carry on like this?'

There was little Bao-yu could say in answer to this. After a long silence he finally came out with:

'But it's not a trifle! It's a tragedy! It's the decline of our entire family that I'm lamenting!'

'Listen to you!' retorted Bao-chai. 'The one thing Father and Mother want is that you should do well and be a credit to the family. If you persist in this folly, how can the family fortunes ever hope to improve?'

Her words received a most unsympathetic reception from Bao-yu, who proceeded to lean over the table and doze off. Bao-chai ignored him, and went to bed, telling Musk and the others to wait on him.

Bao-yu soon awoke, and noticed how few people were left in the room with him.

'I've never had a proper talk with Nightingale since she was transferred to our apartment,' he thought to himself. 'She probably thinks I've been very cold. I feel very bad about it. I can't treat her like Musk or Ripple – they're easy to deal with. Nightingale's different. I remember how she kept me company all those times I was ill – I still have the little mirror she left. She must have felt something for me then, but somehow whenever we meet now, she's very distant and cold. Surely it can't be because of Chai; she and Dai-yu were the closest of friends, and she always treats Nightingale kindly too. When I'm not at home, in fact, she and Nightingale often talk and laugh together. But the moment I walk in, Nightingale leaves the room. It must be because my wedding took place at the very time when Dai-yu was dying . . . Oh Nightingale! Nightingale! Surely a clever girl like you can see the anguish that I suffer!'

His thoughts ran on:

'This is my chance, while they are all asleep or busy sewing, to find Nightingale and have a talk with her. I'll see what she has to say, and if there's still some way in which I have caused offence, I can try to make it up with her.'

He stole quietly out of the room and went in search of Nightingale.

She was living in a maid's room in the west wing. Bao-yu crept up to one of the windows, and seeing that there was still a light burning inside, used the tip of his tongue to moisten a spy-hole in the window-paper and peep through. He saw her sitting idly on her own by the lamp.

'Nightingale!' he whispered. 'Are you still awake?'

Nightingale was startled and sat there stunned for a few moments before asking:

'Who's there?'

'It's me!' replied Bao-yu.

Nightingale thought she recognized Bao-yu's voice.

'Is it you, Mr Bao?'

'Yes!' whispered Bao-yu, to which Nightingale replied:

'What are you doing here?'

'I've something private to talk to you about. Let me in and we can sit and have a chat.'

After a pause, Nightingale replied:

'What do you want to talk about? It's getting late. Please go back to your room now. You can tell me about it in the morning.'

Bao-yu was very disheartened. If he persisted in his efforts, he was afraid Nightingale would bar the door to him; on the other hand, if he went back, how would the emotions that seethed within him find an outlet, emotions that his short exchange with Nightingale had only served to intensify? He made one last attempt to talk her round:

'I haven't a great deal to say. Just one question to ask.'

'Well, if it's only one question, go ahead.'

Bao-yu, however, now suddenly found himself quite bereft of the power of speech, and a long silence ensued. Nightingale, on her side of the window, began to find his silence worrying. She knew his tendency to have fits, and feared that her brusque manner might have caused one of his relapses. She stood up and after listening carefully for a moment, asked:

'Have you gone, or are you still standing there gawping? Why don't you speak your mind instead of spending your time driving people to distraction? You've already driven one person to death; do you want to drive another? It's all so senseless!'

She peeped back at Bao-yu through the spy-hole. There he was, standing, listening to her with a trance-like expression on his face. She felt it advisable to say no more, and walked back and began trimming her lamp. Suddenly she heard Bao-yu sigh:

'Oh Nightingale! You've never been as cold as this before! Why have you not had a single good word for me recently? I know I'm a sorry specimen of humanity, too impure to merit any real respect. But I still wish you'd tell me what it is that I've done wrong. Then I could endure being shunned by you for the rest of my life. At least I could die knowing my faults.'

Nightingale sniffed scornfully.

'Is that all you had to say? Isn't there anything new? I know all *that* by heart. I heard enough of *that* when Miss Lin was alive. But if I've done anything wrong, you should take your complaints to Her Ladyship. She's the one who told me to wait on you. We're only maids anyway, what do *we* count for?'

She started sobbing and snivelling. Bao-yu knew that she was suffering too, and he stamped his foot in frustration.

'How can you talk like that? After being here all these months, surely you must know what's on my mind? And if none of the others will speak for me, won't you let me tell you myself? Do you want me to go on bottling it up inside for ever, and choke to death?'

He too began sobbing his heart out, when a voice was heard behind him, saying:

'Who, pray, should speak for you? Why drag others into it? You've offended her, so you jolly well make it up. It's up to her to decide whether she'll forgive you. Why put the blame on nobodies like us?'

Both Bao-yu on the outside of the window and Nightingale on the inside were greatly startled by this intruder – who turned out to be Musk. Bao-yu felt most embarrassed, as Musk continued:

'What *is* going on here? One grovelling for forgiveness, the other refusing to take any notice. Come on now, you hurry up and apologize; and as for you, Nightingale, you're being altogether too cruel! It's dreadfully cold out here, and he's been pleading with you for ages and not had so much as a breath of a response!'

She turned to Bao-yu:

'It's late, and Mrs Bao's been wondering where you are. To think that you've been here all along, standing out on your own under the eaves! What *are* you up to?'

'Honestly!' protested Nightingale from inside. 'This is ridiculous! I simply asked him to go away. I told him that whatever he had to talk about could wait till the morning. What's the sense in all this?'

Bao-yu still wanted to speak to Nightingale, but now that they were no longer alone, he felt too embarrassed to continue. He resigned himself to returning with Musk, saying as he walked away:

'So be it! I shall never in this lifetime be able to prove my true feelings! Heaven alone will know the truth!'

Tears started suddenly to his eyes and rolled in torrents down his cheeks.

'Mr Bao!' said Musk. 'Take my advice and put the whole thing out of your mind. You're wasting your tears.'

Bao-yu followed her silently to his room. Bao-chai was lying asleep, or rather, as he judged, feigning sleep, but Aroma greeted him with a rebuke:

'Couldn't it have waited till tomorrow? Did you have to go storming out there and work yourself up into another . . .'

Whatever she had been about to say, she thought better of it, and after a short pause went on to ask:

'Are you sure you're not feeling poorly?'

Bao-yu said nothing, but shook his head. Aroma put him to bed and it goes without saying that he spent a sleepless night.

*

Nightingale was most distressed by Bao-yu's visit, and she too lay awake the whole of that night, weeping and reflecting deeply to herself:

'It seems plain that the family conspired together and tricked him into the wedding at a time when he was too ill to understand. Then afterwards, when he knew what he had done, he suffered one of his attacks and that's why he hasn't been able to stop weeping and moping ever since. He's obviously not the heartless, wicked person I took him for. Why, today his devotion was so touching, I felt really sorry for him. What a dreadful pity it is that our Miss Lin never had the fortune to be his bride! Such unions are clearly determined by fate. Until fate reveals itself, men continue to indulge in blind passion and fond imaginings; then, when the die is cast and the truth is known, the fools may remain impervious, but the ones who care deeply, the men of true sentiment, can only weep bitterly at the futility of their romantic attachments, at the tragedy of their earthly plight. *She* is dead and knows nothing; but *he* still lives, and there is no end to his suffering and torment. Better by far the destiny of plant or stone, bereft of knowledge and consciousness, but blessed at least with purity and peace of mind!'

These philosophical reflections cooled the feverish turmoil in Nightingale's mind, and she was tidying up and preparing to go to bed, when she heard a great rumpus break out in the direction of Xi-feng's apartment to the east. But to discover what this portended, you must turn to the next chapter.

CHAPTER 114

*Wang Xi-feng ends her life's illusion
and returns to Jinling
Zhen Ying-jia receives the Emperor's favour
and is summoned to the Palace*

It was the middle of the night when Bao-yu and Bao-chai were awoken and informed that Xi-feng was dying. They rose from bed at once, a maid brought a lighted candle, and they were on their way out of the courtyard, when another message came from Lady Wang:

'Mrs Lian's condition is critical, but she is still alive, and Mr and Mrs Bao should wait a while. There is something odd about Mrs Lian's state; from midnight until two o'clock this morning she wouldn't stop talking, and we couldn't make head or tail of what she was saying One minute she was demanding a boat, the next a sedan-chair; then she was "off to Jinling to be entered on the Register" . . . No one could understand a word, and she just kept on crying and wailing. There was nothing for it but for Mr Lian to go and get a paper boat and sedan made for her. He hasn't come back with them yet, and Mrs Lian is waiting for him, gasping for breath. Her Ladyship wants you both to wait and to come after Mrs Lian has finally passed away.'

'How extraordinary!' exclaimed Bao-yu. 'What does she want in Jinling?'

'Didn't you see some registers in a dream once?' whispered Aroma. 'Perhaps that's where Mrs Lian is going.'

Bao-yu nodded:

'Yes! If only I hadn't forgotten what was written in them. Our lives are clearly preordained by destiny. I wonder where destiny has taken Cousin Lin? What you said just now, Aroma, about the registers, has set me thinking. If I ever have a dream like that again, I must be more observant. I may see things and be able to predict the future.'

'Hark at you!' retorted Aroma. 'It's impossible to have a sensible conversation with you. You insist on taking a chance remark of mine in deadly earnest. Even supposing you *could* see into the future, what good would it do you anyway?'

'It will probably never come to pass,' replied Bao-yu. 'But if I ever did know the future, then at least it would mean an end to all the worries that plague me on your account.'

Bao-chai came up to them:

'What are you two talking about?'

Bao-yu was afraid of being subjected to one of her inquisitions, and merely replied:

'We were discussing Cousin Feng.'

'There she is dying,' exclaimed Bao-chai, 'and you're *discussing* her! You accused me last year of being unduly gloomy and bringing her bad luck; but wasn't my interpretation of that oracle the right one after all?'

Bao-yu thought for a moment, then clapped his hands:

'Of course! Of course you were right! *You*'re obviously the prophet in the family! Well, let me consult you myself. What's in store for me?'

'Off you go on one of your hobbyhorses again!' Bao-chai chided him with a smile. 'Mine was simply an off-the-cuff explanation for the wording of the oracle. There's really no need to take it seriously. You're as bad as Xiu-yan. When you lost your jade, she asked Adamantina to consult the planchette, and the answer was totally unintelligible to everyone; but that didn't stop Xiu-yan from talking to me in private about Adamantina's amazing powers of clairvoyance, saying how enlightened and advanced she was in her Zen practice. And yet look at this calamity that's befallen Adamantina now – why couldn't she have predicted *that*? What sort of clairvoyance is that supposed to be? Just because I said something once about Cousin Feng, that doesn't mean I ever claimed to see into her future, or into my own for that matter. Claims of that sort are fantastic and don't deserve to be taken seriously.'

'All right,' said Bao-yu, 'let's drop the subject. Tell me about Xiu-yan instead. We've been so busy that her wedding seems to have passed us by altogether. That was an important event for your family, and yet it was celebrated with so little ceremony. Didn't you even invite any relatives and friends?'

'You've missed the point again,' replied Bao-chai. 'My own family's closest relatives are the Jias and the Wangs. There's no one respectable left in the Wang family now, and the Jias weren't invited because my mother knew we'd be too busy with Grandmother's funeral. Lian lent a hand, and one or two other relations came – but you wouldn't know about that, as you weren't there. If you think about it, things were much the same for Xiu-yan as they were for me. She was formally engaged to Cousin Ke, and Mama wanted a stylish wedding. But in the first place, Pan was still in gaol, so Cousin Ke wanted to keep it simple; then there was Grandmother's funeral; and Xiu-yan was having such a hard time at Aunt Xing's, especially after the confiscation, when Aunt Xing became stingier than ever. Poor Xiu-yan, she could hardly bear it. I talked to Mama, and in the end she decided to go ahead and make do with a simple ceremony. Xiu-yan seems a lot happier now and she is so good to Mama, far better than her real daughter-in-law ever was. She's a wonderful wife to Ke, and gets on very well with Caltrop. If Ke has to be away for some reason, the two of them still manage very happily together. They are a bit hard up, but Mama is a great deal more relaxed than she used to be. She still gets upset about Pan, and he's always writing to her from gaol and asking for more money. But luckily Cousin Ke has been able to collect some of the debts that were owing, and has sent Pan the money from that. Some of our town properties have had to be mortgaged too. We still have one house left, and that's where Mama is planning to move now.'

'What's the need?' protested Bao-yu. 'It's so much more convenient for you to have them living close by. If they move so far away, it will be a whole day's expedition to visit them.'

'Even when families are as closely related as ours,' said Bao-chai, 'it's really much better in the long run to be independent. Mama can't go on for ever living on charity.'

Bao-yu was about to expand on the reasons for their not moving, when a final message came from Lady Wang, to say that Xi-feng had passed away, and all the family had now arrived in her apartment. Would Bao-yu and Bao-chai please join them there? Bao-yu stamped his foot and seemed about to burst into tears. Bao-chai too was deeply moved, but controlled herself for fear of upsetting Bao-yu any further.

'We should keep our tears for later,' she counselled.

They both made their way directly to Xi-feng's room, where they found a weeping throng gathered. Bao-chai went forward to the bedside, where Xi-feng's body was already laid out, and gave a great cry of grief. Bao-yu held Jia Lian's hand and sobbed loudly, which set Jia Lian off again. Patience, seeing that no one else was capable of offering any comfort, stepped forward, and tried to mask her own grief and urge moderation. Sounds of inconsolable weeping continued to fill the room none the less.

Jia Lian was in a helpless dither. He sent for Lai Da, and told him to make whatever preparations were necessary for the funeral. He himself reported Xi-feng's death to Jia Zheng and then went to see what other arrangements he could make. But there were simply no funds; it was an impossible task. Fond memories of Xi-feng brought tears constantly to his eyes and his distress was made still more acute by the pitiful sight of Qiao-jie, crying her heart out for her mother. The weeping continued all that night. At dawn Jia Lian sent a messenger for Xi-feng's elder brother Wang Ren.

The death of his older uncle Wang Zi-teng had left Wang Ren free to carry on very much as he pleased. Zi-sheng, the surviving younger uncle, was too ineffective a character to control him, and Wang Ren had already by his behaviour succeeded in causing considerable discord in the family. Now, learning of the death of his younger sister, he hurried over (with a slightly ill grace) to perform his duty as a bereaved brother and mourn for her. On his arrival he observed immediately how makeshift the funeral arrangements were and voiced his indignation in no uncertain terms:

'Years my sister toiled for you, did a fine job of it too. The least you owe her is a proper funeral. You should be ashamed of yourselves, making such a poor show of it!'

Jia Lian had never been on good terms with his brother-in-law, and, when he heard him blustering on like this, turned a deaf ear. Wang Ren next called Qiao-jie aside.

'My girl,' he said to her, 'while your mother was alive, she had one shortcoming: she was too anxious to please Lady Jia, and as a result she neglected her own family. But you're old enough now to make decisions yourself, my dear! Look at me, have I ever tried to profit from you? Now that your mother is dead, you must look to me and do as I tell you. Your great-uncle and I are your mother's family. I know your father, he'll go out of his way to bow and scrape to anyone, rather than take any notice of us. When that fancy woman of his, that Auntie You, died, I wasn't in town, but I heard that a lot of money was spent on her. And now he's scrimping on your own mother's funeral. Don't you think you ought to have a word with him about it, and make him see sense?'

'Father would like nothing more than to have a nice funeral,' said Qiao-jie. 'But things have changed. We haven't enough money, so of course we have to be a bit careful.'

'What about your own things?' pursued Wang Ren relentlessly. 'Surely you've something left yourself?'

'It all went in the raid last year,' said Qiao-jie. 'I've got nothing left at all.'

'Are *you* trying me on too?' expostulated Wang Ren. 'I know that Lady Jia gave away all sorts of things. You ought to produce your share now.'

Qiao-jie could not bring herself to admit that her father had already taken her share and sold it, and so pretended not to understand what he was referring to.

'I know!' exclaimed Wang. 'You're keeping it for your trousseau!'

Qiao-jie refused to say another word. Wang Ren had already offended her with his remarks and she began to sob until she was almost choking with emotion.

'If you have anything else to say, sir,' protested Patience heatedly, 'please wait until Mr Lian comes back. Miss Qiao-jie is much too young to understand.'

'As for you, you've just been itching for my sister to die, haven't you!' sneered Wang Ren. 'The lot of you! So you could step into her shoes . . . I'm not asking for much; just a decent funeral. Surely you don't want to disgrace your own family?'

He sat himself down in a surly fashion.

Qiao-jie was feeling very miserable. 'I know Father *does* care,' she was thinking to herself. 'And besides, when Mother was alive, Uncle Ren sneaked off with all sorts of stuff of hers himself, so he's got no right to complain.'

In her eyes Wang Ren was rather a despicable sort of person. He for his part secretly reckoned to himself that Xi-feng must have kept her own private hoard, and that despite the raid there was bound to be silver somewhere in her apartment – and a fair amount of it too.

'They probably think I've come to sponge, and the girl is trying to protect them. She won't be any use to me, the little wretch!'

He began to conceive an intense dislike for his niece.

Jia Lian was far too busy trying to rustle up money for the funeral to take in all these complications. He had delegated the 'outer' formalities to Lai Da, but he still needed a lot of money for the 'inner' reception and could not see how he was going to find it. Patience was aware of his predicament.

'You mustn't overdo things, sir,' she urged him. 'You'll only make yourself ill.'

'Ill!' exclaimed Jia Lian, somewhat histrionically. 'That's the least of my worries! We can't even find the money to get by from day to day, let alone pay for the funeral. And to make matters worse, now I've got this idiot round my neck!'

'There's really no need to work yourself into such a state, sir,' said Patience. 'If you've no money, I've a few things that were not taken in the raid. Use them if you like.'

'What a wonderful stroke of luck!' thought Jia Lian to himself. He smiled at Patience:

'That *would* be a real help. It would save me from having to race around trying to raise the money. I'll pay you back as soon as I can.'

'Whatever I have was given me by Mrs Lian in the first place,' said Patience. 'So there's really no need to pay me back. I just want the funeral to be done properly, that's all.'

Jia Lian accepted Patience's offer with sincere gratitude, and pawned her belongings for the funeral expenses. From then on he made a point of discussing everything with her. Autumn was most put out, and took every opportunity to mutter complaints:

'Now that Mrs Lian is gone, Patience thinks she can take over. The Master gave me to Mr Lian; how can Patience think to climb above me?'

Patience noticed Autumn's disgruntled attitude, but paid no attention. Jia Lian, for his part, found Autumn's resentment (which he observed soon enough) most objectionable, and whenever anything happened to annoy him he vented his bad humour on her. Lady Xing criticized him for this, and he felt obliged to restrain himself. But of this no more.

*

In due course, after Xi-feng's encoffined corpse had been laid out for ten days, it was escorted to the temple. Jia Zheng was still in mourning for Grandmother Jia and was confined to his study during the period of Xi-feng's funeral. His entourage of literary gentlemen had gradually deserted him. Only Cheng Ri-xing still called regularly. On one occasion Jia Zheng was speaking to him on the general subject of the family's decline:

'See how one by one we are dying off! My elder brother and young Zhen are both in exile. Our finances deteriorate daily. And who knows what has become of our country estates in the Eastern provinces. Altogether, a disastrous state of affairs!'

'I have been here many years, sir,' said Cheng, 'and I have seen for myself how busy your staff are, enriching themselves at your expense. Every year sees money draining from your pockets into theirs. It is ruining you. Then there is the money needed for the families of Sir She and Mr Zhen, and the sizeable debts incurred besides, and the loss sustained as a result of the recent burglary, which I hardly think will be recovered. If you wish to put your house in order, sir, the only remedy I envisage is for you to assemble your staff, and to charge your most trustworthy steward with a comprehensive investigation of their accounts. In that way you can judge in which department retrenchment is possible. Deficits should be made good by the individual steward responsible. That way you will at least know where you stand.

'Then there's the Garden. It is too large for anyone to buy. But it is a shame that a place with such potential for profit should have been so neglected. During the years that you have been away, sir, the staff there have been manufacturing all manner of scarifying tales, which have had the effect of deterring everyone from entering the place. All your troubles are, in short, the doing of the servants. You should make a thorough investigation, and dismiss any unsatisfactory elements among them. It is the only remedy that makes sense.'

'My dear Cheng,' replied Jia Zheng, nodding his head gravely, 'you do not seem to realize: I cannot even trust my own nephew, let alone the servants! And if I myself were to try to carry out an investigation such as you suggest, I could never hope to get to the root of the problem. Not that I could engage in such a thing anyway, while still in mourning. Even if I did, I have never paid much attention to household details in the past, so I really have no idea what we are supposed to have and what we don't have. I would not know where to look.'

'You are altogether too charitable and virtuous a man, sir,' rejoined

Cheng. 'In any other family of comparable position, even if things had reached this critical state, the masters would count on being able to stave off disaster for another five or ten years by asking their stewards for money. I understand that one of your men has even been appointed to a district magistracy . . .'

'No!' cut in Jia Zheng firmly. 'When a man stoops to borrowing from his own servants, it is the beginning of the end. We shall simply have to draw in our belts a little. If we still own the property that is down on our books, well and good. But personally I am inclined to believe that there may be very little reality behind some of those entries.'

'Precisely, sir,' replied Cheng. 'That was my very reason for suggesting an inspection of the accounts.'

'Why, have you heard something?' asked Jia Zheng.

'Word has reached me of some of the iniquities perpetrated by those servants of yours,' answered Cheng. 'But I hardly dare mention them in your presence, sir.'

Jia Zheng realized from Cheng's tone of voice that he was speaking the truth.

'Alas!' he sighed. 'Since my grandfather's day, we have always had a tradition in my family of being considerate and generous to our servants. We have never treated them harshly or given them cause for complaint. What is the present generation coming to! And if I were suddenly to start acting the strict master now, I hardly think I would be treated seriously.'

As they were talking, one of the janitors came in and announced that Excellency Zhen of the Nanking family had come to call.

'What brings him to the capital?' asked Jia Zheng.

'I understand, sir,' replied the servant, 'that he has been reinstated by Imperial favour.'

'Show him in at once,' said Jia Zheng.

The servant went out to usher in the visitor. This Excellency Zhen was the father of Zhen Bao-yu; his full name was Zhen Ying-jia, his courtesy name You-zhong (Friend of the Loyal). The Zhens were, it will be remembered, like the Jias, an illustrious old family from Nanking, and the two families had a long-standing family connection and had always seen a good deal of each other. Zhen Ying-jia had lost his post a year or two previously for some misdemeanour, and the family property had subsequently been confiscated. Now His

Majesty the Emperor had shown him a special favour as the descendant of a loyal and deserving subject, had restored him to his hereditary position and had summoned him to the capital for an audience. Knowing that Lady Jia had recently passed away, Zhen had prepared an offering and had chosen an auspicious day in the almanac on which to convey the offering to the temple where her remains were lying. Before so doing he called at Rong-guo House to pay his respects.

Mourning etiquette prevented Jia Zheng from going out to greet his guest, but he welcomed him at the threshold of his outer study. When Zhen Ying-jia saw him, sorrow and joy mingled in his breast. Both gentlemen refrained from any elaborate display of ceremony, and instead clasped each other simply by the hand and exchanged greetings. They sat down at either side of a table, Jia Zheng offered his guest some tea and they continued to talk for some little while.

'When were you received by His Majesty?' asked Jia Zheng.

'The day before yesterday,' replied Zhen Ying-jia.

'His Majesty in his great kindness must surely have favoured you with some words of instruction.'

'Yes indeed. His Majesty, whose kindness exceeds the heavens, has favoured me with a decree.'

'May I enquire as to its import?'

'In view of the recent outbreak of piracy on the South coast, and the unsettled conditions prevailing among the people there, His Majesty has despatched the Duke of An-guo on a mission of pacification against the rebels. Because of my familiarity with the region, he has ordered me to take part in the campaign. I shall have to leave almost immediately. When I learned yesterday that Lady Jia had passed away, I prepared a humble offering of petal-incense to burn before her coffin, as a small expression of my devotion.'

Jia Zheng kowtowed his thanks and replied:

'I am sure this enterprise will be an opportunity for you to set His Majesty's mind at rest, and to bring peace to the nation. I have no doubt too that it will bring you great personal glory! I only regret that I shall not be able to witness it with my own eyes, but will have to content myself with hearing the news of your victories from afar. The present commander of the Zhenhai littoral is a relation of mine, and I hope that when you meet him you will receive him favourably.'

'How are you related to the commander?' asked Zhen Ying-jia.

'During my period of office as Grain Intendant in Kiangsi,' replied Jia Zheng, 'I betrothed my daughter to his son, and they have been married three years now. A protracted coastal disturbance and the continued concentration of pirates in the region have prevented news of them from reaching us for quite some time. I am most concerned for my daughter's well-being, and earnestly beseech you to visit her, when your duties are completed and a convenient opportunity presents itself. In the meanwhile I shall write her a short letter, and if you would be so kind as to have it delivered for me by one of your men, I should be eternally grateful.'

'Children are a source of concern to us all,' rejoined Zhen. 'I myself was on the point of asking *you* a similar favour. When I received my instructions from His Majesty to proceed to the capital, I decided to bring my family with me; my son is of a tender age and we have so few servants at home now. I have had to hurry on ahead, while my family are following at a more leisurely pace and should arrive here any day. I have been given my marching orders already and cannot delay here any longer. When my family arrive they are sure to call on you, and I have instructed my son to kowtow to you in the hope of benefiting from your counsel. Should a suitable offer of marriage make itself known to you, I should be most grateful if you would make representations on our behalf.'

'But of course,' Jia Zheng assured him. After a little more chat, Zhen Ying-jia rose to take his leave, saying:

'I shall hope to see you tomorrow outside the city.'

Jia Zheng knew that Zhen must have many other engagements and would not be prevailed upon to stay. He saw him to the study door, where Jia Lian and Bao-yu were waiting to escort him out (in the absence of a summons from Jia Zheng they had not ventured into the study). The two younger men stepped forward to salute him. Zhen Ying-jia seemed quite stunned by the sight of Bao-yu.

'Take away the white mourning clothes,' he thought to himself. 'and this young man is the very image of our own Bao-yu!'

'It is such a long time since we last met,' he said politely, 'that I have quite forgotten your names.'

Jia Zheng indicated Jia Lian:

'My elder brother She's son, Lian.'

Then pointing to Bao-yu:

'My own second son, Bao-yu.'

Zhen clapped his hands:

'How extraordinary! I heard tell at home that you had a well-loved son born with a jade, and that his name was Bao-yu. I was at first greatly surprised that our sons should share the same name, but later I reflected that such coincidences must be quite frequent. Now I have seen him in the flesh, I am amazed all over again! He is the living likeness of my own son! Not only his features, his whole manner and bearing are the same!'

On being told Bao-yu's age, he commented:

'My son is a year younger.'

Jia Zheng went on to say that he had already gathered a little information about Zhen Bao-yu from Bao Yong, the former Zhen retainer whom Zhen Ying-jia had himself recommended to them. Zhen Ying-jia seemed too engrossed in Bao-yu to enquire after his old servant, but kept exclaiming:

'Most extraordinary! Most extraordinary!'

He took Bao-yu by the hand and was most affable towards him. Their conversation would have been longer had it not been for the fact that the Duke of An-guo was in a hurry to leave. Zhen did not wish to delay his superior, and himself needed to make hasty preparations for the long journey ahead. He therefore forced himself to say farewell and made a dignified departure, escorted by Jia Lian and Bao-yu. All the way he was still plying Bao-yu with questions. At last he mounted his carriage and was gone, and Jia Lian and Bao-yu returned to report to Jia Zheng. When they were dismissed Jia Lian went once more to endeavour to settle the accounts for Xi-feng's funeral.

Bao-yu returned to his own room and told Bao-chai of his encounter with Zhen Ying-jia.

'I never thought I'd have a chance to see that Zhen Bao-yu we are always hearing about, but now I've seen his father, and apparently the son will be coming any day to call on Father. Excellency Zhen called me the "living likeness of his son", which I find hard to believe. If this other Bao-yu does come, you must all be sure to take a peep at him, and judge whether there really is a resemblance.'

'Shame on you!' exclaimed Bao-chai. 'Honestly, you grow more and more thoughtless with every day! First you treat us to a story about some young man who's supposed to look like you, then you want *us* to go and "take a peep" at him! What next!'

Bao-yu realized that he had said the wrong thing, and blushed. He tried to think of some way of rectifying his gaffe, but to learn more you will have to turn to the next chapter.

CHAPTER 115

A private obsession revived confirms
Xi-chun in an ancient vow
A physical likeness verified deprives
Bao-yu of an imagined friend

Before Bao-yu had time to appease Bao-chai, Ripple came in and announced:

'The Master wishes to see Bao-yu.'

Bao-yu did not wait for any second bidding.

'I want to have a word with you,' said Jia Zheng, when he arrived, 'concerning your studies. You are still in mourning and it would therefore be improper for you to attend school; but you can and must revise your compositions. Over the next few days I shall have some leisure, and I want you to write me a few samples at home. I shall then be able to judge for myself whether in all this time you have made any discernible progress.'

'Yes, Father,' said Bao-yu rather miserably.

'I have instructed your brother Huan and your nephew Lan to revise as well. I sincerely hope that your work will be better than theirs.'

'Yes, Father.' Bao-yu dared say nothing more, but stood rooted to the spot.

'Off with you, then.'

As he withdrew from the study, Bao-yu passed Lai Da and the other stewards coming in with their registers.

He was back in his room like a flash, and communicated the substance of his interview to Bao-chai, who seemed rather pleased to hear it. Bao-yu himself groaned inwardly, but knew that it would be inadvisable to appear idle and was preparing to settle down and concentrate, when two nuns from the Convent of the Saviour King arrived to pay their respects to Bao-chai. She told a maid to bring them tea, but was otherwise decidedly offhand towards them, while Bao-yu, who would have liked to talk with the sisters, could tell that Bao-chai found their company distasteful and therefore refrained.

The nuns for their part knew only too well that Bao-chai was un-sympathetic to their cause, and after sitting for a short time they excused themselves.

'Won't you stay a little longer?' asked Bao-chai somewhat dis-ingenuously.

'We have so many calls to make,' replied one of them. 'What with the masses we've been saying at the Temple of the Iron Threshold, we've been kept very busy and haven't called on Their Ladyships and the young ladies in a very long while. Apart from your good self, we've already been to see Mrs Zhu and Their Ladyships, but we still have Miss Xi-chun to call on.'

Bao-chai nodded, and the nuns proceeded to Xi-chun's apartment. They asked Landscape, who received them, where her mistress could be found.

'My mistress hasn't eaten for days,' exclaimed Landscape, 'and now she won't even get up from her bed.'

'Why? What's the matter?'

'Oh, it's a long story. I'm sure she'll tell you all about it when you see her.'

Xi-chun had heard them talking as they came in, and sat up at once.

'How are you both?' she asked. 'I suppose you've stopped visiting us because our fortunes are so altered . . .'

'Holy Name!' came the pious ejaculation. 'Benefactors are bene-factors, whether they be rich or poor. Our convent was founded by your family, and we were always most generously provided for by Her Old Ladyship. We saw Their Ladyships and the young ladies at Her Old Ladyship's funeral, but we didn't see you there, miss, and we were worried about you. That's why we've come here specially to visit you today.'

Xi-chun asked after the young nuns at the temple.

'Ever since that scandal,' was the reply, 'the gatemen won't let them so much as set foot in Rong-guo House.'

'Talking of scandals,' continued the same nun, 'is it true, what we heard the other day, that Sister Adamantina from Green Bower Hermitage has run off with a man?'

'What utter nonsense!' replied Xi-chun. 'People who tell such tales should beware of having their tongues cut out in hell! The poor girl was kidnapped by a gang of ruffians! How can anyone have the heart to spread such malicious gossip!'

'Sister Adamantina was a strange one all the same,' said the nun. 'We always thought she overdid it a bit. Of course, we don't like to criticize her in front of you, miss. Who are we when compared with her, after all? Just ordinary, unrefined people; we chant our liturgy, say our prayers, make intercession for the sins of others, and hope to earn ourselves a little merit, a little good karma.'

'What does good karma really mean?' asked Xi-chun earnestly.

'Well, miss, putting aside the truly virtuous families like your own, which have nothing to fear, of course – other noble ladies and young misses of good family can never be certain how long their prosperity will last. If calamity once strikes, then nothing can save them. Nothing, that is, except Our Lady of Mercy: if Our Lady sees a mortal suffering, her infinite compassion moves her to try to guide that mortal towards salvation. That is why we all pray to her and say: "Hail, Lady of Mercy, Bodhisattva of Boundless Compassion and Grace, Deliverer, Saviour, Hail!"

'A nun leads a hard life, it's true, harder than a young lady in a rich family. But we're *saved*! Even if we can't hope to become Buddhas or Saints, at least by keeping up our devotions we may one day in another lifetime be reborn as men. And that would be sufficient reward in itself. At least then we would escape the endless trials and silent tribulations of womankind. You are still too young to understand, miss; but let me tell you, when once a young lady leaves home and marries, it is all over with her. She must spend the rest of her days a slave to her husband's will.

'In the true religious life, it is sincere devotion that counts. Sister Adamantina always thought herself so gifted and sensitive, so superior. To her we were always vulgar mortals. And yet ordinary folk like us can at least earn good simple karma, while look at this terrible thing that has befallen her.'

Their words found an all too receptive ear. Uninhibited by the presence of her maids, Xi-chun poured out the whole story of how badly You-shi had been treating her, and how she had been made to stay and look after the house, and the disastrous consequence. She showed them where she had already hacked off a part of her hair.

'You think I'm just another worldling, trapped in the fiery pit of delusion! But you're wrong. I've been wanting to be a nun for a long time myself. I just haven't been able to think of a way of achieving my goal.'

The nuns feigned alarm:

'Now, miss, don't you ever say such a thing again! If Mrs Zhen were to hear, she'd give us the scolding of our lives and have us thrown out of the convent. Why, a young lady like yourself, bred in such a good family, you're sure to marry a fine young gentleman and enjoy a lifetime of luxury and ease . . .'

The colour flew into Xi-chun's cheeks:

'What makes you think my sister-in-law can have you sent away, and I can't?'

The nuns realized from this that she was in earnest, and decided to goad her on a little further:

'Don't take offence, miss. But do you honestly believe that Their Ladyships and the young mistresses would let you have your way? You will only stir up a lot of unnecessary trouble for yourself. It's you we're thinking of.'

'We shall see,' was Xi-chun's brief comment.

Landscape thought this augured ill, and gave the nuns a meaningful glance. They took the hint, and too scared to lead Xi-chun on any further, made their farewells. Xi-chun did not detain them, but merely smiled scornfully after them and said:

'Don't imagine yours is the only convent!'

The nuns thought it wiser not to reply.

Landscape was worried by this latest turn of events, and fearing that she might be blamed if anything untoward occurred she crept off to inform You-shi:

'Miss Xi-chun is still set on shaving her head and becoming a nun, ma'am. These past few days she's not been ill, she's been lying at home nursing her grievance. Perhaps it would be safer to take some precautions. If anything were to happen, we would be blamed . . .'

'She doesn't really want to leave home and take holy vows,' said You-shi. 'She just thinks she can take advantage of Mr Zhen's absence to challenge my authority. Well, so far as I'm concerned, she can go ahead and good luck to her!'

Landscape continued none the less in her efforts to dissuade Xi-chun from her drastic course of action. But Xi-chun persisted in her fast, and her only thought now was to take the final step and cut off what remained of her hair. Landscape could bear it no longer, and went to tell Ladies Xing and Wang. They tried talking Xi-chun out of it several times, but their efforts were in vain. She seemed obsessed.

The two ladies were on the point of going to inform Jia Zheng when one of the servants outside announced the arrival of Lady Zhen and young Master Zhen Bao-yu. They hurried out to welcome their guests and escorted Lady Zhen into Lady Wang's apartment, where they all sat down, formal greetings were exchanged and polite conversation was made, details of which we need not record. Lady Wang made a reference to the supposed resemblance between their two sons, the 'two jades', and expressed a desire to see Zhen Bao-yu for herself. He was sent for at once, but the answer returned that he was conversing with Sir Zheng in the outer study, and that they seemed to have struck up an immediate rapport. Bao-yu, Huan and Lan had also been summoned to take lunch in the study, and Master Zhen would call on Lady Wang afterwards.

Presently lunch was served for the ladies.

Jia Zheng, having witnessed for himself the physical resemblance between this Zhen Bao-yu and his own son, proceeded to test the young man's literary and scholastic abilities and was most impressed by the fluent answers that he gave. He sent for his own Bao-yu and the other two boys, in order to exhibit to them this paragon of virtue, as both stimulus and admonition, and in particular to afford Bao-yu an opportunity for salutary self-comparison.

Bao-yu answered the summons promptly, and appeared in full mourning-dress, accompanied by Huan and Lan. When he saw Zhen Bao-yu for the first time, it seemed to him almost as if he were being reunited with an old friend, and the feeling of delight was apparently mutual. They bowed to each other, and Huan and Lan followed suit. Jia Zheng had been sitting on a mat on the floor, and had asked Master Zhen on arrival to sit at a chair, an invitation that Master Zhen had (very properly) declined, since his senior was seated at a lower level. Instead he installed himself on a cushion on the floor. Now that Bao-yu and the other two had joined the company, it would hardly be right for them to sit on the floor with Jia Zheng; nor on the other hand could they remain standing while Master Zhen, their contemporary, was seated below. Jia Zheng resolved the dilemma by standing up himself, and after talking with them for a few minutes, he instructed the servants to serve lunch.

'I shall have to leave you now,' he said to Master Zhen. 'Please excuse me. I hand you over to the younger generation, who will learn much from you.'

'It is I, sir,' replied Zhen, with polite modesty, 'who am most anxious to learn from these gentlemen.'

Jia Zheng said a few more words in reply, and then took his leave, politely preventing his young visitor from accompanying him, but allowing Bao-yu, Jia Huan and Jia Lan, who had preceded him and were waiting outside the threshold, to escort him into the inner study. They returned, prayed Master Zhen to be seated again, and there was a certain amount of conventional chat, with references to this 'long-awaited and much anticipated meeting', details of which we need not record here.

Jia Bao-yu, on seeing Zhen Bao-yu, had instantly been reminded of their earlier dream-encounter 'in the mirror'. From what he knew by report of Zhen Bao-yu, he felt sure that this jade counterpart of his would be a person after his own heart, and that he was destined to find in him a true friend. However, since this was their first 'real' meeting, and since Huan and Lan were present, he felt the need to be somewhat discreet, and therefore addressed him in the polite hyperboles customary on such occasions:

'Long have I admired you from afar, but alas till now I have been denied the honour of a personal acquaintance. Today this great blessing is mine, and lo, I see before me a reincarnation of the Great Bard, a second Li Bo!'

Zhen Bao-yu had also heard a great deal about his namesake, and found that the reality conformed pretty much to his expectations.

'He seems a passable companion in my studies,' he thought to himself, 'but hardly someone to share my aspirations. And yet he has my name, and looks so like me; we must be souls linked by some bond at the Rock of Rebirth. I have made some progress of late in the understanding of Higher Principles, and should therefore seek to impart to him something of what I have learned. Since this is only our first meeting, however, and since I am still ignorant where his sympathies lie, I should tread cautiously.'

He replied to Jia Bao-yu's remarks in what he deemed to be a fitting vein:

'Long have I known of your great gifts. I fear that, before a person of such egregious purity, refinement and grace, I am but an ordinary and foolish mortal, and that by sharing your name I do but tarnish its lustre.'

'He seems a sympathetic enough character,' pondered Jia Bao-yu upon hearing this. 'But why does he flatter me almost as if I were a girl? We are both of us men, and therefore creatures of impurity.'

'Your praise is alas undeserved,' he said. 'I am but a dull and foolish creature, a mere lump of senseless stone! How can I compare with a person of such quality and nobility as yourself? It is I who am unworthy of the name that we both bear.'

'When I was young,' mused Zhen Bao-yu aloud for his new friend's benefit, 'I was blind to my own limitations and entertained ideas far above my station. But then my family fell on hard times, and we have all spent the past few years in greatly reduced circumstances. As a result, although I can hardly lay claim to a comprehensive experience of life's vicissitudes, I feel I may have acquired some slight knowledge of the ways of the world, some meagre understanding of human nature. You, on the other hand, have lived in the lap of luxury all your life, you have lacked for nothing, and you have, I am sure, been able to achieve great distinction in your literary compositions and in the study of public affairs, a distinction that has caused your honourable father to hold you in high esteem, and to view you with great pride and affection. I say again, *you* are worthy of the fine name that we both bear.'

Jia Bao-yu recognized by now the telltale rhetoric of the 'career worm' and fell silent, wondering how best to respond, while Jia Huan for his part began to feel uncomfortable at having been so entirely excluded from the conversation. Jia Lan, however, found Zhen Bao-yu's little sermon most congenial:

'You are altogether too modest, sir. Surely, in the fields of literary composition and public affairs of which you speak, it is precisely from long experience that true ability and knowledge are derived. I am of course too young to claim any knowledge of literary composition, but a careful perusal of the little that I have read has led me to the conclusion that external grace and meretricious refinement are of little worth when compared with the cultivation of a good character.'

Jia Bao-yu found his nephew's remarks nauseatingly priggish, and wondered where on earth he had picked up this way of speaking. He attempted to forestall a reply in like vein from Zhen Bao-yu:

'I had always understood from what I had heard of you that you condemned vulgar and commonplace notions, and had formed your own personal view of the world. I was so happy to have had this

opportunity of meeting you today, and of learning from you something that would help me transcend this mortal realm we live in and
enter a more spiritual plane. I felt sure that such an encounter would
help to cleanse my heart of worldly desires, and open my eyes to a
more profound view of life. Alas, it is clear from your words that
you consider me a coarse creature, and have therefore treated me out
of politeness to this rigmarole of worldly wisdom.'

Young Zhen reflected:

'Clearly he has heard tales of me as a child, and therefore thinks
that I was speaking out of mere politeness, masking my true nature. I
must be frank with him. Who knows, he may even turn out to be a
true friend.'

'I fully appreciate the sincerity of your remarks,' he began. 'When
I was young, I too abhorred anything that smacked of the platitude
and the cliché. But I grew older, and when my father resigned from
his post and had little further inclination for social entertaining, the
role of host devolved upon me. In the course of my duties I observed
that each one of the distinguished gentlemen whom I met had in one
way or another brought honour and glory to his family name. All
their written works or spoken words were of loyalty and filial piety,
their entire lives were devoted to virtue and truth and were indeed a
fitting tribute to the enlightened rule under which we live and a due
token of gratitude for the kind and illuminating instruction bestowed
upon them by their fathers and teachers alike. So gradually I cast off
the intractable theories and foolish passions of my youth. I am still
searching for teachers and friends of a like mind to instruct me and
guide me out of my benighted ignorance, and I consider it a great
blessing to have met you. I feel sure that I have much to learn from
you. Believe me, what I said earlier was in earnest.'

The more Jia Bao-yu heard the more exasperated he felt. For
politeness' sake he mumbled something ambiguous in reply, and was
saved from further embarrassment by a summons from the inner
apartments:

'If the gentlemen have eaten, would Mr Zhen please join the
ladies?'

Bao-yu seized this opportunity, promptly inviting Zhen Bao-yu to
lead the way, and they proceeded to Lady Wang's apartment,
followed by the other boys. Seeing Lady Zhen seated in the place of
honour, Jia Bao-yu paid her his respects, Jia Huan and Jia Lan

followed suit, and Zhen Bao-yu likewise paid his respects to Lady Wang. At last the two ladies and their two 'jades' were face to face. Although Jia Bao-yu was now married, Lady Zhen was old enough not to have to stand on ceremony on that account, especially as the connection between their two families was such a long-standing one. She saw how alike the two of them were, and could not help warming towards Jia Bao-yu; with Lady Wang it was the same, she took Zhen Bao-yu by the hand and plied him with questions, finding him rather more mature than her own son. She glanced at Jia Lan, and reflected to herself that he too cut a fine figure; though not quite on a level with the two 'jades', he could certainly hold his own in their company. Jia Huan's uncouth appearance, on the other hand, aroused all her old antipathy.

When it became known that both 'jades' were present together, all the maids came to have a look.

'How extraordinary!' they murmured to one another. 'It's one thing for them to have the same name; but they even *look* alike – face, build, everything! Luckily *our* Bao-yu is dressed in mourning white or we'd never be able to tell them apart!'

Nightingale in particular seemed momentarily quite stunned. She was thinking of Dai-yu:

'If only she were still alive! They might have married her to *this* Bao-yu. I think she'd have been willing enough . . .'

Even as these thoughts were running through her head, she heard Lady Zhen say: 'A few days ago, I believe my husband, who now considers *our* Bao-yu of an age to be married, asked Sir Zheng to look out for a suitable bride for him.'

Lady Wang was already much taken with Zhen Bao-yu and without any hesitation she replied:

'I should be glad to act as a matchmaker for your son. Of our own girls, two have passed away, and one is already married. Cousin Zhen of Ning-guo House has an unmarried younger sister, but she is a few years too young for the match. I have another idea, though. My elder daughter-in-law, a member of the Li family by birth, has two cousins, both fine good-looking girls. The older of the two is already betrothed, but the younger is not and would make an excellent bride for your son. I will make the proposal on your behalf. I ought perhaps to mention that their family circumstances are somewhat reduced.'

'You are being unnecessarily polite,' said Lady Zhen. 'Nowadays, we are nothing to boast about ourselves. In fact *they* may consider *us* beneath them.'

'But your husband has been given this new commission,' said Lady Wang, 'and I feel certain that in the future he will not only be restored to his former prosperity, but will rise to new heights of glory.'

Lady Zhen smiled:

'I only hope your predictions come true. Well, in that case, I should be most grateful if you would propose the match on our behalf.'

Zhen Bao-yu, on hearing them broach the subject of his betrothal, excused himself and was escorted by Jia Bao-yu and the other boys back to the study, where they rejoined Jia Zheng and stood for a while talking. Presently one of the Zhen servants came to summon Zhen Bao-yu:

'Lady Zhen is leaving now, sir, and requests you to return.'

Zhen Bao-yu made his farewell, and Jia Zheng instructed Bao-yu, Jia Huan and Jia Lan to see him out. And there we must leave him.

Ever since his earlier encounter with Zhen Bao-yu's father, Jia Bao-yu had been looking forward impatiently to the arrival of his supposed *alter ego*, hoping to find in him a true friend. Now that they had met, he was sorely disillusioned, realizing from their conversation that the two of them were poles apart, as far removed from each other as the proverbial ice and coal. He made his way back to his apartment in a mood of profound depression, said not a word, did not even smile, but stared vacantly into space.

'Well?' asked Bao-chai. '*Is* he your "living likeness" then?'

'He certainly looks like me,' replied Bao-yu. 'But I could tell from the way he talked that he was a fool, just another career worm.'

'There you go, finding fault again!' protested Bao-chai. 'How can you suddenly know that he's a career worm?'

'He talked a lot,' replied Bao-yu, 'and there was nothing the slightest bit profound or illuminating in what he said; he just spouted on at me about "literary composition and public affairs", and "loyalty and filial piety". Isn't that the way a worm talks? It's a shame that he looks like me; now that I know what he's like, I wish I could look different . . .'

Bao-chai could see he was on one of his hobbyhorses again:

'The things you say are really laughable! How could you possibly look different? What's more, his ideas sound very right and proper to me. A man should want to set himself up in life and amount to something. Just because you're so sentimental and wrapped up in your own feelings, does that mean that everyone else has to be too? You attack him for being a worm, when it's really *you* who have no strength of character!'

Bao-yu had found Zhen Bao-yu's sermon exasperating enough. With Bao-chai's diatribe on top of it, he felt himself rapidly sinking into a slough of despond. A familiar feeling of overwhelming muzziness seemed to descend on him, and he could sense a relapse coming on. He said nothing, but smiled inanely, to the bewilderment of Bao-chai. She surmised that he was smiling to mask his annoyance with her harsh words, and therefore decided to ignore him. But for the rest of that day he remained in the same stupor, refusing to speak even if Aroma or one of the others deliberately provoked him, and when he rose the next morning he looked exactly as he had done before his recent convalescence.

Lady Wang meanwhile had finally concluded that she must inform Jia Zheng of Xi-chun's determination to shave her head and take holy vows. You-shi had proved incapable of dissuading her and it seemed likely that any further opposition to her will would only drive her to suicide. They were keeping a watch on her day and night, but this was just a temporary measure. She and her aspirations could not be contained in this way for ever. Jia Zheng sighed and stamped his foot:

'Goodness only knows what Ning-guo House has done to deserve an end like this!'

He sent for Jia Rong:

'Go and tell your mother that she must make one last determined effort to talk Xi-chun round. Then if the girl persists in her folly, we will simply have to act as if she is no longer one of our family.'

You-shi did as she was instructed, but her efforts had the very opposite effect, and only elicited more threats of suicide from Xi-chun.

'I'm a girl and you know I can't stay at home for the rest of my life. What if I were to end up with a marriage like Ying-chun's? Look at all the heartache she caused her parents, and Uncle Zheng and Auntie Wang, and then she died . . . If you love me, think of *me* as dead, let me go, let me at least *try* to make something pure of my life. I won't be living away from home anyway, I'll only be in Green Bower Hermitage, which is part of the Garden. Adamantina's women are still living there. *That* can be my nunnery. You can look after my needs there. Please let me do this, and I shall think myself blessed. By continuing to go against me, you will be forcing me to put an end to my life. If I am allowed to follow my own chosen path, then when my brother returns I shall tell him plainly that I did it of my own free will. But if I die, he's sure to say you drove me to my death.'

There had always been discord between You-shi and Xi-chun, and besides, You-shi could see the force of her argument. She went to report to Lady Wang. But Lady Wang was in Bao-chai's apartment, where she had just discovered for herself the recent deterioration in Bao-yu's condition, and was upbraiding Aroma:

'You are altogether too careless! You should have told me at once when Bao-yu fell ill!'

'But your Ladyship,' pleaded Aroma, 'Bao-yu is often ill – some days he may be better, then he's worse again. He's been visiting you and paying his morning duty every day and really he's been quite all right until today, when he seems to have had a bit of a queer turn. Mrs Bao was going to come over and tell you, only she didn't want you to scold us for making a fuss about nothing.'

This scolding of Aroma's, and the fear that she and Bao-chai might suffer on his behalf, seemed to restore Bao-yu temporarily to his senses:

'Don't worry, Mother. There's nothing the matter with me. I just feel a bit low.'

'My child, you mustn't forget you have a tendency to take ill. If only I'd known earlier, I could have sent for a doctor and had some proper medicine prescribed for you in time. If you allow yourself to sink into the dreadful state you were in after you lost your jade, you'll cause us no end of trouble again!'

'If you're still worried, Mother,' said Bao-yu, 'then by all means send for a doctor and I'll take some medicine.'

Lady Wang accordingly sent a maid to fetch a doctor, and was thus far too preoccupied with Bao-yu to think of Xi-chun's predicament. The doctor arrived presently, examined Bao-yu and made out a prescription, after the administration of which Lady Wang returned to her own apartment.

Over the next few days, however, Bao-yu seemed to become more of an imbecile than ever. He stopped eating completely, and his condition began to cause general concern. When the time came for the ceremony to mark the end of the formal mourning period for Grandmother Jia, and since the family were especially busy at the temple, Jia Yun was called in to receive Bao-yu's doctor; and because of the shortage of men in Jia Lian's compound, Wang Ren also had to be asked to attend and help supervise there. Qiao-jie had made herself ill crying day and night for her mother, and in every respect Rong-guo House presented a picture of sad disarray.

When the family returned from the service at the temple, Lady Wang went at once to visit Bao-yu. She found that his condition had greatly deteriorated. He was unconscious, and the servants were in a helpless panic; some were standing there in tears, some had already gone to Jia Zheng's, where they announced:

'The doctor says it's a waste of time to prescribe any more medicine, and we must be prepared for the worst . . .'

Jia Zheng heaved a bitter sigh and went to inspect for himself. Bao-yu indeed showed every sign of being at death's door, and Jia Zheng ordered Jia Lian to make the necessary preparations. Jia Lian did not dare gainsay him, and reluctantly gave instructions for Bao-yu's last things to be prepared. He was just wondering how they could possibly raise the money for yet another funeral, when one of the servants rushed into the room in a state of great agitation, crying:

'Mr Lian! Something terrible! Another disaster!'

Jia Lian had no notion what the man could be referring to and stared at him transfixed with fear:

'What is it?'

'There's a monk at the gate and he says he's brought back Mr Bao's lost jade. He wants ten thousand taels for it . . .'

Jia Lian spat in the servant's face:

'*Hng!* I thought from the fluster you were in that it was something serious. Didn't you hear about that last hoax? And even if this jade *were* genuine, what good could it do now, when the boy's already past hope?'

'That's what I said myself, sir. But the monk swore that Mr Bao would be cured as soon as we paid him the money.'

As he was speaking, another servant rushed in crying:

'The monk's gone berserk! He's crashing his way in and none of us can stop him!'

'This is unbelievable!' exclaimed Jia Lian. 'Send him packing this instant!'

When he learned what had happened, Jia Zheng was as flummoxed as Jia Lian. Meanwhile more cries came from within:

'Bao-yu is sinking!'

Jia Zheng was growing desperate, when he heard the monk's voice calling:

'If you want the boy to live, just bring me the money!'

Jia Zheng suddenly thought:

'It was a monk who cured Bao-yu's earlier illness; perhaps this monk can save him after all. But if the jade *is* genuine, how will we ever raise the money for it?'

After a moment's reflection, he concluded to himself:

'Oh well, we can think of that in due course. Let's cure him first, and bargain later.'

By the time he had reached this decision and despatched a servant with an invitation, the monk was already on his way, and without so much as a bow or a word of acknowledgement went striding into Bao-yu's room. Jia Lian tried to restrain him, saying:

'There are ladies in there! A tramp like you can't go barging in!'

'Any delay,' cried the monk, 'and it may be too late to save him!'

Jia Lian was too flustered to be able to do anything but follow him, calling out in confusion:

'Quiet now! Stop your weeping! The monk has arrived!'

He continued calling out like this, but Lady Wang and the others were far too overwrought by Bao-yu's condition to pay him any attention. When eventually they did look round, they were shocked to see the great burly figure of the monk descending on them, and at the last moment tried unsuccessfully to conceal themselves, while the monk made straight for the kang on which Bao-yu lay. Bao-chai withdrew to one side, but Aroma felt she should stay with Lady Wang, who had remained standing where she was.

'Ladies, I have brought the jade,' proclaimed the monk.

He held it up, as he continued:

'Give me the money, and I can save the lad.'

Shock had utterly incapacitated Lady Wang, and she and the other ladies were certainly in no fit state to judge the authenticity of the stone exhibited to them.

'Just save him,' they cried, 'and the money will be yours!'

The monk laughed.

'I want it now!'

'Don't worry,' said Lady Wang. 'You shall have the money without fail, even if we have to pawn everything we have.'

The monk seemed to find this suggestion hysterically funny, and after a good deal of laughter he held the jade out in one hand, bent down and whispered in Bao-yu's ear:

'Bao-yu! Precious Jade! Your Stone has returned!'

No sooner had he spoken than Bao-yu opened his eyes a slit.

'He lives!' cried Aroma ecstatically.

'Where is it?' asked Bao-yu.

The monk placed the jade in Bao-yu's hand.

At first Bao-yu clutched it tightly, then slowly he turned his hand palm upwards and brought the Stone up to eye-level. He peered at it closely and exclaimed:

'Ah! We are reunited at last!'

Everyone began uttering fervent prayers to the Lord Buddha, and even Bao-chai now seemed oblivious of the monk's male presence. Jia Lian came across to see what had happened, and the sight of a revivified Bao-yu brought momentary cheer to his heart too. Suddenly he slipped out, and without a word the monk raced after him and overtook him. Jia Lian had no choice but to escort the monk to the reception hall and then hurry over to inform Jia Zheng, who was enormously relieved by the news, and sent for the monk straight away, bowing to him and expressing his profound thanks. The monk returned the salutation and sat down. Jia Lian thought to himself apprehensively:

'Now he won't budge till he's been paid . . .'

Jia Zheng scrutinized the monk. It was not, he concluded, one of the two he had seen on the previous occasion.

'From which holy establishment do you hail?' he enquired. 'And what pray is your reverend's own name in religion? Where did you obtain my son's stone talisman? How is it that the sight of it has cured him so quickly?'

The monk greeted this stream of questions with an inscrutable smile:

'Don't ask me. I have not the slightest idea. Just give me my ten thousand taels, and we'll call it a day.'

Jia Zheng could see he was dealing with rather a brusque sort of fellow, and was nervous of offending him:

'The money? Why yes, of course you shall have it . . .'

'I'd like it now. I'm in a hurry.'

'Please be seated for a moment, while I go in and see whether it is ready.'

'You'd better get a move on.'

Jia Zheng went in to the others. He said nothing of his interview with the monk but went straight to the kang where Bao-yu was lying. When Bao-yu saw his father coming, he tried to raise himself up, but was too weak to do so. Lady Wang held him down and told him on no account to move, while Bao-yu smiled from where he lay and handed the jade to his father, with the words:

'You see, *Bao-yu* has returned!'

Jia Zheng was aware of the Stone's reputedly supernatural properties. He glanced at it and said to Lady Wang:

'Now that Bao-yu has recovered consciousness, how are we to pay the monk?'

'Pawn everything I own!' replied Lady Wang at once. 'That should be enough.'

'I hardly think he wants money,' put in Bao-yu. 'Do you?'

Jia Zheng nodded thoughtfully:

'I thought it rather strange, I must say. But he absolutely insists.'

'You must go out and entertain him,' said Lady Wang. 'We'll see what we can do.'

As Jia Zheng went out, Bao-yu began clamouring for food. First he consumed a bowl of congee and then he demanded some rice, which the old women even brought him. But Lady Wang forbade him to eat it.

'It'll be perfectly all right,' protested Bao-yu. 'I'm better now.'

He leant forwards and promptly tucked into a bowl of rice. His spirits seemed greatly revived. He wanted to sit up properly, and Musk came forward and supported him gently. Carried away by her excitement at his recovery she blurted out:

'What a treasure that Stone of yours is! Just *seeing* it has made you better! Thank goodness you never managed to smash it to pieces!'

Her words caused a sudden change to come over Bao-yu's face. He threw the Stone aside and slumped back. But to learn if he survived, you must turn to the next chapter.

CHAPTER 116

Human destinies are revealed in a fairy realm,
and the Stone is restored to its rightful owner
Mortal remains are transported to their terrestrial home,
and duty is discharged by a filial son

Musk's untimely reference to a sensitive episode from the past sent Bao-yu into a sudden swoon and he slumped back onto his bed once more. Lady Wang and the assembled family broke into a fresh bout of wailing and weeping, while Musk herself, realizing that her thoughtlessness was to blame for this terrible turn (though Lady Wang had not yet had time to scold her), began to weep and at the same time made a desperate resolution:

'If Bao-yu dies, I shall take my own life and die with him!'

Lady Wang could see that this time none of their efforts to rouse Bao-yu was having any effect, and sent an urgent message to the monk, begging him to come to the rescue again. But the monk was nowhere to be seen. Jia Zheng had returned earlier to the hall, only to find that his eccentric guest had vanished into thin air. This fresh outcry from the inner apartment now reached Jia Zheng's ears and he hurried back, to find Bao-yu unconscious again, teeth clenched and with no trace of a pulse. He felt his chest, and finding it still quite warm, sent in desperation for a doctor, to attempt resuscitation by forcing down a draught of some kind.

But Bao-yu's spirit had already quit its mortal frame. Then that means he was dead, you say? The exact situation, dear Reader, was as follows: the spirit had flitted in its incorporeal fashion out to the reception hall, where it saw the jade-bearing monk and saluted him with a bow. The monk hurriedly rose to his feet, grasped the spirit by the hand and set off. Bao-yu (spirit) followed, light as a leaf drifting in the breeze. They made their way out not by the main entrance but by a route he failed to recognize, and presently they reached an open space, a wilderness, whence in the far distance he spied a strangely familiar monumental archway. He was on the point of asking the monk what it was, when a misty female form came gliding towards him.

'What is a beautiful creature like that doing in such a desolate place as this?' Bao-yu asked himself. 'She must be some goddess come to earth.'

He approached her and looked more closely. Her face was as familiar as the archway had been, but somehow he was unable to remember exactly who she was. She greeted the monk, and then in an instant vanished from view. In that same instant Bao-yu knew who it was that she resembled: You San-jie. More puzzled than ever (for what could *she* be doing here?), he wanted to question the monk. But before he could do so, the monk was leading him by the hand on through the archway. On the lintel of the arch were inscribed in large characters the words:

THE PARADISE OF TRUTH

A couplet in smaller characters ran down on either side:

> When Fiction departs and Truth appears,
> >   Truth prevails;
> Though Not-real was once Real, the Real
> >   is never unreal.

Having negotiated the archway, they presently came to the gate of a palace, above which ran a horizontal inscription:

> Blessing for the Virtuous; Misfortune for the Wicked

whilst the following words were inscribed vertically on the two sides:

> Human Wit can ne'er unveil the Mysteries of Time,
> Nor Closest Kin defy the Stern Decrees of Fate.

'So . . .' thought Bao-yu to himself. 'It is time I began to learn more about the operation of fate.' Even as this thought was passing through his mind, he saw (of all people) Faithful standing a little way off, beckoning and calling to him.

'All this time and I'm still at home in the Garden!' he reflected in astonishment. 'But why is it so changed?'

He hurried forward to speak to Faithful, but a second later she too had vanished and he was left standing there, more perplexed than ever. He continued to advance towards the place where Faithful had been, and as he did so he observed a range of buildings on either side of him, and above the entrance to each building a board proclaiming its name. He felt no great inclination to inspect any of these buildings closely, but hurried on in quest of Faithful. The entrance beyond the spot where she had stood was ajar, but he did not dare to enter, thinking he should consult his guide first. And yet when he turned to find him, the monk had vanished. The buildings all around him suddenly seemed very grand, and it began to occur to Bao-yu that perhaps this was not Prospect Garden after all. He stood still and raised his head to read the words above the doorway immediately in front of him:

AWAKEN FROM LOVE'S FOLLY

The couplet on either side ran:

> Smiles of gladness, tears of woe, all are false;
> Every lust and every longing stems from folly.

Bao-yu nodded his head and sighed. He still wanted to enter the doorway and go in search of Faithful, to ask her what this place was that he had come to. He felt a growing certainty that he had been here on some previous occasion. Finally he plucked up the courage to push the door open, and went in. There was no sign whatsoever of Faithful. It was pitch dark inside and he was about to give in to fear and retrace his steps when his eyes discerned, looming in the darkness, the shapes of a dozen large cupboards, their doors apparently pushed to but unlocked. A sudden realization swept over him:

'I *know* I've been somewhere like this before. I remember it now. It was in a dream. What a blessing this is, to return to the scene of my childhood dream!'

Somehow in his confusion his original intention of finding Faithful had gone, giving way to a new and more generalized curiosity about what lay before him. He plucked up his courage again and opened the door of the first cupboard. Within it he saw a number of albums, and a thrill of excited delight ran through him.

'People always say that dreams are false,' he thought to himself. 'But it seems that this one was real! How often I've wished I could dream that dream of mine again! And now here I am, and my wish is coming true. I wonder if these are the very albums I saw?'

Stretching out his hand he took the top one, and held it in his hand. It bore the label 'Jinling, Twelve Beauties of, Main Register'.

'I *do* remember seeing this,' he thought to himself. 'I think I do . . . If only I could remember more clearly!'

He opened it at the first page, and found himself looking at a picture, but one that was so blurred he could hardly tell what it represented. There followed a few rows of characters, written in an almost indecipherable hand, among which he could faintly trace the forms of 'jade belt' (*dai yu*) and 'greenwood' (*lin*).

'Surely that must be a riddle for Cousin Lin?' he thought to himself, and read on in earnest. The next line contained the words 'the gold pin beneath the snow (*xue*)'.

'Why that's Bao-chai's surname!' he exclaimed aloud.

He read to the end of the fourth and last line.

'It doesn't seem to say very much. It's just a series of riddles on the names Lin Dai-yu and Xue Bao-chai. There's nothing very exceptional about that. But some of the phrases sound rather ominous. I wonder what it's all supposed to mean?

'Silly me! I'm not really supposed to be here at all,' he rebuked himself. 'If I spend my time daydreaming like this and someone comes, I'll have wasted my chance to look through the rest.'

He continued his inspection of the albums. He did not allow himself time to linger over the next picture, but went straight to the poem, which ended with the words:

> When hare meets tiger, your great dream shall end.

They brought a sudden burst of illumination:

'What a brilliant prediction! It must refer to the death of my eldest sister. If they are all as clear as this, I should copy them down and study them carefully. That way I can find out everything about my sisters and cousins, how long they're going to live, whether they will fail or succeed in life, be wealthy or poor. At home I shall have to keep my knowledge a secret of course. But my inside information will at least save *me* a lot of unnecessary worrying . . .'

He looked everywhere for writing implements, but could see neither brush nor inkstone, and fearing that someone might surprise him, he hurriedly scanned through the rest of the album. The next leaf bore an impressionistic representation of a figure flying a kite. He did not feel in the mood to dwell on the pictures but quickly read the remaining poems in the set of twelve. In some cases he was able to grasp the hidden meaning at a first reading, others required a moment's reflection, while some remained obstinately unintelligible. He committed all of them carefully to memory none the less. With a sigh he took out the next album, labelled 'Supplementary Register No. 1', and began to read. He stopped at the lines:

> You chose the player fortune favoured,
> Unmindful of your master's doom.

At first they meant nothing to him. Then he studied the accompanying picture, a bunch of flowers and a mat painted in the same impressionistic style as the kite-flying girl. Suddenly he burst into tears.*

He was about to read further, when he heard a voice saying:

'Daydreaming again! Come now, Cousin Lin wants to see you.'

The voice was very like Faithful's, but when he turned to look, to his great bewilderment there was no one there. Then suddenly he saw Faithful again, standing outside the doorway and beckoning to him. He ran out after her in delight, but her shadowy form drifted constantly ahead of him and he was unable to overtake her.

'Dear Faithful! Please wait for me!' he cried.

She took no notice but hurried on ahead, while he ran panting after her. Suddenly another vista loomed in front of him, of high buildings and intricately carved roofs, among which he could dimly perceive the figures of palace ladies. In his eagerness to explore this new realm Bao-yu forgot Faithful completely. Wandering in through one of the gateways, he found himself among all sorts of strange and exotic plants and flowers, none of which he could identify. One in particular caught his eye, a herbaceous plant surrounded by a marble balustrade, the tips of its leaves tinged a faint red.

'What rare plant can that be,' he wondered, 'to be accorded such a place of honour?'

A gentle breeze had arisen and the plant fluttered its leaves with a long drawn-out trembling motion. It was small and flowerless, but its delicate charm held Bao-yu's heart spellbound and enraptured his soul. He was still staring at it dumbfounded when a voice beside him spoke:

'Where are you from, you great booby? And what do you think you're doing peeping at our Fairy Plant?'

Startled from his reverie, Bao-yu turned to see a fairy maiden standing at his side. He bowed and said in reply to her questions:

* See Volume 1, Appendix, p. 527.

'I came here to find Faithful. Excuse me if I have clumsily tres-passed on your fairy domain. Please can you tell me, Sister Fairy, what this place is, and why Faithful said that Cousin Lin wanted to see me? Please will you explain?'

'Sister this, Cousin that! Such names mean nothing to me!' replied the fairy. 'All I know is that this Fairy Plant is my responsibility, and that it is strictly forbidden for mortals like you to loiter here. You must leave at once.'

Bao-yu could not bring himself to obey the fairy's command.

'Sister Fairy!' he pleaded once more. 'If you are in charge of a Fairy Plant, then you must be a Flower Fairy yourself. Can you tell me: what is so special about *this* particular plant?'

'That's a very long story,' replied the fairy. 'Once it grew by the banks of the Magic River and then it was called the Crimson Pearl Flower. It wilted and began to die, but was revived and given im-mortal life through the intervention of the Divine Luminescent Page-in-waiting, who generously watered it with sweet dew. Afterwards it descended into the world of men to repay its debt with the tears of a lifetime, and now that this has been done it has returned to its true abode. Fairy Disenchantment has given me instructions to tend it and to stop the bees and butterflies from molesting it . . .'

Bao-yu still did not understand. He had a growing conviction that this really must be a Flower Fairy that he had met, and was deter-mined not to let such a rare opportunity slip through his hands. He asked her politely:

'So you, Sister Fairy, are in charge of this plant. But each of the many other fine flowers must have its own fairy-in-attendance. I hate to bother you, but I wonder if you could tell me which fairy is in charge of the Hibiscus?'

'I don't know. You'll have to ask my mistress about that.'

'Who is your mistress, pray?'

'My mistress is the River Queen.'

'I knew it!' exclaimed Bao-yu. 'That's my cousin Lin Dai-yu!'

'Stuff and nonsense!' retorted the by now highly exasperated fairy. 'May I remind you again that this is a heavenly realm and the abode of fairies. My mistress may be called the River Queen, but she is nothing like your earthly queens and consorts. How could she possibly be related to a mortal? Stop talking such utter nonsense or I shall have you beaten and thrown out by one of our guards.'

Bao-yu was struck dumb by the fairy's words and became painfully conscious of his own uncleanliness. He was taking his leave when he heard someone hurrying towards them, calling:

'They're asking for the Divine Luminescent Page-in-waiting!'

'I know,' replied the fairy. 'I was told to look out for him. That's why I've been waiting here all this time. But I haven't seen any such Page go by. So what am I to do?'

'Surely that was him – the one who left just now!' cried the messenger with a laugh, and rushed out to waylay Bao-yu.

'Will it please the Divine Luminescent Page-in-waiting to return?'

Bao-yu thought she must be addressing someone else. He was afraid of being overtaken and caught, and continued stumbling forwards, in an effort to make good his escape. When he looked up, he saw before him a formidable figure barring his way with a large sword:

'Where are you going?'

Bao-yu was frightened out of his wits, but managed to pluck up enough courage to take another look. He was astonished, and then somewhat reassured, to find himself face to face with You San-jie.

'Oh Cousin!' he begged her. 'Why are *you* after me too?'

'You men, you're all the same!' was her reply. 'There's not a good one in your entire family. You ruin a girl's reputation, then you destroy her marriage. Well I've got you now, and you won't escape me!'

Bao-yu could tell that she was in deadly earnest and was beginning to panic when he heard another voice behind him saying:

'Sister! Stop that man at once! He must not be allowed to leave!'

'I have my orders from the River Queen,' replied San-jie, 'and I've been waiting a long while for something like this. Now you're in my grasp, and with one blow of my sword I shall sever the ties that bind you to the mortal world.'

Bao-yu was terrified. He could not understand what she was saying, and turned and fled, only to see that the face from which the voice behind him had issued was that of Skybright. Joy and sorrow mingled in his heart.

'I'm lost!' he cried pathetically. 'I'm all on my own and I seem to have run into the arms of the enemy. I wanted to escape and go home, but I couldn't find any of you to take me back. Now I shall be safe! Dear Skybright, please will you take me home now?'

'You must not lose heart,' replied the maiden. 'I am not Skybright. I have been specially commissioned by our Queen to escort you into her presence. I will not do you any harm.'

Bao-yu was now utterly bewildered:

'You say your Queen sent you; but who *is* your Queen?'

'Don't ask now,' replied Skybright. 'Soon you will see for yourself.'

Helplessly Bao-yu followed her, and as they walked he studied her more closely. She resembled Skybright in every detail.

'Her face, her eyes, her voice are all Skybright's!' he reflected to himself. 'How can she say she isn't Skybright? Oh dear, I'm in such a muddle. I'd better take no notice of what she says. Whatever it is that I've done wrong, when I am admitted into the presence of her Queen, I can ask her to help. Women have kind hearts, after all. She will surely forgive me.'

They had now reached a magnificent palace, lavishly and brilliantly appointed in every respect. In the courtyard before them grew a clump of bright green bamboo, while by the main doorway stood a row of dark pine-trees. There were several ladies-in-waiting standing under the eaves, dressed in fine palace robes, and when they saw Bao-yu come in they began whispering among themselves:

'Is *that* the Divine Luminescent Page?'

Bao-yu's attendant informed them:

'It is, so you'd better hurry in and announce his arrival.'

One of the ladies beckoned to Bao-yu with a smile, and he followed her in through several apartments, till finally they arrived at what seemed to be the entrance to the main hall of the palace. It was hung with a pearl blind. Stopping before this blind, the lady-in-waiting turned to Bao-yu and said:

'Wait here for your instructions from Her Majesty.'

Bao-yu did not dare breathe a word, but waited obediently outside the doorway. Presently the lady-in-waiting returned and announced:

'Will the Page please enter now for his audience?'

Another attendant began to roll up the pearl blind, and as she did so Bao-yu caught sight of a regal figure seated within, dressed in richly embroidered robes and wearing a crown of flowers on her head. Raising his head a fraction to look more closely, he saw that the Queen did indeed resemble Dai-yu and cried out impulsively:

'Here you are at last, Coz! Oh how I've missed you!'

The lady-in-waiting outside the blind whispered in a shocked tone: 'Ill-mannered Page! Out with you at once!'

She had barely said this when the other attendant lowered the blind again. Bao-yu was too scared to go in, and yet the thought of leaving was inconceivable. He wanted to ask one of the other ladies-in-waiting for an explanation, but when he looked round he realized that they were all of them strangers. They were forcing him out now and he had no choice but to leave. He thought as a last resort of trying to ask 'Skybright', but when he looked for her she was nowhere to be seen. A deep feeling of confusion and foreboding descended on him and he dragged himself dejectedly away, this time without a guide. There was no trace of the way by which he had come and he was beginning to wonder if he would ever be able to find his way back, when to his delight he saw the figure of Xi-feng beckoning to him from beneath the eaves of another building.

'Thank goodness! I'm home again! How could I have lost my bearings so quickly?'

He rushed up to her:

'Here you are! They've all been so cruel to me, and Cousin Lin wouldn't see me. I don't know why!'

He was standing right next to Xi-feng. But on closer inspection it turned out not to be Xi-feng at all but Jia Rong's first wife, Qin Ke-qing. He hesitated for a moment and then asked her where Xi-feng had gone. But the lady made no reply and presently turned and went inside.

Bao-yu stood there in a daze, not daring to follow her in, but staring blankly before him.

'What have I done wrong today,' he sighed, 'that I should be spurned like this wherever I turn?'

Just as he was bursting into tears, a cohort of guards in yellow turbans with whips in their hands descended upon him.

'Where are you from, and who do you think you are to come sneaking into this fairy realm? Off with you! Be gone!'

Bao-yu did not dare say a word, but continued to search for a way out of the place. In the far distance he spied a crowd of ladies laughing and walking in his direction, and thought to his relief that he could recognize among them Ying-chun and some of his other cousins.

'Help!' he cried. 'I'm lost! Save me!'

Even as he shouted, the guards continued relentlessly to push him on from behind, and he stumbled helplessly forward. Then to his horror he saw that his 'cousins' had been transformed into strange ghoulish monsters and were pursuing him too. His nerves were at breaking point. Suddenly the monk appeared before him, and shone a mirror in his face:

'By the order of Her Grace the Imperial Jia Concubine I have come to save you!'

In a trice the monsters vanished, and Bao-yu was spirited back to the bleak stretch of wilderness from which he had first entered the fairy domain. He grasped the monk's hand:

'You brought me here – that I can remember; and then the next thing I knew you had vanished and I saw some of my family but they would have nothing to do with me and in the end they turned into monsters! Was it all a dream, or was it real? Please, Master, I beg you to tell me the truth.'

'When you first entered this place,' said the monk, 'did you steal a look at anything in particular?'

Bao-yu thought for a moment:

'If he can whisk me off to a fairy paradise, he must be an Adept himself, so it's no use trying to fool him. Besides, I want to know more.'

He confessed to the monk that he had seen several registers.

'Hark at you!' exclaimed the monk. 'You have seen the Registers themselves and are *still* blind! Now listen to me carefully: predestined attachments of the human heart are all of them mere illusion, they are obstacles blocking our spiritual path. Ponder deeply on what you have experienced. I shall explain it to you further when we meet again.'

With that he gave Bao-yu a hefty shove.

'Back you go!' he cried.

Bao-yu missed his footing and stumbled forward, calling out in alarm.

The family were standing by his bedside when suddenly he began to show these unmistakable signs of life. They called his name, and he opened his eyes, to find himself lying on his old kang. Before him were Lady Wang, Bao-chai and other members of his family, their eyes red and swollen with tears. He reflected for a moment and tried to compose himself.

'So!' he said to himself. 'I have visited the land of death, and now I have returned once more to the living!'

He lay pondering one by one the experiences of his wandering soul, and as he did so a glazed look came over his eyes. To his great delight, he found that he could still remember every detail of his dream, and he chuckled aloud with satisfaction:

'So! So!'

Lady Wang suspected a recurrence of his old fit and decided that the doctor had better be summoned again at once. She sent a maid and one of the serving-women to inform Sir Zheng that Bao-yu had recovered consciousness and that his previous (and apparently fatal) crisis had only been a temporary mental affliction from which he now seemed to have recovered. Since he was now obviously on the mend, and was even able to utter a few words, they could safely suspend the funeral arrangements. Jia Zheng came hurrying in to verify this news for himself.

'Luckless creature,' he exclaimed. 'Do you want to frighten us all to death?'

He was weeping despite himself. Heaving a few gusty sighs, he went out again and sent for a doctor to take Bao-yu's pulses and prescribe a medicine for him.

Musk, it will be remembered, had only recently been contemplating suicide; but now that Bao-yu was recovered she set her mind at rest. Lady Wang ordered some longan soup, and told Bao-yu to drink a few mouthfuls. She was greatly relieved to see him gradually revive and regain his composure and she did not even scold Musk for her original blunder, but merely told one of the maids to give the newly recovered jade to Bao-chai, who was to hang it once more round Bao-yu's neck.

'I wonder where the monk found it?' she asked out loud. 'It seems so strange. One minute he was demanding his money, the next minute he had disappeared. Do you imagine he was some sort of Immortal?'

'To judge by the "mysterious" way he came,' said Bao-chai, 'and the equally "mysterious" way in which he left, I should say he never *found* it at all, but that it was he who took it in the first place.'

'How could he have taken it from under our very eyes?' asked Lady Wang.

'If he could bring it back, then he could take it,' persisted Bao-chai.

'When the jade was lost,' put in Aroma and Musk, 'Steward Lin consulted a word-diviner – we told you about it ma'am, soon after the wedding. The character he divined was *shang* meaning "reward". Do you remember, ma'am?'

'Yes, you're right,' said Bao-chai. 'You said it had something to do with a pawnshop. But now I can see it was really pointing to the word "monk", which is contained in the upper part of the character *shang*. We were being told by the word-diviner that a *monk* had taken it!'

'The monk was a strange enough creature,' said Lady Wang. 'When Bao-yu was ill before, another monk came, I remember, and told us that Bao-yu had a precious object of his own at home that could cure him. He was referring to the jade. He too must have known all about its magical properties. It is extraordinary that Bao-yu came into the world with the Stone in his mouth! Have you ever heard of such a thing happening, in the whole of history? Who knows what will become of the Stone in the end? And who knows what will become of *him*! It seems to be an inseparable part of his life, in sickness and health, at his birth and . . .'

She stopped short suddenly and tears started to her eyes. Bao-yu felt in his own mind that he now knew the answer to her questions only too well. Thinking back, he understood more clearly the significance of his visit to the 'other world'. But he said nothing, and stored these thoughts silently in his mind.

It was Xi-chun who spoke next:

'When the jade was lost, we asked Adamantina to consult the planchette on our behalf. The reply she received from the spirit contained the lines:

> Gone to Greensickness Peak, to lie
> At the foot of an age-old pine.

It ended with:

> Follow me and laugh to see
> Your journey at an end!

There's much food for thought contained in those two words "follow me". The gate of the Dharma is certainly wide and all-embracing, but somehow I doubt if Cousin Bao could squeeze through it, whoever he happened to be "following" . . .'

Bao-yu sniffed scornfully. Bao-chai noted this reaction of his, and involuntarily she frowned and stared abstractedly into space.

'Trust you to drag the Buddha into it!' snapped You-shi. 'Are you still pining for your nunnery?'

Xi-chun smiled caustically.

'Actually, sister-in-law, I have already taken the first step. Long ago I vowed that meat should never touch my lips again.'

'My child!' said Lady Wang. 'In the name of Lord Buddha himself! You must abandon this foolish idea!'

Xi-chun was silent.

During this exchange Bao-yu recalled two lines from one of the albums he had seen:

> Alas, that daughter of so great a house
> By Buddha's altar lamp should sleep alone.

He could not refrain from uttering a few sighs. Then he remembered the bunch of flowers and the mat, and glanced at Aroma. Tears started to his eyes. When the family saw him behaving in this strange fashion, laughing one minute and crying the next, they could only think it a symptom of his old fit. None of them knew that their conversation had sparked off a flash of illumination in Bao-yu's mind, with the result that he could now remember word for word every poem from the registers in his dream. Although he said nothing, in his mind a new resolve was already formed. But we anticipate.

*

After Bao-yu's sudden recovery, his spirits improved daily, and with the regular administration of medicine he continued to make steady progress. Now that his son was out of danger, Jia Zheng was anxious to proceed with the interment of Lady Jia's coffin, which had been resting for a long while in the temple. He himself was still in mourning and therefore free from official obligations. There was no telling when (or if) Jia She would be pardoned, so Jia Zheng decided to act on his own initiative and arrange for his mother's mortal remains to be transported to the South and given proper burial there. He sent for Jia Lian to discuss the matter.

'Your proposal is an excellent one, Uncle,' said Jia Lian. 'It would be best to proceed with this important task now. Once the mourning period is over, it may be harder for you to find the necessary time. Father is not at home, and it would be presumptuous of me to undertake a task of this nature. My one concern is the cost. You will require several thousand taels. Our stolen property must I am afraid be written off as an irretrievable loss.'

'My mind is made up to do this,' said Jia Zheng. 'In your father's absence I sent for you merely to discuss the best ways and means. You cannot go, since that would leave no one at home. I am proposing to go myself, and to take several coffins simultaneously. I will need some assistance, and am thinking of taking young Rong with me. There will be three coffins altogether, including your wife's and your cousin Lin's. It was your grandmother's wish that her granddaughter should be buried with her in the South. As for the money, we shall simply have to borrow a few thousand taels from somewhere.'

'There is little generosity left in the world these days,' commented Jia Lian bitterly. 'You are in mourning, Uncle, and Father is in exile. I fear that it may prove impossible to borrow the money. We shall be obliged to mortgage some of our property.'

'But our residence was granted us by Imperial decree,' objected Jia Zheng. 'We are not free to dispose of it in this way.'

'That is true,' said Jia Lian. 'But we have other properties available for mortgage. They can be redeemed after your period of mourning, and after Father's return – all the more so if he is reinstated. Our chief concern is that you may overtax yourself, embarking on such a strenuous journey at your age.'

'It is a duty I owe your grandmother,' said Jia Zheng. 'While I am away, I am counting on you to be diligent here at home, and keep things firmly under control.'

'You can set your mind at ease on that score,' said Jia Lian. 'I shall do my utmost. As you will be taking several servants with you, that will mean fewer mouths to feed here, so we should be able to save a little. If you need any help along the way, you will be travelling close by the official residence of Lai Shang-rong, Steward Lai's son, so you can always call on him for assistance.'

'This affair is my responsibility,' commented Jia Zheng drily. 'Why should I need his or anyone else's assistance?'

'Of course,' Jia Lian hastily concurred, and withdrew to make his own financial calculations.

Jia Zheng informed Lady Wang of his plans, exhorted her to keep a careful eye on the household, and selected a day in the almanac auspicious for setting out on his long journey. Then he made his preparations to leave.

Bao-yu was now completely restored to health, and Jia Huan and Jia Lan were earnestly engaged in their studies. Jia Zheng entrusted them all to Jia Lian, reminding him:

'The state examinations will be held this year. Huan will not be able to compete because he will still be in mourning for his mother. There is nothing to prevent Lan from doing so, however, since his mourning period is shorter and will be over by then. He and Bao-yu should attend together. If they can pass the examination and become Provincial Graduates, it will help to redeem the family from its present disgrace.'

Jia Lian hastened to assure him that he would carry out these instructions. Jia Zheng then addressed the domestics at some length, took ceremonial leave at the ancestral shrine, and after a few days spent outside the city attending religious services at the temple, was finally ready to board his barge and set off. Steward Lin and a handful of servants were travelling with him, and a few members of the family came some of the way to bid him farewell and see him on his way. He did not trouble any other relatives or friends.

Now that Bao-yu had been given his orders to attend the next Civil Service examinations, Lady Wang began to apply more pressure and came constantly to see how his work was progressing, while Bao-chai and Aroma added their support in the form of periodic lectures. They observed the daily improvement in his spirits, but remained quite unaware that a great inner change had been wrought within him, drawing him in an unprecedented (indeed for him almost perverse) direction. In addition to his inveterate contempt for worldly success and advancement, he had of late begun to adopt an attitude of indifference towards the whole gamut of romantic attachment – in a word, towards love itself. But this radically new departure was hardly noticed by those around him, and he himself said nothing to enlighten them.

Nightingale was one of the few to detect the early symptoms of this inner change, and she drew her own conclusions. She had just returned from accompanying Dai-yu's coffin to the landing-stage, and was sitting in her room brooding and weeping to herself.

'How cold-hearted Bao-yu is! It doesn't seem to have upset him in the slightest to see Miss Lin's coffin taken away. He didn't so much as shed a single tear. He could see me crying my eyes out, and didn't even try to comfort me, but just stared at me and smiled. What a deceiver! All those fine things he used to say to us in the past were just meant to fool us. Thank goodness I'd seen through him the other evening and didn't fall for it again! But there's still one thing I don't understand. He even seems to have become cold towards Aroma. I know Mrs Bao has never been a very warm or close person by nature – so she probably doesn't mind his change of heart. But what about Musk and the others, don't they feel hard done by? They've let their feelings make fools of them and have wasted half their lives over him, only to be forsaken like this!'

As she was brooding, she saw Fivey coming towards her.

'You're not still weeping for Miss Lin, are you?' asked Fivey, seeing Nightingale's tear-stained face. 'If you want my opinion of Mr Bao, I think it's high time we forgot about his reputation, and looked at what he really is. I was always being told how kind he was, especially towards girls. That's why my mother tried so hard to get me into service with him. Since then I've waited on him from the beginning of this illness of his. But now that he's better, I haven't had so much as a kind word from him! In fact he won't even acknowledge my existence!'

Nightingale burst out laughing at this comical tale of woe.

'Pshh! Why, hark at you, you little vixen!' she exclaimed. 'How do you want Mr Bao to treat you? Really, you should be ashamed of yourself! When he's not even interested in the maids that are closest to him, do you expect him to find time for you?'

She laughed again and drew a reproving finger across Fivey's face.

'What kind of a niche are you carving out for yourself in Bao-yu's affections?'

Fivey blushed at her own foolishness. She was on the point of explaining that it wasn't so much her own treatment at Bao-yu's hands that was worrying her as his whole attitude towards the maids, when they heard someone calling from outside:

'The monk is back! And he's demanding his ten thousand taels! Her Ladyship doesn't know what to do and wanted Mr Lian to go and talk with him, but Mr Lian's not at home! The monk is outside, ranting and raving. Her Ladyship wants Mrs Bao to go over and consult with her.'

To learn how they placated the monk, please read the next chapter.

CHAPTER 117

*Two fair damsels conspire to save the jade, and forestall
a flight from earthly bondage
An infamous rogue takes charge of the mansion, and assembles
a gang of cronies*

Lady Wang sent for Bao-chai to consult with her, while Bao-yu, hearing that the monk was outside, rushed to the front courtyard on his own.

'Where is my Master?' he shouted.

Finally, as there was no sign of the monk there, he went outside, where he found his groom Li Gui barring the monk's way.

'My mother bids me invite His Reverence in,' said Bao-yu.

Li Gui relaxed his grip, and the monk went swaggering in. Bao-yu observed at once the resemblance between this monk and the guide in his dream, and the truth began to grow clearer in his mind. He bowed: 'Master, please forgive your disciple for being so slow in welcoming you.'

'I have no desire to be entertained,' said the monk. 'I just want my money, and then I'll be off.'

This was hardly the way one would have expected a man of great spiritual attainments to talk, reflected Bao-yu. But then he looked at the monk's head, which was covered with scabs, and at his filthy, tattered robe, and thought to himself:

'There's an old saying: "The True Sage does not reveal himself, and he who reveals himself is no True Sage." I must be careful not to waste this opportunity. I had better reassure him about the money, and sound him out a little.

'Father,' he said, 'please be patient. My mother is preparing your money at this very moment. Please be seated and wait a while. May I venture to enquire, Father, whether you have recently returned from the Land of Illusion?'

'Illusion, my foot!' exclaimed the monk. 'I come whence I come, and I go whither I go. I came here to return your jade. But let *me* ask *you* a question: where did your jade come from?'

For a minute or so Bao-yu could think of no reply. The monk laughed.

'If you know nothing of your own provenance, why delve into mine?'

Bao-yu had always been a sensitive and intelligent child, and his recent illumination had enabled him to penetrate to a certain extent the veil of earthly vanity and illusion. But he still knew nothing of his own personal 'history', and the monk's question hit him like a whack on the head.

'I know!' he exclaimed. 'It's not the money you're after. It's my jade. I'll give you *that* back instead.'

'And so you should!' chuckled the monk.

Without a word, Bao-yu ran into the house. He reached his apartment and, finding that Bao-chai, Aroma and the others had all gone out to wait on his mother, he quickly picked up his jade from where it lay by his bed and ran back with it. As he left the room, he collided with Aroma, giving her the fright of her life.

'Her Ladyship was just saying what a good idea it was,' she protested, 'for you to sit and keep the monk company, while she tried to work out a way of raising the money. What on earth have you come rushing in here for again?'

'I want you to go back at once,' ordered Bao-yu, 'and tell Mother she needn't bother about the money. I shall give him back the jade. That will settle the bill.'

Aroma seized Bao-yu at once:

'That's completely crazy! The jade is your very life! If he takes that away, you'll fall ill again for sure.'

'Not now,' replied Bao-yu. 'I shall never fall ill again. Now that I know my true purpose, what do I need the jade for?'

He shook Aroma off and made to leave. She hurried after him, crying:

'Come back! There's something else I want to tell you!'

Bao-yu glanced back at her:

'There's nothing more to be said.'

She pressed after him, casting aside her inhibitions and crying as she ran:

'Don't you remember the last time you lost it, how it was nearly the end of me? You've only just got it back, and if he takes it away again now it will cost you your life and me mine too! You'll be sending me to my death.'

She caught up with him as she was speaking, and held him tightly.

'Whether it means your death or not,' said Bao-yu with strange vehemence, 'I shall still give it back.'

He pushed Aroma away with all his might and tried to extricate himself from her grip. She, however, wound the ends of his sash around her hands and sank to the ground, sobbing and calling for help.

The maids in the inner apartments heard the noise and came running out, to find the two of them locked in this desperate impasse.

'Quickly!' cried Aroma. 'Go and tell Her Ladyship! Master Bao wants to give his jade back to the monk!'

The maids flew to Lady Wang with this message, while Bao-yu grew angrier than ever and tried to wrench his sash from Aroma's hands. She held on for dear life, and Nightingale came rushing out from the inner apartment as soon as she heard what Bao-yu was contemplating. Her alarm and concern seemed if anything greater than Aroma's, and her previous resolution to be indifferent towards Bao-yu seemed to have vanished without trace. She joined forces with Aroma, and Bao-yu, though a man against women, and though he flailed and struggled for all he was worth, could do nothing in the face of their desperate refusal to let go. Unable to set himself free, he could only sigh and say:

'Will you fight like this to preserve a piece of jade? What would you do if *I* left you?'

These words produced a noisy outburst of sobbing from Aroma and Nightingale.

Things had reached this impasse when Lady Wang and Bao-chai hurried onto the scene. Now Lady Wang could verify the truth of the report with her own eyes.

'Bao-yu!' she cried, her voice choking with sobs. 'Have you taken leave of your senses again?'

Bao-yu knew that with the arrival of his mother he no longer stood any chance of escape – and therefore changed his tactics.

'There was really no need for you to alarm yourself so, Mother,' he said, with a placatory smile. 'They always make such a fuss about nothing. I thought the monk was being most unreasonable, insisting on being paid every penny of ten thousand taels. It made me very cross and I came in here with the idea of handing him back the jade and at the same time pretending that it was a fake and worthless to us anyway. If I could convince him that it was of no real value to us, then he would probably accept whatever reward we offered him.'

'Goodness! I thought you were in earnest!' exclaimed Lady Wang. 'I must say, you might have told them the truth – look at the state they're all in!'

'It may seem a good idea to do as Bao-yu suggests,' said Bao-chai. 'But I still think it would be risky even to go through the motions of giving it back. If you ask me, there's something most peculiar about that monk. He could very easily do something terrible and throw the whole family into confusion all over again. We can always sell my jewellery if we need to raise the money.'

'Yes,' said Lady Wang. 'Let's try that first.'

Bao-yu made no comment. Bao-chai came up to him and took the jade from his hand.

'There is no need for you to go,' she said. 'Mother and I can give him the money.'

'Very well then, I won't give him the jade,' said Bao-yu. 'But I must at least see him this once.'

Aroma and Nightingale were still loath to allow him out of their sight. In the end it was Bao-chai who ordered them to set him free:

'He'd better go if he wants to.'

Reluctantly Aroma complied.

'You all of you seem to value the jade more highly than its owner!' said Bao-yu with a wry smile. 'What if I go away with the monk and leave you with the jade? You'll look rather silly then, won't you?'

This revived Aroma's anxiety, and she would have seized hold of him again had she not felt constrained by the presence of Lady Wang and Bao-chai and by the need to preserve some semblance of respect towards Bao-yu. It was too late anyway, for the moment they loosened their grip Bao-yu was gone. Aroma contented herself with despatching a junior maid to the inner gate with instructions for Tealeaf and Bao-yu's other page-boys to keep an eye on him, as he was 'acting rather strangely'. The maid went at once to do her bidding.

Lady Wang and Bao-chai meanwhile walked in to Bao-yu's apartment and sat down. They asked Aroma exactly what had happened and she gave them a full account of all that Bao-yu had said. They were both extremely perturbed and sent another messenger with instructions that the servants were to watch Bao-yu and do their utmost to hear what the monk said. A short while later, a junior maid returned to report to Lady Wang:

'Master Bao is acting very strangely, madam. The pages outside say that since you would not give him the jade, he now feels obliged to offer *himself* in its place.'

'Gracious!' exclaimed Lady Wang. 'And whatever did the monk say to that?'

'He said he wanted the jade, not the man,' replied the maid.

'Not the money?' asked Bao-chai.

'They didn't even mention that. Afterwards the monk and Master Bao started talking and laughing together. There was a lot said that the pages couldn't follow.'

'The little idiots!' complained Lady Wang. 'Even if they couldn't understand it themselves, they could at least repeat it to us. Go and tell them to come here.'

The maid sped to do Lady Wang's bidding. Presently Tealeaf arrived, stood outside in the covered walk and paid his respects through the intervening window.

'Surely,' said Lady Wang, 'if you couldn't understand the meaning of what Master Bao and the monk were saying, you could at least manage to repeat the words to us.'

'All we caught, ma'am,' answered Tealeaf, 'was something about a Great Fable Mountain and a Greensickness Peak. And then something about a Land of Illusion and "severing earthly ties".'

To Lady Wang this made as little sense as it had to the pages; but it seemed to have a startling effect on Bao-chai, who stared dumbfounded in front of her.

They were about to send someone to bring Bao-yu back, when in he came himself, wreathed in smiles, announcing:

'All is well! All is well!'

Bao-chair stared at him in dismay, while Lady Wang asked:

'What have you been raving to that monk about now?'

'It was anything but raving. It was a very serious conversation. It turns out that he knows me, and that all he really wanted was to see me. He never wanted the money. At the most he was hoping for a friendly contribution, which would create good karma. As soon as we had reached an understanding, he got up and went. Just like that. So I think you'll agree, all *is* well!'

Lady Wang could not believe this, and asked Tealeaf, who was still standing on the other side of the window, to verify Bao-yu's story. He hurried out to question the gateman, and returned presently to report:

'It is true. The monk really has left. As he was going he said: "Their Ladyships are not to worry themselves. I never wanted the money." He says he only wants Master Bao-yu to call on him whenever he can. "Let all be fulfilled in accordance with karma; a fixed purpose resides in all things." Those were his parting words.'

'So he was a holy man after all!' exclaimed Lady Wang. 'Did anyone ask him where he lived?'

'According to the gateman, the monk said that Master Bao would know where to find him.'

Lady Wang turned to Bao-yu:

'Well – where *does* he live?'

Bao-yu smiled enigmatically:

'His abode is, well . . . far away and yet at the same time close at hand. It all depends how you look at it.'

'For goodness' sake!' interrupted Bao-chai impatiently, before he had finished speaking. 'Pull yourself together and stop all this nonsense! You know how Mother and Father love you! And Father has told you how important it is for you to succeed in life!'

'Does what I am talking about not count as success?' asked Bao-yu in a droll tone. 'Haven't you heard the saying: "When one son becomes a monk, the souls of seven generations of ancestors go to Heaven"?'

When she heard this Lady Wang was more distressed than ever:

'Our family is doomed! Xi-chun talks of nothing but her nunnery, and now here's another! Why should I bother to drag my life out any longer!'

She began sobbing hysterically. Bao-chai tried to comfort her, but Bao-yu only laughed and said:

'I was joking! There was no need to take it so seriously, Mother.'

Lady Wang ceased her tears:

'How can you joke about such a thing?'

At this juncture a maid came in to report the return of Jia Lian:

'He looks very upset too, ma'am. He would like you to go over and have a word with him.'

This was another shock for Lady Wang.

'Ask him just this once if he can come here. Mrs Bao is his cousin, so he needn't worry about her being here too.'

Jia Lian duly came in and paid his respects to Lady Wang. Bao-chai also greeted him.

'I have just received a letter from Father,' said Jia Lian, 'saying that he has fallen seriously ill. I must go to him at once, or it may be too late!'

Tears were streaming down his cheeks.

'Did the letter say what kind of illness?' asked Lady Wang.

'It began as a cold but has developed into pneumonia, which has now reached a critical stage. A special messenger travelled by day and night to bring us the news, and says that if I delay my departure for even a day or two it may be too late. I must leave as soon as possible. I am concerned that with Uncle away in the South there will be no one left to take charge of things here. You will have to make do with young Qiang and Yun; whatever their shortcomings, at least they are men and can communicate with you about anything that may crop up outside. There's nothing much to worry about in my apartment. Autumn spends her time crying and complaining and says she wants to leave, so I have told her family to come and take her away. That will make life a little more bearable for Patience at any rate. There is no one to look after Qiao-jie, I know, but Patience is not too bad with her. Qiao-jie is quite a sensible girl, but has an even more difficult temperament than her mother, so I hope you will try to offer her guidance whenever you can, Aunt.'

As he spoke, a telltale red came into his eyes and he extracted a little silk handkerchief from the betel-nut bag at his waist and dabbed them with it.

'With her own grandmother so close at hand, what need is there for you to entrust her to me?' asked Lady Wang.

'If you adopt that attitude, I might as well beat myself to death!' said Jia Lian to his aunt in a somewhat histrionic *sotto voce*. 'I won't say any more, just beg you to be kind to me and do what you can.'

He knelt at her feet.

'Get up at once!' exclaimed Lady Wang. Her eyes too were moist with tears. 'What way is this for aunt and nephew to talk to one another? There is one thing we should discuss. The child is of age now. If anything untoward should happen to your father and you should be delayed, and if in the meantime a suitable family should make a proposal of marriage, do you wish me to wait for your return, or shall I let her grandmother decide in your absence?'

'Of course you need not wait for me. As you and Mother will be here, the two of you should do whatever you think best.'

'You had better go now,' said Lady Wang. 'Write your Uncle Zheng a note. Tell him that your father is in a precarious state of health, and that there are no menfolk left at home. Ask him to complete your grandmother's burial rites and come home as quickly as possible.'

'Very well, Aunt.'

As he was on the point of leaving, Jia Lian turned back once more and said:

'There should be enough servants in the house. But there is no one in the Garden. The place is altogether too deserted, especially now that Bao Yong has gone back with the Zhens and Cousin Ke and Aunt Xue have moved out of their old compound next to the Garden to live in an apartment of their own. All the buildings in the Garden are empty and have been neglected. You should send someone round regularly to inspect the place. Green Bower Hermitage is a family foundation, and now that Adamantina has disappeared something must be done about her various attendants. The Sister Superior does not feel she can make the decision herself, and would like someone in the family to take charge.'

'That will have to wait,' replied Lady Wang. 'With our own affairs in such disarray, we are in no position to start taking on extra responsibilities. You must on no account mention this to Xi-chun. It would only encourage her in her own ideas. Oh dear, what are we coming to? A nun in the family would be the last straw!'

'That is something I would not have brought up myself,' said Jia Lian. 'But since you have done so, I should perhaps offer my advice, for what it's worth. Xi-chun belongs after all to the Ning-guo side of the family. Neither of her parents is alive, her elder brother has been sent into exile, and she and her sister-in-law are on bad terms with one another. I hear that she has threatened suicide quite a few times. If her heart is really set on being a nun and we continue to be so inflexible, she may really take her own life. And then we would lose her altogether!'

Lady Wang nodded:

'It is too heavy a burden to lay on my shoulders! This really isn't my responsibility. I must leave it to her sister-in-law to decide.'

Jia Lian said a few more words and took his leave. He summoned the servants and gave them their instructions. Then he wrote a letter to Jia Zheng, and packed his bags. Patience urged him at some length to take good care of himself, while Qiao-jie seemed exceedingly upset by her father's departure. Jia Lian expressed his wish to entrust her to the care of her uncle Wang Ren, but she wouldn't consider it; and when she learned that Jia Yun and Jia Qiang were to be on outside duty she also felt extremely uneasy, though she said nothing. She bade her father farewell, and resolved to lead a quiet life at home with Patience.

Felicity and Crimson had been frequently absent since Xi-feng's death, on some occasions asking for leave, on others pleading sickness. Patience had contemplated asking a young lady from some other branch of the Jia family to come and stay with them, partly to keep Qiao-jie company, partly to help educate her, but the only names that occurred to her were those of Xi-luan and Si-jie, Grandmother Jia's favourites, and of these two Xi-luan had recently married while Si-jie was engaged and due to leave home any day.

Jia Yun and Jia Qiang saw Jia Lian off and then went in to report to Ladies Xing and Wang. The two men took turns on night-duty in the outer study, and during the daytime enjoyed themselves with the servants, throwing parties and inviting a variety of friends, who took it in turns with them to act as host. There was even some serious gambling. The ladies of course had no inkling of this.

One day Lady Xing's brother Xing De-quan and Wang Ren dropped by. Learning that Yun and Qiang were now established at Rong-guo House, and observing the good times that were being had, they began to call quite frequently, to 'see how things were getting on', and had soon formed a regular drinking and gambling foursome in the outer study. All the decent servants had accompanied either Jia Zheng or Jia Lian, and the only menservants left behind were the various sons and nephews of stewards Lai and Lin, who were used to the easy life their parents' good fortune had brought them, and were quite ignorant of the principles according to which a proper household should be run. With their parents away, they were like colts let loose in the meadow. And with the two degenerate young masters to spur them on, their pleasures knew no bounds.

Under this new regime, the family motto might as well have been: Anything Goes.

Jia Qiang thought of inviting Bao-yu to join them, but Jia Yun soon squashed that idea:

'That fellow is an absolute killjoy. It would only be asking for trouble. A year or two ago I had a perfect marriage lined up for him. The girl's father was a tax-collector in one of the provinces, the family owned several pawnshops, and the girl herself was an absolute peach. I went to a lot of trouble and wrote him a long letter about it, but I might as well have saved myself the bother. He's an utter spoil-sport.'

Yun glanced round to make sure there was no one else listening and continued:

'The truth was, he already fancied this new missis of his! And then there was Miss Lin, you must have heard about *that*. She died of a broken heart, it's common knowledge. And it was all his fault. But that's another story. To each his fate in love, I suppose. All the same, I don't see why he had to get so angry with me, and start cutting me dead. Perhaps he thought I was trying to get into his good books or something.'

Jia Qiang nodded and gave up the idea of inviting Bao-yu. What neither of them knew was that, ever since his meeting with the monk, Bao-yu was finally resolved to sever his ties with the world. In his mother's presence he still tried to behave as normally as possible, but there was already a marked cooling-off in his relations with Bao-chai and Aroma. The maids were unaware of this change and continued to tease him as before, only to find themselves totally ignored. He was completely oblivious of practical household affairs; and as for his studies, whenever his mother and Bao-chai chivvied him on, he would feign diligence, but in reality his mind was filled with thoughts of the monk and his mysterious excursion to the fairy domain. Everyone around him now seemed unbearably mundane, and he began to find his own family environment less and less congenial. When he was free of other commitments, it was Xi-chun that he chose as a companion. The two of them found they had more and more in common, and their lively conversations further strength-ened his own resolution. He had little time now for Jia Huan and Jia Lan.

Jia Huan, now that his father was away from home and his mother

Aunt Zhao dead, and since Lady Wang paid little attention to what he did, began to gravitate towards Jia Yun and his cronies. Suncloud, who constantly tried to dissuade him from this course, received nothing but abuse for her pains. Silver observed to herself that Bao-yu was becoming more deranged than ever, and asked her mother if she could be taken out of service. Bao-yu and Jia Huan in their different ways succeeded in alienating the people around them. Jia Lan, by contrast, sat by his mother's side conscientiously studying, and when he had finished a composition would take it to the family school for the Preceptor's comments. Recently the Preceptor had been bedridden a great deal of the time, and consequently Jia Lan had been obliged to work on his own. His mother had always been fond of peace and quiet, and apart from calling on Lady Wang and Bao-chai she did not get about much but sat at home and watched Jia Lan at his work. So although life continued in Rong-guo House, everyone was very much minding his own business, which left Jia Huan, Jia Qiang and company free to indulge themselves unmolested. They were soon pawning or selling all manner of family property in order to subsidize their disgraceful activities. Jia Huan was the worst. His whoring and gambling knew no bounds.

One day Xing De-quan and Wang Ren had called and were in the outer study drinking. They were in high spirits and decided to send for some singsong girls to entertain them with a song or two and join in their carousing.

'This is turning into a downright orgy!' protested Jia Qiang playfully. 'I suggest we have a drinking game to raise the tone a little.'

Everyone agreed that this was a good idea.

'Let's play Pass the Goblet, on the word "moon",' proposed Jia Qiang. 'I shall say a line and count it out, and whoever gets the word "moon" has to drink and then recite two lines – a Head and a Tail – according to my instructions. The forfeit is three big cups.'

Everyone agreed to his rules. First Jia Qiang drank a cup as MC, and then he recited Li Bo's line:

' "The Peacock Goblets fly, the drunken moon . . ." ' The 'moon' fell on Jia Huan.

'For the Head, give me a line with Cassia,' said Jia Qiang.

Jia Huan came up with a line by the Tang poet Wang Jian: ' "A cold dew silently soaks the Cassia flowers . . ." '

'And Fragrance for the Tail,' concluded Jia Qiang.

Jia Huan obliged with a line by another Tang poet, Song Zhi-wen:

' "Beyond the clouds there wafts a heavenly Fragrance . . ." '

'Boring! Boring!' complained Xing De-quan. 'Stop posing, Huan, me old fellow! Fat lot *you* know about poetry! This is no fun at all, it's enough to make you sick! Let's drop it and play Guess-fingers instead. Loser to drink *and* sing a song, a double sconce. Anyone who can't sing can tell a joke instead. But it better be a good one.'

They all agreed to this new proposal and there was a noisy scene as they began to throw out fingers and make their calls. Wang Ren was the first loser. He drank and sang a song.

'Bravo!' they cried and set to again. Next to lose was one of the girls. She sang a song called 'Little Miss Glamorous'. Then it was Xing De-quan. Everyone wanted a song from him, but he protested that he was tone-deaf:

'I'll tell a joke instead.'

'If nobody laughs,' Jia Qiang warned him, 'you'll have to pay another forfeit.'

Xing downed his cup and began his story:

'Ladies and gentlemen: once upon a time, in a certain village, there were two temples – a big one, dedicated to the Great Lord of the North, and by its side a smaller one, dedicated to the Village God. The Great Lord was always inviting the Village God over for a chat. One day something was stolen from his temple, and he asked the Village God to look into the matter. "But there are no thieves in this district," protested the lesser deity. "It must be carelessness on the part of one of your door-gods. Someone must have sneaked in past them and stolen these things." "Nonsense!" replied the Great Lord. "You're in charge round these parts. If there's been a theft, then you're responsible. What's the meaning of this? You should be trying to catch the thief, not accusing my door-gods of being careless!" "What I meant by careless," prevaricated the Village God, "was that your temple must have been badly sited – you know, the Dragon Lines must be at fault . . ." "I had no idea you could read *fengshui*," commented the Great Lord in a tone of disbelief. "Allow me to take a look for you," offered the Village God, "and see what I can see." He walked around the temple, peering into every nook and cranny, and after a while reported: "My Lord, behind your throne there is a double-leaved red door. An unfortunate oversight. Personally I have a good solid brick wall behind my throne, so naturally I never have things stolen. You can easily remedy the present situation by having a wall built in place of the door." This seemed plausible to the Great Lord, and he instructed his door-gods to call in builders and put up a wall. "But we can't even afford a single candle or stick of incense in this temple!" moaned the door-gods. "How can we possibly buy bricks and mortar and hire the labour to build a wall?" The Great Lord could think of no solution. He ordered them to find one, but they were stumped too. Just then the Tortoise General, whose recumbent stone form lay at the Great Lord's feet, stood up and said: "You're a useless lot! I've got an idea: pull down the red door, and use my belly to block up the doorway. I'm sure that will do the job perfectly well." "An excellent plan!" cried the door-gods in chorus. "Convenient, dependable and *free*!" So the Tortoise General became Rear Wall, and peace prevailed – for a while. Then things began to disappear from the temple again. The door-gods summoned the Village God and complained: "You guaranteed our security if we built a wall, but look what's happened! We've got a wall and *still* we're losing things!" "Your wall can't be solid enough." "Have a look at it for yourself," they insisted. The Village God went and did so. It certainly seemed a solid enough wall. All most puzzling. Then he felt it with his hand. "Aaah!" he exclaimed. "No wonder! I meant a properly built wall. Any old thief could push down this false wall (*jia qiang*)." '

They all laughed, even Jia Qiang, whose name had provided the raw material for the joke.

'Come on, Dumbo!' he protested. 'Be fair! I never called *you* names! Drink a forfeit, there's a boy!'

Dumbo, who was already a sheet or so in the wind, willingly complied. They all had a few more cups, and in the general state of intoxication Dumbo let fly a few barbed remarks about *his* sister (Lady Xing), while Wang Ren had a go at desecrating the memory of *his* (Xi-feng), both of them evincing great bitterness. Their example and the wine lent Jia Huan a little courage, and he too had his fling, complaining how heartless Xi-feng had been, and how she had tried to ruin so many of their lives.

'Yes, people ought to show a bit of common decency,' they all agreed. 'The way she used Lady Jia's influence to bully everyone was dreadful. Well, she died without giving birth to an heir; she only ever had a daughter. Retribution in her own lifetime!'

Jia Yun, who remembered only too well how harsh Xi-feng had once been towards him, and how Qiao-jie had started bawling the instant she set eyes on him, allowed himself to wade into the general mêlée with some abuse of his own about the two of them. Jia Qiang tried to steer the party in a less vindictive direction:

'Come on! Drink up! This gossip will get us nowhere!'

'How old is the young lady you mentioned?' enquired the two singsong girls. 'Is she pretty?'

'Oh yes,' replied Jia Qiang. 'Extremely so. She's about thirteen.'

'What a pity, in that case, that she was born into a family like yours!' the girls exclaimed. 'If only she came from a more humble home, she could soon find herself in a position to bring all her family lots of jobs, and pots of money into the bargain!'

'What do you mean?'

'We know of a certain Mongol prince,' replied the girls. 'Quite a ladies' man he is. He is looking for a concubine, and the lady who fits the bill would be able to take her whole family along with her to live in the palace. What a marvellous stroke of luck that would be for somebody!'

None of them seemed to take much notice of this, except for Wang Ren, who looked very thoughtful. For the present he said nothing and continued drinking.

A little later two young lads came in, younger sons of Stewards Lai and Lin.

'You seem to be having a fine time of it, sirs, by the looks of things!' they exclaimed.

Everyone rose to greet them.

'Why have the two of you been such a long time? We've been expecting you for ages.'

They explained:

'Early this morning we heard rather a disturbing rumour that our family was in some sort of official trouble again, so we hurried out to see what news we could glean at the Palace. It turned out to have nothing to do with our family after all.'

'In that case, why didn't you come straight here afterwards?'

'It wasn't *exactly* our family, but it was connected with us. It was that Mr Jia Yu-cun. When we were at the Palace we saw him bound in chains. They told us he was being taken to the High Court for questioning. We knew he was a frequent visitor here, and were afraid that the case might somehow involve us, so we followed them to see what happened.'

'Good thinking, my man!' exclaimed Jia Yun. 'We are most obliged to you. Sit down and have a drink, and then tell us all about it.'

The two sat down after a polite show of reluctance, and as they drank continued:

'This Mr Yu-cun is certainly an able enough fellow, and knows how to pull strings. He'd done extremely well until recently, in fact; but greed was his downfall. There were several charges brought against him, "avarice" and "extortion" being two of them. As we all know, our present August Sovereign is exceptionally wise, compassionate and benevolent. There is one thing that stirs his wrath, however, and that is corruption, any form of tyrannical or bullying behaviour. So His Majesty decreed that the offender in this case should be arrested and brought to trial. If he is found guilty, things will look pretty grim for him; if he is acquitted, then the men who brought the charges will be in for trouble. It is certainly comforting to think what just times we live in! For those lucky enough to be officials in the first place!'

'Like your elder brother,' said one of the company, referring to Steward Lai's eldest son, Lai Shang-rong. 'He's a county magistrate. Done very nicely for himself.'

'True enough,' replied young Lai. 'But his conduct still leaves a lot to be desired, I'm afraid. He may not last long at this rate.'

'Has he been taking squeeze himself?'

Lai nodded and drained his cup.

'What other news did you pick up at the Palace?' they asked them.

'Oh, nothing much. A number of criminals from the coast have apparently been arrested, and sent to the High Court. During their trial they revealed the whereabouts of several others of their kind, lying low here in the capital, watching and waiting for fresh opportunities for crime. Fortunately the present civil and military authorities have such a sound grip on the situation, and are so dedicated to the service of the throne, that these criminal elements will be effectively controlled.'

'If you've heard of such cases, perhaps you have news of *our* burglary?' asked one of the party.

'I'm afraid not,' came the reply. 'I heard something about a man from one of the inland provinces who got into trouble here in town for abducting a girl and running off with her to the coast. She put up a fight and he ended by killing her. They arrested him crossing the border, and executed him on the spot.'

'Wasn't Sister Adamantina from Green Bower Hermitage abducted in similar circumstances?' put in one of the others. 'Couldn't it have been her?'

'Bound to have been!' muttered Jia Huan.

'How could you know?' they asked him.

'She was a sickening creature!' said Jia Huan. 'Always giving herself airs and graces. She had only to set eyes on Bao-yu to get a big smile all over her face. But she wouldn't so much as acknowledge *my* existence! I hope it *is* her!'

'Plenty of people are kidnapped all the time,' someone commented. 'It could easily have been someone else.'

'I can well believe it was her,' said Jia Yun. 'The day before yesterday I heard that one of the sisters at the Hermitage had a dream in which she saw Adamantina being killed.'

This was greeted with derision:

'You can't take dreams seriously!'

'Dream or no dream, it's all one to me,' protested Dumbo. 'Let's get on with the real business of the evening, shall we? Eat up, everyone, and we can start tonight's Big Game.'

This met with general approval, and as soon as they had finished their meal they began gambling in earnest. They were still at it well after midnight, when suddenly they heard a great commotion coming from the inner apartments. They were eventually informed that Xi-chun had been arguing with You-shi, and the upshot of it was that she had cut all her hair off and gone running to Ladies Xing and Wang. There she kowtowed and begged them to relent and let her have her wish. If they would not, she threatened to put an end to her life there and then. The two ladies were at their wits' end, and sent for Jia Qiang and Jia Yun to intervene. Jia Yun however knew that this was something Xi-chun had resolved to do long ago, at least since the fateful night of the burglary when she had been left in charge of the house, and to him there seemed little hope in trying to dissuade her now. He talked it over with Jia Qiang:

'Lady Wang says she wants us to intervene, but I don't see how we can achieve anything. It's a heavy responsibility, and they want to off-load it onto us. We'll have to put on a show of talking Xi-chun out of her decision, and then, when she refuses to listen, we'll have to pass the matter back to the ladies, and meanwhile write a letter to Uncle Lian, absolving ourselves from any blame.'

They both agreed on this strategy, called on Ladies Xing and Wang, and then went through the motions of trying to dissuade Xi-chun, who was every bit as adamant as they had predicted. If she could not take refuge in a convent outside the family mansion, then she said she would make do with a couple of quiet rooms within it, in which to recite her sutras and say her prayers. Eventually You-shi could see that the aunts were not prepared to take the responsibility; her own fear that Xi-chun might commit suicide got the better of her and she forced herself to compromise.

'I can see I shall have to take the blame. Very well then. Let them say that it was I who could not tolerate my own husband's sister and drove her to a nunnery! What do I care! But I cannot allow her to leave home. That is out of the question. She will have to stay here. Aunts Xing and Wang, I call you to witness my decision. Qiang, you had better write a letter informing my husband and Cousin Lian of what has happened.'

Jia Qiang acquiesced in You-shi's decision. But to know whether Lady Xing and Lady Wang did likewise, you will have to turn to the next chapter.

CHAPTER 118

*Provoked by a rankling antipathy, Uncle and Cousin
plot the ruin of an innocent maid
Alarmed by riddling utterances, Wife and Concubine
remonstrate with their idiot master*

Lady Xing and Lady Wang judged from You-shi's words that the situation was irretrievable.

'If our niece wishes to become a nun,' said Lady Wang, in a tone of resignation, 'then it must have been decreed in some earlier life. This is evidently her karma, and there is nothing we can do to prevent it. But none the less, it would look very bad for a girl from a family such as ours to enter a nunnery. That really is unthinkable.'

She turned to Xi-chun:

'Your sister-in-law has given you her permission, and we can only lend our approval to hers. But I must ask you not to shave your head. What matters is your state of mind, not your hair-style. After all, Adamantina never shaved hers. Talking of which, I simply cannot understand that dreadful business! How could she have succumbed to temptation so easily? Anyway, if your mind is really and truly made up, then we shall simply have to consider your present apartment your hermitage. Your maids and servants had better be sent for, and we can give them a choice. Those who wish to stay on with you can do so, and we'll find husbands for the others.'

Xi-chun stopped crying at last, and bowed gratefully to Ladies Xing and Wang, Li Wan, You-shi and the others present.

Lady Wang now addressed Landscape and Xi-chun's other maids:

'Which of you wishes to enter the religious life with your mistress?'

'We will do whatever you command, ma'am,' was their response.

Lady Wang could tell that they were none of them genuinely willing and tried to think who else would be suitable to wait on Xi-chun in her new life. Aroma was standing behind Bao-yu, fully expecting this decision of Xi-chun's to move him to tears and provoke one of his fits, but to her surprise and considerable distress, he merely sighed with admiration and exclaimed:

'What a rare resolve!'

Bao-chai made no comment. But she was constantly on the look-out for telltale signs to help her gauge her husband's innermost feelings and intentions, and could not help but weep at this further evidence (so she thought) of his deluded mind.

Lady Wang was about to summon all the other maids and question them, when Nightingale suddenly came forward and fell to her knees:

'Have you decided yet, ma'am, who would be most suitable to wait on Miss Xi-chun?'

'I have no intention of forcing anyone,' replied Lady Wang. 'Whoever is willing must speak up.'

'Miss Xi-chun has chosen a religious life,' said Nightingale. 'But none of her maids, or so it seems, shares this aspiration of hers. I have something I should like to say, ma'am. It's not that I wish Miss Xi-chun to be parted from her maids. But aspirations differ. I served Miss Lin for a long time, and as you know, ma'am, she treated me with a kindness that I shall never be able to repay. When she died, my one wish was to follow her to the grave; but because she was not a member of this family, and because I also owe so much to all of you, it was hard for me to take that step. Now that Miss Xi-chun wishes to become a nun, I beg Your Ladyships to let me go with her and devote the rest of my days to serving her. If Your Ladyships will only grant me this wish, my life will not have been in vain!'

When Nightingale had finished speaking, and before either Lady Xing or Lady Wang could reply, Bao-yu, who at the initial mention of Dai-yu's name had begun to show ominous signs of being distressed and tearful, suddenly gave a loud laugh and came forward:

'I have no business saying this, I know, but since you were so good as to send Nightingale to work in my apartment, Mother, I hope you will forgive me for speaking my mind. Please grant her this request, and allow her to carry out this fine resolution of hers.'

'If it were any of your other cousins leaving home to get married,' replied Lady Wang, 'you would be crying your heart out. But now, when Xi-chun says she wants to leave home and become a nun, so far from trying to dissuade her, you actually praise her for it. I'm afraid I completely fail to understand what's going on in your mind.'

'First let me know whether this matter is settled,' said Bao-yu. 'Has Xi-chun definitely made up her mind? And has she definitely received your permission? If so, if it is real, then there is something further I should like to tell you, Mother. But if it is still not settled, I shall keep what I know to myself.'

'What a peculiar way to talk!' exclaimed Xi-chun. 'If I were not in earnest, do you honestly think I would have been able to convince my aunts? I feel the same way as Nightingale: if they will let me do as I wish, I shall count myself blessed; if they will not, I should rather die than continue living my present life! So, there's nothing to fear. Whatever you have to say, just go ahead and say it.'

'If I do tell you this, it's hardly divulging a secret,' said Bao-yu, 'since it refers to something already predestined. I want you all to listen while I recite a poem.'

'Honestly!' they chided him. 'At a moment like this, with real people really suffering, all you can think about is poetry! It's sickening!'

'It's not something of my own. It's a poem I once saw somewhere. I'd like you to listen to it.'

'Oh very well. Hurry up then. Enough of your prattling!'

Bao-yu did not try to explain himself any further, but began to recite:

> 'When you see through the spring scene's transient state,
> A nun's black habit shall replace your own.
> Alas, that daughter of so great a house
> By Buddha's altar lamp should sleep alone!'

Li Wan and Bao-chai both cried out in alarm:

'Lord save us! He's bewitched!'

Lady Wang shook her head and sighed:

'Bao-yu, where on earth did you see this poem?'

Bao-yu was reluctant to say any more, and replied:

'Please don't ask, Mother. Just take my word for it.'

As the meaning of the poem gradually sank in, Lady Wang began sobbing again:

'You said you were joking the other day, when you talked of becoming a monk yourself. And now this poem all of a sudden! Enough! I understand. What am I to do? There is nothing I *can* do, but let you go your own ways. If only you could have waited till I was dead and gone! Then you could all have done as you pleased!'

Bao-chai tried to console her, but was in no fit state to do so. The pain she herself felt was like a knife-wound piercing her heart, and eventually she broke down and burst into tears. Aroma was faint with weeping and had to be supported by Ripple. Bao-yu did not shed a single tear, nor did he try to offer them any solace. He maintained a total silence. Jia Lan and Jia Huan had already left, and it fell to Li Wan to do what she could to save the situation:

'I'm sure it's simply that Bao-yu is too upset by this decision of Xi-chun's to know what he is saying. We should not take it seriously. Nightingale must receive an answer, though; we must let her stand up. Is she to be granted her request or not?'

'What difference does it make?' replied Lady Wang. 'Her mind is clearly made up in any case, and when a person's mind is made up there's no stopping them. No doubt Bao-yu will tell us that this decision of Nightingale's is predestined too.'

Nightingale kowtowed, and Xi-chun thanked Lady Wang. Nightingale also kowtowed to Bao-yu and Bao-chai.

'Amida Buddha!' exclaimed Bao-yu piously. 'How noble! How rare! I never thought that you would be the first of us to be saved!'

Bao-chai's self-control failed her again, and Aroma, heedless of Lady Wang's presence, burst out sobbing and cried:

'*I* want to go with Miss Xi-chun too, and spend the rest of my life in prayer!'

Bao-yu smiled:

'Yours is also a fine aspiration. But alas, a life of seclusion has not been decreed you by fate.'

'Then I would rather die!' sobbed Aroma.

Despite his new-found detachment, Bao-yu could not help being moved by this declaration. But he said nothing.

It was already three o'clock in the morning, and he suggested to his mother that she should retire for the night. Li Wan went back to her apartment, and Landscape escorted Xi-chun to her room, where she continued to wait on her for the time being. Husbands were eventually found for each of Xi-chun's maids, and Nightingale spent the rest of her days faithfully serving her. But we anticipate.

*

Jia Zheng, meanwhile, was on his way south with Grandmother Jia's coffin, and had run into an army convoy returning to the capital

after the victorious completion of a campaign. The canal was hope-
lessly congested with military transport boats, and the delay made Jia
Zheng extremely fretful. His one consolation was an encounter with
an official from the Coastal Defence Yamen, who informed him that
the Commandant, Tan-chun's father-in-law, had been recalled to the
capital. Tan-chun would now be able to visit home, although there
was no indication when she would be travelling.

Another consequence of the delay was that Jia Zheng found
himself running short of cash. He was obliged to write a letter and
have it delivered to the yamen of Steward Lai's son, Lai Shang-rong,
who happened to be a mandarin in the vicinity, asking him for a loan
of five hundred silver taels. The servant entrusted with this mission
was told to bring the money and overtake Jia Zheng further along
the canal.

A few days and a dozen or so *li* later, the servant reappeared and
came on board the boat with Lai Shang-rong's reply. The letter was
full of tales of woe of one sort or another, and enclosed fifty taels of
silver. Jia Zhen was furious, and without a moment's hesitation
ordered the servant to return:

'Take him back his money this instant! And he can have his letter
too! Tell him not to bother!'

The poor servant did as he was ordered and returned to Lai's
yamen. Lai, perturbed at having both his letter and his paltry offering
returned, and knowing that he had behaved meanly, made up another
package, this time enclosing an additional hundred taels, and begged
the servant to take it back with him to Jia Zheng. But despite Lai's
pleas and blandishments, the man absolutely refused, and returned to
the boat empty-handed.

Lai Shang-rong was most apprehensive about the consequences of
this episode, and immediately wrote to his father at Rong-guo House,
advising him to take some leave and if possible to buy his way out of
service. When Steward Lai received his son's letter, he asked Jia
Qiang and Jia Yun to plead with Lady Wang for his release. Jia
Qiang knew quite well that it would be futile even to try; he let a day
go by and then gave a false report that Lady Wang had refused his
request. So Lai took a few days' leave, and meanwhile sent a messenger to his son's yamen, advising him also to plead sick and relinquish his official post. Lady Wang knew nothing whatsoever about
all these goings-on.

*

Jia Yun was most disappointed to hear Jia Qiang turn down Lai's request. It (or, rather, the commission it might have brought) had seemed his last chance of recouping the enormous gambling losses he had incurred over the past several days. His only other hope was to apply to Jia Huan for a loan. But Jia Huan was in no position to act as his creditor, having himself never had a penny of his own, and having already squandered his mother's savings. If Yun failed to raise a loan, he did however succeed in stirring Jia Huan to fresh thoughts of revenge. Memories of Xi-feng's cruelty still rankled in Jia Huan's mind; and with Jia Lian away, he was more than ready to vent some of his spleen on Qiao-jie. The loan-seeking Jia Yun seemed an ideal accomplice.

'You're not a boy any longer, Yun!' he grumbled provocatively. 'Why come asking for a loan from a pauper like me when there's a chance of making a nice little profit?'

'Tell us another!' replied Yun. 'We've just been having a bit of a lark. I never saw any chances for profit passing us by.'

'What was that a day or two ago about a Mongol prince wanting to buy himself a concubine? Why not talk it over with Dumbo, and offer the prince Qiao-jie?'

'This may make you cross when I say it, Uncle Huan,' replied Jia Yun. 'But I'd better say it all the same. Supposing the prince *did* buy a concubine from our family, he'd probably never want anything more to do with us afterwards.'

In response to this, Jia Huan whispered something in Jia Yun's ear and Yun nodded casually, judging the proposal to be a passing whim of Huan's and not worthy of serious consideration. At that very moment Wang Ren happened along.

'What are you two plotting?' he asked. 'Trying to keep me in the dark, are you?'

Jia Yun communicated to him, *sotto voce*, the substance of Jia Huan's scheme, and Wang Ren clapped his hands enthusiastically.

'Bravo! A capital idea! Lucrative too! But can you really pull it off? If you've the guts to go through with it, I'll back you up. Don't forget I'm her uncle. It's my decision, after all. You just put the plan to Lady Xing, Huan, old chap, while I have a word with Dumbo. If the aunts start asking questions, we must be sure to back each other up with the same story.'

When this conference was over, Wang Ren went to find Dumbo,

while Jia Yun went to impart the good news to Ladies Xing and Wang, adding many an enticing embellishment. Lady Wang made a note of the proposal, but was somewhat sceptical. Lady Xing on the other hand, when she heard that her brother knew, seemed in favour of the idea and sent for Dumbo to supply her with more details. Dumbo had already been briefed by Wang Ren (and had needless to say been offered his cut in the profits from the enterprise), and therefore when summoned to his sister's apartment he knew what to say:

'This prince is a very important man. Of course, what you're being asked to consent to is not for her to become a proper wife exactly; but as soon as she goes to him I can guarantee that brother-in-law will get his job back and the family as a whole recover a bit of its old pull.'

Lady Xing had no real mind of her own. She was taken in by Dumbo's story and invited Wang Ren to come and talk the matter over with her. Wang Ren's enthusiastic support for the project finally swayed the balance. She communicated her consent to Jia Yun, while Wang Ren went ahead at once and sent word to the prince's palace.

The prince for his part was unaware of all this behind-the-scenes activity. He was merely planning to despatch some of his ladies to examine the girl's physiognomy and suitability to enter his harem. Jia Yun managed to have a word with the ladies in private before-hand:

'None of the girl's own family know the truth about this. So far as they are concerned, the prince is thinking of taking the girl as one of his wives. Once she is installed, everything will be all right, have no fear. Her grandmother has given her consent, and her uncle Wang Ren is acting as go-between.'

The ladies agreed to co-operate. Jia Yun went to give Lady Xing the latest news, and informed Lady Wang of the 'match'. Li Wan and Bao-chai had no inkling of the truth and received the news of the princely 'wedding' with pleasure.

On the day appointed, several splendidly attired palace ladies arrived, and were received and entertained for a while by Lady Xing. They were soon aware that the lady with whom they were dealing was of considerable rank, and were most respectful towards her. As the terms of the transaction had not been finally agreed upon, Lady

Xing had said nothing to Qiao-jie but had merely informed her that some relatives had come to call and asked her to go out and see them. Qiao-jie, who was little more than a child, and too young to suspect anything, went with her old nanny and Patience, who felt a little uneasy and insisted on accompanying her charge. The minute Qiao-jie entered the room the two palace ladies began subjecting her to a penetrating scrutiny, ogling her entire person, top to toe. They then rose to their feet, took her by the hand and looked her over once more, after which they sat down again for a few minutes and then left. Qiao-jie was most embarrassed by all this staring, and when she returned to her room she sat puzzling it over to herself. She could not recall ever having seen these 'relatives' before, and said as much to Patience, who for her part, as soon as she had seen the way the two women were carrying on, had guessed the truth.

'They're obviously examining her with a view to marriage,' she thought to herself. 'But with Mr Lian away from home, the responsibility for this rests with Lady Xing, and I've no idea which family is involved. A family of the same rank as ours would never go in for all this staring. Anyway, those women didn't look as if they came from one of the royal princely establishments. There was something rather outlandish about them. I'd better not say anything to Qiao-jie for the present, but wait until I know more myself.'

Patience set about discovering the truth of the matter, and since the maids and serving-women concerned had all worked under her at one time or another in the past, they were well disposed and immediately gave her the information she wanted. She was horrified, and racked her brains for some means of averting this catastrophe. She still thought it wiser to say nothing to Qiao-jie, but hurried over to inform Li Wan and Bao-chai, begging them to lay the matter before Lady Wang.

Lady Wang herself had already sensed that there was something amiss, and had said as much to Lady Xing. But Lady Xing was quite taken in by her brother and Wang Ren, and instead of paying any heed to Lady Wang's words, rather suspected some ulterior motive in her opposition to the scheme.

'The girl is of age,' she replied. 'With Lian away from home, the decision in this matter is mine. And besides, my brother and the girl's own uncle have both looked into it thoroughly. Surely they know the truth. I am very much in favour of the idea. And you needn't worry; if anything should go wrong, Lian and I are not going to start laying the blame at your door.'

Lady Wang made some perfunctory reply, but was secretly furious with Lady Xing. She took her leave and went back to tell Bao-chai what had been decided. She wept as she spoke, and Bao-yu tried to console her.

'Mother, don't distress yourself. Nothing will come of this scheme. Whatever happens is already written in Qiao-jie's destiny anyway, so please don't try to interfere.'

'Don't be such an idiot!' exclaimed Lady Wang. 'Once they've agreed to this match, they'll be here any day to fetch her away! Patience is right, your cousin Lian will blame me for this when he comes back! I would want the best for *any* member of the family, and especially for Qiao-jie, for her parents' sake. Think of the other girls. We arranged Xiu-yan's marriage to your cousin Ke, and now look how happy they are together! And the Mei family into which Bao-qin has married are by all accounts very comfortably off, so there's no need to worry about her. Xiang-yun, I know, has not been quite so fortunate. That match was her own uncle's idea in the first place, and it would have turned out well if her husband had not fallen ill of a consumption and died. Now the poor girl has vowed to spend the rest of her days a widow. If Qiao-jie falls into bad hands, I shall never forgive myself!'

As she was speaking, Patience came in to consult with Bao-chai and also to learn the results of Lady Wang's meeting with Lady Xing. Lady Wang told her what Lady Xing had said. After a thoughtful silence, Patience fell to her knees.

'Qiao-jie's whole future now depends on you, ma'am!' she pleaded. 'If we deliver her into the hands of those people, it will mean a lifetime of suffering for her. And what do you think Mr Lian will say when he comes home?'

'You are an intelligent girl,' said Lady Wang. 'Stand up now and listen to what I have to say. In the last resort, Qiao-jie is my sister-in-law's granddaughter, not mine. If Lady Xing wants to take a decision, how can I stand in her way?'

'There is really no cause for concern,' insisted Bao-yu. 'The important thing is to have a clear perception of destiny.'

Patience was afraid that Bao-yu would start raving again and commit some indiscretion, and she remained silent. She had said all that she wanted to say to Lady Wang, and now returned to her own apartment.

Lady Wang's mental distress had brought on a pain in her heart. She summoned a maid to assist her and leaning heavily on her arm struggled back to her own room and lay down. She did not ask Bao-yu and Bao-chai to accompany her, saying that she would feel better after a sleep. But she found it impossible to shake off her troubled mood, and later when she heard that old Mrs Li had called, could not bring herself to rise from her bed and entertain her. Then Jia Lan came in to pay his respects and to deliver a message:

'A letter has come from Grandfather. The boys at the gate have brought it in. Mother was going to give it to you, but as my Grandmother Li has just come, she asked me to bring it instead. Mother will be coming over shortly to talk to you, and bringing my Grandmother Li.'

He handed Lady Wang the letter. Lady Wang asked him, as she took it from him:

'Why is your grandmother here?'

'I don't know myself,' replied Lan. 'I just heard say that there's a letter from Cousin Qi's fiancé's family, the Zhens.'

Lady Wang knew that Li Qi had been promised to Zhen Bao-yu, and that the betrothal had already been sealed with the customary gift of tea. It must be that the Zhens wanted to proceed with the wedding, and old Mrs Li had come to discuss some last-minute details. She nodded, and opened the letter from Jia Zheng:

The canal is congested with boats bringing back the army from its successful campaign on the coast, and my progress has thereby been greatly delayed. I have heard that Tan-chun's husband is travelling to the capital with his father, and wonder if you have heard anything from them? A day or two ago I had a letter from Lian, telling me of brother She's illness. Is there any more news?

The time is drawing near for Bao-yu and Lan to sit their examinations. They must study diligently and on no account must they be allowed to fritter their time away. It will be a few days before I can reach Nanking with Mother's coffin. I am in good health, so don't worry about me.

Please pass on my instructions to Bao-yu and Lan.

Zheng.

Dated the __ day of the __ month
PS Rong will be writing separately.

After reading the letter, Lady Wang handed it back to Jia Lan, saying:

'Give this to Bao-yu and tell him to read it. And then give it back to your mother.'

While she was speaking, Li Wan and old Mrs Li came in and paid their respects. They seated themselves, and old Mrs Li spoke about the Zhens and Li Qi's wedding. They discussed this for a while, and then Li Wan asked Lady Wang:

'Have you read Father's letter?'

'I have.'

Jia Lan handed the letter to his mother, who read it herself and said:

'Tan-chun has been away for over a year and not once come home. It will be such a relief for you now that they are moving up to the capital.'

'Yes,' replied Lady Wang. 'I was in some pain just now, but this piece of news has made me feel much more comfortable. We still don't know when they'll be arriving, mind you.'

Old Mrs Li asked how Jia Zheng's journey had been, while Li Wan turned to Jia Lan and said:

'I hope you have taken note of what your grandfather says in his letter? The examination is drawing closer, and he is very concerned about you both. You'd better hurry and take the letter for Bao-yu to read.'

'Please tell me,' enquired old Mrs Li, 'how it is that the two of them can take the second examination without having acquired their first degree?'

Lady Wang explained:

'Before he set out on his posting as Grain Intendant, my husband arranged for the purchase of the Licentiate degree for the two of them.'

Old Mrs Li nodded, and Jia Lan went off with the letter to find Bao-yu.

Having taken his leave of Lady Wang earlier, Bao-yu had returned to his apartment, where he picked up his copy of the 'Autumn Floods' chapter from *Zhuang-zi* and began reading it with fascination. When Bao-chai came out from the inner room and saw him so totally absorbed in his reading, she wandered across and glanced at the book's title. It disappointed her greatly that it should be a Taoist classic.

'Still the only thing he takes seriously is nonsense like this about "quitting the world and rising above the mortal plane",' she reflected to herself. 'He's truly a hopeless case!'

It seemed futile to remonstrate with him, so she just sat by his side, gazing at him reproachfully. Observing her expression, Bao-yu asked:

'What's all this about, then?'

'Since we are husband and wife,' she replied, 'I should be able to look to you for lifelong support. Our life together should be built on something more than the passion of a moment. Glory and wealth are as insubstantial as a cloud – that I can understand. But since ancient times, what the sages have prized most has always been virtue, not . . .'

Before he had heard her out, Bao-yu put his book down, smiled and said:

'You talk of virtue and the sages of ancient times. But do you know that the sages also held up as an ideal the "heart of a new-born child"? What *virtues* has the new-born child? None, only a complete absence of knowledge, of consciousness, of greed, of envy. All our lives we sink deeper and deeper into the quagmire of greed, hatred, folly and passion. The great question is, how to rise above all this, how to escape the net of this mortal life? "This floating life, with its meetings and partings" – I can see now why in all the ages since it was first uttered the true meaning of this expression has never been fully grasped. As for your "virtue", who has ever attained the true pristine state of virtue?'

'What the ancients meant by the "heart of a new-born child",' retorted Bao-chai, 'was a heart full of loyalty and filial devotion, not this mystical, escapist notion of yours. The Emperors Yao, Shun, Yu, Tang, the Duke of Zhou, Confucius – they all spent their lives improving the lot of mankind. Their "heart of a new-born child" was simply their spirit of compassion and concern for others. Whereas yours, it would seem, leaves you so blissfully unconcerned that you would be willing to forsake your own family. It doesn't make any sense to me.'

Bao-yu nodded and smiled:

'Yao and Shun were not able to prevail upon Chao-fu or Xu You to abandon their mountain retreats; nor could King Wu or the Duke of Zhou induce Bo Yi and his brother Shu Qi to involve themselves in the world . . .'

'You are becoming more and more absurd!' interrupted Bao-chai. 'If all the men of old had been hermits like those four you mention, then there would never have been sages like Yao, Shun, the Duke of Zhou and Confucius. And besides, it's ridiculous to compare yourself with Bo Yi. Both he and Shu Qi lived in the declining years of the Shang dynasty, and their lives were beset with difficulties of one kind or another. So they had a good pretext for escaping their responsibilities. But your case is totally different. Ours is a golden age, and we ourselves have received numerous favours from the throne, while our ancestors enjoyed lives of luxury. And you yourself have been treasured all your life, both by our late grandmother, and by Mother and Father. Reflect a little on what you said just now. Don't you think that I'm right?'

Bao-yu listened in silence. His only response was to stare at the ceiling and smile.

'Since you're stuck for an answer,' Bao-chai continued, 'you should listen to my advice. Pull yourself together from now on, and work as hard as you can. Do well in the examination, and even if you never achieve anything else in your entire life, that will at least be some return for Heaven's favour and for your ancestors' virtue.'

Bao-yu nodded and heaved a sigh:

'Doing well in the examination is not that difficult. And what you say about *never achieving anything else* and making *some return for Heaven's favour and our ancestors' virtue* is very much to the point . . .'

Before Bao-chai could reply to this, Aroma put in her word:

'I didn't really understand what Mrs Bao was saying about the sages of old. All I know is that we've all stuck with you through thick and thin since we were children, tending you with more devotion than I can say. Of course, I know that's only as it should be, but shouldn't *you* show *us* a little consideration in return? And look at the devotion Mrs Bao has shown to the Master and Her Ladyship, all for your sake! Even if you don't set great store by your marriage, surely you owe her a simple debt of gratitude for what she has done? As for all that stuff about immortality, that's just a lot of hot air. Who ever actually saw an immortal set foot in this world of ours? Some monk turns up from goodness knows where, talking a lot of rubbish, and you go and take him seriously! You're an educated man, surely you don't give more weight to his words than you do to the Master's and Her Ladyship's?'

Bao-yu bowed his head in silence.

Aroma had more ammunition ready, but just then footsteps were heard outside, and a voice came through the window:

'Is Uncle Bao at home?'

Bao-yu recognized Jia Lan's voice, stood up and said pleasantly: 'Come in!'

Jia Lan entered, his face wreathed in smiles. He paid his respects to Bao-yu and Bao-chai, and exchanged greetings with Aroma, before presenting Bao-yu with Jia Zheng's letter, which Bao-yu took from him and read.

'So my sister is coming back to town, then?'

'Judging from the letter it seems more than likely,' was Jia Lan's reply.

Bao-yu nodded his head in thoughtful silence, and Jia Lan continued:

'You see at the end of the letter, Uncle Bao, Grandfather urges us to get down to some serious work. I don't suppose you've been doing many compositions recently, have you?'

Bao-yu laughed:

'I'd like to do a few, just to keep my hand in. Why not? May as well pull the wool over their eyes!'

'In that case,' suggested Jia Lan, 'why don't you propose a few themes, and we'll write them together. That will help us prepare for the exam. I certainly don't want to hand in a blank sheet and make a fool of us both.'

'I know you will do nothing of the kind,' said Bao-yu.

Bao-chai asked Jia Lan to take a seat. Bao-yu sat down again himself in his original chair, while Jia Lan perched politely nearby, and they chatted for a while about their compositions, their conversation becoming quite animated. Bao-chai, seeing the two of them thus engrossed, discreetly withdrew, thinking to herself:

'It almost seems as if Bao-yu may have seen the light. But I wonder what he meant just now by picking on my words "never achieving anything else" and repeating them so emphatically?'

She was still greatly puzzled. Aroma on the other hand was delighted to hear him talking about compositions and the examination.

'Praise be to Buddha!' she exclaimed silently to herself. 'What a sermon it took though, to bring him to his senses!'

The boys continued their discussion, and Oriole made them some tea. Jia Lan rose to his feet to receive his cup, and talked a little longer about the regulations governing the examination, adding that he would also like to invite Zhen Bao-yu over one day. Bao-yu seemed willing that he should do so.

After a while, Jia Lan returned to his apartment, leaving Jia Zheng's letter behind with Bao-yu. Bao-yu read it through again, and with a smile on his lips went in and handed it to Musk to put away. Then he returned and removed his copy of *Zhuang-zi* from the table, collecting up at the same time some of his other favourite esoteric books (a collection that included *The Hermetic Clavicule*, *The Secret of the Primordial Flower* and *The Compendium of the Five Lamps*). He gave instructions to Musk, Ripple and Oriole to store all of these away. Bao-chai was amazed to see him do this, and wished to sound out his true motives.

'It's very commendable of you to forgo reading such books,' she said with a quizzical smile. 'But why do you have to move them out of sight altogether?'

'Because now I understand,' replied Bao-yu. 'None of those books is worth anything. It would be best to burn the lot and be rid of them once and for all!'

Bao-chai was delighted to hear him saying this. But the very next minute she heard him recite, as if to himself:

> 'True Buddha Mind Within
> Is not in Sutras to be found;
> Beyond the Crucible,
> There leads a path to Higher Ground.'

Bao-chai did not catch every word, but 'Buddha Mind Within' and 'Higher Ground' were enough to fill her once more with gloomy forebodings. She watched him anxiously. He told the maids to prepare a quiet room for him, looked out all his old copies of books like Zhucius's *Neo-Confucian Primer*, and collections of examination essays and verses, and assembled them all in his new room. Then he sat down in earnest and began quietly working. Bao-chai felt she could finally set her mind at rest.

Aroma could hardly believe the evidence of her eyes and ears. She smiled conspiratorially at Bao-chai:

'You certainly know how to talk him round, ma'am! Just that one lecture from you and he's a new man! I only hope he hasn't left it too late. The exams are looming very close.'

Bao-chai nodded and smiled:

'These things are in the hands of fate. His success will not turn on how soon or late he begins preparing. I just hope that from now on he will learn to be more adult, and give up his old antics.'

Checking first that she and Aroma were alone in the room, she added in an undertone:

'I'm certainly very pleased at this change of heart. But there is still one thing that worries me. His old weakness. We ought to try to isolate him from our own sex.'

'You are quite right, ma'am,' said Aroma. 'So long as he was under the influence of that monk, he seemed to be quite indifferent to the girls around him. But now that he's changed course again, we must once more be on our guard for a revival of his old habits. I don't think he's likely to show much interest in either of us, ma'am. With Nightingale gone, that only leaves the four other maids. Fivey is the little vixen among them, but I hear that her mother has been asking for permission to take her out of service to get married, so she'll be leaving in a few days' time. Musk and Ripple have never been particularly close to Master Bao, but we shouldn't forget that they used to fool about with him when he was a child. That leaves Oriole. He doesn't seem at all interested in her, and she's a very dependable girl. I suggest that for day-to-day duties, like pouring tea and carrying water, Oriole should take charge, with a few of the junior maids to help her. What do you think, ma'am?'

'I have been worrying about the same thing myself,' replied Bao-chai. 'Your proposal is a very sensible one.'

So from then on Oriole was put in charge. Bao-yu never left his room now. Every day he sent someone else to pay respects to his mother on his behalf. Lady Wang's delight at this new regime of his needs no description.

When the third of the eighth came round (Grandmother Jia's birthday), Bao-yu went early in the morning to kowtow at her shrine and then returned to his 'quiet room'. After breakfast, Bao-chai, Aroma and some of the maids had gone to sit in the front room and were chatting with Ladies Xing and Wang, and he was sitting alone in his room, deep in concentration, when Oriole came in with a tray of sweetmeats.

'Her Ladyship asked me to bring these for you,' she said. 'They are offerings left over from Her Old Ladyship's sacrifice.'

Bao-yu rose to his feet to thank her and then sat down again.

'Put them over there,' he said.

As she placed the tray to one side, Oriole said to him in an undertone:

'Her Ladyship has been speaking very highly of you in the front room.'

Bao-yu smiled. Oriole continued:

'She said that now you are studying so hard, you are sure to pass your exam and then if you go on and become a Palace Graduate and an official, your parents' hopes for you will not have been in vain.'

Oriole suddenly remembered what Bao-yu had once said to her, the day she had knotted tassels for him.

'I hope you *do* pass!' she went on animatedly. 'It will be such a blessing for our mistress. Remember what you said that day in the Garden, when you asked me to knot you a plum-blossom tassel? You wondered what lucky household the mistress would take me to when she married? Well, you were the lucky one after all!'

There was something about what she said and the way she said it that aroused in Bao-yu once more an old and all too human emotion. But the nostalgia soon passed; he composed himself again and said with a gentle smile:

'So, according to you, I am lucky, and so is your mistress. But how do *you* feel about it?'

Oriole flushed at once, and forced a smile:

'We're just maids. Being lucky or not doesn't really enter into it for us.'

Bao-yu smiled again:

'As a matter of fact, even if you did spend your whole life as a maid, you might turn out to have been luckier than either of us.'

This sounded to Oriole like more of his foolishness. She was afraid of being responsible for another of his scenes, and deemed it prudent to leave, but before she could do so, Bao-yu laughed:

'Silly girl! Let me tell you something.'

If you want to know what it was, you must turn to the next chapter.

CHAPTER 119

*Bao-yu becomes a Provincial Graduate
and severs worldly ties
The House of Jia receives Imperial favour
and renews ancestral glory*

As we told in the last chapter, Oriole, perplexed by Bao-yu's words, had been about to leave when she heard him speak again:

'Silly girl! Let me tell you something. If your mistress is lucky, then so are you, since you are her maid. Aroma cannot be depended upon. In future, mark my words, you must look after your mistress with care and devotion, and in the end you may receive a fitting reward for your years of service.'

To Oriole Bao-yu's speech, although it began with some semblance of sense, tailed off into rambling nonsense.

'Well,' she replied, 'I'd better be going now. Madam is waiting for me. If you want any more sweets, Mr Bao, just send one of the junior maids to fetch me.'

Bao-yu nodded and Oriole went on her way. Shortly afterwards, Bao-chai and Aroma returned from the front room.

*

The time drew near for the examination. All the family were full of eager anticipation, hoping that the two boys would write creditable compositions and bring the family honour. All except for Bao-chai; while it was true that Bao-yu had prepared well, she had also on occasions noticed a strange indifference in his behaviour. Her first concern was that the two boys, for both of whom this was the first venture of its kind, might get hurt or have some accident in the crush of men and vehicles around the examination halls. She was more particularly worried for Bao-yu, who had not been out at all since his encounter with the monk. His delight in studying seemed to her the result of a somewhat too hasty and not altogether convincing conversion, and she had a premonition that something untoward was going to happen. So, on the day before the big event, she despatched

Aroma and a few of the junior maids to go with Candida and her helpers and make sure that the candidates were both properly prepared. She herself inspected their things and put them out in readiness, and then went over with Li Wan to Lady Wang's apartment, where she selected a few of the more trusty family retainers to accompany them the next day, for fear they might be jolted or trampled on in the crowds.

The big day finally arrived, and Bao-yu and Jia Lan changed into smart but unostentatious clothes. They came over in high spirits to bid farewell to Lady Wang, who gave them a few parting words of advice:

'This is the first examination for both of you, and although you are such big boys now, it will still be the first time either of you has been away from me for a whole day. You may have gone out in the past, but you were always surrounded by your maids and nurses. You have never spent the night away on your own like this. Today, when you both go into the examination, you are bound to feel rather lonely with none of the family by you. You must take special care. Finish your papers and come out as early as possible, and then be sure to find one of the family servants and come home as soon as you can. We shall be worrying about you.'

As she spoke, Lady Wang herself was greatly moved by the occasion. Jia Lan made all the appropriate responses, but Bao-yu remained silent until his mother had quite finished speaking. Then he walked up to her, knelt at her feet and with tears streaming down his cheeks kowtowed to her three times and said:

'I could never repay you adequately for all you have done for me, Mother. But if I can do this one thing successfully, if I can do my very best and pass this examination, then perhaps I can bring you a little pleasure. Then my worldly duty will be accomplished and I will at least have made some small return for all the trouble I have caused you.'

Lady Wang was still more deeply moved by this:

'It is a very fine thing, what you are setting out to do. It is only a shame that your grandmother couldn't be here to witness it.'

She wept as she spoke and put her arms around him to draw him to her. Bao-yu remained kneeling however and would not rise.

'Even though Grandmother is not here,' he said, 'I am sure she knows about it and is happy. So really it is just as if she were present. What separates us is only matter. We are together in spirit.'

Li Wan feared that this scene might provoke Bao-yu to one of his fits. Besides, she sensed something inauspicious. She hurried forward:

'Mother, today we should be filled with joy. You mustn't upset yourself like this. Think how sensible and dutiful and hard-working Bao-yu has been of late. All he needs to do now is to sit the examinations with Lan, write his papers properly and come home early. Then he can show copies of what he has written to some scholars connected with the family, and we'll just wait for the good news.'

She told one of the maids to help Bao-yu to his feet. Bao-yu turned and bowed to her:

'Sister-in-law, you are not to worry. Lan and I are sure to pass. What is more, Lan has a brilliant future ahead of him, while you yourself will one day become a lady of noble rank and dress in the finest robes.'

Li Wan smiled:

'If all this were ever to come true, it would at least be some compensation . . .'

She stopped short, fearing to cause Lady Wang further distress. Bao-yu felt no such inhibition:

'If Lan does well and upholds our family tradition, my late brother may not have lived to witness it, but you will at least see his dearest wishes fulfilled.'

It was getting late, and since Li Wan did not wish to prolong this exchange any further, she contented herself with a brief nod. Bao-chai had already perceived the strangeness of the conversation. Not only were Bao-yu's remarks ominous in themselves, but every word uttered by Lady Wang and Li Wan seemed laden with inauspicious meaning as well. Not daring to express this presentiment of hers openly, Bao-chai held back her tears and remained silent. Bao-yu came up to her and made her a deep bow. It seemed to them all such an eccentric way to behave, and no one could imagine what it was supposed to mean; nor did anyone dare to laugh. The general amazement increased when Bao-chai burst into floods of tears, and Bao-yu bade her farewell:

'Coz! I'm going now. Stay here with Mother and wait for the good news!'

'It is time for you to go,' replied Bao-chai. 'There is no need to embark on another of your long speeches.'

'Strange that you should be urging me on my way,' said Bao-yu. 'I know it is time to go.'

He glanced around him and saw that Xi-chun and Nightingale were absent.

'Say goodbye to Xi-chun and Nightingale for me,' he said. 'I shall certainly be meeting them again.'

Everyone was forcibly struck by the strange blend of sense and nonsense in Bao-yu's words. They thought him momentarily confused, in part by the unprecedented nature of the occasion, in part by Lady Wang's injunctions. To all of them the best course of action in the circumstances seemed to be to speed him on his way and get the thing over with.

'They're waiting for you outside. No more dilly-dallying now, or you'll be late.'

Bao-yu raised his head and laughed.

'Off I go! Enough of this foolery! It's over!'

'Well – off you go then!' they all cried, laughing nervously. Only Lady Wang and Bao-chai were sobbing inconsolably, as if they were parting from him for ever. Finally Bao-yu walked out through the door and on his way, giggling like a half-wit.

> Entering the lists of worldly renown,
> He breaks the first bar of his earthly cage.

*

We must leave Bao-yu and Jia Lan on their way to the examination, and return to Jia Huan. The excitement surrounding the candidates' departure had left him feeling even more peeved and sour than usual, and with their absence he was now free to carry out his plan:

'My own mother *will* be avenged! Now there's not a man left in the house, and Aunt Xing will do as I say. I need fear no one.'

With determined stride he hurried over to Lady Xing's to pay her his respects, and then conversed with her for a while in a most obsequious tone. She was naturally flattered, and said to him:

'Now you are speaking like an intelligent child! Or course I'm the one who ought to take the decision in an affair such as this of Qiao-jie's. It was very stupid of your cousin Lian to ignore his own mother and place this in someone else's hands.'

'So far as the prince is concerned, your side of the family is the one that he recognizes,' said Jia Huan. 'The whole thing is settled, and now they are preparing to send you a large consignment of presents. With this prince married to your granddaughter, Uncle She is bound to be given an important position. It will benefit us all. I don't want to sound critical of Mother, but all the time sister Yuan-chun was an Imperial Concubine, it didn't prevent them from treating some of us very shoddily. I hope Qiao-jie will be less ungrateful. I must have a word with her.'

'Yes, you should speak to her,' said Lady Xing. 'It will give her a chance to see how much you've done for her. I am sure if her father were at home he would never have found her such a good match! That foolish creature Patience has been saying things against it and protesting that your mother disapproves. It is probably nothing more than sour grapes on their part. We must lose no time, or Lian will be back and then they will set him against the idea too and we'll never be able to go through with it.'

'So far as the prince is concerned, the matter is already settled,' said Jia Huan. 'They are only waiting for you to send over the horoscope. Then, according to their princely customs, she will be fetched three days later for the wedding. There is however one condition that you may object to. They say that in view of the circumstances, because it is not quite proper to marry the grand-daughter of a disgraced official, they will have to take her away quietly without any ceremony. Later, when Uncle She has been pardoned and reinstated in office, they can celebrate the union with all the usual festivities.'

'Of course I agree,' said Lady Xing. 'What they suggest is only correct.'

'In that case all you have to do now is give them the Eight Characters for Qiao-jie's horoscope.'

'Silly boy! What can we womenfolk do? You'd better ask Yun to write them out for you.'

Jia Huan was delighted by Lady Xing's response and agreed at once to this proposal, which suited him perfectly. He hurried over to have a word with Jia Yun, and asked Wang Ren to go to the prince's palace to sign the contract and receive the money.

The conversation between Jia Huan and Lady Xing had been overheard by one of Lady Xing's maids who owed her appointment to Patience and who therefore, as soon as an opportunity presented itself, went straight to see Patience and told her the gist of what was happening. Patience had known all along that no good would come of this marriage plan, and had already told Qiao-jie all that she knew about it. When she first learnt that she was to be married, Qiao-jie had cried all night long; she demanded that they wait for her father's return before making a decision, and insisted that there was no need to obey Lady Xing. Now, when this latest news arrived, she began howling and wanted to go and complain to Lady Xing herself. Patience hastened to prevent her:

'You must calm down, miss. Lady Xing is your own grandmother, and with your father away she has every right to make these decisions. Besides, your own uncle is acting as go-between. They're all in this together, and you're on your own. You'll never make them change their minds. And I am only a maid, I can say nothing. We must try to think of a plan ourselves, and not do anything rash!'

'You'd better be quick,' advised Lady Xing's maid, 'or it will be too late. The bridal chair will be here any day now and then Miss Qiao-jie will be taken away.'

With these gloomy words she returned to Lady Xing's apartment.

Patience turned round to see Qiao-jie huddled up and weeping disconsolately to herself. She reached out a hand to comfort her:

'It's no use crying, miss. There's nothing your father can do for you now. From what they've been saying, it seems as if . . .'

Before she could complete her sentence, a messenger arrived from Lady Xing's and announced:

'This is indeed a happy day for Miss Qiao-jie! Will Patience please prepare whatever Miss Qiao-jie will need to take with her. Her trousseau can wait until Mr Lian's return.'

Patience was going through the motions of obeying these instructions, when Lady Wang arrived. Qiao-jie hugged her tightly and wept into her bosom. Lady Wang was in tears herself:

'Try not to worry, child. I've spoken to your grandmother and done everything I can for you, and I've received nothing but insults for my pains. I can't make her change her mind. We can only go along with it, and try to delay things as much as possible. Meanwhile we must send someone straight to your father to tell him what is going on.'

'But haven't you heard, ma'am?' said Patience. 'Early this morning Master Huan was over at Her Ladyship's. According to this prince's custom the bride will be fetched in three days. Her Ladyship has already asked Mr Yun to prepare the horoscope. By the time Mr Lian returns it will all be over!'

When she heard that Huan was involved, Lady Wang was speechless with rage. Eventually she stammered out, 'Bring him to me! Bring him to me at once!' A servant went in obedience to her command, but returned to report that Master Huan had gone out early that morning with Mr Jia Qiang and Mr Wang Ren.

'Where's young Yun?' asked Lady Wang.

'We don't know,' was the reply.

The people gathered in Qiao-jie's room stood staring impotently around them. Lady Wang lacked the nerve to go and challenge Lady Xing directly. They all wept bitterly on each other's shoulders.

Just as their spirits had sunk to these depths of gloom, a serving-woman came in to announce that Grannie Liu had arrived at the back gate of the mansion.

'We're all at sixes and sevens,' was Lady Wang's comment. 'How can we start receiving guests at a moment like this? Find some excuse and ask her to leave.'

'Perhaps you should ask her in, ma'am,' said Patience. 'After all she is Qiao-jie's godmother. We should tell her what is happening.'

Lady Wang said nothing. The serving-woman left the room and reappeared shortly with Grannie Liu, who exchanged greetings with all the ladies present. Seeing their eyes red from weeping, and having no idea what the matter was, Grannie Liu asked, with some hesitation:

'What is the trouble? It's Mrs Lian you're grieving for, I'll be bound.'

The mention of her mother set Qiao-jie weeping with renewed abandon.

'There's no point in avoiding the issue, Grannie,' said Patience. 'As her godmother you ought to know the truth.'

She went on to tell Grannie Liu the whole story. At first the old dame was aghast. Then, after a long silence, she suddenly laughed.

'A smart young woman like you ought to be able to hit on something without much difficulty. Look at the drum ballads, they are full of clever plots and schemes for getting people out of scrapes like this one.'

'Oh, Grannie!' begged Patience. 'If you can think of a way, please tell us quickly!'

'It's easy,' said the old dame. 'We mustn't tell a soul, though, and we must be sure to make a quick getaway and hide – that's all that's needed.'

'You can't be serious!' protested Patience. 'Where could someone from a family like ours possibly hide?'

'Well,' said Grannie Liu, '*if* you're willing – and that's the only if – then you can both come to our village. I can keep Miss Qiao-jie hidden and at the same time I'll tell my son-in-law to send a man with a letter (which Miss Qiao-jie must write with her own hand) straight to Mr Lian. Once *he* arrives on the scene, everything can be mended well enough.'

'And if Lady Xing finds out meanwhile?' asked Patience.

'Do they know that I'm here?' asked Grannie Liu.

'Lady Xing is living at the front, and as she treats people so harshly no one ever tells her what's going on. If you'd come in by the front gate she might have known. As it is, we have nothing to fear.'

'Well then,' said Grannie Liu, 'let us agree on a time, and then I'll tell my son-in-law to send a cart for you both.'

'There's not a moment to be lost,' urged Patience. 'I'll be as quick as I can.'

She went into the inner room with Lady Wang, and having dismissed all the servants explained Grannie Liu's plan to her. Lady Wang considered it carefully, and judged it altogether too risky.

'But it's our only hope!' pleaded Patience. 'I can speak my mind to you, ma'am. This is what I think you should do. You must pretend to know nothing about it; later you can even go to Lady Xing's and ask her where Qiao-jie has gone. We'll send a message to Mr Lian, and surely he won't be long coming.'

Lady Wang was silent, and heaved a deep sigh. Qiao-jie had heard them talking and added her entreaties to those of Patience:

'Oh Auntie, please! Save me! I know how grateful Father will be to you when he returns.'

'We *must* go ahead with our plan,' said Patience decisively. 'You can return to your own apartment, ma'am. But please send someone to keep an eye on Qiao-jie's room.'

'Very well then – but be secret about it!' urged Lady Wang. 'And both of you, remember to take plenty of clothes and bedding with you.'

'We must leave quickly if we are to succeed,' said Patience. 'If they come back with the contract signed, we'll be done for!'

This seemed to bring Lady Wang to her senses:

'Yes! Of course! You must hurry! You can depend on me!' Lady Wang returned to her own apartment, and then went to engage Lady Xing in conversation and thus hold her at bay.

Patience despatched a servant to prepare their things, with instructions not to seem too furtive about it. 'If anyone comes in and sees what you are doing, just say that you are acting on Lady Xing's instructions, and that you're ordering a carriage for Grannie Liu to go home in.' Meanwhile the men on the back gate were bribed and told to hire a carriage. Patience dressed Qiao-jie to look like Grannie Liu's granddaughter Qing-er, and hurried out with her. She pretended to be seeing the 'Liu family' off, and then at the last minute jumped into the carriage herself. Although the back gate had recently been kept open, there were only one or two men on regular duty; as for the various other domestic servants, the mansion was so large and understaffed – indeed almost deserted – that their departure was sure to go virtually unnoticed. Besides, Lady Xing had a reputation for meanness with the servants, and they disapproved of what they knew she was planning to do to Qiao-jie. They were therefore very much on Patience's side and only too willing to connive at Qiao-jie's escape. Lady Xing was thus successfully engaged in conversation with Lady Wang, and remained completely unaware of the escape.

Lady Wang was still most apprehensive. After talking to Lady Xing she made her way to Bao-chai's, trying to attract as little attention as possible, and sat there, her mind filled with doubts as to the safety of the enterprise. Seeing how distracted she was, Bao-chai asked her what was on her mind, and Lady Wang explained everything to her in confidence.

'How very dangerous!' exclaimed Bao-chai. 'We must find Yun quickly and order him to halt matters at his end at once.'

'But I can't even find Huan!' complained Lady Wang.

'You must carry on as if you know nothing at all,' advised Bao-chai. 'I shall find someone to inform Aunt Xing.'

Lady Wang nodded and left Bao-chai to proceed with her plan.

*

Our story now turns to the Mongol prince himself. This gentleman was in fact doing no more than looking for a couple of presentable young concubines to add to his harem, and on the strength of a professional broker's recommendation had sent two of his women to examine Qiao-jie. When they returned, and when their master questioned them about the young lady's provenance, they did not dare conceal the truth. The prince was deeply shocked to learn that she was from such an old and noble family:

'But this is monstrous! Such a thing is strictly forbidden! I have come close to committing a grave crime! Besides, I have already been received in audience by His Majesty and will shortly be choosing a suitable day to start on my return journey. If anyone should come to pursue this matter further, send him packing!'

This was precisely the day on which Jia Yun and Wang Ren were delivering Qiao-jie's horoscope to the palace. When they arrived they met with a brusque reception:

'His Highness has instructed that any person daring to misrepresent a member of the Jia family as a common citizen is to be arrested and dealt with according to due process of law! What an outrageous way to behave in these peaceful times!'

Wang Ren and Jia Yun skulked off at once with their tails between their legs, grumbling to themselves that someone had betrayed them and going their separate ways in extremely low spirits.

Jia Huan was at home waiting for news, and had become very agitated when he received Lady Wang's summons. He saw Jia Yun returning home on his own, and rushed up to him:

'Well? Is everything arranged?'

Jia Yun stamped his foot frantically:

'It's terrible! Something's gone badly wrong! I can't think who can have given us away.'

He told the whole story to Huan, who was at first speechless with rage, then burst out:

'Only this morning I was at Aunt Xing's singing the praises of this match; now what am I supposed to do? You're all trying to ruin me!'

Just as they were wondering how to save the situation, a confused hubbub reached them from the inner apartments. They heard their own names called, 'wanted by Their Ladyships', and slunk shamefacedly into Lady Wang's apartment.

'A fine mess you've made of things!' exclaimed Lady Wang, waiting for them with fury written on her face. 'Well, now you've driven Qiao-jie and Patience to their deaths! The least you can do is bring me back their corpses!'

They both knelt at her feet. Jia Huan did not dare to open his mouth, but Jia Yun bowed his head and said:

'I would never have dared to do it myself. We only mentioned this match to you, Great-aunts, because Great-uncle Xing and Uncle Wang suggested it. It was all their idea. Then Great-aunt Xing agreed to it and asked me to write out the horoscope. Now the other party wants to back out. How can you accuse us of driving Qiao-jie to her death?'

'Huan told your great-aunt Xing that they would be arriving in three days to take the girl away,' said Lady Wang. 'Whoever heard of a proper wedding being conducted in such a hurry? I shall ask no more questions. Just give me back Qiao-jie. We shall see what Sir Zheng decides to do with you when he returns.'

Lady Xing wept in silent shame. Lady Wang turned next on Jia Huan:

'That harpy Aunt Zhao evidently left behind her a son every bit as vile as herself!'

She called one of her maids to support her and retired to her bedroom.

Left on their own Jia Huan, Jia Yun and Lady Xing began to indulge in mutual recrimination, until finally one of them said:

'What's the use of blaming each other like this? The girl probably isn't dead at all. Patience has almost certainly taken her off to hide in the home of a relative.'

Lady Xing summoned the janitors from the front and rear gates and after giving them a good scolding asked them where Qiao-jie and Patience had gone.

'It's no good asking us, ma'am,' they replied with one voice. 'Ask one of the stewards, they're the ones who ought to know. We wouldn't advise you to make a scene, ma'am. If Lady Wang should choose to question us, there's plenty we could tell. And if one person is beaten or given the sack, it will have to be everyone. Since Mr Lian left it's been a sheer disgrace what has been going on in the front of the mansion. We haven't even received our wages or monthly grain allowance, but *they*'ve been drinking and gambling away, fooling around with pretty little actors, inviting girls into the house – is that how masters of the family are supposed to behave?'

Jia Yun and Jia Huan were silent. A servant arrived from Lady Wang's with renewed orders to 'hurry up and find Patience and Qiao-jie', which sent them into another flurry of desperate activity. They did not even bother to question the servants in Qiao-jie's own apartment, knowing they would be too hostile to reveal the whereabouts of the missing pair (though this was hardly something they could say to Lady Wang). Instead they had to go asking at the home of every relative, and still failed to unearth the slightest clue. Lady Xing in the inner apartments and Jia Huan in the outer spent a hectic few days and nights.

At last came the day when the examinations were due to be concluded and the students released from their cells. Lady Wang was eagerly awaiting the return of Bao-yu and Jia Lan, and when midday came and there was still no sign of either of them, she, Li Wan and Bao-chai all began to worry and sent one servant after another to find out what had become of them. The servants could obtain no news, and not one of them dared to return empty-handed. Later another batch was despatched on the same mission, with the same result. The three ladies were beside themselves with anxiety.

When evening came, someone returned at last: it was Jia Lan. They were delighted to see him, and immediately asked:

'Where is Bao-yu?'

He did not even greet them but burst into tears.

'Lost!' he sobbed.

For several minutes Lady Wang was struck dumb. Then she collapsed senseless onto her couch. Luckily Suncloud and one or two other maids were at hand to support her, and they brought her round, themselves sobbing hysterically the while. Bao-chai stared in front of her with a glazed expression in her eyes, while Aroma sobbed her heart out. The only thing they could find time to do between their fits of sobbing was to scold Jia Lan:

'Fool! You were with Bao-yu – how could he get lost?'

'Before the examinations we stayed in the same room, we ate together and slept together. Even when we went in we were never far apart, we were always within sight of each other. This morning Uncle Bao finished his paper early and waited for me. We handed in our papers at the same time and left together. When we reached the

Dragon Gate outside there was a big crowd and I lost sight of him. The servants who had come to fetch us asked me where he was and Li Gui told them: "One minute he was just over there clear as daylight, the next minute he was gone. How can he have disappeared so suddenly in the crowd?" I told Li Gui and the others to split up into search parties, while I took some men and looked in all the cubicles. But there was no sign of him. That's why I'm so late back.'

Lady Wang had been sobbing throughout this, without saying a word. Bao-chai had already more or less guessed the truth. Aroma continued to weep inconsolably. Jia Qiang and the other men needed no further orders but set off immediately in several directions to join in the search. It was a sad sight, with everyone in the lowest of spirits and the welcome-home party prepared in vain. Jia Lan forgot his own exhaustion and wanted to go out with the others. But Lady Wang kept him back:

'My child! Your uncle is lost; if we lost you as well, it would be more than we could bear! You have a rest now, there's a good boy!'

He was reluctant to stay behind, but acquiesced when You-shi added her entreaties to Lady Wang's.

The only person present who seemed unsurprised was Xi-chun. She did not feel free to express her thoughts, but instead enquired of Bao-chai:

'Did Bao-yu have his jade with him when he left?'

'Of course he did,' she replied. 'He never goes anywhere without it.'

Xi-chun was silent. Aroma remembered how they had had to waylay Bao-yu and snatch the jade from his hands, and she had an overwhelming suspicion that today's mishap was that monk's doing too. Her heart ached with grief, tears poured down her cheeks and she began wailing despondently. Memories flooded back of the affection Bao-yu had shown her. 'I annoyed him sometimes, I know, and then he'd be cross. But he always had a way of making it up. He was so kind to me, and so thoughtful. In heated moments he often would vow to become a monk. I never believed him. And now he's gone!'

It was two o'clock in the morning by now, and still there was no sign of Bao-yu. Li Wan, afraid that Lady Wang would injure herself through excess of grief, did her best to console her and advised her to retire to bed. The rest of the family accompanied her to her room, except for Lady Xing who returned to her own apartment, and Jia Huan who was still lying low and had not dared to make an appearance at all. Lady Wang told Jia Lan to go back to his room, and herself spent a sleepless night. Next day at dawn some of the servants despatched the previous day returned, to report that they had searched everywhere and failed to find the slightest trace of Bao-yu. During the morning a stream of relations including Aunt Xue, Xue Ke, Shi Xiang-yun, Bao-qin and old Mrs Li came to enquire after Lady Wang's health and to ask for news of Bao-yu.

After several days of this, Lady Wang was so consumed with grief that she could neither eat nor drink, and her very life seemed in danger. Then suddenly a servant announced a messenger from the Commandant of the Haimen Coastal Region, who brought news that Tan-chun was due to arrive in the capital the following day. Although this could not totally dispel her grief at Bao-yu's disappearance, Lady Wang felt some slight comfort at the thought of seeing Tan-chun again. The next day, Tan-chun arrived at Rong-guo House and they all went out to the front to greet her, finding her lovelier than ever and most prettily dressed. When Tan-chun saw how Lady Wang had aged, and how red-eyed everyone in the family was, tears sprang to her eyes, and it was a while before she could stop weeping and greet them all properly. She was also distressed to see Xi-chun in a nun's habit, and wept again to learn of Bao-yu's strange disappearance and the many other family misfortunes. But she had always been gifted with a knack of finding the right thing to say, and her natural equanimity restored a degree of calm to the gathering and gave some real comfort to Lady Wang and the rest of the family. The next day her husband came to visit, and when he learned how things stood he begged her to stay at home and console her family. The maids and old serving-women who had accompanied her to her new home were thus granted a welcome reunion with their old friends.

The entire household, masters and servants alike, still waited anxiously day and night for news of Bao-yu. Very late one night, during the fifth watch, some servants came as far as the inner gate, announcing that they had indeed wonderful news to report, and a couple of the junior maids hurried in to the inner apartments, without stopping to inform the senior maids.

'Ma'am, ladies!' they announced. 'Wonderful news!'

Lady Wang thought that Bao-yu must at last have been found and rising from her bed she exclaimed with delight:

'Where did they find him? Send him in at once to see me!'

'He has been placed seventh on the roll of successful candidates!' the maid cried.

'But has he been *found*?'

The maid was silent. Lady Wang sat down again.

'*Who* came seventh?' asked Tan-chun.

'Mr Bao.'

As they were talking they heard a voice outside shouting:

'Master Lan has passed too!'

A servant went hurrying out to receive the official notice, on which it was written that Jia Lan had been placed one hundred and thirtieth on the roll.

Since there was still no news of Bao-yu's whereabouts, Li Wan did not feel free to express her feelings of pride and joy; and Lady Wang, delighted as she was that Jia Lan had passed, could not help thinking to herself:

'If only Bao-yu were here too, what a happy celebration it would be!'

Bao-chai alone was still plunged in gloom, though she felt it inappropriate to weep. The others were busy offering their congratulations and trying to look on the cheerful side:

'Since it was Bao-yu's fate to pass, he cannot remain lost for long. In a day or two he is sure to be found.'

This plausible suggestion brought a momentary smile to Lady Wang's cheeks, and the family seized on this opportunity to persuade her to eat and drink a little. A moment later Tealeaf's voice could be heard calling excitedly from the inner gate:

'Now that Mr Bao has passed, he is sure to be found soon!'

'What makes you so sure of that?' they asked him.

'There's a saying: "If a man once passes the examination, the whole world learns his name." Now everyone will know Mr Bao's name wherever he goes, and someone will be sure to bring him home.'

'That Tealeaf may be a cheeky little devil, but there's something in what he says,' agreed the maids.

Xi-chun differed:

'How could a grown man like Bao-yu be lost? If you ask me, he has deliberately severed his ties with the world and chosen the life of a monk. And in that case he *will* be hard to find.'

This set the ladies weeping all over again.

'It is certainly true,' said Li Wan, 'that since ancient times many men have renounced worldly rank and riches to become Buddhas or Saints.'

'But if he rejects his own mother and father,' sobbed Lady Wang, 'then he's failing in his duty as a son. And in that case how can he ever hope to become a Saint or a Buddha?'.

'It is best to be ordinary,' commented Tan-chun. 'Bao-yu was always different. He had that jade of his ever since he was born, and everyone always thought it lucky. But looking back, I can see that it's brought him nothing but bad luck. If a few more days go by and we still cannot find him – I don't want to upset you, Mother – but I think in that case we must resign ourselves to the fact that this is something decreed by fate and beyond our understanding. It would be better not to think of him as having ever been born from your womb. His destiny is after all the fruit of karma, the result of your accumulated merit in several lifetimes.'

Bao-chai listened to this in silence. Aroma could bear it no longer; her heart ached, she felt dizzy and sank to the ground in a faint. Lady Wang seemed most concerned for her, and told one of the maids to help her up.

Jia Huan was feeling extremely out of sorts. On top of his disgrace in the Qiao-jie affair, there was now the added humiliation of having to watch both his brother and nephew pass their examinations. He cursed Qiang and Yun for having dragged him into this trouble. Tan-chun was sure to take him to task now that she was back. And yet he dared not try to hide. He was altogether in a state of abject misery.

The next day Jia Lan had to attend court to give thanks for his successful graduation. There he met Zhen Bao-yu and discovered that he too had passed. So now all three of them belonged to the same 'class'. When Lan mentioned Bao-yu's strange disappearance, Zhen Bao-yu sighed and offered a few words of consolation.

The Chief Examiner presented the successful candidates' compositions to the throne, and His Majesty read them through one by one and found them all to be well balanced and cogent, displaying both breadth of learning and soundness of judgement. When he noticed two Nanking Jias in seventh and one hundred and thirtieth place, he asked if they were any relation of the late Jia Concubine. One of his ministers went to summon Jia Bao-yu and Jia Lan for questioning on this matter. Jia Lan, on arrival, explained the circumstances of his uncle's disappearance and gave a full account of the three preceding generations of the family, all of which was transmitted to the throne by the minister. His Majesty, as a consequence of this information, being a monarch of exceptional enlightenment and compassion, instructed his minister, in consideration of the family's distinguished record of service, to submit a full report on their case. This the minister did and drafted a detailed memorial on the subject. His Majesty's concern was such that on reading this memorial he ordered the minister to re-examine the facts that had led to Jia She's conviction. Subsequently the Imperial eye lighted upon yet another memorial describing the success of the recent campaign to quell the coastal disturbances, 'causing the seas to be at peace and the rivers to be cleansed, and leaving the honest citizenry free to pursue their livelihood unmolested once more'. His Majesty was overjoyed at this good news and ordered his council of ministers to deliberate on suitable rewards and also to pronounce a general amnesty throughout the Empire.

When Jia Lan had left court and had gone to pay his respects to his examiner, he learned of the amnesty and hurried home to tell Lady Wang and the rest of the family. They all seemed delighted, though their pleasure was marred by Bao-yu's continued absence. Aunt Xue was particularly happy at the news, and set about making preparations for the payment of Xue Pan's fine, since his death sentence would now be commuted as part of the amnesty.

A few days later it was announced that Zhen Bao-yu and his father had called to offer their congratulations, and Lady Wang sent Jia Lan out to receive them. Shortly afterwards Jia Lan returned with a broad smile on his face:

'Good news, Grandmother! Uncle Zhen Bao-yu's father has heard at court of an edict pardoning both Great-uncle She and Uncle Zhen from Ning-guo House, and restoring the hereditary Ning-guo rank to Uncle Zhen. Grandfather is to keep the hereditary Rong-guo rank and after his period of mourning will be reinstated as a Permanent Secretary in the Board of Works. All the family's confiscated property is to be restored. His Majesty has read Uncle Bao's composition and was extremely struck by it. When he discovered that the candidate concerned was Her Late Grace's younger brother, and when the Prince of Bei-jing added a few words of commendation, His Majesty expressed a desire to summon him to court for an audience. The ministers then told him that Uncle Bao had disappeared after the examination (it was I who informed them of this in the first place), and that he was at present being looked for everywhere, without success, whereupon His Majesty issued another edict, ordering all the garrisons in the capital to make a thorough search for him. You can set your mind at rest now, Grandmother. With His Majesty taking a personal interest in the matter, Uncle Bao is sure to be found!'

Lady Wang and the rest of the family were delighted and congratulated each other on this new turn of events.

*

Meanwhile Jia Huan and his accomplices were still on tenterhooks, searching everywhere for Qiao-jie, who having left the city with Patience and Grannie Liu had meanwhile arrived in the village and been installed in Grannie Liu's best room, specially cleaned out for the occasion. Although their daily diet was simple village fare, it was wholesome and clean, and with little Qing-er to keep them company they had relatively few cares. There were a few quite well-off families in the village, who when they heard that there was a Miss Jia staying at Grannie Liu's insisted on coming to have a look for themselves. They all waxed eloquent on the subject of her fairylike appearance and sent presents of fruit, fresh produce and game. In fact, Qiao-jie's presence caused a considerable stir. The richest family were the Zhous, whose wealth was composed partly of money and partly of extensive holdings of land. They had one son in the family, a cultivated, fine-looking lad of fourteen, who had studied with a family tutor and had recently passed the preliminary Licentiate exam. When his mother set eyes on Qiao-jie she was lost in admiration.

'What a pity!' she thought to herself, with a deep inner sigh of regret. 'A boy from a country family like ours would never be thought fit for such a well-bred young lady.' She stood there for some time deep in thought, and Grannie Liu soon guessed what was on her mind.

'I know what you're thinking,' she said. 'Why don't I propose the match for you?'

Mrs Zhou laughed:

'Don't go making fun of me! A great family like theirs, stoop to the likes of us!'

'Well, it'd do no harm to suggest it,' replied Grannie Liu. 'And we shall see.'

The two of them left it at that and went their separate ways.

Grannie Liu was concerned to know the latest developments at Rong-guo House and sent Ban-er into town to find out. He reached Two Dukes Street to find a throng of carriages outside the two mansions, and stationed himself close by to glean what news he could. This is what he overheard:

'Both families have had their ranks restored and all their confiscated property returned. Things are looking up for them again. But young Bao-yu has disappeared without trace after passing his exams.'

Ban-er was delighted to hear of the family's restoration to favour and was just setting off home to carry the good news back to his grandmother when he saw several horses pull up outside the gates. The riders dismounted and the gatemen saluted with one knee on the ground:

'Welcome home, sir! And congratulations! How is Sir She's health?'

'Better,' replied the young man who had first dismounted. 'And he has received His Majesty's gracious permission to return home.' After a short pause he asked: 'What are those men doing over there?'

'His Majesty sent an official here with a decree. They require a member of the family to receive back all the confiscated property.'

The young master strode in cheerfully, and Ban-er, concluding that it must be Jia Lian, did not wait for any further news but hastened home to inform Grannie Liu. A smile spread across the old lady's face when she heard, and she went at once to tell Qiao-jie and congratulate her on the good news.

'We owe everything to you, Grannie,' said Patience with a grateful smile. 'Without your help Miss Qiao-jie would never have lived to see this happy day.'

Qiao-jie herself was even more excited. Presently the messenger who had been sent with a letter to Jia Lian returned.

'Mr Lian says he is extremely grateful. He asks me to escort Miss Qiao-jie home at once, and to give you this handsome reward.'

Grannie Liu was highly satisfied that all had turned out for the best, and she sent someone to fetch two carts. When she asked Qiao-jie and Patience to make use of them for their return journey, they seemed reluctant to leave. They had grown accustomed to Grannie Liu's home, and little Qing-er was in tears because her new friends were being taken from her. Grannie Liu, seeing how attached they had become to one another, told Qing-er that she could travel with them in the carts into town. And so they hurried back to Rong-guo House.

*

It will be remembered how Jia Lian, on hearing of his father's grave illness, had hurried to his place of exile. When father and son met there was a tearful scene, which we need not describe in detail. Jia She gradually recovered his health, and when Jia Lian received a letter with the latest (and none too cheerful) news from home, he asked his father for permission to return. On his way he heard of the amnesty, and two days later arrived home on the very day that the Edict was delivered to Rong-guo House – at the very moment in fact when Lady Xing was wondering who could receive the Edict on behalf of the family. Jia Lan was now theoretically entitled to perform this function, but he was rather too young. Then Jia Lian's arrival was announced. He exchanged greetings with them all, and the re-union was an occasion for expressions of both sorrow and joy. There was no time for much talk, however, and Jia Lian hurried to the main hall to make his kowtow to the Imperial emissary, who enquired after Jia She's health and said:

'Tomorrow you must proceed to the Imperial Treasury to receive your compensation. The Ning-guo residence will be restored to your family.'

The men rose to their feet, and the emissary took his leave. Jia Lian saw him off to the front gate, where he noticed a couple of country carts pulled up. The gatemen were refusing to allow the carts to stop there and a noisy argument was taking place. Jia Lian realized at once that these must be the carts bringing his daughter home and began shouting angrily at the gatemen:

'You pack of misbegotten curs! While I was away you turned on your own masters and drove my daughter from home. Now you want to prevent her from returning! Are you trying to take ven-geance on me?'

The servants had been dreading Jia Lian's return, since he would be sure to find out sooner or later what had occurred in his absence and would certainly punish them for their part in it. It still came as something of a shock to them to hear him speaking like this so soon, as if he had already discovered everything (how this could be they did not understand). They rose to their feet and protested:

'While you were away, sir, some of us were sick, some were away on leave; it was all the doing of Master Huan, Mr Qiang and Mr Yun, sir, it had nothing to do with us.'

'Stupid incompetents!' cried Jia Lian. 'I'll deal with you when I'm finished. Hurry up and let those carts in!'

When Jia Lian went in he said nothing to Lady Xing. He went to Lady Wang's apartment, knelt before her and kowtowed:

'It is thanks to your foresight, Aunt Wang, that my daughter has returned safely. I shall say nothing of Cousin Huan's conduct in this matter. I hardly need to. But so far as that creature Yun is concerned, the last time he was left in charge there was trouble, and now, in the few months that I've been away, he has allowed the rot to set in. In my opinion he should be sent packing and never given a job of any kind here again.'

'What about your own brother-in-law, Wang Ren?' exclaimed Lady Wang. 'What induced him to behave in such a despicable manner?'

'Don't waste your breath on him,' replied Jia Lian. 'I shall deal with him later.'

Suncloud came in to announce the arrival of Qiao-jie. When Lady Wang saw her, although the separation had not been a long one, the agonizing suspense of the days leading up to her escape flooded back into her mind, and she broke down and wept profusely. Qiao-jie cried a great deal herself. Jia Lian came over to thank Grannie Liu. Lady Wang bade her be seated, and together they discussed the whole adventure. When Jia Lian saw Patience again, he was overcome with gratitude for what she had done, and although he could hardly express his true feelings at such a family gathering, he could not help shedding a few tears. From this day on he held Patience in greater and greater esteem and resolved to promote her to the position of proper wife as soon as his father returned. But we anticipate.

Lady Xing had been sure there would be trouble as soon as Jia

Lian learned of Qiao-Jie's disappearance. When she heard that he was at Lady Wang's she became most anxious and sent a maid to eavesdrop, who returned to inform her that Qiao-jie and Grannie Liu were both there talking, having just arrived back together. It suddenly dawned on Lady Xing what had happened. She knew that she had been hoodwinked and felt very peeved with Lady Wang:

'Stirring up trouble between me and my son! I wonder who it was that told Patience our secret in the first place!'

At that moment she saw Qiao-jie and Grannie Liu come in, accompanied by Patience. Lady Wang followed them and spoke to her, laying the blame for everything on Jia Yun and Wang Ren:

'You were taken in by what they said, Sister-in-law. You only meant the best. How could you have known the tricks and schemes they were up to!'

Lady Xing felt truly ashamed of herself. She saw that Lady Wang had acted rightly, and respected her for it. From now on relations between the two sisters-in-law became less strained.

Patience spoke to Lady Wang, and then took Qiao-jie to say hello to Bao-chai. The two of them exchanged commiserations.

'With the Emperor's favour now restored,' said Qiao-jie, 'our family is sure to prosper once more. And *surely* Uncle Bao will come back.'

As they were talking, Ripple came running into the room in a great lather, crying:

'Help! Aroma's been taken poorly!'

But for the outcome, you must read the next chapter.

CHAPTER 120

*Zhen Shi-yin expounds the Nature
of Passion and Illusion
And Jia Yu-cun concludes the Dream
of Golden Days*

As soon as she heard from Ripple that Aroma had been taken seriously ill, Bao-chai hurried in with Qiao-jie and Patience to see her. They found her lying unconscious on the kang, having had what seemed to be a heart seizure. They forced some cool boiled water through her lips and eventually she came round, whereupon they settled her down to sleep and sent for the doctor.

'How could Aroma have been taken like this so suddenly?' asked Qiao-jie.

'The other evening,' replied Bao-chai, 'she wept herself into a terrible state and had a sudden giddy spell. Mother told one of the maids to help her up from the ground and in the end she went to sleep. There was so much else happening at the time that we never sent for a doctor. That must be what has brought this on.'

The doctor arrived presently, and the ladies withdrew. When he had taken Aroma's pulses, he diagnosed her condition as the consequence of undue excitement and anger, wrote out a prescription accordingly and took his leave.

Aroma had in fact overheard (or *thought* she had overheard) someone saying that if Bao-yu failed to return all of his maids would be dismissed. It was the shock of hearing this that had upset her and aggravated her illness. When the doctor had departed, and when Ripple went out to prepare her medicine, Aroma was left lying alone on her bed, and in her confusion she thought she could see Bao-yu standing before her. Then the dim figure of a monk appeared before her eyes, holding the pages of an album open in his hand and saying:

'You are not destined to be mine. In days to come another will claim you for his own.'

Aroma was about to speak to him, when Ripple returned.

'Your medicine's ready,' she said. 'You'd better take it now.'

Aroma opened her eyes and knew that it had all been a dream. She did not confide in Ripple, but swallowed her medicine and lay there brooding to herself:

'Bao-yu must have gone away with that monk. I remember that day when he tried to take the jade out and give it to the monk, he seemed bent on escaping. When I tried to stop him he wasn't his normal self, pushing and shoving me off like that. He didn't seem to care about me any more. And ever since then, he has been so cool with Mrs Bao, and quite indifferent towards the rest of us.

'I suppose you think this is enlightenment. But what sort of enlightenment is it, for you to abandon your own wife? Her Ladyship asked me to serve you, but although my monthly pay has been that of a chamber-wife, I have never been officially recognized as one. Now if the Master and Her Ladyship dismiss me and I insist on staying, out of respect to your memory, people will think me ridiculous. But how can I bear to leave, remembering how things were between us?'

She agonized over her dilemma, and recalling the ominous words Bao-yu had spoken to her in her dream she vowed to herself that if her destiny could not be shared with Bao-yu she would rather not live at all.

With the medicine, however, the pain in her heart gradually subsided. She felt guilty to be lying down all the time, but forced herself to rest and struggled through the next few days until she was able to get up and about again and wait on her mistress. Bao-chai herself, although she was constantly thinking of Bao-yu and shed many a tear in private over her own unhappy fate, was kept busy helping her own mother to arrange for the payment of Xue Pan's commutation fine, by no means an easy task. But of this no more.

*

Jia Zheng had arrived in Nanking with Grandmother Jia's coffin, accompanied by Jia Rong and the coffins of Qin-shi, Xi-feng, Dai-yu and Faithful. They made arrangements for the Jia family members to be interred, and then Jia Rong took Dai-yu's coffin to her own family graveyard to be buried there, while Jia Zheng saw to the construction of the tombs. Then one day a letter arrived from home, in which he read of the success achieved by Bao-yu and Jia Lan in their examinations – which gave him great pleasure – and of Bao-yu's disappearance, which disturbed him greatly and made him decide to cut short his stay and hurry home. On his return journey he learned of the amnesty decreed by the Emperor, and received another letter from home telling him that Jia She and Cousin Zhen had been pardoned, and their titles restored. Much cheered by this news, he pressed on towards home, travelling by day and night.

On the day when his boat reached the post-station at Piling, there was a sudden cold turn in the weather and it began to snow. He moored in a quiet, lonely stretch of the canal and sent his servants ashore to deliver a few visiting-cards and to apologize to his friends in the locality, saying that since his boat was due to set off again at any moment he would not be able to call on them in person or entertain them aboard. Only one page-boy remained to wait on him while he sat in the cabin writing a letter home (to be sent on ahead by land). When he came to write about Bao-yu, he paused for a moment and looked up. There, up on deck, standing in the very entrance to his cabin and silhouetted dimly against the snow, was the figure of a man with shaven head and bare feet, wrapped in a large cape made of crimson felt. The figure knelt down and bowed to Jia Zheng, who did not recognize the features and hurried out on deck, intending to raise him up and ask him his name. The man bowed four times, and now stood upright, pressing his palms together in monkish greeting. Jia Zheng was about to reciprocate with a respectful bow of the head when he looked into the man's eyes and with a sudden shock recognized him as Bao-yu.

'Are you not my son?' he asked.

The man was silent and an expression that seemed to contain both joy and sorrow played on his face. Jia Zheng asked again:

'If you are Bao-yu, why are you dressed like this? And what brings you to this place?'

Before Bao-yu could reply two other men appeared on the deck, a Buddhist monk and a Taoist, and holding him between them they said:

'Come, your earthly karma is complete. Tarry no longer.'

The three of them mounted the bank and strode off into the snow. Jia Zheng went chasing after them along the slippery track, but although he could spy them ahead of him, somehow they always remained just out of reach. He could hear all three of them singing some sort of a song:

'On Greensickness Peak
I dwell;
In the Cosmic Void
I roam.
Who will pass over,
Who will go with me,
Who will explore
The supremely ineffable
Vastly mysterious
Wilderness
To which I return!'

Jia Zheng listened to the song and continued to follow them until they rounded the slope of a small hill and suddenly vanished from sight. He was weak and out of breath by now with the exertion of the chase, and greatly mystified by what he had seen. Looking back he saw his page-boy, hurrying up behind him.

'Did you see those three men just now?' he questioned him.

'Yes, sir, I did,' replied the page. 'I saw you following them, so I came too. Then they disappeared and I could see no one but you.'

Jia Zheng wanted to continue, but all he could see before him was a vast expanse of white, with not a soul anywhere. He knew there was more to this strange occurrence than he could understand, and reluctantly he turned back and began to retrace his steps.

The other servants had returned to their master's boat to find the cabin empty and were told by the boatman that Jia Zheng had gone on shore in pursuit of two monks and a Taoist. They followed his footsteps through the snow and when they saw him coming towards them in the distance hurried forward to meet him, and then all returned to the boat together. Jia Zheng sat down to regain his breath and told them what had happened. They sought his authority to mount a search for Bao-yu in the area, but Jia Zheng dismissed the idea.

'You do not understand,' he said with a sigh. 'This was indeed no supernatural apparition; I saw these men with my own eyes. I heard them singing, and the words of their song held a most profound and mysterious meaning. Bao-yu came into the world with his jade, and there was always something strange about it. I knew it for an ill omen. But because his grandmother doted on him so, we nurtured him and brought him up until now. That monk and that Taoist I have seen before, three times altogether. The first time was when they came to extol the virtues of the jade; the second was when Bao-yu was seriously ill and the monk came and said a prayer over the jade, which seemed to cure Bao-yu at once; the third time was when he restored the jade to us after it had been lost. He was sitting in the hall one minute, and the next he had vanished completely. I thought it strange at the time and could only conclude that perhaps Bao-yu was in some way blessed and that these two holy men had come to protect him. But the truth of the matter must be that he himself is a being from a higher realm who has descended into the world to experience the trials of this human life. For these past nineteen years he has been doted on in vain by his poor grandmother! Now at last I understand!'

As he said these words, tears came to his eyes.

'But surely,' protested one of the servants, 'if Mr Bao was really a Buddhist Immortal, what need was there for him to bother with passing his exams before disappearing?'

'How can you ever hope to understand these things?' replied Jia Zheng with a sigh. 'The constellations in the heavens, the hermits in their hills, the spirits in their caves, each has a particular configuration, a unique temperament. When did you ever see Bao-yu willingly work at his books? And yet if once he applied himself, nothing was beyond his reach. His temperament was certainly unique.'

In an effort to restore his spirits, the servants turned the conversation to Jia Lan's success in the exams and the revival of the family fortunes. Then Jia Zheng completed and sealed his letter, in which he related his encounter with Bao-yu and instructed the family not to brood over their loss too much, and despatched one of the servants to deliver it to Rong-guo House while he himself continued his journey by boat. But of this no more.

*

When Aunt Xue heard of the general amnesty pronounced by the Emperor she sent Xue Ke to borrow money from wherever he could, to add to what she herself had collected for Xue Pan's commutation fine. The Board of Justice finally gave its approval and agreed to receive the money in settlement, whereupon an official document was issued authorizing Xue Pan's release. When he was reunited with his family, there was a great deal of news for him to catch up on, some of it sad, some more cheerful. But this we can safely leave to the reader's imagination. Xue Pan for his part uttered a solemn vow:

'If I ever behave like that again, may I be hacked to death piece by piece!'

Aunt Xue held her hand over his mouth:

'Just make your mind up to mend your ways! There's no need for all these blood-curdling oaths! But what are you going to do about Caltrop? Jin-gui died by her own hand, and though we may be poor, you can still afford to fill her place. After all Caltrop has been through on your account, I think you owe it to her to make her your proper wife. What do you think?'

Xue Pan nodded his head in consent, while Bao-chai gave Aunt Xue's suggestion her full support. Caltrop herself seemed overwhelmed and flushed a deep crimson:

'It's the same to me if I continue to serve Mr Pan,' she said. 'There's no need to change things.'

From then on all the servants began calling her Mrs Pan, and looked up to her with great respect.

Xue Pan next went to call on the Jias and offered them his thanks for all that they had done. He was accompanied by his mother and Bao-chai, and there was quite a family gathering at Rong-guo House. Greetings were exchanged, and they were still chatting when a messenger arrived and presented the letter which Jia Zheng had written on the boat.

'The Master will be arriving in a matter of days,' he reported.

Lady Wang told Jia Lan to read the letter out aloud. When he reached the passage where Jia Zheng described his encounter with Bao-yu, they all wept bitterly, Lady Wang, Bao-chai and Aroma most bitterly of all. Then they listened as Jia Lan read out Jia Zheng's words of advice, that they were not to grieve but to understand that this was Bao-yu's destiny, that he was the reincarnation of a Buddhist Immortal.

'If he *had* ever risen to become an official and his career had then ended in disaster, it would have been much worse,' they consoled themselves. 'That would have meant public condemnation and ruin. Better that we should at least enjoy the honour of having had a holy man in the family. After all, it was his own father's and mother's karma, their virtue, that enabled him to be born into this family.

Without wishing to be disrespectful, even Sir Jing from Ning-guo House who practised yoga all those years failed to become an Immortal. Bao-yu's is no mean achievement. If you think of it in this light, Auntie' (referring to Lady Wang), 'it should be possible to have an easier mind.'

'Do you think I hold it against Bao-yu that he has abandoned *me*?' sobbed Lady Wang to Aunt Xue. 'No, what grieves me is the thought of his wife's unhappy fate. After little more than a year of marriage, how could he be so unfeeling as to desert her like this?'

Aunt Xue found this quite heart-rending, while Bao-chai had already wept herself into a faint. Since all the menfolk had adjourned to the front hall, Lady Wang continued to pour her heart out to her sister:

'After all the alarms and excursions I had to endure on his behalf, I finally had the comfort of seeing him marry and pass his exams, and could even look forward to the birth of a grandchild. And now this! If I'd known it would end like this I would never have let him marry in the first place! I would never have let him bring such unhappiness on the poor girl!'

'These things are all decreed by fate,' Aunt Xue consoled her. 'What else could we possibly have said or done in the circumstances? We must count ourselves blessed that my daughter is with child, and that you will have a grandchild. I am sure that he at least will do well and bring some good out of all this. Look at Li Wan: her son has passed his Provincial examination, and no doubt next year young Lan will go on to become a Palace Graduate and an official. After all that his mother has suffered, now at last she can reap her reward. As for my daughter, you know that she is not a fickle or flighty girl. You have no cause to worry on her account.'

Lady Wang found her sister's words convincing and reassuring.

'Bao-chai was always so demure and restrained as a child,' she reflected to herself. 'Always fond of plain, simple things. Perhaps that is why she has ended up in this predicament. Perhaps everything in this world really is fated! Though Chai has wept a great deal, she has never lost her sense of dignity. In fact she has even on occasion tried to comfort me. What a rare girl she is! So unlike her poor husband, who clearly was not meant for any joy in this world.'

Comforted somewhat by these thoughts, Lady Wang turned her mind to Aroma:

'None of the other maids presents much of a problem. The older ones can be married off, the younger ones can continue to wait on Bao-chai. But what am I to do with Aroma?'

She did not feel she could raise such a sensitive matter at a large family gathering, and decided to wait until the evening when she could discuss it privately with her sister.

Aunt Xue did not go home that night but stayed to comfort Bao-chai, afraid she might weep to excess. But in the end, as it turned out, Bao-chai was extremely reasonable. She reflected stoically on the whole course of events and concluded that since Bao-yu had always been a very strange creature, and since no doubt all that had happened had been preordained, there was little point in fighting against it. She expressed this in a very level-headed way to her mother, who was most relieved to hear her adopt this attitude and communicated it to Lady Wang when she next saw her. Lady Wang nodded and sighed:

'If I really were a wicked woman, fate would never have given me such a wonderful daughter-in-law!'

She started to become tearful again, and Aunt Xue tried to calm her down. She brought up the subject of Aroma:

'She has grown so terribly thin of late. All she ever does is brood about Bao-yu. It's right and proper for a wife to exhibit loyalty to her husband, even when he is a true husband to her no longer. And a chamber-wife may do the same if she wishes. But Aroma was never formally declared to be Bao-yu's chamber-wife, even though in fact we know that she was.'

'Yes, I was thinking about this only a short while ago,' said Lady Wang. 'I was waiting for a chance to talk it over with you in private. If we simply dismiss her from service, I'm afraid she won't want to go, and may even try to take her own life. We could keep her on, but I am afraid Sir Zheng would not approve. It is a tricky problem.'

'I hardly think Sir Zheng would want her to remain single and make a show of faithfulness to Bao-yu,' said Aunt Xue. 'He doesn't even know that she was Bao-yu's chamber-wife. He has always thought of her as just an ordinary maid, so it would seem rather absurd to him to want to keep her on. The only solution is for you to send for a member of her own family and impress upon them the importance of arranging a decent marriage for her. We can give her a generous send-off. She is a good-natured girl and still quite young. You should do what you can for her after all the years she has worked for you. Let me explain things carefully to her. There's no need to let her know straight away. First we should get in touch with her family and let them arrange a match; next we should make some enquiries ourselves; and then if it seems that the prospective husband's family are in a position to support her properly, and if the young man himself seems suitable, we can let her leave and get married.'

'That's a very good idea. You've thought it all out very well,' replied Lady Wang. 'If we do not take the initiative, Sir Zheng may go ahead himself and deal with her in a very tactless way, and then I will be responsible for yet another misfortune.'

'Exactly the same thought had occurred to me,' said Aunt Xue nodding her head.

After they had chatted a while longer, Aunt Xue took her leave and went to Bao-chai's apartment. She found Aroma in floods of tears and did her best to console her, speaking so far as possible in vague generalities. Aroma was at heart a simple girl and not much of a talker, and she merely gave the appropriate responses to whatever Aunt Xue said.

'I am only a servant,' she said in the end, 'and it is very kind of you to think to speak to me like this, ma'am. I have never dared to go against any wish of Her Ladyship's.'

'There's a good girl!' said Aunt Xue, more pleased than ever with her. Bao-chai added a few high-sounding words of her own and when she and Aunt Xue parted from Aroma their minds were considerably more at ease.

*

A few days later Jia Zheng came home and was greeted on his arrival by all the family. Jia She and Cousin Zhen had also returned from their exile by now, and they spent some time with Jia Zheng, catching up on each other's news. Then Jia Zheng went in to see the womenfolk. Bao-yu's absence cast a shadow of gloom over the gathering, which Jia Zheng tried to dispel as best he could.

'There was a reason behind all this!' he said. 'It is up to us men now to maintain a high standard of public life, and I hope that all of you meanwhile will lend us your support here at home. There must be no hint of any slipping back into the lax old ways. Each apartment can look after its own affairs, and we've no need of a general manager.

Everything in our own apartment I leave to you' (this was addressed to Lady Wang), 'to deal with in a fitting manner.'

Lady Wang informed him that Bao-chai was with child, and that all Bao-yu's maids would be dismissed. Jia Zheng nodded in silence.

The following day he attended court to receive his instructions from the chief ministers.

'I am extremely grateful for His Majesty's gracious favour,' he said. 'But since this is still within my period of mourning, I beg you to instruct me how I should express my gratitude.'

The ministers offered to present a memorial on his behalf. The Emperor most magnanimously granted Jia Zheng a special audience, and after listening to his formal expression of thanks favoured him with several Imperial instructions and enquired after his son, the successful Provincial Graduate. Jia Zheng told him the full story of Bao-yu's disppearance. The Emperor marvelled at it and declared that Bao-yu's compositions had indeed manifested a remarkable originality, the very quality one would expect of a soul from another plane. Such a person could have excelled at court if such had been his destiny; but since he had not deigned to earn honours of a worldly nature, it was His Majesty's pleasure to confer upon him the religious title *Magister Verbi Profundi* – Master of the Profound Word.

Jia Zheng kowtowed again to express his thanks for this great honour, and took his leave. On his return home he was received by Jia Lian and Cousin Zhen, who were delighted to hear the latest news from court.

'Ning-guo House has been set in order,' said Cousin Zhen, 'and with your consent we intend to take up residence there again. Green Bower Hermitage in the Garden has been set aside for my sister Xi-chun's devotions.'

After a pause for reflection Jia Zheng gave them a long homily on their debt of gratitude to the throne for all these favours. Jia Lian took the opportunity of raising the issue of his daughter's marriage:

'Both Mother and Father are willing that Qiao-jie should be married to this Master Zhou.'

Jia Zheng had heard the full details of Qiao-jie's story the previous evening, and replied:

'If that is their decision, then so be it. There is nothing against a country life. What matters is that the family should be an honest one and the lad should be prepared to study and make his way in the world. Not every official at court is from a city family, after all.'

Jia Lian replied appropriately and continued:

'Father is advanced in years, and is moreover afflicted with a chronic phlegmatic condition. He plans to retire for a few years and leave everything in your hands, Uncle.'

'A quiet retirement in the country would suit me well enough,' commented Jia Zheng. 'But alas my obligations to the throne do not permit it.'

Jia Zheng went in to see Lady Wang, while Jia Lian sent someone to invite Grannie Liu over. When she was informed that the match had been approved by the Master, she proceeded to favour Lady Wang and the other ladies with a long speech on the certain future success of the young man, how his family was sure to come up in the world, and what a prosperous multitude of sons and grandsons the couple were sure to breed.

While she was talking one of the maids came in to announce that Hua Zi-fang, Aroma's brother, had sent his wife to convey his respects. Lady Wang spoke to the woman and ascertained from her that a match had been proposed by the Hua family to a certain Mr Jiang living south of the city, a young man with property and land and a pawnshop business of his own. He was a few years older than Aroma but had never married and was exceptionally good-looking. Lady Wang was satisfied with this description of the match.

'Tell them I agree,' she said. 'In a few days' time your husband can come and fetch his sister and take her away to be married.'

She also sent some of her own people to make discreet enquiries, and received confirmation of the man's character, whereupon she informed Bao-chai, and asked Aunt Xue to break the news gently to Aroma. Poor Aroma was inconsolable at the prospect of leaving Rong-guo House, but she could not offer any resistance. She remembered the visit Bao-yu had paid her at home many years previously, and the oath she had sworn afterwards, never to leave him even in death. 'Now Her Ladyship is making me do this against my will, and if I insist on remaining single and faithful to his memory, people will call me shameless. But if I do go, it is not of my own wishing.'

She wept until she was choking with tears. Aunt Xue and Bao-chai did their utmost to talk her round, and eventually she thought to herself:

'If I were to die here, it would be a poor return for all Her Ladyship's kindness to me in the past. I had best die at home.'

So she bade farewell to them all, her heart heavy with sorrow. It was equally painful for her to part from the other maids. Resolved to end her own life at the first opportunity, she mounted a carriage and set off for home. When she saw her brother and his wife, there were more tears, but she could not bring herself to say what was on her mind. Her brother showed her one by one all the presents sent by the Jiang family, and the trousseau that he himself had made ready for her, a part of which, he explained, had been given by Lady Wang, while a part he had provided himself. This kindness made it harder than ever for Aroma to express her sorrow, and after spending two days at her brother's home, she thought things over carefully again: 'He has done everything so nicely for me. If I were to die here, wouldn't I be hurting him?' She turned it over and over in her mind, and no course of action seemed easy and right. Her heart was wound into a tight knot. She could only bear her fate stoically and bide her time.

The auspicious day in the almanac arrived for her to be taken to her husband's home, and not wishing to make a scene she concealed her grief and let herself be helped into the bridal sedan. At her new home, she thought to herself, she would make plans afresh. But once she arrived at the Jiang household, she found them so sincere and respectful towards her, deferring to her in every way as a young married lady, with the maids and serving-women all calling her Mrs Jiang the minute she set foot in the house, that death seemed impossible again: to die there would be to do *them* a great injury, she thought to herself; it would be a poor return for all *their* kindness. On her wedding night she wept without ceasing and would not at first yield to her husband's embrace, but gradually he won her over with gentle affection.

The next day, when they were unpacking her cases together, Jiang noticed among her things a crimson cummerbund. From this clue he deduced that his bride must have been one of the maids in attendance on Bao-yu, to whom he had once presented this cummerbund. Earlier he had thought that his bride was just one of Grandmother Jia's maids; he had certainly never dreamed that he was marrying Aroma. Jiang Yu-han (for it was he, Bao-yu's actor friend Bijou) was greatly moved when he remembered all the warmth shown him by Bao-yu in the past, and as a consequence he treated Aroma with still greater courtesy and consideration. He showed her the viridian sash that Bao-yu had given him in exchange for the cummerbund, and this visible proof of her husband's friendship with her erstwhile master inspired Aroma to believe that her life too lay in the hands of fate, that this marriage was indeed predestined. This in turn gave her the courage to open her heart to her husband. Jian proved himself worthy of her trust and showed her a great depth of feeling and a sincere respect, never venturing to steer her forcibly into any new direction, but showing her an ever more gentle affection and regard. Aroma was finally deprived of her last opportunity to take her own life.

Gentle Reader, it is indeed true (as Aroma concluded) that life is predestined and that 'there's naught to be done'. But unfortunately this argument is too often adduced by sons and statesmen who find themselves out of favour, or by faithful widows and widowers, as an excuse for moral torpor. It was this very streak in her personality that relegated Aroma to the 'Second Supplementary Register'. As a poet of former times once wrote, when passing by the temple built in memory of the Lady of the Peach Blossom:

> Throughout the ages death has been the hardest choice;
> Lady Xi was not alone in lamenting her weakness.*

*

Aroma's married life is the first chapter of another history. Our narrative returns to Jia Yu-cun, who, having been convicted of avarice and extortion, was also released under the general amnesty and allowed to return to his native city as a common citizen. He sent his family on ahead and himself travelled with a young page and a cartload of baggage. His journey brought him once more to Wake Ness Ferry at Rushford Hythe, and as he approached the river he saw a Taoist hermit emerging from a thatched hut by the water's edge, clasping his hands in greeting. This time Yu-cun recognized him at once as Zhen Shi-yin and promptly bowed in response.

*In the Spring and Autumn period, King Wen of the state of Chu (ruled 689–676 BC) defeated and put to death the ruler of the state of Xi. He then took the Lord Xi's widow as his concubine and had two sons by her. She refused to communicate verbally with her new master, however, and when King Wen asked her the reason for her silence she eventually replied: 'I, a widow, now serve a second husband. Having thus failed to seek death, what is there that I can say?'

'Esteemed Mr Jia,' began the old hermit, 'I trust you have been well since we last parted?'

'So you, sir, are indeed my erstwhile patron Mr Zhen, in Immortal form!' exclaimed Yu-cun. 'Why did I not know you at our last encounter? Afterwards, when I heard that your hermitage had been destroyed by fire, I was most concerned for your safety. I am fortunate indeed to have been granted this second opportunity to marvel at the profundity of your spiritual attainments. Alas, I am as benighted as ever, as you can see from my present condition.'

'On the previous occasion,' replied Zhen Shi-yin, 'your position was so exalted that I dared not presume an acquaintance. Because of our old friendship, I said a few words, which you ignored altogether. Wealth and poverty, success and failure, none of these are coincidental. Nor is our meeting again like this today a coincidence, but rather a meaningful and marvellous event. We are not far from my lodge and I would be delighted if you could stop by and pass the time of day with me.'

Jia Yu-cun consented with pleasure and the two men walked hand in hand, the page following them with the baggage-cart to the little thatched hermitage. Shi-yin ushered Yu-cun in, and he sat down and was brought tea by the old man's acolyte. Yu-cun asked to hear the story of his mystical conversion, and Shi-yin smiled:

'In an instant my world was transformed. You yourself, sir, hailing as you do from the realm of luxury and opulence, must surely have heard there of a person by the name of Bao-yu?'

'Of course,' replied Yu-cun. 'Recently I heard a rumour to the effect that he too has taken refuge in the dharma. I saw something of him in the past and it certainly never occurred to me that he would take a step like this.'

'There is nothing unexpected about it,' said Shi-yin. 'I have known of his strange destiny for many years. Ever since that day long ago, in fact, when I met you outside my abode in Carnal Lane and we had that little chat. I had already encountered him then.'

'But the capital is a long way from your old home,' said Yu-cun in great surprise. 'How could you possibly have set eyes on him at that time?'

'We had long enjoyed a spiritual communion,' replied Shi-yin darkly.

'In that case, sir, you must know of his present whereabouts?'

'Bao-yu,' replied the old man, 'is the Stone, the Precious Jade. Before the two mansions of Rong and Ning were searched and their worldly goods impounded, on the very day when Bao-chai and Dai-yu were separated, the Stone had already quit the world. This was in part to avoid the impending calamity, in part to permit the consummation of the union. From that moment the Stone's worldly karma was complete, its substance had returned to the Great Unity. All that remained was for it to demonstrate some small fraction of its spiritual powers by achieving academic distinction and by leaving behind an heir to bring honour to the family name. Thus its precious nature, its magical power, its capacity for spiritual transformation, these were made manifest, and all could know that it was no ordinary stone of this world. To this end the Buddhist mahāsattva Impervioso and the Taoist illuminate Mysterioso first brought it into the world, and now that its destiny is fulfilled it is they who will take it back once more to its place of origin. That is the sum of my knowledge concerning Bao-yu and, as you put it, his "present whereabouts".'

Although Yu-cun could not take all of this in, he was able to follow about half. He nodded his head and sighed:

'So that is the truth of the matter. And I never knew. But if Bao-yu is a person of such a remarkable spiritual pedigree, why did he first need to be blinded by human passion before he could reach enlightenment?'

Shi-yin smiled:

'Even though I may seek to expound this, I fear you may never be able to understand it fully. The Land of Illusion and the Paradise of Truth are one and the same. Could two readings of the registers and a whole lifetime's experience fail to bring enlightenment? Could he fail to see the Alpha and the Omega? If the Fairy Flower regained its true primordial state, then surely the Magic Stone should do likewise?'

This time the hermit's words were truly beyond Yu-chun's powers of comprehension. He knew only that they must contain some esoteric meaning, and did not venture to probe any further.

'It is so kind of you to tell me all this about Bao-yu,' he said. 'But may I ask you another question: why is it that of all the ladies in these noble families, none, including Her Grace the Imperial Jia Concubine, has come to more than an undistinguished end?'

On hearing this Shi-yin sighed:

'Do not take my words amiss, sir! The fact of the matter is that all these noble ladies to whom you refer hail from the Skies of Passion and the Seas of Retribution. Since olden times their sex has been under a natural obligation to remain pure, pure from lust, pure even from the slightest taint of passion. Thus amorous beauties such as Cui Ying-ying and Su Xiao-xiao were fallen fairies, their celestial hearts polluted with the base desires of this world, while romantic poets such as Song Yu and Si-ma Xiang-ru sinned in like manner through the written word. Consider for a moment: how can any being ensnared in human attachment hope to "come to more than an undistinguished end", as you put it?'

As he listened to the hermit's words, Jia Yu-cun found himself stroking his beard meditatively and heaving a long sigh.

'May I ask, sir,' he ventured, 'whether the Ning and Rong houses will ever rise again to their former heights of prosperity?'

'It is preordained that prosperity comes with virtue, and calamity with evil,' replied Shi-yin. 'At present in these two houses the virtuous have turned to the true path, while the wicked have at least repented of their ways. In time to come, orchid and cassia will bloom, and the family fortunes will indeed prosper again. This is natural and right.'

Yu-cun lowered his head in thought for a while, then suddenly laughed:

'Yes! Of course! There is one among them called Lan (Orchid), who has recently passed his examinations. As for the cassia you mention, could this be in some way connected with what you said earlier about Bao-yu achieving academic distinction and leaving behind a creditable heir? Is his posthumous son a Jia Gui (Cassia) destined for glory?'

Shi-yin gave an inscrutable smile:

'Time will show. It would be wrong to make predictions about this now.'

Yu-cun had still more questions to ask, but Shi-yin was clearly unwilling to provide any further replies. He told his boy to lay the table and bring in the food, and invited Yu-cun to eat with him. When they had finished their meal, Yu-cun was still curious, this time wanting to know the secrets of his own future; but his luck had run out.

'Rest awhile, sir,' said Shi-yin, 'in my humble hermitage. I still have a duty to perform, and today is the day for its completion.'

This took Yu-cun by surprise:

'In view of the exalted spiritual state you have achieved, I cannot conceive what karma can remain for you to fulfil?'

'It concerns the love between a man and a woman.'

This amazed Yu-cun even more.

'Pray explain, sir.'

'There is something of which you are ignorant, my respected friend,' replied Shi-yin. 'My daughter Ying-lian was, as you know, kidnapped when she was a little girl. You yourself gave judgement in the case when you first held office. Now she is married to a certain Mr Xue and is about to give birth to his child. In so doing she will die. She will leave behind her a son to continue the Xue family's ancestral rites. Now is the moment for her earthly life to cease, and I must be at hand to receive her spirit.'

With a shake of his sleeve Shi-yin was gone. Yu-cun began to feel very dozy and had soon fallen asleep in the little hermitage at Wake Ness Ferry by Rushford Hythe.

Shi-yin went to receive Caltrop's soul across the threshold of death and to escort her to the Land of Illusion, there to be handed over to the Fairy Disenchantment and to have her name entered on the register. As he passed through the great archway he saw the monk and the Taoist drifting towards him, and approaching them he said:

'Mahāsattva! Illuminate! My felicitations! Is the love karma fulfilled? Have all those souls involved been duly returned and entered in the registers?'

'The karma is not yet complete,' they replied. 'But that senseless Block has already returned. Now all that remains is to restore it to its place of origin and to record the last instalment of its story. Then its little trip into the world will not have been in vain.'

Shi-yin clasped both hands together in salutation and took his leave. The monk and the Taoist continued on their way bearing the jade, until finally they came to the foot of Greensickness Peak and there, in the very place where Nu-wa had once smelted her fiery amalgam to repair the vault of Heaven, they carefully deposited their burden and each drifted off on his way.

> An otherworldly tome recounts an otherworldly tale,
> As Man and Stone become a single whole once more.

*

One day Vanitas the Taoist passed again by Greensickness Peak and saw the Stone 'that had been found unfit to repair the heavens', lying there still, with characters inscribed on it as before. He read the inscription through carefully again and noticed that a whole new section had been appended to the gātha with which the earlier version concluded. This new material provided several dénouements and tied up various loose ends in the plot, completing the overall design of fate that underlay the original story.

'When I first saw this strange tale of Brother Stone's I thought it worth publishing as a novel and copied it down for that purpose. But at the time it was unfinished; the cycle within it was incomplete. There was in the earlier version none of this material relating the Stone's return to the source. I wonder when this rather admirable last instalment can have been added? From it the reader can indeed see that Brother Stone's experience of life sharpened the edge of his spiritual perception, and brought him to a more complete awareness of the Tao. At the end he had no cause for remorse or regret. But with the passing of the years the characters of this new version of the inscription may wear away and be misread. I had better copy it down again in this complete form and find someone in the world with leisure on his hands to publish it and transmit its message: that things are not as they seem, that the extraordinary and the ordinary, truth and fiction, are all relative to each other. Perhaps my fellow humans whom the dream of life has ensnared may find in this tale an echo, may be summoned back by it to their true home; while free spirits of the high hills may find in the record of Brother Stone's transformations, as in that older tale of the Migration of the Magic Mountain, a reflected light to quicken their own aspirations.'

So Vanitas copied it all down and slipping this new version into his sleeve took it off with him to the luxurious, opulent world of men, to seek out a suitable mortal for the task of publication. But all the men he encountered were either too busy establishing themselves in their careers, or else too preoccupied with their day-to-day survival, to have the leisure or inclination to prattle with a Stone. Then at last Vanitas came to the little hermitage at Wake Ness Ferry by Rushford Hythe; there he found a man asleep (from which he deduced him to be a man of leisure) and thought he would give him this Story of the Stone to read. But however many times he called out, he could not rouse him from his slumber. Eventually he heaved him up and gave him a good shake, and the man slowly opened his eyes. He skimmed through the book and let it fall from his hands, saying:

'I have seen all this myself at first-hand. As far as I can see your record contains no errors. Allow me to tell you of a man who can transmit this story to the world on your behalf, and by so doing bring this strange affair to a proper conclusion.'

'Whom do you mean?' asked Vanitas eagerly.

'You must wait until the year ___, the __ day of the __ month. At the __ hour, you must go to a certain Nostalgia Studio, where you will find a certain Mr Cao Xue-qin. Just tell him: "Jia Yu-cun says . . ." and ask him to do such-and-such and so forth . . .'

Yu-cun dozed off again, and Vanitas made a careful note of his instructions. Sure enough, after an incalculable number of generations, an infinity of aeons, there was indeed a Nostalgia Studio and in it a Mr Cao Xue-qin, perusing the histories of bygone days. Vanitas did as he had been instructed; he repeated Yu-cun's words and handed him the Story of the Stone to read. This Mr Cao smiled and said:

'Rustic fiction indeed (*Jia Yu Cun Yan*)!'

'How is it that you know the man, sir? May I deduce from this that you are willing to transmit this tale for him?'

'You are aptly named Vanitas,' exclaimed Cao. 'You have a Nothing in your Belly, a very Vanity. These may be rustic words, but they contain no careless errors or nonsensical passages. It would be a pleasure to share this with a few like-minded friends, to help the wine down after a meal or to while away the solitude of a rainy evening by a lamplit window. No need for some self-important being to commend it or publish it. You in your insistence on ferreting out facts are like the man who dropped his sword in the water and thought to find it again by making a mark on the side of his boat; you are like a man playing a zither with the tuning-pegs glued fast.'

Vanitas lifted his head and guffawed at this, dropped the manuscript to the ground and went breezily on his way. As he went he said to himself:

'So it was really all utter nonsense! Author, copyist and reader were alike in the dark! Just so much ink splashed for fun, a game, a diversion!'

A later reader of the manuscript added a four-line gātha, to expand a little on the author's original *envoi*:

> When grief for fiction's idle words
> More real than human life appears,
> Reflect that life itself's a dream
> And do not mock the reader's tears.

ADAMANTINA a genteel and eccentric young nun residing in Prospect Garden

AMBER maid of Grandmother Jia

AROMA principal maid of Bao-yu

AUNT XUE widowed sister of Lady Wang and mother of Xue Pan and Bao-chai

AUNT ZHAO concubine of Jia Zheng and mother of Tan-chun and Jia Huan

AUNT ZHOU Jia Zheng's other concubine

AUTUMN concubine given to Jia Lian by his father

BAN-ER see WANG BAN-ER

BAO-CHAI see XUE BAO-CHAI

BAO ER servant employed by Cousin Zhen

BAO-QIN see XUE BAO-QIN

BAO YIN domestic in employment of Jia Hua

BAO YONG Zhen family servant now employed by the Jias

BAO-YU see JIA BAO-YU

BIG JIAO an old retainer of the Ning-guo Jias

BIJOU stage name of JIANG YU-HAN

BRIGHTIE
BRIGHTIE'S WIFE } couple employed by Jia Lian and Wang Xi-feng

CALTROP Xue Pan's chamber-wife; the kidnapped daughter of Zhen Shi-yin

CANDIDA maid of Li Wan

CASTA maid of Li Wan

CENSOR LI responsible for the impeachment of the magistrate of Ping-an

CHAI see XUE BAO-CHAI

CHENG RI-XING one of Jia Zheng's literary gentlemen

COOK LIU in charge of the kitchen for Prospect Garden; mother of Fivey

COUSIN BAO (1) see JIA BAO-YU (2) see XUE BAO-CHAI

COUSIN CHAI see XUE BAO-CHAI

COUSIN DAI see LIN DAI-YU

COUSIN FENG see WANG XI-FENG

COUSIN KE see XUE KE

COUSIN LIAN see JIA LIAN

COUSIN LIN see LIN DAI-YU

COUSIN PAN see XUE PAN

COUSIN QIN see XUE BAO-QIN

COUSIN SHI *see* SHI XIANG-YUN

COUSIN TAN *see* JIA TAN-CHUN

COUSIN WAN *see* LI WAN

COUSIN XI *see* JIA XI-CHUN

COUSIN XUE *see* XUE PAN

COUSIN YING *see* JIA YING-CHUN

COUSIN YUN *see* SHI XIANG-YUN

COUSIN ZHEN son of Jia Jing; head of the senior (Ning-guo) branch of the Jia family

CRIMSON maid employed by Xi-feng

DAI *see* LIN DAI-YU

DAI LIANG foreman in charge of the granary at Rong-guo House

DAI-YU *see* LIN DAI-YU

DIME *see* NI ER

DISENCHANTMENT an important fairy

DOVE concubine of Cousin Zhen

DUKE OF AN-GUO, THE entrusted by the Emperor with pacification of the South

DUMBO *see* XING DE-QUAN

FAITHFUL principal maid of Grandmother Jia

FELICITY maid attendant on Xi-feng

FENG *see* WANG XI-FENG

FIVEY daughter of Cook Liu; taken on as one of Bao-yu's maids

FROWNER *see* LIN DAI-YU

GAFFER LI proprietor of Li's bar

GRANDMOTHER JIA née Shi; widow of Bao-yu's paternal grandfather and head of the Rong-guo branch of the Jia family

GRANNIE LIU an old country-woman patronized by Wang Xi-feng and the Rong-guo Jias

HALF-IMMORTAL MAO fortune-teller and expert in *The Book of Changes*

HER GRACE *see* JIA YUAN-CHUN

HE SAN Zhou Rui's adopted son, expelled from Rong-guo House

HU-SHI Jia Rong's second wife

HUA ZI-FANG Aroma's elder brother

HUAN *see* JIA HUAN

IMPERVIOSO Buddhist mahāsattva

JIA BAO-YU incarnation of the Stone; the eldest surviving son of Jia Zheng and Lady Wang of Rong-guo House

JIA DAI-HUA son of Duke of Ning-guo and father of Jia Jing

JIA DAI-RU the Preceptor, in charge of the Jia family school

JIA FAN hereditary noble of the third degree

JIA HUA Grand Preceptor and Duke of Zhen-guo

JIA HUAN Bao-yu's half-brother; the son of Jia Zheng and his concubine, 'Aunt' Zhao

JIA LAN Li Wan's son

JIA LIAN son of Jia She and Lady Xing and husband of Wang Xi-feng

JIA QIANG a distant relation of the Ning-guo Jias patronized by Cousin Zhen

JIA QIAO-JIE little daughter of Jia Lian and Wang Xi-feng

JIA QIN a junior member of the clan employed by the Rong-guo Jias to look after the little nuns from Prospect Garden

JIA RONG son of Cousin Zhen and You-shi

JIA SHE Jia Zheng's elder brother; father of Jia Lian and Ying-chun

JIA SI-JIE younger sister of Jia Qiong, made much of by Grandmother Jia

JIA TAN-CHUN daughter of Jia Zheng and 'Aunt' Zhao; half-sister of Bao-yu and second of the 'Three Springs'

JIA XI-CHUN daughter of Jia Ling and younger sister of Cousin Zhen; youngest of the 'Three Springs'

JIA XI-LUAN younger sister of Jia Bin, made much of by Grandmother Jia

JIA YING-CHUN daughter of Jia She by a concubine; eldest of the 'Three Springs'

JIA YU-CUN a careerist claiming relationship with the Jia family

JIA YUAN-CHUN daughter of Jia Zheng and Lady Wang and elder sister of Bao-yu; the Imperial Concubine, now dead

JIA YUN poor relation of the Rong-guo Jias, once employed by Xi-feng in Prospect Garden

JIA ZHENG Bao-yu's father; the younger of Grandmother Jia's two sons

JIA ZHI obscure junior member of the Jia clan occasionally present at family gatherings

JIA ZHU deceased elder brother of Bao-yu; husband of Li Wan and father of her son Jia Lan

JIANG YU-HAN a female impersonator, now turned actor-manager

JIN-GUI see XIA JIN-GUI

LADY JIA see GRANDMOTHER JIA

LADY WANG wife of Jia Zheng, and mother of Jia Zhu, Yuan-chun and Bao-yu

LADY XING wife of Jia She and mother of Jia Lian

LADY ZHEN wife of Zhen Ying-jia and mother of Zhen Bao-yu

LAI DA Chief Steward of Rong-guo House

LAI SHANG-RONG Lai Da's son, educated and enabled to obtain advancement under the Jia family's patronage

LAI SHENG Chief Steward of Ning-guo House

LANDSCAPE maid of Xi-chun

LENG ZI-XING an antique dealer; friend of Jia Yu-cun and son-in-law of Zhou Rui

LI GUI Nannie Li's son; Bao-yu's foster-brother and chief groom

LI QI Li Wan's cousin; younger sister of Li Wen

LI TEN porter on Jia Zheng's staff in the Kiangsi Grain Intendant's yamen

LI WAN widow of Bao-yu's deceased elder brother, Jia Zhu, and mother of Jia Lan

LI WEN Li Wan's cousin; elder sister of Li Qi

LI XIAO magistrate of Soochow, responsible for charges brought against household of JIA FAN

LIN DAI-YU incarnation of the Crimson Pearl Flower; orphaned daughter of Lin Ru-hai and Jia Zheng's sister, Jia Min; now dead

LIN ZHI-XIAO ⎱ domestics holding the highest position in the
LIN ZHI-XIAO'S WIFE ⎰ Rong household under Chief Steward Lai Da

LOVEY concubine of Cousin Zhen

MASTER BAO see JIA BAO-YU

MASTER ZHOU son of a wealthy family in Grannie Liu's village

MISS BAO see XUE BAO-CHAI

MISS LIN see LIN DAI-YU

MISS QIAO-JIE see JIA QIAO-JIE

MISS SHI see SHI XIANG-YUN

MISS XING see XING XIU-YAN

MONGOL PRINCE, THE a tributary prince, almost tricked into buying Qiao-jie

MOONBEAM maid of XIA JIN-GUI, taken as concubine by XUE PAN

MOTHER MA a Wise Woman; Bao-yu's godmother

MR LIAN see JIA LIAN

MR MEI son of Academician Mei (now deceased); betrothed to Xue Bao-qin

MR QIANG see JIA QIANG

MR QIN see JIA QIN

MR SUN see SUN SHAO-ZU

MR YUN see JIA YUN

MR ZHEN see COUSIN ZHEN

MRS LI Li Wan's widowed aunt; mother of Li Qi and Li Wen

MRS LIAN see WANG XI-FENG

MRS XIA mother of Xia Jin-gui

MRS XUE see AUNT XUE

MRS YOU You-shi's mother

MRS ZHANG née Wang; impoverished rustic, mother of Zhang San

MRS ZHAO see AUNT ZHAO

MRS ZHEN see YOU-SHI

MRS ZHOU see ZHOU RUI'S WIFE

MRS ZHU *see* LI WAN

MUSK maid of Bao-yu

MYSTERIOSO Taoist illuminate

NANNIE LI (1) Bao-yu's former wet-nurse (2) Qiao-jie's nurse

NANNIE LIU another of Qiao-jie's nurses

NANNIE WANG Dai-yu's former wet-nurse

NI ER 'the Drunken Diamond'; gangster neighbour of Jia Yun

NIGHTINGALE principal maid of Dai-yu

ORIOLE principal maid of Bao-chai

PARFUMÉE ex-actress, now a nun at Water-moon Priory

PARROT maid of Grandmother Jia

PATIENCE chief maid and confidante of Wang Xi-feng

PEARL maid of Grandmother Jia

PERFECTA nun from the Convent of the Scattered Flowers

PRECEPTOR, THE *see* JIA DAI-RU

PRINCE OF BEI-JING, THE princely connection of the Jias, friendly with Bao-yu

PRINCE OF XI-PING, THE princely connection of the Jias

PROSPER maid of Aunt Xue

QIAO-JIE *see* JIA QIAO-JIE

QIN KE-QING first wife of Jia Rong, now deceased

QING-ER *see* WANG QING-ER

QIN-SHI *see* QIN KE-QING

QIU SHI-AN Eunuch Superintendent of the Inner Palace

RIPPLE maid of Bao-yu

ROPEY one of Bao-yu's pages

SHI FU man claiming to be servant in household of Jia Fan; accused of attempted rape and murder

SHI XIANG-YUN orphaned great-niece of Grandmother Jia, niece of Shi Ding, the Marquis of Zhong-jing

SI-JIE *see* JIA SI-JIE

SILVER maid of Lady Wang; younger sister of her deceased maid Golden

SIR SHE *see* JIA SHE

SIR ZHENG *see* JIA ZHENG

SKYBRIGHT one of Bao-yu's maids, now dead

SNOWGOOSE maid of Dai-yu

STEWARD LIN *see* LIN ZHI-XIAO

SUN SHAO-ZU Jia Ying-chun's callous husband

SUNCLOUD ⎱
SUNSET ⎰ maids of Lady Wang

SUNSHINE page employed by Wang Xi-feng for clerical duties

TAN-CHUN *see* JIA TAN-CHUN

TEALEAF Bao-yu's principal page

UNCLE ZI-SHENG *see* WANG ZI-SHENG

UNCLE ZI-TENG *see* WANG ZI-TENG

VANITAS a Taoist in quest of immortality

WANG BAN-ER Grannie Liu's little grandson

WANG QING-ER Grannie Liu's little granddaughter

WANG REN Wang Xi-feng's elder brother

WANG XI-FENG wife of Jia Lian and niece of Lady Wang, Aunt Xue and Wang Zi-teng

WANG ZHONG Governor of Yunnan Province

WANG ZI-SHENG younger brother of Wang Zi-teng

WANG ZI-TENG elder brother of Wang Zi-sheng, Lady Wang and Aunt Xue, now dead

WU GUI Skybright's cousin

WU LIANG Xue Pan's fair-weather friend

XI-CHUN *see* JIA XI-CHUN

XI-FENG *see* WANG XI-FENG

XI-LUAN *see* JIA XI-LUAN

XIA JIN-GUI wife of Xue Pan; a termagant

XIA SAN adopted brother of Xia Jin-gui

XIANG-YUN *see* SHI XIANG-YUN

XING DE-QUAN Lady Xing's good-for-nothing brother

XING XIU-YAN Lady Xing's niece; gifted daughter of improvident and sponging parents, betrothed to Xue Ke

XIU-YAN *see* XING XIU-YAN

XUE BAO-CHAI daughter of Aunt Xue

XUE BAO-QIN niece of Aunt Xue and younger sister of Xue Ke

XUE KE Xue Bao-qin's elder brother, betrothed to Xing Xiu-yan

XUE PAN the 'Oaf King'; son of Aunt Xue and elder brother of Bao-chai

YING *see* JIA YING-CHUN

YING-CHUN *see* JIA YING-CHUN

YOU ER-JIE Jia Lian's mistress, now dead

YOU-SHI wife of Cousin Zhen and mother of Jia Rong

YU-CUN *see* JIA YU-CUN

YUAN-CHUN *see* JIA YUAN-CHUN

YUN (1) *see* SHI XIANG-YUN (2) *see* JIA YUN

ZHAN HUI granary clerk in the Kiangsi Grain Intendant's yamen

ZHANG DE-HUI manager of Xue Pan's largest pawnshop

ZHANG HUA dissolute young gambler betrothed since infancy to You Er-jie

ZHANG SAN waiter, only surviving son of Mrs Zhang

ZHAO QUAN Commissioner of the Embroidered Jackets